GW00758642

In Her Name
Dead Soul

By
Michael R. Hicks

This is a work of fiction. All of the characters and events portrayed in this novel are products of the author's imagination or are used fictitiously.

IN HER NAME: DEAD SOUL
Copyright © 2012 by Imperial Guard Publishing, LLC
ISBN: 978-0984673032

*This book is dedicated to all the readers like you
who gave this unknown author a chance
and helped him achieve his dreams.*

ACKNOWLEDGEMENTS

Dead Soul was an interesting writing experience for me for a couple reasons. First and foremost, this is the first novel I'll have published working as a full-time, self-published author, and I want to thank you, dear reader, for making that possible.

The second reason that this book was particularly interesting to write is the composition of the editing team. There were, of course, many of the usual suspects, including my wife Jan, who played the part of "alpha reader," Mindy Schwartz as the primary editor, and beta readers Geoff Thomas, fellow author Jeff Hepple, and Will "Cush" Cushman.

For the first time, however, we had an international contingent, Frode Hauge and Marianne Søiland, both from Norway. I met both of them on Facebook, and their different perspective on the English language and comments on the story were enormously helpful.

To all those folks, thank you so much for your friendship and the time you took out of your lives to hammer my scribbles into something that I hope you, the reader, will find worthwhile.

ONE

Three Years After First Contact

"Happy Birthday, Allison!"

Allison Murtaugh, now fourteen years old, smiled as her friends and parents clapped and shouted happily. Even her older brother, Shaun, who was nearly ancient at the age of seventeen and almost always a grouch, smiled and slapped his hands together.

Kayla, Allison's mother, gave her a tight hug. "Blow out the candles, honey!"

Allison looked at the cake her mother had made, now blazing with fourteen flames. The candles danced in her inquisitive green eyes and added highlights to her wild copper-colored hair as she leaned closer to the cake and drew a full breath.

"Don't forget to make a wish, Ali!" Elena, Allison's best friend, held both hands up, fingers crossed.

She'd thought a hundred times of what to wish for, but still wasn't sure. It was hard to wish for anything more than she already had. It was a perfect day, with clear weather and a light breeze that carried the scents from the fields around the farmhouse to the big porch where they'd gathered. Her parents and brother were here with her, as were her friends, and they'd all had a great time that morning, playing and riding horses.

She'd even gotten everything she'd wanted for her birthday, and more. A new reader to replace the one she'd worn out. Shaun's favorite hunting rifle, which she'd always wanted but had never expected to have, especially freely given as a gift. And best of all, she'd gotten a brand new saddle, her very own, for her horse, Race, to replace the worn out hand-me-down saddle that had been Shaun's when he was a little boy.

It was the best birthday she'd ever had, and had been an awesome day so far.

But it was one awesome day out of an endless string of days that were carved from sheer boredom. Her family made ends meet on the farm, but that was about it. They didn't have money to take trips, and you couldn't just up and leave a farm to take a nice vacation for a week or more.

Her family didn't even have a vid in the house, let alone a virtual gaming system or any of the other cool things that some of Allison's friends had.

Then there was school. It was utter torture, and she was always relieved when school went out of session for the harvests, even though that was really hard work. But she'd rather help her parents in the fields or go hunting with her brother than be cooped up in a stifling class room with Mr. Callaway. They had virtual teachers for many of their subjects, but old Callawag, as the kids called him, felt compelled to comment on nearly everything the virtual teachers said.

Allison would have preferred to live in one of the cities, or maybe even sail through space on a starship, traveling to faraway exotic planets, or maybe even visit Earth. She wouldn't want to go anywhere the Kreelans might be lurking, of course, but they couldn't be everywhere.

That's it, she knew. *That's what my wish is, for a little excitement around here.*

"Come on, Ali!" Elena was leaning forward, her face only inches now from the flickering candles and the glistening cake icing. Allison knew why she and the other girls were so eager. Allison's mother made the best cakes in the province, and won first place every year at the fair.

Before Elena could get any ideas about blowing out the candles herself, Allison released her pent-up breath and snuffed the flames to a thunderous round of applause.

As the applause tapered off and Allison's mother moved in with the knife to cut the cake, an unfamiliar, eerie sound reached them.

"What's that?" Allison looked up at her father, Stephen.

"That's not what I think it is..." Kayla set the knife down and moved beside Stephen, taking hold of his arm. They both stared in the direction of Breakwater, a few kilometers away.

"It is." Stephen, his brow knitted in concentration, turned to Shaun. "Get the truck, son. Right now."

"Yes, sir." Shaun had rarely heard his father speak that way, but when he did, Shaun knew to obey right away. He vaulted over the porch railing and ran for the vehicle shed behind the house.

"Daddy?" Allison's voice seemed like that of a little girl to her ears, and she didn't like it. Not at all. "Daddy, what is it?"

"It's nothing, honey." Her mother said, turning and taking Allison's hands. "Don't worry..."

"It's the invasion alert." Her father glanced at her mother, who glared at him. "She needs to be worried, Kayla. That might help keep her and the others alive." He knelt down in front of Allison and gathered the five other girls closer. "You remember the tests of the new emergency sirens we had last month?"

They all nodded, and Allison said, "But those were in case there was a fire in town."

Stephen frowned. "That's what they told you. But that's not the truth." He glanced up at his wife. "The mayor told everyone to say that because he didn't want to scare folks. But you girls are old enough to know the truth, aren't you?"

They all nodded, although Allison thought the others were nodding just because they respected her father. The looks in their eyes told her they were all afraid.

She was worried, but unafraid. She was her father's daughter, and had learned to ride a horse, to fish and hunt. She'd even been with him when he'd killed a neo-bear, one of the few indigenous predator species, that had come after the horses.

And from her brother she had learned how to defend herself at school from a couple of bullies who had tormented her last year. She'd been suspended for breaking both their noses, and had been grounded at home for a month. But she had overheard her parents talking, and both of them had secretly been proud of her. When she'd asked Shaun about it, he'd only smiled.

"The truth is, that's the alarm in case the Navy thinks the Kreelans might be coming." Her father squeezed Allison's hand. "It's to give us a heads-up so we can get ready for them, and get you kids to safety."

They all looked up as three light utility trucks came tearing down the road that led toward town. One of them turned into the long drive to the house, while the other two, both packed with men and women who briefly waved, raced toward Breakwater and the still-screaming sirens.

"Elena, girls," Kayla called, gathering them up when she recognized who was driving the truck. It was Elena's older sister, Danielle. "Time to go."

"We'll see you soon," Elena said, hugging Allison as Danielle brought the truck to a skidding stop, sending up a cloud of dust. Allison hugged the other girls, who all lived right next to Elena's house, as they filed off the porch and climbed into the open truck bed.

"What news, Danielle?" Allison's father called.

Danielle's father was the fire chief and the mayor. His house had one of the new network communication systems the Confederation had brought, but most of the rest hadn't been installed yet, and the local communications network had never worked properly. There was little profit to be made from it here from farmers like Stephen who didn't see the sense in spending money on it, and the only places that had reliable communications were the government and volunteers who manned the local fire station.

"Daddy only told me that it's not a drill." She glanced at the dust trail left by the trucks. "And us *kids*," she spat the word, "have to stay behind." Danielle was old enough to drive on Alger's World, where the legal license age was fourteen, but wasn't old enough for the Territorial Army training or equipment, which the Confederation had mandated was for ages seventeen and older. "It's not fair."

"Let's just hope it's a false alarm, shall we?" Stephen didn't hold out much hope that would be the case, but miracles were always possible. His older brother had seen combat on Saint Petersburg over twenty years before, and had returned home with his left arm and leg missing and his mind caught in an endless nightmare. Stephen had thanked God every day since then that he himself had never had to see combat. He prayed now that his streak of luck would hold.

"Not likely." Danielle glanced in the mirror to make sure the girls were all sitting down in the old truck's cargo bed. "Daddy said the alarm would only be triggered by the Navy defense station."

Stephen's hopes sank. The defense station was the first and, so far, only orbital weapons platform defending the planet. It was manned by regular Confederation Navy personnel and supported by two corvettes. If they had sounded the alarm, it was for real.

"Damn." Stephen turned to see his own battered truck pull up, a grim-faced Shaun at the wheel. "Get going, then, and good luck to you, Danielle. You, too, kids," he called to the other girls. "You be damn careful!"

"Yes, Mr. Murtaugh," they echoed in unison as Danielle backed away. Putting the truck into drive, she spun the wheels and kicked up a huge cloud of dust as she raced back down the drive to the road, then turned back the way she'd come toward home.

"Maybe we should have sent Allison with her." Kayla gave him a worried glance.

"No, she's better off here where she knows her way around." He looked down at his only daughter. "And we've got a better storm shelter than just about anybody, don't we?"

Allison nodded. The family had always had a storm shelter, because this part of Alger's World sometimes suffered from tornadoes and violent storms.

But after the stories of the Kreelans had come across the news channels, after the Confederation had formed to help protect humanity from them, Stephen had taken some precious time from the fields to build a new one. He and Shaun had disappeared into the barn one day with a backhoe, where they dug a tremendous hole in the ground that was nearly four meters deep. Then they built a framework of molds using wood, and filled them with concrete to make a structure that was a third of a meter thick throughout. Steps led toward the surface, with the entrance capped by a ten-centimeter thick steel door operated by an ingenious counterweight mechanism, so even Allison could open it easily. Her father had thought of everything, even a bathroom that only used a little water, pumped in through a pipe from the creek that ran behind the barn.

After backfilling over the top of the structure, about two meters below the surface, the dirt floor of the barn was packed down and again ready for use. Then they stocked the new shelter with enough food, water, and other supplies to last the family at least a month.

Once it was finished, the shelter had instantly become Allison's favorite hangout. It had annoyed her mother for a while, but her father had said, "Let her be. If we ever need it, she'll feel comfortable there."

Reluctantly, her mother had relented, not happy with her daughter spending her free time with her friends, playing in the shelter like it was some sort of entertaining dungeon.

But now, while the rest of her family went into town to draw their weapons and equipment, the last thing Allison wanted to do was cower in the shelter.

"Daddy, can't I go with you? Just to get your weapons and stuff?"

"I wish you could, baby. But you've got to stay here. We've talked about this."

Allison nodded, unhappily giving in. "We've talked about this" was her father's way of saying that he wasn't going to tolerate any further discussion or argument on the subject. He rarely said it, but when he did, nothing short of a supernova would move him.

"Yes, Daddy." She looked down, afraid he might see the tears that threatened to run down her face.

"Don't worry, Ali," he told her softly, drawing her into a tight embrace. "You'll be fine. We'll only be in town for a bit to get our gear and find out what's going on, then we'll make sure we let you know what's happening."

His warmth and strength comforted her, and her nose filled with the scent that was uniquely his, a mix of sweat, earth, and all the many other things that were part of the farm, part of him. She hated feeling like a little girl, but at that moment she was.

"Come on, now." He let go of her and lifted her chin with a callused hand. "You get to where you need to be. We've got to get going." He kissed her on the forehead before taking the steps to where Shaun waited in the truck. "Love you, big girl."

"I love you, too, Daddy."

"We'll be back soon, honey," her mother said, giving Allison a fierce hug, and Allison wrapped her arms tightly around her mother's neck. "Just be careful and keep the door on the shelter locked until we get back, okay?"

"I will, Mom." Allison was crying now, but no longer ashamed of it. Fear took hold of her heart, which felt heavy in her chest, as her father held the door open for her mother. "I love you."

"I love you, too, baby."

They squeezed into the cab next to Shaun, who leaned out the window and said, "Don't forget the present I gave you if you need it." He pointed at the table next to her that held the cake and her presents, including the hunting rifle he'd given her. "And you better not eat all the cake before we get back or I'll paddle you!"

He gave her a big smile and a wave before he pulled away.

* * *

Two hours had passed since her parents and Shaun left for town. A parade of trucks and cars had streamed down the road behind them, and Allison had felt more abandoned and alone with each one.

She'd gone to the shelter as soon as her parents had left, but after sitting there alone for what could only have been ten minutes, she couldn't stand it anymore.

"I'll know when the Kreelans come. I'll have time to run back." Even knowing that her father and mother would be angry, it had been an easy rationalization. Stomping up the stairs, she opened the heavy metal door that was located in the front right corner of the barn. She checked on her horse, Race, who wasn't at all concerned about an alien invasion, but was content to munch on the hay in his feed trough, before she went back to the porch.

After carving a huge piece of her birthday cake, even though she had no appetite to eat it, she had sat there and watched everyone else head to town.

The last of them had gone by nearly half an hour ago, and most of her cake still sat on the table, uneaten.

She knew some of the families had left a parent or older sibling behind to care for the younger children, and part of her was jealous. She wanted more than anything right now for her father or mother, or even Shaun, to be here with her.

But her parents trusted her to take care of herself, and so she would. Her new rifle, the one that Shaun had given her, sat across her knees, the ten-round magazine loaded and a round in the chamber. She wasn't as good a shot as her older brother, but she could hit what she was aiming at, and had brought down her share of the deer that lived in the woods, one of the many Terran species that had been released into the wild when the colony had first been founded here on Alger's World.

She was about to force herself to eat a huge bite of cake that would have brought an indignant rebuke from her mother about poor table manners when she saw them. White trails in the sky, streaking across the horizon.

The invasion alert siren continued its mournful wail, the changes in pitch eerily in step with the wide S-turns made by the white streaks.

Dropping the fork, she stood up and moved to the porch railing for a better look. Some of the streaks were moving north and south, quickly fading from view. Another group, maybe a dozen, spiraled in toward Breakwater.

The house was shaken by what sounded like explosions, but she realized were sonic booms as some of the streaks passed right overhead.

It dawned on her what those streaks were. Kreelan ships, coming in to land. The only other time she'd seen streaks in the sky like that was when her father had taken her to one of the space ports when her uncle had come to visit a few years ago.

A few moments later, the streaks that circled high over the town in graceful arcs resolved into tiny specks as the ships lost their contrails and dove for the ground.

Allison gasped as three small pillars of fire rose from where the town was, each followed by a crackling roar. The anti-air missiles flew unbelievably fast, aimed at three separate landing ships. Two of the missiles exploded well short of their targets, the noise loud enough to force Allison to put her hands over her ears.

The third missile found its target, tearing one of the stubby wings of one of the incoming ships. The craft tumbled out of control, and as she watched a group of smaller things fell away from it like seeds from a pod.

Parachutes fluttered from the tiny things, and they began gliding toward the town, following the other ships that had passed out of view beyond the low rise between the Murtaugh farm and Breakwater.

Over the roar of the ships' engines, Allison heard a sudden eruption of pops from the direction of town.

Rifle fire.

"Oh, no." She stood there, gripping her new hunting rifle, uncertain about what she should do. If her parents were here right now, she knew they would be terribly upset that she wasn't hunkered down in the shelter with the door bolted shut. But they weren't here. They were over there. In trouble.

Before she even realized she was doing it, she was running for the barn. Not for the shelter, but for her horse.

"Easy boy," she soothed as she quickly slipped the bridle on old Race. He was a nine year-old Percheron with a midnight black coat who'd carried Allison since her father had first set her in a saddle when she was four. Race was descended from the genetically modified stock brought by the original colonists to help with clearing and working the land. While most farming tasks were now done with machines, horses still had abundant uses on Alger's World, especially on small farms like this one.

Not to mention they were fun for young girls to ride.

Allison didn't bother with a saddle. There wasn't time. Slipping the rifle's sling over her shoulder, she grabbed a handful of Race's thick mane and jumped up, folding herself over his broad back before sitting up, her legs on either side of his wide rib cage.

Race huffed and tossed his head up and down as the sound of a thunderous explosion rolled across the farm, making the timbers of the barn shake.

"I know, boy," she said as she signaled him forward. "Don't be afraid. I've got to know what's happening."

With one last toss of his head, as if telling her this was a terrible idea, Race dutifully trotted out of the barn, then hit a full gallop as Allison squeezed him with both legs and leaned forward on his back.

She gasped as she looked toward town. Smoke billowed upward, black greasy snakes that curled and undulated into the sky.

The roar of the ships' engines died away as the aliens shut them down, and Allison's ears were filled with the non-stop pops and cracks of even more rifle fire.

Race flew across the fields, taking the shortest route to where Allison could get a glimpse of the town.

To her left, a truck roared over the small hill on the road from town, so fast that the wheels momentarily lost touch with the ground as it sailed over the top.

It was burning. As Allison watched, a web of what looked like lightning arced across the vehicle's body. There were three people in the cab and five in the back, desperately holding on. All of them wore Territorial Army uniforms.

When the lightning touched them, they screamed.

The scene played out like a slow-motion horror vid as the web of lightning grew more intense, wrapping around the entire vehicle. The body of the truck began to melt, and the people writhed in agony as they were electrocuted and charred black.

She was shaken from the horrific scene when the truck finally swung off the road into one of the fields, rolled over and exploded.

"Oh, God. Oh, God." She murmured the words over and over as Race took her up over the rise, where she brought him to a sudden stop with a firm pull on the reins.

The alien ships were in a rough ring around the town, and dozens of black-armored figures were making their way along the streets and alleyways. She immediately saw that almost all the gunfire was coming from her people. None of the Kreelans even seemed to have rifles. Instead, as the news reports had said, they held swords and strange throwing weapons.

She witnessed just how deadly the throwing weapons were when she saw a man poke his head around a corner, rifle at his shoulder. He got off a shot at a warrior, who crumpled to the ground. But before the man could duck back behind the corner, another warrior threw one of the things at him.

Allison saw it pass by him, but it didn't seem to hit him. The man stood there for a moment, as if stunned. Then his face and the front half of his head simply fell away as the warrior who'd killed him ran by, snatching up the weapon she'd thrown before moving deeper into the town.

The horror was overwhelming, and for a moment Allison simply sat there, tears streaking down her face and her mouth open in numb disbelief.

Then she saw them. Two men and a woman lay near one of the missile launchers. Dead. She remembered Shaun bragging about how important his job was, loading one of the fancy missile systems the Confederation had brought in. The helmet of one of the men had come off, and while the body was covered in blood, she could see enough of her father's red hair to know it was him. Her father, her mother, and her older brother. All dead.

"No." The word caught in her throat as she saw a warrior near one of the ships happen to turn her way.

Only then did she realize that she was completely exposed, silhouetted on the top of the rise. And sitting astride a horse, yet. Every warrior in town would be able to see her.

But at that moment, she didn't care. A flare of rage, the likes of which she'd never known, flowed through her at the thought of her murdered family.

The warrior called to one of the others near the ship, and the two of them bolted toward where Race and Allison stood.

"Come on, then." Allison raised the rifle Shaun had given her. It wasn't fancy, but it was incredibly accurate out to three hundred meters. It was also powerful enough to stop a neo-bear.

She had never fired from horseback before, but knew that Shaun had fired his rifle while riding Race, and the big horse had barely flinched.

Laying the sights on the chest of the first alien, who was running flat out toward her, Allison let out her breath and stroked the trigger.

Sitting on Race without a saddle or stirrups, she had no way to absorb the rifle's recoil, and it nearly knocked her backwards off the horse's back. She grabbed his mane just in time and managed to pull herself upright.

"Good boy!"

Race had stood rock-steady, but snorted at her compliment, clearly unhappy to be there.

Her target was down, a crumpled heap of black armor and blue skin on the ground. But the second one was gaining fast, and other warriors had turned around at the sound of the shot.

Allison aimed and fired.

This warrior was smarter, pitching herself to the side at the last instant.

Allison fired again and missed, then once more. Another miss.

The warrior grabbed one of the throwing weapons from her shoulder and cocked her arm back as Allison squeezed the trigger a fourth time, cringing as the warrior's head exploded in a shower of blood and gore.

More warriors were now heading her way.

Time to go, she thought.

"Come on, boy!" She turned Race around and squeezed him hard with her legs. The big horse ran as fast as Allison could ever remember him moving.

She wasn't heading back toward the farm and the safety of the barn and the shelter. Not yet. As fast as the warriors ran, they'd be able to see where she was going if she went straight back home. Her only chance was to make it to the woods that lay a couple hundred meters to the north, then work her way back home.

Glancing behind her, praying that the aliens wouldn't top the rise before she made it into the trees, she urged Race on.

She was almost to the woods when she heard one of the ships starting its engines.

Looking back, a shiver of fear ran up her spine as she saw the black ship, its shimmering black sides covered with strange alien writing in the same color as the lightning that had killed the people in the truck, rise above the hill and turn toward her.

"Come on, boy! Come on!"

She didn't see the laser blast that killed Race. She only heard a brief thrumming sound before the horse make a strange grunt and he fell.

Allison went sailing over his head as he went down, and the rifle flew from her hand.

Rolling as she hit the ground, just as her father had taught her, she quickly got to her knees and looked back at her fallen horse.

Race stared at her with dead eyes. His body had been sheared in half, just behind where she'd been sitting. Smoke rose from the blackened ends of his severed body, and she smelled the stench of burning meat and hair. His rear hooves twitched.

The tree next to her crackled with heat and burst into flame as the ship fired again, and she caught sight of several warriors running toward her. She couldn't see how the ship could have missed her with the laser as she knelt there. They must have killed Race just to keep her from getting away.

"Goodbye, boy," she whispered before she turned and fled into the woods.

* * *

It took Allison nearly six hours to make her way home. Kreelans were scouring the area, and Allison had been forced to hide in a secret spot along the creek until the aliens went away. Waist deep in the burbling water of the creek, she cowered in a tiny cave formed by a group of rocks. Before her father had built the shelter, it had been her favorite hideaway when she played with Elena and the other girls, although her parents and Shaun knew perfectly well where it was.

But the Kreelans didn't. She heard them moving around in the woods outside, but stayed put until late at night, long after the voices of her alien pursuers had faded away.

There, in the dark, she had listened to the continued sounds of gunfire coming from town. The defenders weren't giving in easily. She didn't know anything about armies and fighting, but she knew the Territorial Army, her townsfolk, would probably lose. A lot of Kreelans had come out of those boats.

At last, she forced herself out of the little cave. She was afraid that if she didn't go now, she never would.

After looking and listening carefully for any sign of the aliens, she made her way along the creek that formed the northern boundary of the farms on this side of town, careful not to make any noise.

Finally reaching her own farm, she paused again. Kneeling in the gently burbling water, she carefully watched the barn, which was only a short run from the creek, and listened.

There was nothing but the sounds of battle coming from town. She also heard more shots being fired from the west and south.

Getting up, Allison crept across the open ground to the rear of the barn, then slipped inside. The other animals were still there, and after a moment's deliberation, she freed them. The four cows and two horses wandered out the open doors and began grazing, unconcerned that aliens had invaded their world.

Opening the door to the shelter, Allison entered the stairwell, then closed and locked the door behind her, shutting away the awful sounds of the fighting.

Leaving the lights off, as if the aliens could somehow see them here underground, she crawled into the small bed that was hers. She didn't bother to take off her wet clothes.

After a moment, shivering with cold and the agony of all she'd lost that day, Allison quietly wept in the darkness.

Two

Ku'ar-Marekh, high warrior priestess of the Nyur-A'il, walked alone on an airless world whose existence in the cosmos was unworthy of an entry in the Books of Time, save that she had set foot upon it.

She stopped a moment and looked up at the protostar that was forming far above, an accretion of gas and dust that someday would achieve sufficient mass for fusion to begin, for a star to be born. It was a swirling, glowing cloud whose beauty had never been witnessed by any sentient being other than herself.

Her armor, a light-drinking black that was so smooth it could be used as a mirror, except for the cyan rune of the order of the Nyur-A'il in the center, reflected the subtle hues. The reds and yellows and blues that she could see, but whose beauty could not touch her soul.

Her jet black hair, woven into the braids that were an ancient tradition of her people, hung down to her waist, glistening in the ghostly light. Her eyes, flecked with silver, looked at the scene through slitted pupils. Her skin, a cobalt blue, in this light was so dark as to be nearly black. Black as the empty space around her, a reflection of the emptiness within her.

Around her neck she wore the black collar of living metal that every one of Her Children wore, the many rows of pendants that hung from it proclaiming her accomplishments for the peers to witness. The front of the collar also bore an oval device of glittering metal, the same living steel from which Kreelan swords were made, with her order's rune etched into the surface. It proclaimed that she was a priestess, although the warriors around her knew who and what she was through their very blood. They could sense her spirit in the Bloodsong that united their people across the ten thousand suns of the Empire, and across the boundary that separated life and death.

Indeed, she was a high priestess, but it was an empty honor, the name of her order ash on her tongue. The Nyur-A'il was not the oldest of the orders that served Her, the Empress, for that honor was accorded to the Desh-Ka and its last living disciple, the great priestess Tesh-Dar.

But while the Desh-Ka might be considered the most powerful in the Empire, it could be said that the Nyur-A'il were the most feared.

Yet fear was an emotion that Ku'ar-Marekh no longer felt. Nor was love, joy, or anger. Among the peers she had heard whispers of a name that some had for her. They called her Dead Soul.

Had they spoken the name to her, she would not have taken them to task for it, for it was too close to the truth.

Reaching out her hands toward the protostar, she yearned to touch it, to become one with it over the ages yet to come. The invisible energy bubble surrounding her body flexed, matching her movement. It held the air she needed to breathe and shielded her from the radiation of the star-to-be, but it was not an artifact of technology. It was an act of will, a gift of the Change that had made her far more than a mere warrior, just as was the ability to flit among the stars, merely by wishing it so. Few high priestesses had that particular power, for the sacred crystals which powered the Change were fickle, their gifts not easily predicted.

For her, the Change had not been as expected. While it had brought her powers that made her greatly feared, even among the other warrior priestesses, it had robbed her of much more.

She knew she could not touch the cloud, but yearned to be part of it, to be reborn. To have been chosen to take her place as a warrior priestess among the Children of the Empress had been a great honor, the greatest to which any of the peers could aspire.

But for Ku'ar-Marekh, it had been the end of her happiness. The great cloud of glowing dust at which she longingly stared would know more of happiness than did she.

For long cycles after the Change, after she had become her order's highest and last priestess, she had wandered the galaxy far beyond the Empire's vast domain. She had walked upon a hundred worlds such as this, had floated through great rings of fire and ice, and had seen sights among the stars that no other of her race had ever glimpsed. She sought to find something, anything, that would kindle the faintest emotion in her heart, the tiniest sense of wonder or awe. Even fear or loneliness.

Yet she had felt nothing. Views that would have paralyzed her sisters with their celestial grandeur left her unmoved.

All she could do was live, to survive from day to day without hope or solace. She breathed the air she took with her during her leaps through space. She ate and drank when her body demanded, rested when her endurance was at an end. She existed. No more.

Even the Bloodsong, the emotional river that flowed from the Empress and bound Her Children together, was like a fire that cast light but not the warmth that Ku'ar-Marekh remembered from before the Change. She could sense her sisters, their joys and sorrows, the fierce ecstasy of those fighting the far-distant humans. But their fates were bound to the Universe around her, and in the end did not matter to Ku'ar-Marekh. Nothing did.

Nothing...except the Empress Herself. From Her alone could Ku'ar-Marekh sense in the Bloodsong a trace of the love that she had once known, as if the Empress were a great star, now far distant. That was the only reason Ku'ar-Marekh had not surrendered her honor and taken her own life. Even the eternal dark beyond the love of the Empress could not be worse than the dark and empty torment of her existence.

Ku'ar-Marekh lowered her arms, letting them fall to her side. All she felt now was a great weariness. It was a familiar sensation, and meant that it was time to move on yet again.

That was when she felt a sudden surge in the Bloodsong, a great upwelling that could only have one source, the Empress Herself. Ku'ar-Marekh sighed as she opened herself to her sovereign's power.

She knelt and closed her eyes as she felt space and time whirl around her, bending to the will of She Who Reigned. There was but a brief moment of freezing emptiness as she crossed the vast span of the galaxy to her destination. Toward the home of her race.

"Rise, priestess of the Nyur-A'il."

Ku'ar-Marekh opened her eyes to find the Empress standing before her. She wore only a simple white robe and a golden collar around the deep blue skin of her neck. Unlike the peers, Her collar bore no embellishments, no testimony to her feats from the time before she had surrendered her Collar of Honor and her birth name, things every Empress gave up when ascending to the throne.

The braids of Her hair, unlike that of the peers, was white, not black. It was a rare trait among Her race, and only those warriors born with white hair could ever become Empress.

She Who Reigned had once been a powerful warrior, but since ascending to the throne had become far, far more. She was the heart and soul of the Empire, and embodied the souls of all those who had reigned before Her. All except for Keel-Tath, the First Empress, and the most powerful. The Empress who had cursed Her Own people in a fit of rage and anguish, and whose spirit Her successors had sought for tens of thousands of generations.

Ku'ar-Marekh and the Empress were alone in a corner of the Imperial Gardens that were part of the palace on the Empress Moon orbiting the Homeworld.

Ku'ar-Marekh did as the Empress commanded and rose, yet kept her eyes downcast in respect.

"Walk with me, child." The Empress turned to follow the winding path made of stones taken from all the worlds the Empire had ever touched. Somewhere, Ku'ar-Marekh knew, there was a stone from each of the dead worlds she herself had set foot upon in her travels, and that someday the Empress would touch those stones with Her feet as she guided the Empire with Her words and the power of the Bloodsong.

The thought of how long Ku'ar-Marekh had been away, how she had intentionally shunned the peers, even the Empress herself, should have made her feel great shame. She knew this, but did not feel it.

"It has happened before." The Empress walked slowly, one hand on her belly. She was heavy with child, one of many she had borne. She was older than most of the peers, but would yet outlive nearly all of them, and would bear children for many cycles more. For She was bound by the same curse as were the others of Her people. Fertile adult females had to mate every cycle or they would die. Powerful as She was, the living Empress, too, fell under the same Curse.

"What has happened before, my Empress?"

"What happened to you, child." The Empress stopped and turned to face Ku'ar-Marekh. "I know the emptiness you feel, priestess of the Nyur-A'il. It is a rare thing, for when a priestess passing on her legacy dies in the Change, as did yours, the disciple nearly always dies, as well. But sometimes..."

"Yes, my Empress?"

"Sometimes, the body lives."

"I..." Ku'ar-Marekh stopped, her mind grappling with the unpleasant possibilities. "I do not understand."

"Your soul is caught between life and death, child. That is why you feel no fire in your heart from the Bloodsong, why joy and sorrow have no meaning. Why even pain has no sting. Why you do not feel this."

The Empress raised Her hand to Ku'ar-Marekh's face, and as their flesh touched, Ku'ar-Marekh was flooded with the power of the Bloodsong as she remembered it, with feeling, emotions. With life. It was as if one of the great tapestries that hung in the throne room, drained of color, was returned to its original glory.

"Oh," she gasped, instinctively covering the Empress's hand with her own, pressing it firmly against her cheek, never wanting to let Her go.

Ku'ar-Marekh fell to her knees, and it took all her will not to cry out in joy that she could feel again, and in anguish at the knowledge that this was but a fleeting moment that would vanish as soon as the Empress took away Her hand.

She bit her tongue, one of her fangs piercing it clean through, to keep from begging the Empress to take her life, to not consign her to another moment of living death. For Ku'ar-Marekh was a warrior priestess, and she could not dishonor herself or her order. She would not.

"Your Way is a difficult one, child." The Empress gently ran the fingers of Her other hand over Ku'ar-Marekh's black braids. While the priestess was not a child of Her body, she was a child of Her spirit, and the Empress felt the fear and anguish in her heart now. Yet She was warmed by Ku'ar-Marekh's strength and her refusal to give in, to beg for mercy. "It is a path that very few have been fated to walk during the long ages of our history. Yet it is a path that you must follow to its end, where you shall find peace."

Slowly, the Empress took away Her hands, and Ku'ar-Marekh felt the warmth fade from her heart. In but seconds, her soul was as it had been since the terrible day of the Change. Dead. Empty.

"What must I do, my Empress?" Ku'ar-Marekh's tongue felt heavy, wooden in her mouth.

"You are a warrior priestess, and the Empire is again at war. We know the measure of the enemy, the humans, and they are worthy opponents." She paused. "And if we are to find the One who shall release us from the Curse, we must find him among these animals. For if we do not, in but a few generations our race shall perish from the stars."

Ku'ar-Marekh merely nodded, for the ancient prophecy was no secret among the priestesses and the elder mistresses of the clawless ones.

"A scout force has landed on one of the smaller human colonies, but they have no priestess attending them. Your presence there will redress this."

"As you command, my Empress." Ku'ar-Marekh saluted, hammering her gauntleted fist, her silver talons clenched, against the armor of her breast. The silver signified that she was sterile, barren. Another legacy of the change, and one whose irony had not escaped her.

"I will deliver you to the command ship." The Empress paused, looking at Ku'ar-Marekh with great sorrow. "May thy Way be long and glorious, my child."

To Ku'ar-Marekh, the ancient words of parting were a curse that echoed in her mind as the Empress again sent her across the stars.

THREE

Her name was Valentina. It was not the name she had been given at birth, and she had gone by many others in her life. Those few who knew her true identity called her only by her old codename, Scarlet. But Valentina was her chosen name, the one she planned to carry with her to the grave.

A year of agony, sweat and tears had passed since she had awakened from her coma to endure a brutal physical therapy regimen designed to rebuild her body and recover her strength. Beyond the psychological trauma from the implants, she had been hit five times at point blank range by an assault rifle, and only the implants she had been given as a special operative, the ones that could inject painkillers, adrenaline, and hormones into her blood stream, had kept her alive.

As her body mended, so did her mind. She had brought under control the soul-numbing coldness of the machines that she had merged with, that had nearly driven her insane. She had not banished the frigid darkness entirely, for it still haunted her dreams, but it no longer ruled her mind.

Now, her dark brown hair was pulled back in a tight ponytail, and her face was dripping sweat as she hammered at a well-worn punching bag with her hands and feet. Where she had once cried with joy at being able to hold her arms up from the bed for an agonizing thirty seconds, she now worked out hard every day for at least two hours, kicking and punching the bag with lethal moves taken from a variety of martial arts before she went running through the surrounding woods. She was not as strong or as fast as she had been before she had been shot, for there was some damage to her body that the surgical team had not been able to fully repair. Even at that, once again she was a lethal weapon, even though there was no one for her to kill.

Her days were spent with Dmitri and Ludmilla Sikorsky, her adopted parents, in peaceful pursuits on their horse farm in what had once been the American State of Virginia. During the days and in good weather they were mostly outdoors, working the garden, tending the horses and riding, and enjoying the beauty of the surrounding woods. Inside, especially during the winter, reading had become a favorite pastime. The Sikorskys had grown up on a world where the only books allowed were those published by government-approved authors, and with their sudden immersion in a society where they could read whatever they wanted, where authors could write whatever they pleased, reading had become an instant addiction. Valentina had always loved to read, but never had the time, and had happily gone along with this new family tradition.

Valentina - Scarlet - found that she was, for the first time in her life, at peace.

She had just landed another low kick against the bag, a hit that would have shattered the leg of a human opponent, and was about to follow up with an open-hand strike when her wristcomm chimed.

"Security alert." It was the soft female voice of the house's central security system. It had been installed by the CIS to protect Valentina and the Sikorskys from anyone who might have somehow learned her true identity and come to take revenge for her previous operations. "An unidentified vehicle is approaching."

Valentina immediately went from the workout room to the front door. Next to it was a cabinet on the wall. Opening the cabinet, she pulled out a large-bore pistol that could put a hole through centimeter-thick armor plate. She and the Sikorskys had some local friends who periodically came to visit, but no one ever came to the house unannounced. While she considered herself out of the death-dealing business, she would never hesitate to defend herself or her adopted parents, and there was an impressive arsenal hidden throughout the house.

Taking a look at the video monitor that was tracking the vehicle's progress along the lengthy driveway toward the house, she did a double-take.

It was a Marine utility vehicle.

"What the hell?" She wondered who it could possibly be. While she had been in a coma, she had received a pile of get well cards and flowers from the Marines she had helped to save from the Saint Petersburg debacle, but none of them had ever stopped by to see her. Most of them, she knew, were either still in combat zones or had been killed in action. Very few had been able to return home, and most probably never would.

The dark green- and brown-painted vehicle, an ugly, angular beast on four oversized tires that could drive through or over virtually any terrain, pulled to a stop in front of the house, about a dozen meters from the front door.

The driver side door opened, and a big, broad-shouldered man with close-cropped dark blond hair stepped out. He was wearing a Marine dress uniform that was a stark contrast to the dark forest colors of the vehicle's camouflage paint: a dark blue coat with polished brass buttons and crimson piping over slightly lighter blue trousers sporting a broad crimson stripe down the leg, with the bright red and gold stripes and rockers on the sleeve proclaiming him a first sergeant.

He carefully placed his white "wheel" cap on his head with his white-gloved hands, the black visor shielding his eyes from the bright sun, before he headed toward the house.

With a warm smile, Valentina opened the door and stepped outside to meet him.

"Mills." She was unable to keep the tears from her eyes. "Roland Mills."

"Valentina!" His handsome face turned up in a devilish grin. "Bloody hell, woman," he said in his public school English accent, "but you're looking good!"

She wrapped her arms around his muscular frame, hugging him. He returned her embrace with rib-cracking force.

"It's good to see you." She pulled away, looking up into his intensely green eyes.

"Were you, ah, expecting someone?" He cocked his head at the pistol she was still holding.

"Well, a girl can't be too careful these days." She set the safety on the pistol and hooked an arm through his and led him into the house. "Come on. Let me make you some tea."

When they reached the kitchen, Valentina made some tea from an ornate samovar perched on one of the counters. She smiled every time she looked at it, thinking of how excited Dmitri and Ludmilla had been when they had come home one day and found it there. They had always wanted a nice samovar, which had long been used by Russians to boil water for tea, but had never been able to afford a good one. Valentina had this one custom made for them in Tula, Russia, where samovars had been made since the late sixteenth century. It was ridiculously ornate by modern standards, with an intricate floral design in silver over a bright blue enamel surface, and had cost her a small fortune. But it had been worth every credit for the joy it had brought to her adopted parents.

She turned around to look at Mills, who now sat at the cozy wooden table where the Sikorsky family normally ate breakfast. Having taken off his hat and gloves, he was giving her an openly appraising look.

"I'm not in the market, Roland." She frowned at him as she handed him the glass of hot tea.

"Pardon?"

She stood there, hands on hips, and stared at him. "If you came here looking for some female companionship while you're on shore leave, you came to the wrong place."

He sat there for just a moment, dumbfounded. Then he covered his face with his hands, and she could see his shoulders begin to quiver. She thought he was crying until he threw his head back and roared with laughter.

Valentina, unable to help herself, started laughing, too, as she sat down next to him.

"No, girl." He finally brought himself under control, wiping tears from his eyes after laughing so hard. "Christ, no, I'm not here to try and crawl in your knickers, although Lord knows a lad could do worse."

She took the complement for what it was, and knew that plenty of women would gladly have welcomed the attentions of Roland Mills. He was unarguably good looking, with a ruggedly handsome face bearing a mouth that could light the room when he smiled, and a scowl that could make hardened Marines shrink away in fear when he was angry. Nearly any man would be frankly envious of his body. He was big, tall and broad shouldered, with a tight waist and powerful arms and legs, his muscles perfectly defined under his lightly bronzed skin. While he often enjoyed giving others the impression that he was an ignorant ape, he had a keen mind and a big heart, a heart that she knew had been gravely wounded when the woman he loved, Emmanuelle Sabourin, had been killed by the Kreelans on Saint Petersburg.

Valentina had only met him briefly before she had been shot during the battle, but he had been one of the few visitors she had received during her recovery from her coma. He had been on temporary duty to Earth and had made special arrangements to see her, appearing in his dress uniform, just as he had today, to thank her in person for what she had done to get him and his Marines to safety.

She had still been bedridden then, her muscles so atrophied that she could barely lift up her hands to hold his. They had talked for a long time, and even managed a few jokes, but she could tell that the pain he felt inside, just like her own, would take a long time to heal. They had become friends that day, and she still remembered the feeling of his lips on hers as he had gently, like a shy schoolboy, kissed her goodbye before starting the long trip back to the ongoing battle for Saint Petersburg. They had exchanged emails since then, but getting anything other than military communications into or out of the spreading war zones was hit or miss, at best.

Looking at him now, she could tell that he had come a long way from the last time they had spoken, despite what must have been an incredible strain from having been engaged in nearly non-stop combat operations. She knew there was still a reservoir of pain under the surface, but he could smile now without forcing it, just as she herself could.

"Seriously, Valentina," he told her, "you're looking fantastic. When I came to visit you that first time, I...I didn't think you'd ever even be able to walk again. You were a bit of a fright, you know."

She laughed. "Thanks for the compliment! You really know how to impress a woman, you know that?" Then, more seriously, she asked, "And how about you? How are you doing?"

He shrugged, an uncomfortable look on his face. Like most men, she was sure he hated talking about his emotions, but he hadn't shied away from it when he visited her last time, or in their correspondence.

"Okay, I suppose." He looked down into his tea as he slowly spun the glass around on the table. "Still in one piece, as you can see." He was silent a moment, then went on softly, "I still think of her, Emmanuelle, but I guess I've moved on, mostly. Combat has a way of focusing your attention on more immediate matters." He sighed. "But for most of us there isn't much beyond that now, is there?"

Valentina had a sudden premonition that his last words were more significant than he had meant to let on. Understanding the truth behind a casual statement was a talent she had honed into a useful skill that had saved her life on more than one occasion.

After taking a sip of tea, she set the glass down and looked the big Marine in the eyes. "All right, Roland, you didn't come here just for another social visit, did you?"

Mills had to look away for a moment, a feeling of guilt knotting up in his stomach.

Bloody idiot, he cursed himself. *You should have just gotten to the point right from the start. She's not a damn fool.*

He turned back to her, once again stunned by the transformation she had undergone in the months that had passed since he had last come to visit her. Where there had once been a bullet-riddled body housing a tormented mind, he now saw a strikingly beautiful woman in superb physical and, from what he had read from her files before he had come here, mental shape. With muscles that were lithe and strong as any champion athlete, even without the additional strength her implants might offer, she remained profoundly feminine, with a full bust and invitingly curved hips, her features accentuated by her tight black workout clothes. Valentina's face was graced with sensuous lips and deep brown eyes that were now locked with his own.

Despite his earlier joking about not wanting to get into her knickers, he couldn't deny the attraction he felt toward her. He hadn't been with another woman since Emmanuelle had died, and he felt a warm shiver ripple down his spine.

Now's not the time, you fool, he counseled himself. *She'd kick your arse.*

He couldn't suppress a grin at his own foolishness. Valentina cocked an eyebrow at his change of expression, but she didn't offer up a smile in return.

"Fair enough." He let out a sigh. "You caught me. The truth is, I did come here to pay a social visit, but it's...business, as well." His grin disappeared and his expression grew serious. "I'm putting a team together, Valentina. It's a special recon team that's tasked to go in ahead of an assault force to scout Kreelan positions and report back. The Kreelans keep defeating our technology, or at least selective bits of it, and they completely bugger every kind of technical reconnaissance, seemingly at will. Satellites, drones, even the stealth microsats the CIS has come up with. They just stop working. Poof. The boffins don't have a clue how the blue girls are doing it."

"All of them fail?" Valentina leaned back as she considered the dreadful implications of what Mills was saying. Any combat force that was blind to what the enemy was doing was already halfway to being defeated.

"No." Mills shook his head. "That's what makes it even stranger. Sometimes they work fine, but if they seem to touch on something the enemy doesn't want them to see, the sensor or weapon just dies. Drones fall from the sky. Satellites just stop working. Guided missiles lose their guidance and merrily sail off course.

"And sometimes things don't really go dead, but just stop working for a while. Data-links will drop, then come back on sometime later. It's like the Kreelans just wave some sort of magic wand when they don't want us peeping in on them or don't like the weapons we happen to be using," he snapped his fingers, "and we're bollixed."

"Jesus." Valentina hadn't fought the Kreelans on Saint Petersburg, as she had been injured before they aliens had attacked. She had heard of their seemingly supernatural powers, but that had only been rumor. Until now.

"Ships can help a bit from orbit," Mills went on, "as the Kreelans don't seem to hamper them so much, but our Navy is usually too busy trying to beat back Kreelan warships to help much with the ground battle. But on the ground, our boys and girls are dead without decent battlefield intel."

"So what is it that you have in mind?"

"We need boots on the ground," he told her firmly, "people who can put eyes and ears on the target area, sort out what's going on and report back, and who can move quietly and quickly through enemy territory without being seen. I also need people who are good enough to fight their way out of a tough scrap if things turn—"

"I'm not going back to Saint Petersburg." She said it before he could finish, a haunted look shrouding her face. She would never go back there.

Mills shook his head. "It won't be Saint Petersburg. The target for the first operation hasn't been announced yet, but I know it won't be there, or any of the six other worlds the enemy attacked in the first round after the invasion of Keran."

"Why not?"

"Because," he went on grimly, "those worlds are as good as lost. That's obviously not being trumpeted from the Presidential Complex, but it's the truth. The fighting will probably go on for some time yet, maybe even a few more years, but the Kreelans are too well entrenched on the ground, and the Navy can't prevent the enemy from bringing in reinforcements."

He took a sip of tea, noting Valentina's shocked expression. "Every so often a Kreelan task force appears and drops another big load of warriors to the surface. The big transports jump out, while their warships rough up the Navy until our ships finally wipe them out. Meanwhile, the warriors they leave behind continue hacking and chopping away at us on the ground.

"Don't get me wrong. We kill them in droves, even without using the really high-tech weaponry that they somehow bedevil. But there are always more of them to kill, and they have to be killed, because they don't surrender. Ever. We haven't had one single prisoner, Valentina, in all the battles being fought now across over a dozen worlds. Not one. And we haven't been able to break them psychologically, get them to rout or retreat in a single battle. All the things we've always taken for granted as part of warfare amongst humans," he flicked his fingers in the air, "is good for nothing at all. They come at us like they're berserkers and just go on fighting until they die. Then more come to replace them."

"This operation you're talking about, is it part of the strategic offensive that President McKenna has been alluding to?"

Natalie McKenna was the first president of the newly formed Confederation. Working under incomprehensible pressure and driving herself mercilessly, she had managed to forge a working interstellar government amidst a massive alien invasion, using the industrial might of Earth and the worlds of the Francophone Alliance to forge an arsenal that could defend humanity.

"Yes." Mills nodded. "It was originally going to be launched months ago, but the second wave of attacks set back the timetable. And now there's been a third."

"How many colonies have been hit so far?"

"Fifteen," Mills told her. "The Empire attacked seven, including Saint Petersburg, in the first wave of invasions after Keran was wiped out. A few months later, while you were still in a coma, they attacked six more. And just last week they attacked two, Alger's World and Wuhan. The couriers came in this morning with that news.

"McKenna's tired of letting the blues having the initiative, and she's given the green light for a full counteroffensive to take back one of our worlds so we'll have some good news. So we can give people hope. Because frankly, love, we're getting our arses pounded."

He took a long sip of tea, then set the glass down. "Now we're just trying to put the last pieces together. I'm to lead one of the recon teams that'll be first on the ground." He paused, looking at her pointedly. "I have one slot on my team left to fill. I need a sniper, and God strike me dead if you're not the best shot I've ever seen, with that circus shooting you did on Saint Petersburg.

"On top of that, you know all about intel, and I know you've had extensive training in first aid and communications. Plus," he added with a playful leer, "you'll bring up the average for good looks on the team by quite a few points."

"How much do you know about my background?" Valentina narrowed her eyes at the mention of her background in intelligence. Only two people had ever seen her complete file and knew everything about her. One was Vladimir Penkovsky, the Director of the Confederation Intelligence Service. The other was her controller, Robert Torvald. There was information in there that she would never want anyone else to know, information that was dangerous enough that she would kill someone, even a friend, to keep it secret.

Mills held up his hands toward her, seeing the change in her expression and the sudden tension in her body that he knew could erupt into lethal violence. He was far larger than she was, but despite his size advantage and experience in close combat against the Kreelans, he wouldn't have wagered money on his own survival in a fight against her. From what he had been told and seen in her file, she could tear him to pieces without breaking a sweat.

"Hold up, Valentina. Your old friend Torvald briefed me on your training and abilities that were pertinent to our mission needs. That was all. Nothing about your past or what you've done; nothing about any of that spooky stuff from your former life. I don't care, and I don't want to know. Confirm it with him if you like." He chuckled. "Director Penkovsky had to order Torvald to talk to me, and even then it was like pulling teeth to get the bugger to tell me anything useful. He's a bit of a constipated sod, isn't he?"

With that, Valentina relaxed. She would double-check what Mills had told her with Torvald, with whom she'd kept in periodic contact, but she could tell Mills wasn't lying. And thinking about his ribald description of Torvald, she couldn't help but chuckle herself. It was too close to the mark.

"All right. I guess I won't have to kill you. This time."

"Whew!" Mills puffed some air through his lips and theatrically wiped a hand across his brow, but inwardly he was relieved. Torvald had warned him that if he lost "Scarlet's" trust and she thought Mills knew too much about her past, she wouldn't hesitate to kill him. "So that brings us to the big question of the day. Will you do this?"

Valentina looked out one of the kitchen windows at the woods beyond, considering. She had given up everything for her career with the CIS. She had traded away her true identity and had made a profession of spying on and killing other human beings. Sometimes it had been justified, sometimes it had simply been necessary.

But with every life she had taken, she had felt like a piece of her soul had been carved away and cast into Hell. Even now that she was no longer officially in the employ of the CIS, her past guaranteed that she would never be able to live the ordinary, normal life that so many others took for granted. She was still young, and often wished for a man to share her life and her bed, but that, too, had been something she had decided could never happen. She could never expose anyone else to the risks that she and the Sikorskys already lived under, the perpetual fear that her identity might be compromised and the demons of her past deeds would come to claim their vengeance. She did not have to worry about such threats to any children she might have, for the bullets that had ravaged her body at Saint Petersburg had put an end to that possibility.

She had more than paid her dues to the Confederation government, she knew, and to the Terran government before that. She had even paid the price for getting Mills and his fellow Marines away from Saint Petersburg, spending months in a coma that wasn't dreamless, but had been a never-ending nightmare until the day she finally awakened. She owed nothing more to humanity.

But the threat now was not from another group of human beings with which her star nation was in competition or conflict, but from an alien menace that seemed determined to wipe her kind from the Universe.

Turning her eyes to the beautiful samovar on the counter, she realized that everything good that humanity had ever done was now at risk. Humanity had a dark and ugly side, and she had seen far more than her share of it. But she believed there was far more that was good, that was worth saving. Things of beauty like the samovar, and things that money could not buy, like the love and devotion of Dmitri and Ludmilla as they waited for her to wake from her coma.

If the Kreelans had their way, all of that, and so much more, would be erased, gone forever.

She knew that she couldn't prevent that from happening single-handed. But standing on the sidelines, comfortably tucked away on this little horse farm in the deep woods, wouldn't help win the war.

And Mills was right. There was probably no one, anywhere, who was more qualified for what he needed than she was.

With a deep sigh, Valentina turned back to him. "Okay, Mills, I'm in."

FOUR

Allison spent the first three days after the invasion in the shelter. She heard strange sounds on the second day, muffled and indistinct through the concrete and earth above her. The third day was quiet.

By the fourth day, she had to get outside to take a look before she went crazy.

Waiting until the clock told her night had fallen, she crept up the steps to the thick shelter door and tried to open it, but it was stuck. She checked the counterbalance mechanism to make sure it wasn't jammed. As far as she could tell, it looked fine.

That meant that something was blocking the door.

It took her nearly fifteen minutes of desperate pushing and shoving before she finally managed to get the door open far enough to see what was blocking it.

Charred wood. It wasn't hot or smoking, but the smell of it was so strong it made her cough.

An hour of hard, messy work later, she had cleared the wood away by poking and prodding it through the slim opening with long screwdrivers and the pry bar.

Finally able to open the door enough to stick her head outside, she could see in the starlight that the barn was nothing but a burned out ruin. The front half had collapsed, with some of the rafters falling across the door to the shelter. That's what had been blocking her way.

She suppressed a gasp when she saw someone sprawled on the dirt floor toward the rear of the barn, which still stood.

Letting the door close quietly behind her, Allison crept over to the person.

"Hello? Can you hear me?"

She flicked on the tiny flashlight she carried, and bit back a cry of

It was a man wearing a Territorial Army uniform. She didn't recognize him, but he was clearly dead, a deep gash through his throat. His eyes stared, unseeing, at the underside of the ruined barn's loft.

She looked around with her flashlight, but couldn't see any other bodies. Afraid now that one of the aliens might see the light, she switched it off and sat there in the dark, shivering.

Some soldiers must have hidden in the barn, she thought, and then the Kreelans found them. That would explain the noises she'd heard earlier. They were the sounds of a battle taking place right over her head. A battle that the humans had again lost, and during which the barn had been set ablaze. She was only amazed that the whole structure hadn't burned to the ground.

Moving back toward the front of the barn, picking her way carefully through the wreckage, she found a spot that had a clear view of the house.

Or where the house should have been. She stared open-mouthed at the sight of her home. It looked like it had been destroyed by a tornado of fire. There was wreckage everywhere, like the house had blown up, and everything was singed and blackened.

Moving slowly, she made her way to what was left of the porch where she'd been sitting only a few days ago, enjoying her birthday party.

Clambering up on the burned and broken wood, she could only get as far as where the door would have been, because it ended in a big hole that had once been the basement.

Allison sat down, her legs dangling into the hole, wanting to vomit from the smell of smoke.

After sitting there a while, she thought of the body back in the barn, and knew she couldn't just leave the man as he was.

"That wouldn't be right." Her father spoke those words when he used to talk to her about making choices, and she fought back a sudden hot flash of tears as she thought of him.

As she returned to the barn, she saw with dismay that the vehicle shed, too, had been destroyed. Moving to the rear of the barn, which was still largely intact, she looked and listened for any signs of the enemy.

Nothing moved in the starlit darkness between the barn and the nearby creek, beyond which lay the woods. The night creatures made their normal chirruping and occasional hoots, and she knew that nothing was hiding out there, waiting for her.

Already exhausted from prying open the door to the shelter, she knew that what had to be done would only be harder the longer she waited. The body hadn't begun to smell yet, but she knew it would.

Taking hold of the dead man's wrists, she pulled him outside the barn and into the nearest corner of the family garden where the earth was soft. After retrieving a shovel from the mess in the barn, she began to dig.

* * *

Not content to stay put in the shelter and wait for rescue that she now doubted would ever come, Allison ventured out at night to learn what she could of the enemy. While many children her age were still afraid of the dark, especially in the woods, she had spent enough time hunting with her father and brother that the woods held no fears for her other than the packs of Kreelan warriors that sometimes passed by.

The first night, she was able to reach a place where she could see into the town. There wasn't a single light shining from any of the buildings. The power was out, which didn't surprise her.

But it wasn't completely dark. In the town square she could see the flickers of what must have been a number of fires, and off in the woods beyond the town she could see the faint glow of what must have been many more. The dark shapes of warriors moved here and there, the glow of the firelight sometimes glinting from their shiny black armor.

She also noticed that the landing ships had all gone.

"At least they can't go around shooting horses." She thought bitterly of poor Race.

She stayed in the shelter on the second night when a storm passed through. Allison had cracked the door to the shelter, but rain was pouring down outside. After a moment's consideration, she closed the door and went back inside.

On the third night she had reached the edge of town when she was stopped cold by a Kreelan patrol. She had come around the corner of a big storage building where the town kept its communal equipment, which was the farthest building that was generally considered part of the town itself, when she ran into them.

She had reached the back of the building and moved toward one of the corners. Stopping, she listened for any sounds, and after about thirty seconds she rounded the corner.

And there they were. For a moment, she just stood there, stupefied, while not ten paces away three alien warriors stood facing her, dark shadows against the star light.

The warriors stiffened, and two of them began to move toward her. But the third uttered something in their strange language, and the others stopped, flexing their claws in their armored fists.

Afraid to so much as breathe, Allison backed slowly around the corner, then turned and ran.

Terrified as she had been, she came back the next night and made it into the town proper, sneaking down the alley behind the town's small theater.

She paused a moment near the back door, remembering how the theater's owner, Mr. Bernson, always gave the kids free popcorn during the matinees. Allison knew that he was almost certainly dead, and the thought brought with it more sadness than she'd expected. Mr. Bernson had been a very nice man who had loved the town's kids. She would miss him.

On a whim, she tried the door handle. It was unlocked. Opening the door just a few centimeters, she looked inside, but couldn't see anything. It was pitch black.

She waited a moment, listening for any sign of movement, then quickly stepped inside. She pulled the door closed behind her, wincing as it clicked shut.

Then she waited, trying to muffle the sound of her own breathing as she listened. She was in the small store room where Mr. Bernson kept the supplies for the refreshment stand. Flicking on the pocket flashlight she'd brought, she saw that she was surrounded by neat stacks of cups and containers holding popcorn bags and candy.

With a vague sense of guilt, she reached out and took a package of her favorite candy from one of the boxes. Then two more.

The store room had another door that led to the main hall where the refreshment stand and the entrance to the theater were. As she was pocketing the candy and considering taking more, she heard something out there.

Whispers.

Quickly switching off her light, she moved to the hallway door, which stood ajar.

She heard something else now, too. Footsteps on the carpet beyond the door. Slow and stealthy.

Allison had no weapon. She had looked near where Race had been killed, but hadn't been able to find her hunting rifle, and her father hadn't been able to afford a separate set of weapons just to store in the shelter.

The guns had all been in the house, and had been lost when the house was blown up.

With the furtive sounds of the footsteps growing steadily closer, she backed up behind the door next to one of the stacks of boxes.

The door was pushed open, very slowly. A dark shape, then another, came into the room, illuminated by the ghostly starlight glow from the theater's front windows down the hall.

"It should be in here," one of the shadows said softly, just above a whisper.

It was Vanhi, a girl from her school. She was only eight, but Allison had spoken to her a few times in their small school's cafeteria. Vanhi had a very distinctive singsong voice that Allison instantly recognized. The other shadow with her, about the same size, must be her twin brother Amrit. They lived on a small farm on the far side of town, and had only arrived on Alger's World a year ago, immigrants from Earth.

"Vanhi," Allison whispered, reaching out a hand to touch the girl's shoulder.

Both Vanhi and Amrit screamed in fright, jumping away from Allison to crash into a floor to ceiling stack of plastic cups that clattered to the floor.

"Be quiet!" Allison turned on her flashlight and held it up to the ceiling to provide a little illumination without blinding any of them. It was a trick her brother had shown her.

"Allison?" Amrit's voice trembled, his dark brown eyes wide with terror.

"Allison Murtaugh?" Vanhi lay on the floor amongst the jumble of cups, staring up at the older girl.

"Yeah, it's me." Allison reached out her free hand to help Vanhi up. "It's okay. But we've got to get out of here. Now." She knew that the racket they'd just made would have alerted any Kreelans who might be nearby. "Come on. Follow me." Reaching into a box of chocolate bars, she stuffed a bunch into her jacket, then took Vanhi's hand.

Allison pushed the outside door open just a crack, then looked and listened for any signs of patrolling warriors. There was nothing.

"You've got to be really quiet." Allison's whisper broke the silence of the darkened alley, and she quickly glanced around.

They were still alone.

Behind her, the twins nodded their heads side to side in a way that some of the other kids in school had thought funny, but that Allison had always found endearing.

Allison led the way out, with Vanhi holding tightly to one of her hands, and Amrit holding onto Vanhi's other hand to make sure they didn't get separated in the dark. They followed Allison down to the end of the alley.

Once there, she had the twins sit down and gave them each a chocolate bar from her pocket. She was shocked to see how they both ripped off the wrapper and devoured the bars in but a few bites.

"We're starving."

Allison could barely understand what Amrit said, his mouth was so full of chocolate, but the message was clear. She gave them both a couple more bars.

The twins sat right next to each other as if they were freezing, even though it was a warm spring night. Allison sat cross-legged across from them, and their foreheads almost touched as they leaned in close to talk.

"What were you doing in there?" Allison asked.

"Looking for food." Vanhi's singsong voice was flat, desperate. "We haven't had anything to eat since the aliens came."

"Nothing at all? Didn't your family have a storm shelter or anything?"

"We didn't have a chance to get to it." Amrit's voice quivered, and Allison reached out a hand and took his to reassure him. "One of the alien ships landed right next to the house. Our parents..."

Vanhi let out a quiet sob, and it was a moment before Amrit went on in a raspy voice. He was a small boy, no bigger than his sister, but he didn't lack for courage. Allison had seen him stand up to one of the class bullies once. The older boy had nearly beaten Amrit to a pulp before the teachers could intervene, but Amrit had stood his ground.

"The aliens killed them and set fire to the house. We were playing in the barn." He paused. "We saw everything."

"I'm sorry." Allison couldn't think of what else she could say. After a moment, she asked, "How did you get away?"

"There is a big pipe under the drive between the barn and the main road for water to run through."

"We hid there for two days," Vanhi added. "We got some water from a sprinkler line that still held some water, but that was all. Without power, the well pump stopped working."

"Since then we've been trying to get to Mr. Bernson's theater, because we knew there would be some food and things to drink there. And we wouldn't have to go far into town to where the restaurants are." Amrit paused. "Because there are lots of *them* there."

Nodding, Allison understood their reasoning. She had noticed that, too. After the initial battle, the aliens seemed to have concentrated in the center of Breakwater. She'd heard strange things and seen weird lights, like flickers of lightning coming from the town square area, but she hadn't yet mustered the courage to investigate any further.

"Well," she told them, "you won't have to worry about a place to stay. I want you to come back with me. I've got lots of room in a nice shelter back at our farm."

"You have food and water?" Vanhi's voice had taken on more of its singsong quality, and it made Allison smile.

"Yes, I've got plenty for all of us."

* * *

Over the next week, Allison's optimistic appraisal of the food situation radically changed as she found seven more children, all younger than herself, who were desperate enough for food to brave the dangers of being caught by the aliens. All of them had been starving, and one had been so weak that she'd had to carry him to the shelter on her back.

Ravenous as they were, they had quickly eaten their way through most of the food supplies in the shelter. Allison had gone to look for food at the adjoining farms, but without exception the houses, barns, and any other buildings had been destroyed.

Foraging in town was the only option. Deciding that they needed something more than the candy in the town theater (and the popcorn was useless, as she had no way to cook it), she began to explore deeper in the town. While many of the buildings had suffered heavy damage, the contents were still largely intact, especially the market and the hunting store, which had prepackaged food they could eat. She had tried to get a gun at the hunting store to replace the rifle she'd lost, but had given up. While she could get to the guns in the display cases, the ammunition was locked in a big safe.

While gathering food and looking for other children had become her main goals in her nightly forays, Allison's expeditions into town also made her feel like she was doing something useful. She didn't have a weapon to fight back, but just learning what she could of the aliens and finding out what they were up to, aside from simply killing humans, made her feel good.

But it wasn't easy sneaking past the Kreelans who had set up their main base in the town square and the warriors constantly moving in and out of the area. Like the third night after the attack when she had run into a group of warriors who had just let her go, she was sure that warriors had seen her more than once on her nighttime runs, but had simply ignored her. They must have only been concerned with older humans. Every once in a while she heard the distant sound of gunfire, so she knew there were still people fighting back.

While the aliens didn't seem all that interested in her, she wasn't taking it for granted. She did everything she could to move unseen and unheard.

Now, almost two weeks to the day since the attack, she was deep into the town, moving down an alleyway, probing toward the town square. It was the focus of whatever the aliens were doing here, and she wanted to know what it was.

She paused, then put her back against the wall as a pair of Kreelans walked by a few meters away, their black armor and talon-like fingernails glistening in the bonfires that the aliens kept burning at the center of the town square each night. They strode right past her, unaware that two hateful young eyes were boring holes in them, wishing them dead and gone back to whatever hellish world had spawned them.

The two warriors had just reached the end of the alley and Allison took a step away from the wall when she heard the aliens make a slight gasp. Quickly backing up to the wall again, she saw that the warriors were rooted to the ground, their eyes staring up at the sky, as if they could see something among the stars that was invisible to Allison's gaze.

A moment later the two warriors turned around and ran back toward the square, and Allison could hear alien cries and the sound of more running feet and the clatter of weapons and armor as the entire Kreelan garrison came alive.

This can't be good, she told herself. Deciding to take advantage of the situation, she darted into the market and stuffed her backpack full of packaged food, napkins (that were used mainly for toilet paper), and the short list of other essential items she had come for.

Back out in the alley, she paused. The Kreelans in the square, hundreds of them, if not more, were making a lot of noise in their guttural language. She hadn't seen them act this way before, and knew that whatever was happening must be important.

Reluctantly setting down her backpack and concealing it in a pile of empty boxes, she crept down the alley toward the end that opened onto the main street and the square beyond to see what was happening.

The aliens had formed themselves into a military-style formation, the warriors arrayed in semicircular rows facing an open area of the square. There were hundreds of them, maybe even a few thousand. It was hard to tell. She hadn't realized there were so many, and an involuntary shiver ran up her spine at the sight of the orderly ranks of alien killers.

A warrior who stood in front of the formation bellowed a command, and the warriors fell silent and stood ramrod-straight.

Allison looked up as she heard the growing roar of an approaching shuttle, and watched with slitted eyes as it settled to the grass in the square, its hover engines blowing dust and debris in a swirling cloud that swept through the Kreelan ranks.

As the shuttle's engines spun down, a ramp extended from the rear. Allison had a clear view, as the ramp faced directly toward her, and watched in frightened awe as the Kreelan warriors knelt and hammered their right fists against their left breasts as one, the sound of their armored gauntlets against their chest armor echoing through the square.

* * *

Ku'ar-Marekh stepped down the shuttle's gangway into the smoke-shrouded square. She had chosen to arrive in the shuttle because she knew that many of the warriors found her more accustomed means of appearing out of thin air...disturbing.

She looked upon the ranks of kneeling warriors with silver-flecked eyes, her gaze taking in everything, missing nothing.

Unlike the peers who knelt before her, the porcelain-smooth blue skin of her body bore not a single scar. Scars were considered a prize among her people, trophies of combat or great deeds done in service of the Empress. Ku'ar-Marekh had seen more than her share of battle from the time she was a young *tresh* learning the Way of Her Children, and had gathered an impressive collection of scars through the cycles before she had become a priestess.

But the Change that took place when her mentor had passed on her powers to Ku'ar-Marekh had stripped her skin bare of her trophies. While she still wore a sword and dagger, and three *shrekkas* on her left shoulder, the powers she had inherited when she became a priestess had made combat by sword and claw largely irrelevant.

She looked out upon the warriors the Empress had put in her care, and could barely see them through the swirling dust kicked up by the shuttle's engines.

With a gentle wave of her hand, the gusts of air stilled, and the tiny particles fell to the ground in a silent rain. Some of the warriors bowed their heads even further, for they could sense the power of her spirit in their blood like a great, frigid wind.

Ku'ar-Marekh could of course sense the warriors, but she also sensed something else, and stopped at the bottom of the ramp, casting her second sight into the world around her.

A human.

While the blood of the animals did not sing as did that of Her Children, priestesses such as Ku'ar-Marekh could see beyond the senses of the flesh. She turned to stare at the creature, which cowered in the shadows of a nearby building. It was plainly visible to Ku'ar-Marekh's eyes, for her race could see well in the dark. She knew that the warriors could only have overlooked the tiny human simply because it posed no challenge to their skills. Killing it would have brought no honor to the Empress, and no doubt they thought it better to leave it die of starvation.

Ku'ar-Marekh was not concerned with honor, but thought instead that killing the human would bring the Empire one step closer to exterminating these unworthy animals from the universe. Its blood did not sing, so it could not be the One the Empress so eagerly sought.

Staring at the creature, Ku'ar-Marekh reached out with her mind, seeking the human's heart. She could feel it, beating rapidly with fear in the tiny chest, and in her mind she imagined her fist gripping the pulsating organ, her talons sinking into the muscle. Then she began to squeeze...

* * *

Allison felt a shiver pass through her as the warrior walked down the ramp. The Kreelan looked much the same as the others, but there was something about this one that was different. She didn't know why, but a sudden surge of fear swept through her.

The alien stopped and turned to stare right at her.

She can see me! Allison realized, and her stomach fell away into a dark abyss as terror took hold and she turned to run.

It was then that she felt an uncomfortable pressure in her chest. She gasped as the sensation turned into icy needles that speared her heart, and she collapsed to the ground, gasping in agony.

She felt as if her heart was being torn, still beating, from her chest.

* * *

"My priestess?" Ri'al-Hagir said quietly. She was to serve as the First to Ku'ar-Marekh, to act as her right hand in all things. She had never before met the priestess, although she had heard many fearful tales from other warriors, and of course could sense the priestess through the Bloodsong.

Ri'al-Hagir glanced at where the human child writhed, perplexed as to why one such as Ku'ar-Marekh, who stood twelfth from the throne among all the souls in the Empire, would trifle with such a thing.

"We decided to leave the pups be," she explained as the human writhed in torment. "We have hopes that those that are resourceful may survive to be warriors worthy of our attention, as the adult human animals of this planet have been."

For a moment she was unsure if Ku'ar-Marekh had heard her words, for the attention of the priestess remained fixed on the human child, whose struggles were rapidly weakening. Ri'al-Hagir could sense the power flowing from the priestess, and was not so proud to admit, at least to herself, that it caused her fear such as battle never had.

Then, with a barely audible sigh, the priestess turned to look at her, and Ri'al-Hagir quickly lowered her gaze.

"I meant no offense, my priestess."

"Had any been taken, you would now be with our ancestors in death." Ku'ar-Marekh barely breathed the words, but every warrior kneeling before her heard them. Each and every one bowed her head even lower. In a louder voice, cold as any machine could be, she went on, "However, I honor your wisdom. If such as that can grow to pose a challenge to us, then I shall allow it to live."

* * *

Allison heaved a desperate gasp of air into her lungs as the icy spikes that had been crushing her heart disappeared. She lay on the hard pavement of the alley, her body wracked with tremors as her heart sluggishly returned to its life-sustaining duty.

She managed to turn on her side just before she vomited.

Looking up, spitting the awful taste from her mouth, she could see the Kreelan who had come on the shuttle, moving through the ranks of warriors, who still knelt before her.

"Get up," Allison told herself. She was afraid that if she didn't leave now, paralyzed by pain and fear, she never would. "Get up!"

She pushed herself to her knees, and then to her feet, leaning against the outside wall of the market for support. With unsteady steps she went to where she had hidden her backpack and hoisted it onto her shoulders, wincing at the weight.

After she'd gone a short way down the alley, Allison looked one last time at the Kreelans.

The newly-arrived warrior was staring at her. She pulled her lips back in a silent snarl that revealed a set of glistening ivory fangs.

Allison turned and ran.

FIVE

"We're ready."

Those simple words, spoken by Fleet Admiral Phillip Tiernan, commander of the Confederation Navy, sent a wave of excitement through every person sitting in the briefing room in the Presidential Complex.

At the head of the conference table sat President Natalie McKenna. The dark skin of her face that was a gift of her African heritage was deeply lined from stress and worry, but the hard look from her dark eyes was proof of indefatigable determination to defeat the Kreelan Empire and save her people.

"Go ahead, admiral." McKenna nodded. "Let's hear it."

"Yes, Madam President." Tiernan turned to the wall-sized display at the front of the room that showed a star map of the human sphere. Not all human-settled worlds had yet joined the Confederation, but there were very few holdouts after the latest wave of Kreelan invasions. "Just to recap the strategic situation, there are now a total of eighteen colonies currently under attack by forces of the Kreelan Empire. Only one, Keran, where the enemy struck us first, has been completely...assimilated."

According to the last intelligence information the Navy had been able to obtain, the Kreelans had likely exterminated every human soul on Keran, then had begun to terraform the planet to better suit their needs.

What had happened there had driven home to everyone in the government that humanity was not simply in a battle for territory, riches, or ideology. Humanity was fighting for its very existence.

"The other planetary campaigns," Tiernan continued, "are essentially long-term battles of attrition. From what we can tell of the enemy's intentions, it's basically to try and kill as many of us at close quarters as possible. They don't seem interested in simply taking our worlds from us, because we know from the information we gained during the first contact encounter that they're radically more advanced than we are, or at least some portion of their Empire is. Our assessment is that if they wanted to simply take something from us, or just wipe us out, they could. But for some reason, they're taking their time about it."

"So, you're saying we have no chance against them?" Secretary of Trade Raul Hernandez asked the question of Tiernan, but his eyes darted to the President.

"Not at all, Mister Hernandez. Perhaps the best thing for me to say is that we simply don't understand their intentions. We understand some of their potential capabilities from what Commodore Sato," he nodded to a man with Japanese features who sat at the table, looking absurdly young compared to the other flag officers around him, "brought back from first contact, but we don't understand why they do what they do, or what their strategic goals are, other than killing us one by one." He looked around the room, finally resting his gaze on the president. "They've kicked us hard, and if they wanted to they could take us down.

"But I didn't come here," he went on, his voice deepening with resolve, "to tell you that we don't have a chance, or that we're just going to roll over and let them have their way."

Hernandez, clearly not convinced, simply nodded and rested his chin on his hands, focusing on the map of humanity's outposts among the stars, eighteen of which were displayed in red.

"What's the target, admiral?" McKenna asked.

"Alger's World."

The screen zoomed in on one of the red-flagged planets, and data appeared in a pop-up. It was a rare cousin of Earth, capable of supporting human life without domes or respiration equipment. It had a population of just over five million, with a planetary economy that was based primarily on agriculture. Before the arrival of the Kreelans, Alger's World had been a quiet, modestly successful colony in a location that had no particular strategic significance.

"Why Alger's World?"

The question had come from Vice President Laurent Navarre, who was leaning forward, studying the information on the screen. The former ambassador of the Francophone Alliance to the Terran Government, he had been the logical choice for McKenna's right-hand man. He had been of inestimable help to her in both forging the Confederation government and in setting in motion the largest industrial mobilization in the history of humankind to provide the weapons and material with which to fight humanity's enemy. "Not to belittle the suffering of any of our citizens, but

Alger's World doesn't strike me as a strategic target. Its entire population is less than some of the major cities on some of the other besieged worlds, and it has no industrial capacity to speak of. I do not ask this to sound heartless, admiral, Madam President," he turned and nodded his head to McKenna before turning back to Tiernan, "but what do we gain strategically by mounting a major operation there?"

"In short, our plan for Alger's World gives us the best possible chance of winning a decisive victory, Mr. Vice President." Turning to McKenna, he went on, "Madam President, your orders to me were to find a way to strike back at the enemy and give the Confederation a success in the wake of so many invasions. The battles being fought on every planet other than Alger's World are battles of attrition that we will likely lose in the end." He paused, glancing momentarily at a naval officer who was new to the Confederation Navy, but who wore the stars of a full admiral. "As an example, I'm sure Admiral Voroshilov can tell you that we have very little hope of mounting a successful counteroffensive against the Kreelan forces on Saint Petersburg."

"Our world is lost." Lavrenti Voroshilov confirmed Tiernan's statement without preamble. He had been the commanding officer of the Saint Petersburg Navy when Confederation forces had come to confiscate his government's illegal nuclear weapons, and he had fought the Confederation Navy before the Kreelans had arrived.

Now, Saint Petersburg was a charnel house, and the surviving units of his fleet had been merged with that of the Confederation. Most of Saint Petersburg's surviving population, those the Confederation had been able to evacuate, had been sent to the colony of Dobraya, where even now a massive industrialization program was underway to help build more ships that the Confederation needed to survive.

"We could send in the entire fleet and every Marine, and still we would lose. The battle is not over, but it has already been decided."

Tiernan nodded, his expression grim. "The other larger colonies under attack are in similar straits. In a two years, if we can ramp up production of the new ship designs fast enough and expand the Marine Expeditionary Forces as rapidly as our plans are calling for, we could think about trying to take back a world like Saint Petersburg. Now..." He shook his head. "We had to choose a smaller colony that had not been completely overrun, did not have an enormous number of Kreelan warriors, and was still central enough to our primary fleet elements that we could mass an overwhelming number of ships quickly, get the job done, and then get them back on station as rapidly as possible. We've been waiting for this opportunity for months, and Alger's World is it. We don't expect that a victory there is really going to hurt the Kreelans in a strategic sense, but it will give us some good news to tell the people."

"It will not hurt the morale of the fleet and Marines, either," Voroshilov added.

"So this is like the so-called 'Doolittle Raid,' is it not?" Navarre asked.

Tiernan nodded, impressed at the vice president's historical knowledge, but there were blank looks from everyone else around the table.

"Forgive my dredging up ancient history," Navarre apologized. "It was during Earth's Second World War, when the United States was reeling from a succession of defeats by the Empire of Japan. Then-President Roosevelt needed a victory to give the American people hope, and the United States Navy and Army Air Corps came up with a plan to bomb Japan using land-based bombers flown from a naval aircraft carrier. The raid caused little real damage, but was a blow to Japanese morale as much as it was a boon to that of the Americans." He gestured toward the map. "This strikes me as similar, at least in terms of our morale. The effect on the Kreelans, we may never know."

"Ladies and gentlemen," McKenna told them, "what the vice president said cuts to the heart of what we're trying to accomplish here. The success of this operation is vital from a political perspective, regardless of any military gains. Many of the planetary governments, not to mention their citizens, are near panic. After the last wave of attacks, there has even been talk of secession, with some people believing that the formation of the Confederation has somehow encouraged the Kreelans to attack more of our worlds."

"Rubbish!" Voroshilov spat.

"I agree, admiral, but people everywhere are terrified, with every one of them wondering if their world will be the next to sound the invasion sirens. And that's without the knowledge of how thinly spread the fleet really is. With the current campaigns underway, there aren't enough ships to mount a credible defense against more than half a dozen worlds, including Earth."

Tiernan and Voroshilov exchanged a look, then Tiernan nodded unhappily.

"We're not just fighting the Kreelans now," McKenna went on. "We're fighting the worst enemy mankind has ever known: unreasoning fear. And I have very little with which to fight it. The Confederation has no deep-rooted traditions or other social fabric to hold it together, no historical flag around which I can rally our people. Right now the Confederation is still a relatively loose alliance of worlds brought together by the need for common defense, and it's held together by little more than treaty and this government's commitment to help member worlds build up their defenses.

"We're doing that, but the chronic fear our citizens are suffering, especially after the most recent attacks, is leading to irrational beliefs that can't be defeated by reason. Secession may sound like a crazy idea from where we sit, but if people don't believe the Confederation can protect them, cutting their ties and trying to lay low starts to look like an attractive option." Her expression hardened. "Make no mistake. If the Confederation splinters and breaks apart, our species is doomed. That's why this operation *must* succeed, because a victory, even on a small, backwater colony world, will show our people that all is not lost and give them hope. And hope is a weapon I can use to combat their fears."

"We will succeed, Madam President," Tiernan assured her. "I can't say at what price, and I hope I don't sound arrogant when I say this, but we're going to win this one." He turned and gestured toward Sato. "And I'd now like to introduce Commodore Ichiro Sato, who's going to go over the details of how we're going to do it."

McKenna watched as the young commodore moved to the podium and stood at attention. Sato had become a household name throughout the Confederation. The sole survivor of the ill-fated ship that had made first contact with the Kreelans, he had gone on to have two more ships shot out from under him, one at Keran and the other, his first command, at Saint Petersburg. Unlike most of his peers, who wore several rows of ribbons, Sato only had two. The lower one held his campaign decorations for Keran and Saint Petersburg, while the top one held the ribbon for the Medal of Honor, which McKenna had presented to him.

Sato was fifteen years younger than the next youngest flag officer in the room, and had gone from a midshipman aboard the ill-fated *Aurora* to commodore in a mere three years. Many senior officers had complained about Sato's rapid promotion to commander, but none had complained about him receiving his first star as commodore. Most of his detractors had died in combat.

Looking at the younger man as he stepped up to the podium, Tiernan knew that Sato didn't have everything a peacetime flag officer needed to be successful. But this wasn't peacetime, and Tiernan needed warriors. More importantly, he needed leaders of warriors. And that's exactly what Sato was.

"Madam President," the young commodore began, bowing his head slightly, "Admiral Tiernan, ladies and gentlemen. As the admiral already noted, our target is Alger's World, which the Kreelans invaded nine days ago. Most of the human population is settled in small towns distributed through open country that is well-suited for agricultural production, which was another important consideration for the ground phase of the battle plan, which we'll cover shortly.

"Navy reconnaissance missions into the target system have indicated that the Territorial Army probably no longer exists as a cohesive force, but radio transmissions clearly show that there is continued organized human resistance. We have no idea how many survivors there may be, but based on projections derived from the assimilation of Keran, we believe that the majority of the population is still alive."

"How old is this information?" McKenna asked.

"Six days, Madam President. The emergency courier departed for Earth as soon as the naval detachment there sounded the invasion alert, and we dispatched a reconnaissance vessel as soon as we received the alert at Naval HQ."

Courier ships were used to route communications between star systems, storing up batches of data in one system before jumping to another to download it to a relay and upload another batch for the next jump. It was a huge hindrance for military planning, because some of the star systems under siege were weeks away by hyperlight travel.

Fortunately, Alger's World was much closer.

"Please continue."

Sato turned to the map on the wall, which now showed a glowing green icon that moved in a graceful arc toward Alger's World. "The first part of the operation involves the covert insertion of several ground reconnaissance teams. The Kreelans are able, through means we do not yet understand, to selectively defeat or disrupt our high technology weapons and sensors, apparently at will. We're hoping that these teams will be able to provide the reconnaissance we need for the ground phase of the operation without involving high-technology assets that may not work.

"The ships transporting the teams are modified courier vessels that are already on their way to the system. We sent them in as quickly as possible so they'll be able to get the teams on the ground with as much lead time as possible."

"You sent them in before the operation was approved?" McKenna asked.

"Yes, ma'am." Sato made no attempt to dodge what some might have considered a freight-train sized bullet. "You see, we have another courier standing by that will deliver your 'go' order to the reconnaissance teams. If for any reason the teams don't receive that order, they'll automatically abort the mission and return home."

"Very well, commodore. I applaud the initiative, and as Admiral Tiernan can confirm," she smiled, "I try very hard not to micromanage the fleet's operations."

That earned a number of grins and a few chuckles from those around the table.

"Then what happens?"

"Concurrent with the deployment of the scout teams," Sato continued, "we'll be sending couriers with orders for Fleet elements from fourteen systems. Those ships will deploy from their current duties to participate in the assault." A list of ships appeared on the display, with lines connecting them to the fourteen different systems. "As you can see, we are taking only a handful of vessels from each system to minimize the impact on operations, as eleven of these systems are currently under siege.

"The main drawback is that the assault fleet will not have had the opportunity to train as an integrated unit, but this will allow us to bring a very potent force to bear at Alger's World quickly. Based on reconnaissance data, we should initially have a ratio of at least four to one in warships, and nearly ten to one in total tonnage."

He paused as the map display showed a depiction of the courier ships heading out from Earth with orders for the other systems, then the warship flotillas jumping in sequence to Alger's World.

"I must point out that the most critical aspect of the operation is the sequencing of the jumps for the assault fleet. We intend to have all of our warships arrive over Alger's World within a window of only sixty seconds. The main risk factor is that they'll be jumping deep into the planet's gravity well using techniques pioneered by Admiral Voroshilov at Saint Petersburg." He nodded toward the Russian admiral, whose attention was fixed on the screen. "This should give us complete tactical surprise and allow us to deploy the Marine assault force under a solid shield of warships." He paused. "But I must advise you that this is the first time, during war or peace, that any navy has attempted such a complex navigational maneuver."

"Admiral Voroshilov," McKenna asked quietly, "you don't look very happy."

"I am not," Voroshilov replied, turning to look her in the eye. "Do not misunderstand, please. The plan is a good one, and Commodore Sato and his planning staff have done an amazing job of bringing it together.

"The danger is that we are pushing right to the limits of our computational capabilities for navigation. After a long and lively debate, we decided not to stage the fleet closer and then jump in. That would take precious additional time to reach Alger's World, and would also prolong the time the ships are away from their other vital duties, as well as lead to further civilian casualties on Alger's World.

"But there is great risk, Madam President. If the fleet arrives out of sequence, we run the risk of being defeated in detail by Kreelan forces and newly arriving warships interpenetrating with existing ones when they come out of their jumps.

"I also worry about the accuracy of our navigational data for jumping so deep into the gravity well. We were able to test and verify our mapping many times in Saint Petersburg before the Confederation fleet arrived. This time we will have only the remote sensor data from surveillance vessels. It will be difficult. And that is not all." He frowned.

"Admiral?" McKenna prompted.

"We will also be taking nearly two-thirds of the ships from Home Fleet. Earth's defenses will temporarily be greatly weakened."

McKenna looked to Tiernan. "Are we taking too much of a risk here, admiral? I want to hit back at the enemy, but I don't want to wipe out the fleet in the process or leave Earth open to invasion."

"Ma'am," Tiernan said, "as Admiral Voroshilov noted, there was a great deal of debate over how we should do this. But what it boiled down to in the end was that we're past the time for half-measures. We haven't thrown caution or prudence to the wind. Thousands of hours have been spent in very meticulous planning for this operation. We started this as a contingency plan months ago, using it as a framework. That's why Sato was able to bring it together so quickly.

"But we're not going to win this war by being careful. We're going to win it by taking daring, calculated risks." He gestured to the map. "As you know, I named Admiral Voroshilov as the fleet commander for this operation because he has unique expertise in the navigation aspect, and a significant number of the fleet units involved were formerly of the Saint Petersburg Navy, all of which have seen combat. And I told Lavrenti straight up that if he didn't think this mission would succeed to say so. He's frowned a lot, but hasn't said he wouldn't lead it."

Voroshilov only grunted, but the others in the room visibly relaxed.

"As for the invasion threat to Earth," Sato interjected darkly, "if the Kreelans wanted to invade, they would have. They know exactly where we are."

A round of quiet murmurs swept through the room. Sato, as the sole survivor of the ship that had made first contact, had unique first hand experience with the Kreelans. When the aliens had finished massacring his crew, they had sent him alone in his ship back to Earth in a feat of navigation that humans had thought to be impossible.

"That may be, commodore," McKenna said, "but there is a political dimension beyond any military realities. There would be a panic if Earth's population felt their defenses had been stripped. We have to at least keep up the appearance that Home Fleet can stop the enemy."

"That appearance, and the reality," Tiernan told her firmly, "will remain, Madam President. Aside from some of the Francophone Alliance worlds, Earth is the most heavily defended planet in human space, even without the Home Fleet units we plan to detach for this operation. We've taken this into account by putting ships that would normally be in dry dock on extended defense patrols until we can bring the deployed ships home. If the Kreelans come calling, they'll be in for the fight of their lives."

Still concerned, but satisfied with Tiernan's reasoning, McKenna nodded. "Very well, admiral."

"Go on, Commodore Sato." Tiernan gestured for the younger man to proceed.

"Yes, sir." Sato again turned his attention to the president. "Once the fleet has jumped in, its first mission will be to gain orbital supremacy to protect the assault carriers and, if possible, to destroy any Kreelan ships in-system. Once that is accomplished, the battleships and cruisers may also be tasked to provide fire support for the ground operation.

"And with that, I would like to hand the briefing over to Lieutenant General James Sparks, the ground force commander."

"Thank you, commodore." McKenna smiled at Sato as he took his seat.

She caught Tiernan's sigh as a wiry officer stood up from a chair along the wall. The man wore a Marine dress blue uniform with the three stars of a lieutenant general, but something was...odd about it.

It took her a moment to realize that rather than the regulation gloss black shoes, he was wearing calf-high black leather boots that made a clinking sound with each step. She nearly guffawed when she saw that he was wearing riding spurs, as if he was expecting to go and hop onto a horse as soon as the briefing was over. He also wore a saber strapped to the gold belt of his uniform. And his cap, which was held by an aide sitting behind him, wasn't the regulation cap of the Confederation Marines, but was a wide-brim black hat with gold braid around it and an insignia with crossed sabers at the front.

She couldn't suppress a smile, thinking that while he was clearly out of regulation, the unusual attire seemed to suit him perfectly.

Her smile quickly faded as she realized that while the man might be a bit of a theatrical dandy, he was one of the few survivors of the disastrous defense that had been mounted against the enemy at Keran, the first world that had been attacked. She had read the full report of the battle, and Sparks had acquitted himself well. Like Sato, he was a leader of warriors. Also like the much younger commodore, Sparks had been rapidly promoted to flag rank.

"Ma'am," he began without preamble in a heavy drawl from the American South, looking at some hand-written notes on crumpled paper he'd taken from a pocket inside his uniform, "we've allocated three full divisions, each with roughly eighteen thousand Marines, to conduct the ground campaign. We'll be using the most advanced weapons and systems we have available, but we're also going into this battle prepared to lose them."

McKenna frowned. "I'm not sure I understand that, general."

"Ma'am, it's because of the Kreelans' ability to selectively defeat our technology. This has had a huge impact on how we wage war. It's hard to emphasize just how much. And weapons and sensors aren't the only things the enemy has meddled with. They do the same thing to the command, control, and communications systems that we normally rely on. I've read reports of some combat units having to resort to voice communications over radio using equipment that they've had to cobble together in the field, because their normal comm systems and data-links inexplicably die on them. The Kreelans don't seem to have a problem with us using radio."

"Radio?" Navarre didn't try to conceal his amazement. "But that technology is, well, practically ancient!"

"Yes, sir," Sparks told him, "it is. But I believe in using what works. We haven't had any reports of the Kreelans jamming or disrupting radio where it's been put into use, so I've had radio equipment retrofitted on all of our vehicles and infantry gear."

"We have also installed radio equipment in the ships and assault boats so they can communicate with the ground forces in case our primary systems go down," Tiernan added. "The Kreelans sometimes still let us use the data link systems, but most of the time they limit us to voicecomm in the fleet. It seems to depend on their mood."

McKenna shook her head in dread and wonder. She'd been briefed on this before, and knew that the best and brightest minds of humanity were trying to figure out how the Kreelans were interfering with the technology that humanity had long taken for granted. But so far there was no news. It was as if the Kreelans were using magic. "Go on, general."

"Our units will be deployed based on the intelligence information we receive from the forward recon teams once the fleet jumps in." Drawing his saber (which caused some momentary consternation among the presidential protective detail) he used it as a pointer, jabbing the tip at illuminated areas of the wall display, which now showed a map of the main continent. "We believe these will be the most likely areas, as they hold the greatest population concentrations, and we'll deploy units tailored to the size of each threat. We can drop a single battalion or a whole division in any given area, depending on the situation, with the assault boats providing close air support unless we need to call on the Navy for heavier firepower."

Sparks looked over the attendees, his eyes focusing on each face in turn before he locked eyes with the President. "We're going to kick their asses, ma'am. That's all I have."

With that, Sparks sheathed his saber and left the podium, his spurs making a ching-ching-ching sound with every step until he sat back down.

Tiernan turned to the president from his seat at the table. "After we've destroyed the Kreelan ground forces, transports will bring in defensive equipment and support personnel that will make it very expensive for the Kreelans to try and come back to Alger's World any time soon. We're hoping to give them such a bloody nose in this operation that they won't want to try."

"Wouldn't it make more sense to just evacuate?" Everyone turned to Secretary of Industry Johann Thurmond, whose question had several others around the room nodding their agreement.

"It's going to be a huge additional burden on the fleet and the Territorial Army to fortify Alger's World to the point where they might stand a chance against another attack." With a look toward Voroshilov, he added, "Its population is much smaller than many of the other colonies. We should consolidate so we can better concentrate our forces."

Tiernan opened his mouth to answer, but didn't get the chance.

"No." McKenna hadn't raised her voice, but that single word echoed through the room like a gunshot. "No. The Kreelans have already taken too much from us. Eighteen worlds are under siege and millions have already died, with more dying every day. We're not going to give them anything without a fight, and we're going to take back everything we can. We're also going to rapidly build up the survey arm of the fleet so we can find more habitable worlds and establish more colonies. We need to expand our presence in the galaxy, not withdraw, because every time we do that we move one step closer to extinction."

McKenna looked around the room at her cabinet members and the other attendees, her eyes cold and hard. "We'll fight them on every planet, give up nothing that we aren't forced to, and kill every last one of them if we must to achieve victory."

The president turned to Tiernan. "The operation is a go, admiral."

* * *

"Madam President?" Stephanie Guillaume-Sato, President McKenna's press secretary, stood at the door to McKenna's office.

"Steph!" McKenna looked up from the pad on her desk where she'd been making notes for an upcoming speech. "Please, come in."

Closing the door behind her, Steph crossed the office's dark blue rug to stand in front of McKenna's mahogany desk. The wall behind the president was armor glass that looked out over the Hudson River from where the Presidential Complex stood on Governors Island. From where

Steph was standing, the Statue of Liberty was just behind the president. It was an image captured more than once by the president's official media artist.

"You wanted to see me, ma'am?"

"Yes, I did, Steph. Please, sit down." McKenna gestured to one of the armchairs in front of her desk, and Steph sat down. "You read the briefing on the Alger's World operation, didn't you?"

"Yes, Madam President, I went through the entire briefing." Steph suppressed a rush of guilt. She should have attended, but had been on an assignment on the west coast and had been delayed by a foulup in her transportation arrangements, a foulup she had purposely engineered. The truth was that she had known Ichiro was going to be at the briefing, and she hadn't wanted to see him. *Not exactly*, she amended to herself. *He wouldn't want to see me.* "And let me apologize once again for not making it. It won't happen again."

McKenna waved the apology away. "I'm sure it won't."

Looking into the president's eyes, Steph could tell that McKenna knew the truth. It wasn't any secret that Steph and Ichiro had parted company a few months before, and Steph was ashamed that she had let her personal situation interfere with her job.

"Yes, ma'am." She dropped her gaze.

McKenna paused a moment before asking, "Steph, are you tired of this job?"

Looking back up at her boss, Steph said, "Tired of it? No. No, of course not."

A glint of anger flared in McKenna's eyes. "Don't tell me two lies in a row."

"Madam President..." Steph was momentarily at a loss for words. She had loved the job as press secretary for most of the two years that she'd held it, but McKenna was right. It had become a grind, a chore. More and more, Steph was just going through the motions, and she'd been growing increasingly restless. "I'm sorry, ma'am. I didn't mean for it to sound like that. I...I don't want you to think I'm disloyal. You gave me an incredible opportunity, and I can't tell you how much I appreciate what you did for me by giving me this position. But if you put it like that, then yes, I'm getting tired of it."

"Good." McKenna sat back and smiled, enjoying the confused mix of emotions on Steph's face. "Because I have a job that I think is right up your alley." She leaned forward, completely serious now. "Steph, you know as well or better than anyone else how the Confederation is faring. So you know just how fragile things are now."

Steph nodded. "If the Kreelans breathe hard against one more planet, the Confederation is finished." While the members of the president's cabinet had access to channels of information that Steph didn't, no one in McKenna's entire administration had a better handle on the pulse of the Confederation's citizenry than Steph. She was plugged into every news service for every human-settled world that was part of the interstellar courier network. She had seen how the political landscape had transformed from one of hope and optimism in the aftermath of the Confederation's formation to weariness as the war dragged on, and near-hysteria after the latest round of Kreelan invasions. "If we don't pull a rabbit out of the hat," she told McKenna, "the only thing we'll have left is what we started with, Earth and the Francophone Alliance."

"That's right. That's why this operation is so important. And that's why I want someone in on it from the start to document what I hope and pray will be our first decisive victory."

Stunned, Steph sat there for a moment. Her mind suddenly filled with the nightmare images of the Battle of Keran, where she had been an embedded journalist with the 7th Cavalry Regiment. She was incredibly lucky to have survived.

At the same time, she felt her pulse quicken, not in fear, but anticipation. She also realized that it wouldn't have been long before she would have resigned her position to return to being a journalist in the field. That was her passion, and she was one of a very few journalists who had not only survived, but had helped fight.

"I want to be clear," McKenna went on, "that this is strictly a volunteer assignment. There will be other journalists going in with the main force, but I've given a lot of thought to something I hadn't considered earlier. I want someone to tell the story from the very beginning of the operation, which means going in with one of the reconnaissance teams and documenting what they find. There aren't many people who could do that, and I wanted to give you first crack at it."

Steph didn't have to think about her answer. "When do I leave?"

McKenna pressed a control on her desktop pad. Five seconds later a Marine staff sergeant opened the door and stood at attention beside it. "The courier's waiting for you. It's the one taking the execution orders to the teams. I've already ordered your field equipment and travel bag loaded on the shuttle you'll be taking up to Africa Station. You just have to decide which team you want to go with."

That was another easy answer. Steph had studied the operations files long before the briefing and had seen some familiar names. "I'll go with the team led by First Sergeant Roland Mills."

"Done. Now get going, and good luck." McKenna stood and offered her hand.

"Thank you, ma'am!" Steph stood up and shook the president's hand, then turned to go.

As she boarded the shuttle on the roof of the complex, she thought about contacting Ichiro to let him know, but decided against it. *He went his own way*, she told herself. *I don't care if he knows.*

It was the third lie she'd told that day.

Six

Ku'ar-Marekh strode toward what had been the open center of the human town. She could not abide what passed for human architecture, where all the structures were square and blocky, bereft of the pleasing curves inherent in all the works of Her Children and the graceful script of the New Tongue. While she knew that she should be hoping that the One would be found soon, she could not help wishing the humans gone from the universe. They were unsightly creatures, whose ugliness was reflected in all they made.

Her warriors were building the first *Kalai-Il* to be erected on this world, making the first step in reshaping the planet for the pleasure of the Empress.

A massive stone edifice, the *Kalai-Il* comprised a large central dais surrounded by two rings of stone pillars that supported enormous capstones. It was central to Kreelan society, and was a place of atonement for those who had fallen from Her grace. Rarely was it used, for few were the transgressions of the peers severe enough to warrant such punishment. It stood as a reminder to all of the terrible price of dishonor.

She watched as hundreds of warriors labored, hauling the stones from a nearby quarry cut into the rock by the landing ships. Beyond that, no modern machines were used. The *Kalai-Il* was built on every world of the Empire the same way as it had been since before the time of the First Empress, with simple machines of wood and stone, powered by the straining muscles of the warriors who served Her will.

Around the *Kalai-Il*, hundreds more warriors hauled in smaller stones to build the five arenas that tradition demanded for ritual combat. Once they and the *Kalai-Il* were complete, contests between her warriors and the humans would commence, and would continue through all hours of the day and night until no humans remained, or the One had been found.

When the last of the humans was gone, this world would be turned over to the builder caste, who would fashion it into whatever form the Empress required.

There had been a time when that knowledge had thrilled Ku'ar-Marekh, knowing that her people could shape the face of a world, or even create a planet in the void of space. Or destroy one, or even an entire star system. These things and more had the Empire done in the long ages since the First Empress, Keel-Ta'th, had forged it.

But the wonder of what was in the power of the Empress to accomplish, to create or destroy, was gone.

All that remained to her was duty.

Ri'al-Hagir strode up to Ku'ar-Marekh and knelt as she saluted. "My priestess, the *Kalai-Il* and the arenas will be finished in another three turns of the sun."

"And have you made arrangements to hold the humans who will await their turn in the arenas?"

"Yes, my priestess. Pens are being constructed for the animals."

"When are the first humans due to arrive?"

"This evening. A column of the animals is being marched from the south."

"How many are there?" Ku'ar-Marekh ran her eyes across the arenas, watching as warriors hauled the sand on which the combats would be fought.

Ri'al-Hagir glanced up, then returned her eyes to the safety of the ground. "Thousands, my priestess. That is just in this first catch. There are many, many thousands more that we can take at our leisure."

"So many allowed themselves to be captured?"

"There were few warriors here, it seems. Some still fight on in small groups, but most are as our clawless ones, unable to defend themselves."

Ku'ar-Marekh grunted in surprise. The clawless ones of her race, those such as the builders and the healers, the armorers and many more, were never allowed in harm's way, for they were precious beyond their skills. They were the sacred legacy of those priestesses who had cut off their talons as a proclamation of faith and honor to the First Empress after She had been betrayed, over a hundred thousand cycles ago.

To leave any such as their own clawless ones undefended, vulnerable to attack, was unthinkable to any warrior.

"Animals, indeed." Ku'ar-Marekh made a flicking gesture with her talons, indicating disgust. "Be they human clawless ones or merely untrained warriors, they will fight and die in the arenas."

"As you command, my priestess." Ri'al-Hagir again saluted, then stood and hurried away to fulfill her duties.

* * *

That evening, Ku'ar-Marekh found herself restless despite a long day of accompanying some of the hunting parties that ranged across the planet, looking for humans to capture.

It had been a dull, empty day in a lifetime of such days since the Change.

Despite her weariness from covering many leagues on foot and whisking herself from place to place across the planet, she found that sleep eluded her.

With a sigh, she finally got up from her bed of animal hides and, on her knees, began to dress. Like everything else that was of the Way, there was a ritual to guide it. Unlike many of the peers, she normally slept in the nude, wearing only the collar about her neck and the pendants that hung from it.

Now she knelt beside her bed and carefully unfolded the black gauzy undergarment that was worn by all Her Children. It fit close to her skin, molding itself to her as she stood to put on the bottom, then the top, and she sealed it closed with a stroke of her hand.

Kneeling again, she began to put on her armor, drawing each piece in sequence from the neat stack she had made when she undressed. First came the sections of black leatherite that formed a layer covering her body from her ankles to just below her collar, and along her arms to her wrists. Then came her sandals which, like everything else, had been created by a senior armorer to fit her body perfectly. She tied the leather laces around her calves.

Last came the armor plate, which always gleamed like a black mirror, the cyan rune of the Nyur-A'il at the center of her breastplate glowing in the darkness. She put on the armor protecting her shins and thighs, then her upper and lower arms. She attached her breast and back plates, which molded themselves to her body. Then she put on her armored gauntlets, which had openings in the ends of the fingers for her black talons.

She cinched the leatherite belt around her waist and slid her sheathed sword into the holding ring. Her dagger was already attached, the deadly blade shrouded by the scabbard. Last, she attached three of the deadly *shrekkas*, throwing weapons, to her left shoulder.

Standing up, she pulled aside the white cloth that formed the door of her temporary quarters, which was little more than a large domed tent. Like all things, it was traditional, but she would have much rather slept in the open so she could see the stars before sleep took her away into blissful darkness for a few hours. Sleep that had passed over her this night.

Walking past the warriors who continued to labor on the *Kalai-Il* and the nearby arenas, she nodded her head as they saluted her, even though she felt completely isolated from them.

Ku'ar-Marekh did not know or care where she was going. It did not matter. Her warriors had the situation on this world well in hand, and the ships of Her fleet in space above were vigilant. All was quiet.

Too quiet.

She wandered the dark streets of the human settlement, her footsteps making no sound and leaving no mark, marveling at how ugly it was. Wishing she were of the builder caste, she imagined how she might remake it to be more pleasing.

Then she sensed it. The same small human she had seen the night she had arrived on this world. She did not need to cast forward her second sight to know it was the same creature, for she could sense its heartbeat, which was as unique to Ku'ar-Marekh as a face.

Curious, she silently glided toward the young animal.

* * *

Allison crept down the street along the side of the market, heading toward the front of the building. The back door was locked, and she hadn't wanted to risk trying to break in.

She felt guilty for having gone out tonight, because they really didn't need any more food right now. But the truth was that Allison needed some breathing room, some freedom from being cooped up with the kids all day, and it wouldn't hurt to have a little extra.

A quick smile crossed her lips as she thought of the word. Kids. She wasn't a kid anymore, she knew. She was an adult. For a moment she was proud of that, before she remembered how it had come to be. The smile faded as she thought of the contrails in the sky and the sirens, of her family, dead in the street.

The bodies, both human and Kreelan, had all been removed, along with all the weapons. Allison had planned to go see the bodies of her parents and brother, but they and all the others had been taken away before Allison had first ventured into town.

She didn't know what the Kreelans had done with them. The vids she
had seen about the aliens had only made clear how little humans really
knew about them. No one had said for sure that they didn't eat people,
and their fangs made it pretty clear they were meat eaters.

Allison shuddered and shoved the grisly thought aside as she moved
up to the corner of the market, crouching low. The building didn't face
onto the town square where the Kreelans were busy with their
construction project, but it was close enough that warriors passed by
frequently. She always had to be careful here.

She took a quick peek around the corner, then pulled back. It was
clear.

Taking a deep breath, she took the corner quickly, still staying low.

There, right in front of her, was the warrior who had landed that
night. The one who had absolutely terrified Allison, and who somehow
had grabbed her heart.

Even though the street was pitch dark and the warrior's features were
indistinct, a shadow that blocked the glow of the star light, Allison knew
it was her. A faint glow shone from the strange rune on her chest armor, as
if it was lit from within.

Allison knew she couldn't get away if the alien wanted to get her. She
had no idea where the Kreelan had even come from in the second between
when Allison had checked that the coast was clear and when she turned
the corner. There had been nowhere for the alien to hide. She was
simply...there.

"What...what do you want?" Allison cursed herself for asking such a
stupid question, but she wasn't sure what else to say. What was the proper
thing to ask a member of an alien race that was bent on annihilating
humanity?

The Kreelan, of course, said nothing. She simply stood there,
unmoving, starlight glinting from her eyes.

Allison tensed as she saw the alien clench her hands, and felt a sudden
stab of fear at the sight of the Kreelan's claws. They were five, maybe six
centimeters long, and Allison knew they were wickedly sharp.

"Can't we talk about this?" She could barely hear her own whisper
above the blood pounding in her ears.

Then the alien did something Allison never would have expected in a
million years. The Kreelan stood aside, and made a clear gesture for

Allison to pass, holding her hand out, palm up, in the direction Allison had intended to go.

Stunned, Allison simply stood there a moment, wondering if it was some sort of trick. But she quickly realized that the alien had no need to trick her. Allison's life was entirely in the alien's hands. Or claws.

Biting her lip, Allison was tempted to turn and run, but didn't. Not so much because of what the warrior might do, but because running would be like surrendering. And one thing both her parents had taught her was that the worst thing you could ever do was give up.

"Okay, then." Steeling herself, she took a step forward. Then another, which drew her up next to the warrior, who kept her eyes fixed on Allison, but otherwise made no move.

With the next step, Allison passed the Kreelan. She wanted to turn around to keep her eyes on the alien and back away from her, but resisted the urge.

Instead, she walked slowly to the market's front door, which had been blasted from its hinges. Shards of glass still littered the walkway, and the sound of it crunching under Allison's shoes sounded like a long string of gunshots in her ears. Her nose wrinkled at the sickening smell at the threshold, but she knew it was only spoiled food.

Glancing over her shoulder to see if the warrior was still there, Allison saw that the alien was following right behind her, barely an arm's length away.

Growing a bit bolder now, Allison asked, "So, I guess you're hungry, too?"

* * *

Ku'ar-Marekh was intrigued by the industrious human. While obviously little more than a pup, the animal had repeatedly come into the human settlement, no doubt seeking sustenance for the other pups that Ku'ar-Marekh knew had taken refuge at a destroyed homestead beyond the settlement. The young animal had taken great risks to do so, even coming back after an encounter with a group of patrolling warriors.

Through the numbness in her soul, she felt a tiny sliver of warmth: respect. It would not change the eventual fate of the pup and those sheltering with it, for when they were old enough to pose a credible threat to her warriors, or when Ku'ar-Marekh grew tired of their existence, they would be put to the arena.

For now, however, the young animal provided an interesting diversion.

It stood at the entrance to what must have been an indoor market for food, much of which had spoiled. The reek was overpowering to Ku'ar-Marekh's sensitive nose, but it was hardly the worst thing the priestess had endured.

The human said something in its incomprehensible language.

Ku'ar-Marekh again gestured with her hand in a way that she hoped the human would understand, urging it onward.

* * *

Allison saw the alien raise her hand again, palm up, simultaneously nodding toward the market's dark interior.

She found herself nodding back, then took out her flashlight and flicked it on. There was no reason to be stealthy, now that she had a Kreelan chaperone.

"Unreal," she breathed as she moved into the market. She moved quickly down the aisles, stuffing her backpack with boxes of breakfast bars, freeze-dried food packets, and some medicine that she hoped would cure what she knew was an infection in the hand of one of the kids. With every step she hoped that the warrior wouldn't decide to kill her. But every time Allison glanced back, the warrior was right behind her, intently watching everything she did like a curious but deadly puppy.

With the backpack nearly full, Allison tried to jam in a package of dried fruit. As she did, one of the closures on the pack flew opened and everything spilled out.

None of it hit the floor. Allison stood there, mouth agape, as the spilled contents of her backpack floated in the air as if they were in zero gravity in space, reflecting the light cast by the tiny flashlight that was clamped in her teeth.

Looking up at the Kreelan, she saw that one of the warrior's hands was out, fingers spread, as if she were going to pluck the items from the air. With a graceful turn of the warrior's wrist, everything magically flew back into the pack as Allison's shaking hands held it open.

As the troublesome dried fruit joined the other items, the pack closed itself, sealing tight. Then, as Allison stared at the warrior, she felt the pack lift up and seat itself on her shoulders.

Allison gulped. "Thank...thank you," she stuttered.

The Kreelan just stood there.

Carefully, as if she were stepping past a tame but hungry tiger, Allison moved toward the market's entrance. Glancing behind her, she saw that the warrior was gone. The Kreelan had disappeared as mysteriously as she had appeared in the first place.

"Oh, my God." Allison sighed with relief as she moved quickly along the front of the store and turned the corner back the way she had come.

And there stood the warrior, waiting for her.

"You know, that's really getting annoying." Allison didn't try to mask the anger in her voice. It was a more comforting feeling than unbridled fear, and even a tiny bit of jealously. She wished that she had powers like the alien did. It was like - she hated to use the word - magic. It was impossible.

But Allison knew that she wasn't just seeing things. She didn't imagine it. She wondered if all the aliens possessed such powers. If they did, what chance did humans have?

Not wanting to take that line of thought any further, she hastened down the street, heading toward home. The only difference was that she didn't take her normal route along the creek to try and stay out of sight. She walked right down the road, this time ignoring the aliens who passed by.

The alien warrior stayed right behind her the entire way.

* * *

Ku'ar-Marekh padded silently behind the human, marveling at the animal's courage as it marched right past the warriors moving through the night on their appointed tasks.

Other than a curious glance, the warriors paid the human no mind, seeing that Ku'ar-Marekh was with it. She felt intense curiosity from them through the Bloodsong, but they only saluted her as they continued on. Warriors did not question the affairs of a high priestess, especially of the Nyur-A'il.

When the human reached the path to the homestead that led from the main road, it stopped and turned to her. The animal held out its clawless hands toward her, as if pushing Ku'ar-Marekh away. The meaning was clear enough. Come no farther.

Ku'ar-Marekh pondered the peculiarities of the situation. Save the Empress and those who stood higher upon the steps to the throne than Ku'ar-Marekh herself, she would have instantly killed any other member of her race for such an egregious act. She would never even have given it thought before striking. She would have demanded ritual combat from any of the priestesses who stood above her had they done such a thing.

And yet, this human, this tiny thing that Ku'ar-Marekh could slay with the barest thought, gave her pause. The pup must eventually die in the arena, if Ku'ar-Marekh or another of her warriors did not kill it first. So why let it live?

The realization came to her with sudden clarity. She saw in this human something of what she herself had once known as a young warrior, fiercely proud. This animal clearly was not the One, for Ku'ar-Marekh could tell it was female and its blood did not sing.

Yet for the first time she gave some credence to the belief that the salvation of Her Children might be found among the humans. While she did not entirely accept the notion as fact, she no longer dismissed the possibility.

The human said some more words, shaking Ku'ar-Marekh from her reverie. Looking deep into the human's strange eyes, she bowed her head slightly.

* * *

Allison stood there, her arms still raised to ward the Kreelan off, hoping that the alien wouldn't become angry and decide to kill her.

The warrior shifted her gaze momentarily, as if looking at something beyond Allison. Glancing over her shoulder, Allison couldn't see anything behind her.

Looking more carefully at the warrior, who stood just beyond arm's reach, Allison thought the alien must have been deep in thought. Even in nothing but the starlight, Allison could see that the Kreelan's eyes, which looked much like those of a cat and in their own way were beautiful, were empty. Dead. Allison had seen enough of other warriors, had seen their expressions through the binoculars, to know that this alien was different. The other aliens showed expression, even if Allison couldn't read them. This one didn't. Her face was an unmoving mask, her eyes lifeless mirrors.

And if she was entertaining herself by following a human child around, rather than going to kill other humans, she was probably alone, too. Perhaps an outcast, even though she was clearly the leader here from the way the other warriors acted around her.

For a moment, Allison felt an unfamiliar sensation toward the warrior. Pity. She could never forgive the Kreelans for what they had done, but she couldn't help but feel sorry for this one, all alone out here, with no one for company but Allison.

But she wasn't about to invite the warrior in for dinner. "Go away, now. Please."

The warrior refocused her attention on Allison, spearing her with a gaze that sent a cold rivulet of fear through Allison's stomach.

Then, much to Allison's astonishment, the warrior bowed her head.

Not trusting herself to say anything, Allison slowly backed away, then turned and began walking down the drive toward the ruined house and barn.

After half a dozen paces, she threw a glance back at the warrior, but she had already vanished.

SEVEN

Valentina wiped her face with the waterless cleansing cloth, then stared into the mirror of the tiny lavatory, savoring a few precious moments alone.

She, Mills, and the other four members of the recon team had been crammed aboard a hastily modified courier ship that had originally been designed for a crew of two. The two pilots kept mostly to the cramped cockpit, leaving the Marines to fend for themselves in the midships area, which had been stripped of equipment and expanded with some welded-on sections that held the Marines' bunks. There was enough room in an aisle to move around, if you could make your way past the crates of equipment and weapons that were bolted to the walls and floor. There was no exercise equipment and nothing with which to entertain themselves but the ship's library of vids and books, and the Marines' imaginations, of course.

The ship reeked of stale sweat and unchecked body odor. Aside from the waterless wash towels, which never got their bodies truly clean and left an oily residue, they had no way to clean up. There was enough water aboard for drinking, and that was all. The deodorants the pilots tried to use to mask the smell only made it worse, and after some dire threats from the Marines, they wisely chose to stop using them.

They had only been cooped up in the courier for three days, but the overly close quarters, complete lack of privacy, and the stress of the high stakes mission had made the trip seem like weeks. Tempers were running high, and Mills had been forced to break up arguments that had threatened to erupt into potentially lethal violence.

The Marines were counting the nanoseconds until they could get off what they had begun calling the "pig boat."

The only place anyone could have any privacy was in the tiny lavatory, which some naval architect had the foresight to modify to accommodate the extra waste produced by the tiny ship's oversize crew.

Both of the courier's pilots were women who kept largely to themselves in the cockpit, and Valentina was one of only two women on the recon team. The other woman, Ella Stallick, who was the team's demolition specialist, was built like a champion wrestler and had a face to match, replete with a scar and twice-broken nose.

That left Valentina to deal with the brunt of the overdose of testosterone from the men on her team. In an effort to avoid any unpleasantness, she had taken to spending most of her time out of her bunk in the door to the cockpit, standing silent vigil with the pilots as the point of light that was Alger's World slowly grew brighter.

Almost there, she thought. Soon they'd be making their final approach to the planet, with the courier darting in to land the team.

The biggest question was what the Kreelans had in the system. So far, it was all good news. There were only seven destroyers, all in orbit over the planet. A heavy cruiser had appeared the day before, but had quickly departed.

The pilots were confident that they would be able to dodge the destroyers easily enough, drop the Marines, and then jump to safety.

Now all they needed was the final execution order. It was a failsafe in case the mission had been called off or delayed. If they didn't get the final go order within the next twelve hours, they would jump back to Earth space and terminate the mission.

Part of Valentina wanted desperately to go home, to be out of this stinking sardine can and be back in the safe and sweet-smelling woods around her home in Virginia.

Another part of her, the part that had defined most of her adult life, wanted to get on the ground and do nothing but kill Kreelans. Unlike the Marines (she had refused to formally join the Corps, but had deployed as a civilian contractor), she had never fought the aliens, only humans. But she had no doubt she could kill them better than any of the Marines could.

The door to the lavatory, which was only a glorified closet with a waterless toilet, mirror, and a small medicine cabinet, opened. The door wasn't equipped with a lock or occupancy indicator.

"I'm not done yet-" was all she managed to say before a large hand roughly clamped down on her mouth.

It was Ely Danielson, the team's communications technician. He had been extremely persistent in his amorous pursuit of Valentina until Mills had finally put him in a painful headlock and threatened to break his neck.

"Just keep your mouth shut," Danielson breathed as he shoved her backward against the bulkhead, using his other hand to close the flimsy door behind him. "I just want to-"

Her right hand shot upward in a sword strike, the rigid fingers jabbing into the vulnerable spot under his jaw, then drove her knee into his unprotected groin.

Gagging, he let her go and sagged to his knees, his hands instinctively going to his groin.

Valentina wasn't quite finished with him. She shoved both thumbs into his mouth and stretched it open so violently that the skin at the corners split and began to bleed.

Danielson screamed.

"When a girl says no," she said softly, her breathing barely above its normal slow rhythm, "she means no. The only reason I'm going to let you live is because we need you for this mission. But if you ever try to touch me or the other women again, I'm going to kill you. Do you understand?"

He nodded emphatically, or gave the impression of doing so as best he could. She was still holding his mouth stretched open with her thumbs while her fingertips dug into the nerves behind his ears.

Letting one side of his mouth go, she reached for the door latch.

Before she could touch it, the door flew open. Mills stood there, his face red with fury. He held a combat knife in his hand.

"No need." She shoved Danielson out of the lavatory. He fell backward into a groaning heap in the narrow aisle.

Putting his knife back into its scabbard, Mills shook his head. "Danielson, you have no idea how far out of your league you are, mate."

"I...just...had to pee." Dannielson wheezed out the words as he struggled to get to his knees. "She was hogging the head."

That caused Valentina, who wasn't easily given to laughter, to chuckle. "Well, sorry, then." She hoisted him up by the belt and shoved him into the lavatory before closing the door. "It's all yours."

"Jesus," Mills muttered. "What a fuckup. I'm sorry."

"It's not your fault. He's here for the mission, not his personality. He just needs to grow up a little."

"Well, after what you did to him, we may not have to worry about him propagating his genes."

That brought a big smile to Valentina's face, and Mills threw back his head and laughed.

"Mills," the courier's senior pilot called, "we've got the go order!"

"About time!" He grinned at Valentina.

"That's not all," the pilot went on, a strain of worry creeping into her voice. "We've had a last minute change in plans."

"What kind of change?" Mills didn't like last minute changes in missions. They had a tendency to get people killed.

"The courier that laser-linked the orders to us is coming in to dock. It looks like someone else is going to be joining your little party."

* * *

Ku'ar-Marekh crept silently through the woods two dozen leagues from the human town where her warriors had made their main encampment. She was alone, save for the unfamiliar forest creatures around her and the sense of the humans who lay ahead, those she was hunting.

She could have found them easily enough with her second sight, casting her spirit from her body to search the world around her.

Yet she chose not to, for that would have given her unfair advantage. It was for the same reason that she was making her final approach in daylight, for she knew the humans had poor night vision. While she could also slaughter the animals without ever coming in sight of them, this would bring no honor or glory to the Empress. That one thing, that duty to honor and glorify Her, was the closest thing she had left to any feeling.

She paused behind a large tree and knelt to the ground, closing her eyes. She listened to the sounds of the woods around her and smelled the air, her sensitive nose picking out the scents of the animals, the different varieties of trees. The faint stench of human body odor.

She could not entirely tune out the sense that the humans were near, for the powers she had inherited when she became priestess of the Nyur-A'il were as much a part of her as the heart that beat in her breast. Some of those powers she used or not, as she willed. Others simply fed her mind, as did her sight or hearing.

Opening her eyes, she found herself staring down at the cyan rune that graced her breast plate, thinking of the great honor it had been to accept the Way of the Nyur-A'il, and also of what it had cost her. She remembered, as if it were yesterday, kneeling in the ancient temple of her order, her hands locked with those of her priestess as the blazing light from the sacred crystal first touched her flesh, consummating the Change. Even with all her years of training and discipline, it was all she could do to not scream in agony as every cell in her body seemed to burst into flame. For to have done so, to have screamed or shown weakness, would have invited instant death.

When she had awakened, her priestess lay dead, and Ku'ar-Marekh's own clothing and armor was burned to ashes. Her skin, once proud with the scars of many contests of sword and claw, was now flawless, unblemished. While she did not then know how to control them, she could sense the powers that she had inherited from her now-dead priestess. She could tell instantly that she was more than she had been before.

And yet, something else that she had once had, like the scars on her skin, had vanished. Looking at the body of her priestess, who had stood on the sixth step from the throne in the rank of Her Children, she had felt...nothing. No anguish at her death, no pride that she had gone to join the Ancient Ones in the afterlife. Not even a shard of self-pity that she would not be able to teach Ku'ar-Marekh about her new powers. All emotion, all feeling, was gone. Her memories, even of the ceremony of the Change, when she had never been more honored, elated, and frightened, did not stir her soul or quicken her heart. It was as if they were the memories of someone else, gray and empty.

The Bloodsong, which bound together the Children of the Empress, still flowed in her veins, but only as a source of power. The tide of emotions from her sisters in blood that ebbed and flowed within it were no more to her now than the rise and fall of the waves of a long dead sea. All the feelings that made up the complex tapestry of her soul were gone.

Even the knowledge that all the Children of the Empress, every soul in an empire that spanned ten thousand suns, would die if they failed in their search for the First Empress and the One failed to move her. That their race was within but a few generations of extinction had become nothing more than a dry fact.

Drawing her mind away from what she could not change, Ku'ar-Marekh focused on the present. Somewhere ahead was a small band of humans that had proven particularly adept at inflicting serious losses on her warriors before melting away into the woods. They were well-armed with weapons of which the Empress would approve, without any of the more advanced systems that made the battle more between machines than true combatants.

She had tracked them this far mainly by scent. The humans, for all their cunning, could not completely mask their odor, or that of the weapons they used. She could identify eleven unique human scents, along with traces of oil and chemical residue of weapons that had been recently fired. They had covered their tracks extremely well, and...

She heard the faint mechanical sound of a trigger being pulled back ever so slightly. In a blur of motion, she drew one of her three *shrekkas* and hurled it at a patch of leaves on the ground at the base of a pile of large rocks not far ahead of her. As the weapon left her hand, she leaped into the air toward where the human animal lay in ambush, her body sailing between the trees as if she were borne on the wind.

The *shrekka* tore into her prey, and Ku'ar-Marekh was rewarded with the animal's shriek of agony as the *shrekka's* blades ripped down the human's spine.

She drew her sword in mid-air and did a graceful forward flip. Landing with her legs astride the writhing human, she stabbed the sword downward, the gleaming tip spearing the creature through the heart.

Ku'ar-Marekh snatched another *shrekka* from her shoulder and hurled it at a human whose head had poked out from among the rocks above her. The creature had no time to cry out as the whirling blades took its head from its neck in a spray of crimson.

She leaped again, this time to the top of the rock outcropping where she found two more humans armed with rifles. She took the head from one with her sword, and simply grabbed the other one and tossed him bodily from the rock, ignoring his scream as he fell to the ground below.

Four. Ku'ar-Marekh mentally tallied the kills, knowing there were at least seven more. She could feel the surge of power in the Bloodsong, but the elation, the ecstasy she had once felt were missing. It was a bright light that flared in her heart, but brought no warmth to her soul.

Four humans emerged from where they had been sheltering in the rocks. All of them opened fire on her with their rifles.

The bullets came within an arm's length of her body and simply fell from the air, so hot that they instantly melted into small pools of metal that set the leaves smoldering.

Pausing to gape at what their eyes told them, yet clearly not believing what they saw, the humans continued to fire, and the other three she had knew must be here stepped from behind the rocks and joined in.

Between them, they fired hundreds of rounds at her, until their magazines ran dry and a pool of molten metal sizzled on the ground before Ku'ar-Marekh.

Two of the humans tried to run, and she was upon them in an instant, her sword flashing as she leaped beyond the ring of fire that now surrounded her.

Another charged at her, brandishing a knife, and in the blink of an eye she slammed her sword back into its scabbard and faced her opponent with only her claws. He was skilled and fearless, but was no match for her. After toying with him enough to satisfy her honor, she clawed the knife from his hand, then drove the talons of one hand into his throat.

She whirled as the remaining four humans attacked her. She did not bother to draw her sword. One of them came at her with a knife, but only used it as a diversion. When the human was close enough, he simply grabbed her in a bear hug and shoved her backward, no doubt hoping to pin her to the ground while the remaining humans finished her off.

Using the animal's momentum, she leaped backward, sailing into the air with the human clinging to her, terrified. She grasped its head and twisted it until the neck snapped, then tossed the animal away before landing on her feet.

Looking up, she saw that the surviving humans, which she had expected to try and run, were instead coming straight at her, bellowing what must have passed for war cries.

Then she noticed what they held in their hands. Explosive grenades.

A fair contest, then, she told herself. Focusing on them, she reached out with her spirit and found their hearts. Then she began to squeeze.

The three humans collapsed in mid-stride, the grenades, all of them armed, rolling from their twitching hands.

Ku'ar-Marekh released her hold on their hearts and watched just long enough to see the realization dawn in their eyes of how their lives would be ended.

By their own grenades.

Then she leaped away, gliding to the ground below.

Behind her, the three humans were consumed by thunder and flame.

* * *

"I don't fucking believe this." Mills stood between the pilots as they guided the ship to rendezvous with the incoming courier. "If the Kreelans don't pick up on this stunt, I'll eat my drawers."

"You're probably safe on that count, Mills." The pilot's voice was tense as she watched the head-up display that showed the soft-dock approach of the other ship. "Our buddies here had good timing. The ESM sensors aren't chirping at us."

The Electronic Surveillance Measures, or ESM, suite on the ship was designed to warn the crew if any signals from enemy ships were strong enough to detect them. When they were near the detection threshold, the system warned the crew with a variety of chirps and automated voice warnings.

"I don't give a bloody damn. We're exposed as hell and on a tight timeline now. Whoever comes aboard had better have a good reason or I'll wring his neck for putting us and the mission in such danger."

A few moments later, the two ships were flying side-by-side, and there was a gentle thunk outside the airlock as the soft-dock tubes linked up. They didn't bother to pressurize it.

"The link's good." The pilot confirmed the hookup to her counterpart in the other ship. "Send over your cargo."

A few minutes later a figure in a vacuum suit moved awkwardly though the tube to enter their air lock, then turned to hit the control to close the outer door.

When the lock indicator showed it was pressurized, Mills slid the hatch open and stood in the doorway, glaring at the suited figure.

Whoever it was fumbled with the helmet catches, but Mills didn't offer to help. He was furious.

As soon as the newcomer managed to undo the catches and began to take off the helmet, Mills lit into whoever it was.

"I don't give a fuck if you're the goddamn Chief of Naval Staff," he said coldly. "Your coming here may have put the knife to all of us, and..."

"Oh, my God." Valentina, who stood beside him, put a hand up to her mouth in surprise as the face behind the helmet was revealed.

"And here I thought you two would be happy to see me." A woman with brunette hair handed her helmet to a stunned Roland Mills.

Mills heard someone behind him blurt, "Who the fuck is that?"

"That," Valentina said, unable to suppress a smile, "is Stephanie Guillaume-Sato, Commodore Ichiro Sato's wife."

EIGHT

"What the devil are you doing here, Steph?" Mills helped Steph strip out of her vacuum suit, revealing combat fatigues identical to his own, but without any badge of rank.

The other members of the team grabbed the suit and the small case she'd brought along as the courier accelerated away from the rendezvous point, racing now toward Alger's World.

Behind them, the ship that had brought Steph leaped away into hyperspace.

Mills had met Steph during the battle of Keran on the assault boat that had extracted them from the disastrous ground battle. She had been one of the embedded journalists attached to the 7th Cavalry Regiment, and Mills had been in what had been the Francophone Alliance's Foreign Legion, the remnants of which had been absorbed into the new Confederation Marine Corps after being decimated at the battle of Keran. It had been designated as a regiment in the Corps, but had taken on the unofficial name of the Red Legion for the blood that had been spilled from its ranks in its final battle.

While Steph had started out in the battle as a journalist, by the time she and the other handful of survivors had escaped the abattoir the Kreelans had made of the planet, she had also become a combat veteran.

After her return to Earth, she became something of a celebrity, and that had helped catapult her to a position she had never even dreamed of, President McKenna's press secretary. That's the role she'd been playing in service of the Confederation.

Until now.

"The president decided that we needed a unique view of this operation to give the public." She met his glaring gaze without the slightest trace of guilt. "She wanted someone on one of the recon teams, and I wanted to go. When I found out you were leading one, it was pretty much a given which team I'd choose."

"And she just let you go, did she?" Mills didn't try to mask his sarcasm as he folded his tree trunk-sized arms across his chest.

"Yes, Mills, she did. In fact, she asked me to go." She stepped closer to him, tilting her head back to stare up at him. "You were going to be stuck with someone, regardless. So just go ahead and name another journalist who has my qualifications for this type of assignment, or that you'd rather have with you."

Mills glared at her a moment more, then broke out into a grin. "Well, I guess better you than some fat-headed dolt who doesn't know how to handle a weapon when the Kreelans get in sword range." He slapped her on the shoulder, nearly knocking her off her feet. "Welcome aboard, then, girl."

"Speaking of weapons," Steph said, rubbing her shoulder as she regained her balance, "I take it you've got a spare rifle for me?" While Steph was a journalist first, she would never again go into a combat zone unarmed.

"I think we can arrange that. Do you know the op?"

"Yes, I've been fully briefed. I can also be a backup for Danielson." She nodded to the comms specialist, who had just emerged from the lavatory, where he'd been trying to recover from Valentina's knee smashing into his groin. "I went over the information for your communications gear and procedures on the trip out."

"All right, then." Mills sighed, not happy about the situation but resigned to the reality of it. "I just hope your surprise appearance didn't give us away too early."

"Maybe not too early," the pilot called, having listened in to the conversation over the intercom, "but they're definitely on to our game. Four of the ships in orbit are changing course."

"Are any after us yet?" Mills called.

"I can't tell, but they're definitely hot and bothered now. Some of them look like they're going after the drones, but we're still too far away to be sure."

The courier ships carrying the Marine recon teams weren't the only ones that had been sent to the system. There were another two dozen smaller vessels, drones, that were programmed to follow flight profiles similar to the real ships. They were decoys designed to appear identical to the real ships to the enemy's sensors. It was hoped they would give the couriers a better chance to slip into their insertion positions.

"Well, let's get ready for the big game, then, shall we?"

As the others began unpacking their equipment and double-checking their weapons, Mills cornered Steph and asked quietly, "Does the commodore know you've come along?"

Steph looked up at him, and he saw a brief flash of pain in her expression before she could hide it. "I don't know, Mills." She averted her eyes, looking down at the deck. "We...we haven't spoken in the last couple months. We separated not long after he came back from Saint Petersburg."

"Oh." Mills felt a fool, not quite sure what to say. "Sorry for that."

Steph looked back up into his eyes. "Ichiro was different after he came back. The only thing he could focus on was the Kreelans, and how we could defeat them. He lost himself in working on the new ship designs. Nothing else seemed to matter. Nothing. And no one."

Mills was feeling increasingly uncomfortable, hearing of the marital problems between a commodore and his former press secretary wife. But he couldn't just walk away. He hadn't known Steph all that well, but the survivors of Keran, both those who'd fought on the ground and in space, shared a special bond. There had been few enough of them.

As if reading his mind, Steph smiled, masking her inner pain. "And why am I telling a big lug of a Marine about all this? Aren't you supposed to be yelling at people or something?"

Mills mustered a smile, but his eyes betrayed his concern for her. The mission was going to be tough enough without someone with a lot of emotional baggage weighing them down.

"Don't worry, Mills." She touched his arm to reassure him. "I've got it together."

"Right, then," he said, nodding. "Come on, let's get you fitted out with proper kit. Valentina?" he called. "Could you give our, ah, journalist extraordinaire a bit of a hand?"

"Sure." Valentina took Steph back to the crowded center aisle where the Marines were busy getting ready. She shot a glance at him over her shoulder when Steph wasn't looking, and Mills gave her the thumbs-up sign.

She's okay.

Valentina, who hadn't known Steph personally, shrugged as she turned back around and helped Steph pick out weapons and other combat gear.

Mills made his way to the cockpit. "How long?"

The luminous disk of Alger's World was huge now in the forward viewscreen. He saw a sudden bright flash against the black of space to the left.

"One of the drones just bought it." The pilot shook her head as a green icon flickered and died on her display. A red icon depicting a Kreelan destroyer swept through the space where the drone had been just a moment before.

"Have any of the other insertion ships bought it?"

"None, yet. But...oh, shit."

"What is it?"

The pilot pointed to a pair of red icons on the head-up display, or HUD. They were two Kreelan destroyers that had appeared from around the far side of the planet. Even Mills, who didn't understand the trajectory data displayed on the HUD, could see that they were coming at his ship on a converging course.

The pilot turned to glance up at him. "Looks like we've got company."

* * *

After killing the group of humans, Ku'ar-Marekh spent the rest of the day gathering wood from the forest to build funeral pyres for their bodies. It was an ages-old tradition to honor worthy opponents who had fallen in battle, and she had judged these to be worthy. They had inflicted many casualties upon her warriors since the Children of the Empress had come to this world, and had acquitted themselves well in the brief battle she had fought with them.

That they had never stood a chance against her was irrelevant. She nonetheless honored their sacrifice as tradition demanded.

As with most things, she did this alone. She realized that the warriors placed in her charge were deathly afraid of her, for she was not given to tolerance of the slightest flaw and had taken the lives of many who had displeased her. It was not an uncommon thing for a warrior priestess to act so, for their place among the peers of the Empire was only below the Empress Herself. But some would say that Ku'ar-Marekh's lethal punishments were...excessive. It was yet another reason why she had spent as much time as she could alone, among the stars.

None, however, even the other warrior priestesses, had ever said as much to her, save one: Tesh-Dar, the last priestess of the Desh-Ka, the oldest order that served the will of the Empress.

Of all the priestesses who still lived, she was the only one who did not fear Ku'ar-Marekh. Tesh-Dar had once counseled Ku'ar-Marekh against being so heavy-handed with her warriors. It had been in private, as much as anything could be private when their entire race was linked through the Bloodsong, for Tesh-Dar's intention had clearly been to instruct, rather than humiliate.

But Ku'ar-Marekh, high priestess of the Nyur-A'il, was not about to be lectured by anyone, even such as Tesh-Dar.

Ku'ar-Marekh could have issued a challenge to the elder priestess, but had instead settled for giving the great priestess of the Desh-Ka a taste of the Nyur-A'il's power. Ku'ar-Marekh no longer felt fear herself, but she knew how to instill it in others.

She reached out with her mind to take hold of Tesh-Dar's heart.

Such was her surprise when she discovered that her ethereal claws collided with a solid wall of power. She could sense Tesh-Dar's heart, feel it beating in the great warrior's chest, but try as she might, Ku'ar-Marekh could not reach it.

"Try as you may, child," Tesh-Dar whispered, "you shall fail. Issue a challenge for combat in the arena, as that is your right, but do not play such childish games with me."

Knowing that she should feel shame, but unable to taste even those bitter ashes in her mouth, Ku'ar-Marekh knelt before Tesh-Dar and offered her neck to the elder warrior's sword. She knew that she had disgraced herself, and that death was the only possible reward. In the cold place that was her heart, she silently wished for it. Her only hope was that in the Afterlife she might recover what the Change had taken from her.

"Take my life," she begged. "I offer it freely."

"No, child." Tesh-Dar, a giant among Her Children, placed a great hand upon Ku'ar-Marekh's head to stroke the braids of the younger priestess's raven hair. "I can sense the emptiness in your heart, the chill of your spirit. The peers call you Dead Soul, and with good reason. I would grant your wish out of compassion, but this is not the will of the Empress. And that, above all else, must we obey. Even you, I know, can sense that much."

Ku'ar-Marekh nodded, then stood to face Tesh-Dar. "I will not thank you for your kindness, priestess of the Desh-Ka."

Then she had turned and left.

That had been many cycles ago. Now, kneeling before the burning pyres of the humans, Ku'ar-Marekh stared into the flames, replaying Tesh-Dar's words. Of all those in the Empire, save the Empress Herself, Tesh-Dar was the only one who had understood Ku'ar-Marekh's pain, a pain she herself could not feel for the emptiness inside her.

And now Tesh-Dar was gone, locked away in the ancient temple of the Desh-Ka, perhaps forever.

Fire and flame. It would be so easy to simply hurl herself into one of the flaming pyres and purge herself of this empty life. Yet she could no more do that than feel the long-gone warmth of the love of her sisters in the Bloodsong. She remained subject to the will of the Empress, a yoke around her spirit, binding her to this life.

As the flames licked higher into the sky and the bodies of the humans were gradually consumed in the fire, Ku'ar-Marekh knelt on the ground and fell into a deep meditative state. Focusing her concentration inward, she slowed her breathing until it stopped, then stopped her heart. It was the closest she could come to death, and she sought this state as often as she could, hoping to force time ahead to the moment of her blessed demise. Her only lament was that she could not hold herself in this state indefinitely.

But there, in the depths of the nothingness that shielded her from herself, she felt a sudden stirring in the Bloodsong, a surge in the excitement of her sisters. Casting her mind's eye outward, following the strands of the chorus of the song, she found herself among the orbiting warships.

The humans had sent tiny ships into the system.

Unlike the sensors of the warships, which had intentionally been made to match the primitive capabilities of the human vessels, Ku'ar-Marekh's second sight could tell which ships held living beings and which did not.

She would never have revealed that information to the warriors aboard her own ships, of course, for that would have violated the will of the Empress. The humans had proven themselves worthy opponents, and would be given equal or better advantage in any combat. Priestesses had more leeway in the matter in their own personal challenges, but the peers would never confer undue advantage upon themselves.

Fastening her attention upon a single human vessel that was closer than the others, Ku'ar-Marekh watched as its fate was decided.

* * *

"They've got us," the pilot called back to where Mills now sat, strapped into one of the fold-out seats against the inner wall of the hull.

"Damn." Mills shook his head, looking at Valentina. The plan had called for the courier to set down on the planet. If that wasn't possible for any reason, the Marines were to jump from high altitude using parasails. Mills had made the decision to prepare to jump, but had hoped they could land. They had the bulky packs strapped to their chests, with their equipment stuffed into backpacks. They also had face masks and oxygen cylinders. If they had to jump at high altitude, they would need oxygen to breathe.

"Mills," the pilot shouted, "we have to abort! We haven't gotten too far into the gravity well that I can't jump out-"

"No!" Mills barked through the microphone in his face mask. "There's no aborting this one, missy. The fleet and Marines are coming in behind us and they need to know what the hell they'll be facing here. We either make it or we die trying. Got that?"

The pilot muttered a string of curses as she and the copilot fought to get the courier into the atmosphere. If they could make it that far, the Kreelan destroyers wouldn't be able to follow them, as the sensors suggested that these particular ships weren't designed to operate in the atmosphere.

The courier lurched. Then it began to roll, the arc of the planet below spinning in the forward view screen. Mills felt a wave of nausea as his inner ear went crazy. The gravity compensators were failing.

The pilot shouted something just before everything went to hell. There was an explosion at the rear of the main cabin that sent shards of metal and plastic flying, but the screams of the men and women of his team were drowned out by the roar of the ship's air streaming through the hole punched into the engineering section by a Kreelan shell.

The explosion had weakened part of the hull wall, and the seat of Staff Sergeant Rajesh Desai, the team's heavy weapons specialist, tore loose. Still strapped to his seat, the NCO tumbled through the cabin, screaming. His screams were cut off as he slammed into the torn metal in the aft bulkhead. Mills watched in horror as the man was pinned there for a moment, then in a spray of blood was blown out through the hole, which was much smaller than Desai.

The ship was wallowing in the atmosphere now as the pilots fought the controls, and the only thing that kept them alive were the shields. If those failed, they would burn up in an instant.

"Is anyone injured?" Mills bellowed through the face mask comm system. "Sound off!"

"Ephraim is gone." Valentina spoke loud enough to be heard through the scream of the air still streaming out, but her voice was completely calm.

Mills turned to look to where Jeremy Ephraim sat. The upper half of the man's body had been torn to ribbons by shrapnel from the shell hit. "Bloody hell. Anybody else hit?"

He received a brief volley of no's from Valentina, Steph, Ella Stallick, and Danielson.

"Mills!" the pilot shouted. While the air had by now vented out, the cabin was filled with the whistling roar of the atmosphere through which the courier was now tumbling, out of control. "You have to jump!"

"Are you off your nut?" Mills shouted back, his mask fogging up slightly as he did. "We're not even close to our release altitude! We'll burn up out there!"

"We're through the worst of it! We redlined our descent, using the shields as a brake. We're high but not too fast now. You don't have any choice! If you don't jump now, you-"

The pilot's words were brutally cut off by a brace of Kreelan shells that blew the nose from the courier. Mills stared in horror as the entire forward part of the ship sheared away, the pilot and copilot carried with it. He could hear the pilot screaming as she fell, her voice echoing in his earphones from the comm system, when he looked up to find Valentina in front of him, clinging to his chair.

"Come on! We've got to go! Now!"

Fighting against the roller coaster motion of the courier's hulk, Mills pushed away his fear and focused on what had to be done.

Taking hold of a nearby conduit running along the wall, he unstrapped himself with his free hand and got to his feet. Stallick and Danielson followed his example, but Steph was still in her chair, struggling with her seat harness.

"Go on!" Mills shouted at Valentina and the others. "Get out! I'll help her!"

"No!" Valentina grabbed his arm. "I'll get her. You get the others and the weapons!"

Mills didn't argue. He understood Valentina's intent. He was the mission leader, and the mission was the most important thing. Everything else was secondary, and he didn't have the luxury now for any heroics.

"Stallick! Danielson! Get one ammo and both supply containers!" Aside from their personal weapons and other gear that was on each Marine's weapons harness, the team's equipment was in a set of containers that had their own parachutes. Mills would have liked to take everything, but having enough to eat and at least some ammunition were the top priorities.

The two Marines nodded. Fighting the tumbling motion of the courier, they began to unstrap the containers from the deck.

In the meantime, Valentina had made her way to where Steph still struggled. The former spy could see Steph's mouth moving, but couldn't hear anything.

"Steph!" She leaned closer to better see Steph's face. "Can you hear me?"

Steph nodded, then pointed to her face mask. A tiny sliver of shrapnel from the hit that had taken the courier's forward section had damaged the microphone's electronics. Had it been a few centimeters to either side, it would have sliced into her mask and her face.

Looking down at the buckle of Steph's harness, Valentina saw that shrapnel had done its work there too. Another shard had bent the buckle's latch mechanism, somehow glancing away from Steph.

"God, you're lucky." Valentina pulled her combat knife from its scabbard and quickly sawed through the tough straps. "Come on!"

Valentina turned to make her way forward toward Mills after Steph was free.

But Steph didn't follow her. Instead, she headed aft.

Valentina was about to go after her when she saw that Steph was going after the small case she'd brought aboard, and which had been stowed in one of the lockers near the smoking wreckage of the lavatory.

Steph grabbed the case and strapped it to her side.

While Valentina waited for her, she told Mills, "Steph's all right, but her mic's not working. She can receive but not transmit."

"That's not a bad thing for a woman sometimes," Mills quipped as he helped Danielson move the second supply container.

"Fuck you, Mills." Stallick, who was silhouetted against the spinning planet in the opening at the front of the hull, was holding down the first supply container and the ammo container.

The ship lurched again, and Stallick reached out to brace herself, taking hold of some bent conduits. The Kreelan destroyers had given up the chase, but the air currents were tossing the ship around as it plummeted toward the surface. "If you-"

The ship dropped, and the container that Mills and Danielson had been shepherding down the aisle toward Stallick got away from them.

"Down!" Mills tried to warn Stallick, but it was too late.

With a single bounce, the fifty kilo container caught Stallick right in the face and carried her out of the ship. Unconscious or dead, she silently spiraled out of sight.

"Goddammit!" Danielson turned to Mills, his eyes wide behind his oxygen mask. "That one had our commo gear!"

Mills slammed a fist into the bulkhead. "Fuck!" Not only had they lost Stallick, they'd also probably lost the container. She had been the one setting the automatic parachute deployment systems, and obviously hadn't been able to take care of that container. It would just fall to the ground like a rock, smashing everything inside it.

We'll have the devil's own time trying to communicate with the other ground teams and the fleet when it arrived, Mills thought bitterly, but he knew that was something they'd have to sort out later. If they survived.

"Come on!" He gathered the others close together. "Let's get off this bitch!"

Danielson checked that the chute controls for the other two containers had been set before kicking them out. Then Mills grabbed the three survivors of his team and leaped out the gaping hole where the cockpit had been.

As they fell away, Mills and Danielson spread their arms to control their fall, moving slightly apart. Valentina did the same, but held onto one of Steph's hands to help stabilize her. Steph had said she'd made a few jumps in simulators before shipping out here, but had never made a real jump, and certainly not one like this.

The four of them fell toward the ground, keeping their eyes fixed on the black dots that were the two containers. They could also see Stallick's body, still spinning lazily below them.

The hulk of the courier tumbled away from them, finally smashing into an empty field where it exploded.

"Stallick!" Danielson called. "Stallick, can you hear me?"

"She's gone," Valentina told him quietly. "Mills, how far from the target are we?"

"We're in bloody bumfuck!" Mills fought to bring his anger under control. "We're not even close to our planned drop zone. I think we're over the right continent, but that's about it."

Looking down, Valentina could see orderly patches of farmland far below. The neat patches of the farms were interspersed with large stretches of forest.

"Well, at least we're not falling into the ocean."

"Now there's a bright side." Mills looked at the digital map display in the face mask. "At least there's a town near here. Breakwater, it's called. Maybe there are some Territorial Army blokes we can hook up with to help get us to where we need to be."

They saw the chutes for the containers open below them. They were set to open at two hundred meters.

Stallick's body continued to plummet downward, and Mills winced when it hit the ground. "Damn."

"Altitude," Valentina called. They were nearing three hundred meters. They could open the chutes lower, but she didn't want to risk it with Steph never having made a combat drop before, and not being able to communicate.

Mills gave the thumbs-up. "Go!"

Danielson activated his chute, and it fluttered out of his pack to form a graceful camouflage-colored parasail.

Valentina let go of Steph and moved away to give her chute room to open. She watched as Steph hit the control to release it...and nothing happened.

Steph frantically worked the chute control again. Nothing. Wide-eyed with terror, she looked up at Valentina, who was already arrowing in toward her.

"Mills, Steph's chute failed. I'm going to double up with her."

"You're too bloody low!" Mills warned. "Valentina!"

Ignoring him, she grabbed Steph and quickly hooked their harnesses together.

"Hang on," she said grimly as she hit her chute's controls. If hers didn't work...well, they wouldn't have to worry about it for very long.

"Valentina!" Mills shouted again. Cursing in frustration, he deployed his own chute. He was too heavy to risk going any lower, or the chute wouldn't be able to slow him enough before he hit the ground.

Valentina's parasail blossomed from her pack and snapped full open. She guided it toward a field not far from where the two containers had fluttered to the ground on their chutes.

Steph clung to her like a terrified child, her eyes fixed on the ground. They were coming down fast, really fast.

Valentina judged the distance. It was going to be close. Really close. "Okay Steph, roll with me when we hit. Ready...ready...now!"

They slammed into the ground. Valentina took the brunt of it as the two of them awkwardly collapsed and rolled into the soft earth of the field. Steph wound up on top, panting heavily.

Valentina undid the buckle that linked them, and Steph rolled off onto her back before tearing off her face mask and throwing it aside.

"Jesus," she gasped. "And to imagine that some idiots pay good money to do this sort of thing."

Valentina, taking off her own mask, couldn't help but laugh. "Actually, for something like this, you'd have to pay extra."

That had them both laughing, happy to be alive.

"I'm glad you two girls are getting along so well," they heard Mills call from where he was busy gathering up his chute about fifty meters away, "but it's time to stop socializing and get to work, dearies. Go get the containers and haul them into the woods, then inventory what we've got and divide up the ammo we need. Danielson, you're with me."

"What are you going to do?" Valentina asked.

Mills turned to her, his expression grim. "We've got to bury Stallick."

* * *

Ku'ar-Marekh withdrew her second sight from watching the humans fall from the sky, returning her spirit to the sanctum of her body.

Her heart again began to beat, and her chest slowly rose and fell as she began to breathe. After a moment, she opened her silver-flecked feline eyes.

With the pyres still burning brightly, she moved off into the forest, toward where the humans had landed.

NINE

Commodore Ichiro Sato stood on the flag bridge of the newly commissioned battleship *CSS Orion*, intently watching the combat information display that took up the entire forward wall of the compartment.

Orion and her three sister ships, *Monarch*, *Conqueror*, and *Thunderer*, made up the Confederation Navy's First Battleship Flotilla, and were the most powerful warships humanity had ever built. Yet even as the four ships were being launched, larger and more powerful ships were being designed.

For their main armament, *Orion* and her sisters had twelve thirty centimeter main guns, able to fire a variety of munitions ranging from basic armor-piercing to what amounted to a gigantic shotgun shell to repel Kreelan boarding parties. While their rate of fire was slower than the fifteen centimeter guns carried by most heavy cruisers, the shells were nearly fifteen times larger by mass, packing an incredibly massive punch.

The battleships also had a pulse cannon running along the keel that could spear even a heavy cruiser. Having learned both the power and the limitations of the weapon through bitter experience during the battle of Keran, Sato had worked with the shipwrights who designed the *Orion* class to maximize the weapon's advantages and minimize its limitations.

The ships had an impressive secondary armament of both kinetic weapons and lasers, which by themselves would be more than a match for any Kreelan warship the humans had yet encountered.

But even as powerful as the new ships were, Sato knew that the enemy had vessels that were vastly beyond humanity's technology. He had seen them with his own eyes. For reasons of their own, the Kreelans had chosen not to use them, instead preferring to match the humans, "dumbing down" their own weapons and systems.

He knew the advantage that *Orion* and her sisters would enjoy during their first battle would be short-lived, for the Kreelans would soon build ships to match them. But he believed that for at least this once, the four battleships would reign supreme.

Half of the display he was watching showed the bright blue and white curve of Earth as the battleships and their escorts maneuvered away from the naval base at Africa Station. The other half showed a tactical map with the icons of the ships of Home Fleet, including *Orion* and her sisters, that were preparing to jump.

The formation, Sato saw with satisfaction, was perfect. All the crews had trained hard for this mission, and Sato had drilled the battleship crews nearly to the point of mutiny.

The battleship captains, all of whom were senior to Sato in time in service, finally complained that he was driving their crews too hard.

"Let me make something perfectly clear," Sato had told them, his voice cutting through the conference room when he'd finally called the captains together to hear their complaints. "This is the first time since the war began that we may have a chance to beat the Kreelans. You've all seen combat and you know some of what the enemy is capable of." He paused, his mind replaying the nightmare visions of the first contact encounter with the Kreelans, of which he had been the sole survivor. Their giant warships had technology that centuries, and perhaps more, beyond what his own people had. "They are relentless, merciless killing machines, and the only way we stand any chance of winning this war..."

He paused in spite of himself, knowing in his heart of hearts that it simply wasn't possible that humanity could win against the Empire. Just the few gigantic, fantastic ships the Kreelans met the *Aurora* with during the first contact encounter would have been more than enough to obliterate the entire Confederation fleet.

"The only chance we have," he went on, "is to be like them in combat. To be the blade of a sword, forged in the hottest flame. And that is what these ships are, the true swords of the fleet. We can't afford to be easy on our crews, because the outcome of the coming battle may very well depend on what those men and women do when all hell is breaking loose around them. We have to be merciless with them, and they have to be merciless with themselves. They must be ready. And they will be, no matter the cost."

No matter the cost. Sato's own words echoed dully in his mind as he considered the price that he himself had paid. After his return from the battle at Saint Petersburg he had become obsessed with the war. He had spent every waking moment at Naval Headquarters or in the yards at Africa Station, working on the new ships and the tactics to employ them, focusing on the day that he knew must eventually come, the day when he would again be able to sail into harm's way. For that, he had given up everything. Even his wife.

A dull pain welled up inside him as he thought of Steph. He hadn't simply drifted away from her, but had intentionally isolated himself, pushing her away, so he could focus his entire being on the fight against the Empire. It had broken his heart when she finally told him that she was leaving him.

The cold, calculating part of his brain considered this a step forward, while the man and husband inside him wept bitter, lonely tears. She had begged him to help her understand what was going on inside him, but he couldn't, wouldn't, tell her.

Part of it was the illogical pursuit of vengeance for what had happened to the crews of all three ships he had served on since encountering the Kreelans. The *Aurora*, the unlucky ship to make first contact; the *McClaren*, named after *Aurora's* captain, which had been destroyed in the battle for Keran; and the heavy cruiser *Yura*, Sato's first true command, which had been destroyed at Saint Petersburg.

Many in the fleet thought he was an incredibly lucky man. He thought he was cursed.

Sato knew he carried an enormous amount of grief and guilt inside him, but he had used it to help forge the weapons that would now finally strike a decisive blow against the enemy. He knew that in the interstellar war the Kreelans had begun, his own personal feelings weren't important. But that didn't keep him from feeling the pain in his heart every time he thought of Steph, which seemed like every minute of every day.

At least she's safe on Earth, he consoled himself, knowing that she was doing vital service as the president's press secretary. She was as safe as anyone could be.

He only wished that he'd had the courage to at least call her before he again sailed into battle. He had told himself every day since this operation had been announced that he would. Every day his hand had hovered over the comm unit as he sat at his console in his cabin, wondering what he would say.

And every day he had taken his hand away, then gone to the flag bridge, his heart a cold stone in his chest.

"Admiral," the operations officer called, breaking him from his reverie, "*Guadalcanal* has initiated the jump timing sequence."

"Very well," Sato told him, shoving his regrets aside. "First Battleship Flotilla," he said over a communications circuit that repeated his voice to the crews of the four battleships under his command, "prepare for jump. *Guadalcanal* has primary control."

While each ship did its own jump calculations, the assault carrier *Guadalcanal*, which was Admiral Voroshilov's flagship, made the primary calculations that were fed into each ship's navigation systems to help ensure that their jump emergence would put every ship where it was supposed to be. Across human space, other groups of warships were going through the same process, with all of them timed to appear over Alger's World.

The ships would be using a single jump, with no mid-course correction or staging points. The navigation for every ship had to be perfect to avert disaster over the target.

Sato could tell that the crew was tense, and with good reason. Nothing like this had ever been attempted before, and everything now rode on this one calculated risk.

"Standby for transpace sequence," an automated female voice announced over the *Orion's* public address system, and Sato could sense a slight change in the tremor of the ship's rhythm, a deepening of the thrum that was the beating of her metal heart. "Transpace sequence in five... four... three... two... one...Jump."

Humanity's four most powerful warships and the bulk of Earth's Home Fleet vanished into hyperspace.

* * *

It had taken four days of slow and deliberate movement for Mills and the others to make their way to the outskirts of Breakwater. They had been forced to lay low for hours at a time to avoid groups of patrolling Kreelan warriors. And the closer the team moved to the town, the larger and more frequent were the patrols.

Mills was convinced that there was some sort of a buildup in the town, and they had finally found a spot on a wooded hill a few kilometers away that had a view into the town center.

"Okay, I see the town square." Mills zoomed in with his binoculars, the digital stabilizer keeping the image steady. "Or what's left of it. Looks like they've cleared out more buildings." He took the binoculars away from his eyes, then looked again. "A couple of the surrounding buildings look like they've been partially sliced away, like someone hacked them apart with a knife."

"What are they building?" Valentina was looking at the town through the scope of her sniper rifle. "Have you ever seen anything like that?"

"I've never seen anything like this from any of the combat footage that's come in." Steph was looking at the town through her vidcam, while Danielson lay prone beside her, his own binoculars fixed on the town and a grim look on his face. "I feel like we're looking at something through a time tunnel back into ancient history."

They watched as well over a thousand straining warriors moved huge stone blocks with primitive cranes and winches made of trees, using thick rope and block and tackle rigs to lift and tilt them into position. More stones, resting on wooden sleds rolling over cut logs, were being moved into position.

The construct was circular in shape, maybe twenty meters across, with some stones, each of which must have weighed hundreds of tons, placed vertically, while others were being raised to bridge the tops.

"Where the hell are they getting the stones?" Valentina checked her mission data. If it was up to date, the nearest quarry was nearly three hundred kilometers away.

"They must have dug a new quarry nearby." Mills lowered his binoculars. "It must be taking thousands of them to quarry and move those bloody things. The warriors we see here can only be the tip of the iceberg."

"Well, I don't know what that twin of Stonehenge is," Steph said quietly, "but I know very well what those are around it. They're a perfect match for what Ichiro," it almost hurt to say his name, "saw during the first contact massacre. They're dueling arenas."

Mills and the others shifted their view slightly. Not far from the ponderous structure was a set of five circular rings that the warriors had built from much smaller rough-cut stones. Each ring was perhaps thirty meters in diameter and looked to be about chest high, with pillars that rose to about two meters and were evenly spaced around the circumference. In the center of each ring was a raised dais of stone, and there was a single entrance to each ring that faced the larger structure, with the two linked by a stone walkway. White sand covered the ground in each one.

"Bloody hell," Mills breathed. "I'll take your word for it."

Valentina lowered her rifle and turned to look at him. "Maybe it was lucky we landed here after all."

"Why?" Steph asked as she filmed both the Kreelans below and the other members of the team. The miniaturized and combat-hardened vidcam that she'd taken from the case she'd brought with her was strapped to her helmet and followed the movement of her head.

"Because we want to find out where the bitches are concentrated," Danielson chimed in. Glancing at Mills, he added, "I doubt anybody ever would have expected there'd be so many here in a podunk little town."

Mills grunted agreement. "We were supposed to land near one of the major cities. Or at least as major as they are on this planet, because we expected most of the enemy would be concentrated there. They probably only needed a few dozen to take this town, but there's at least a thousand, maybe two, in the town alone."

"You can probably double or triple that," Valentina said, aiming her rifle at the woods on the far side of the town. "I can't make out specifics, but I'm picking up a lot of thermal signatures over there through the trees. A few that look like fires, and a bunch that I'll wager are more warriors. They're all over the place over there."

"Look!" Danielson hissed, pointing off to their left. "Down there!"

Along the main road that passed through Breakwater and linked it to two much larger towns to the north and south, a column of figures came into view, marching around the base of the hill the team occupied.

"Oh, my God." Steph focused on the tiny figures, her vidcam able to zoom in more than even Mills's binoculars. "Prisoners."

There were a few thousand people being marched along by at least as many enemy warriors. Men, women, and even children were in the mass of ragged, shuffling figures. She could see their tattered clothes and dirty faces, the helpless defeat in their expressions. The warriors walked along the side of the road, content to leave the humans alone as long as they kept moving.

"We've had reports of civilians being rounded up like this, but never had any hard intel on what happened to them." Mills bit his lip as he looked over the prisoners, his stomach knotting with anger. "We assumed they were killed, but..." He broke off, not sure what else to say.

"Well," Valentina said woodenly, resisting the urge to take out some of the warriors with her rifle, "now we know what the arenas are for."

"What are we going to do?" Steph asked.

"Not a bloody thing," Mills grated, "but take note of what we see and be ready to pass on our information when the fleet jumps in."

"But we can't just leave them!" Steph argued. "They'll be slaughtered!"

"Listen to me," Mills said coldly, turning to face her. "In case you lost count, there are four of us. Just four. I'd sacrifice myself in a heartbeat to help those poor buggers if it would make the slightest difference, but we'd be throwing our lives away.

"Worse, we'd be throwing away their only chance, which is to make sure the fleet knows what they'll be facing down here so the Marines coming in behind us can blow these bitches to hell." Steph turned away, and Mills went on more softly, "Don't believe for a second that I don't want to do something, but-"

"Listen!" Danielson hissed, holding his hand up for silence as he turned to look behind them, up the slope of the hill.

They fell silent, listening intently. For a moment, they heard nothing but the gentle rustling of the leaves.

It was quiet. Too quiet.

Then Mills saw dark shadows moving among the trees, coming toward them. With a silent curse, he made a hand signal for Danielson to take point. The comms specialist moved out, heading silently down the hill to the right, toward a burned out barn and farmhouse in the middle of a patchwork of tilled fields.

Gripping her assault rifle, Steph followed close behind him. Then came Valentina, who slung her big sniper rifle, which was unwieldy for close-in work, over her shoulder. Then she drew her pistol.

Mills hung back for a moment, watching the dark figures as they approached. He knew that if his team was forced into a fight now, they wouldn't stand a chance. Even if they defeated the warriors coming at them, they'd be cornered and wiped out by the warriors now moving down the road.

He'd fight if there was no alternative, but the only real chance they had was to get away.

Hoping the Kreelans weren't very good trackers, he turned and quickly followed after Valentina.

* * *

Ku'ar-Marekh had been watching the humans for hours when a small group of patrolling warriors stumbled upon their trail.

She could have simply killed the alien animals, of course, but watching them had provided an entertainment, of sorts, in which she chose to indulge herself.

The warriors, unaware of her presence, had been hunting for more humans believed to be in this area when they came upon the tracks of those who had fallen from the sky.

These particular warriors had not yet seen battle, and they were eager to prove themselves against some humans to bring glory to the Empress.

Ku'ar-Marekh held back as the warriors excitedly began to follow the trail, and was curious now to see what the humans would do.

* * *

"Follow the creek." Mills pointed as they reached the bottom of the hill. "If we can move along it far enough, it should cover our trail."

"It's going to slow us down," Danielson cautioned, looking at the water that was running shin-deep.

"Yes, but it's either that or make a break for it across the open fields to the barn over there." Mills nodded toward the burned-out structure. "If we can make it around to the woods behind the barn, maybe we can-"

"Down!" Valentina shouted as one of the Kreelan flying edged weapons came whistling through the air at them.

She shoved Steph aside and Mills dropped flat into the water. Danielson tried to dodge the thing, but it clipped his left arm, slicing deep into the muscle. With a grunt of pain, he fell into the creek, which began to run red with his blood.

Four alien warriors emerged from the woods, moving toward them with swords drawn.

Mills raised his assault rifle, but never got a chance to fire. He heard a sound like a mechanical cough that came four times in under a second.

One after the other, all four warriors collapsed into the creek, each with a hole drilled neatly between the eyes.

Whipping his head around, he saw Valentina, still aiming her pistol at the woods in case any more aliens appeared. The weapon now had a large cylinder attached to the muzzle. A suppressor.

"Good God, woman," Mills said, the amazement plain in his voice. Aside from her incredible shooting, he had no idea how she'd gotten the suppressor onto the weapon so quickly. "That was a neat bit of work."

Before anyone could say anything else, a groan got their attention.

"Danielson!" Mills got to his feet, soaking wet now, and went to where the other man was trying to sit up in the creek.

Danielson was holding the wound in his arm with his free hand, but blood was streaming from between his fingers and his face had already turned pasty white.

"Come on, mate, it's only a scratch."

But when Mills pulled Danielson's hand away to take a quick look, he saw why the man was going into shock. The Kreelan throwing star, which is what it was called sometimes, had cut Danielson's arm right down to the bone, almost completely severing the biceps muscle.

"Here," Steph said, kneeling next to Danielson and wrapping a field dressing around the wound. "I got some basic first aid training before I deployed for the Keran operation," she explained. "Don't expect me to take out your appendix or anything, but I can apply a field dressing with the best of them."

"Thanks." Danielson gave her a weak smile after she'd finished wrapping his arm.

"I think we'd better go." Valentina knelt behind them, her pistol held level and steady. While she didn't see or hear anything unusual in the woods behind them, she felt certain there was someone there.

"Capital idea." Mills hauled Danielson to his feet. "Can you move?"

"Yeah," Danielson rasped, grasping his assault rifle in his right hand. "Let's get the fuck out of here."

"I'll take point," Mills said. "Valentina, cover our asses, if you please."

Mills turned around to start moving along the creek again when he found himself staring at a teenage girl, peering at him from around a rock near a bend in the creek a few yards away.

All four of the adults just stood there, dumbstruck with surprise.

"*She's* following you," the girl said cryptically, just barely loud enough for them to hear over the gurgling water of the creek. "I can't save you from her if she wants you. But if you come with me, the others won't bother you."

Then she turned and disappeared along the creek toward where the wrecked farmhouse stood.

Still stunned speechless, Mills and the others followed quickly behind.

* * *

After the adult humans had followed the young animal, Ku'ar-Marekh stepped from the shadows of the trees to where the four warriors had been slain by the single human female. That one, she knew, would be worthy of her personal attention. But Ku'ar-Marekh had decided that she would save these particular humans for later.

In the meantime, the first batch of survivors of the larger population centers were being brought here. There was no special reason for her having chosen this place over any other for the Challenges soon to be fought; it had merely been convenient.

Soon, the humans and her warriors would fight and die in the arenas for the glory of the Empress.

TEN

"Lord God." Mills sat back against the cold concrete wall, unable to keep the awe from his voice after Allison Murtaugh finished her tale.

They were in the shelter under the barn, where Allison had taken him and the others after the encounter with the alien warriors. He looked at the dozen children who were clustered around him and his team. Neither the adults nor the children could quite believe that the other was actually real.

"And you not only survived, but gathered up these other children here and saved them." Steph stared in rapt fascination at Allison, her vidcam having captured the girl's every word. While Steph didn't really care anymore about such things, she knew that what she was recording now would be in the running for the next Pulitzer Prize.

Making the grand assumption, of course, that she and the footage survived.

"Yes," Allison answered simply, nodding her head while offering Steph a shy smile.

The other children voiced their assent, and one by one told their own story of how Allison had saved each of them. By the end, Mills and the other three adults were in tears.

One thing still wasn't quite clear to Mills. Allison had explained it, but he still couldn't quite believe it. "Allison, you said that the Kreelans don't come here to your little hideout. I'm still not clear on that."

"They don't bother us because *she* seems to like me."

"That's this other warrior you mentioned at the creek when you found us?" Valentina asked. "The one who you said would get us if she wanted to?"

Allison visibly shivered. "She looks the same as the others, except she has more of the jewel or bead things hanging from the collar around her neck. Oh, and there's some sort of round or oval thing on the front of her collar that none of the others have, and some fancy bright blue design on her chest."

Mills and Steph simultaneously stared at one another. They had both seen another warrior with a special collar and a bright blue design on her chest armor. The warrior had beaten Mills twice, apparently purely for entertainment, and had killed the woman he loved.

"Is she big?" Mills clenched his huge fists to focus his rage. "As big or bigger than me, much taller and stronger-looking than the others?"

Allison shook her head. "No, not at all. Other than those two things, you couldn't tell her from any of the others." She paused. "Well, except for her eyes. They're dead."

"What do you mean by that?" Steph asked.

"Since the night she landed, the night she did...whatever it was that she did to me, when I felt like she was driving ice picks through my heart, I've seen her a number of times. She's followed me around, watching what I do." She wrapped her arms around herself as if to ward off a chill, even though the shelter was quite warm. "One time, when I was hunting for food in town, I went around a corner and she was right there." She held out her arm and touched Mills on the chest. "That close. I thought, 'That's it, Allison. You're dead.'

"But she just stood there and stared down at me. And her eyes, her face...she's not like the others. The others have expressions, you know? I don't know what all of them mean, but their faces change, a lot like ours do when we're happy or sad. But looking into her face is like looking into nothing, like her eyes are empty wells that just go down forever, but there's no water in them. I don't know how to explain it."

"And she just let you go that time, too?" Valentina was having as difficult a time as Mills believing it.

Allison nodded again. "Yes. I figured that I was still alive, so I'd better get moving. I could've just run back here, but then figured I may as well still get the food. I knew she could find me whenever she wanted. She followed me all night after that, even when I came back here, and she's followed me around other times, too."

"Oh, great!" Danielson blurted. "So you lead us back here so the enemy knows exactly where we are? Brilliant!"

"She already knew where you were," Allison told him bluntly. "She was in the forest, following you."

"How do you know that?" Mills asked her.

"Because I was following her when I saw you escape down to the creek, and I came to help you," Allison explained. "I've followed her before." Mills and the others exchanged a disbelieving glance. "No, really! I think she enjoys it, like I'm a pet or something, trotting after her.

"Don't get me wrong, she terrifies me, but after she followed me that first time and didn't do anything, I decided that fair's fair." She paused, looking defiantly at Danielson. "I don't like being bullied."

Valentina covered up her smile with one hand and Steph suppressed a giggle as Danielson turned red.

Mills shook his head. "You've got some guts, girl. I'm not so sure about your smarts in following a warrior around like that, but I'm glad you did. You saved our lives."

Allison beamed at the big Marine's praise.

"But now I'm hoping you can help us solve a little problem we've got."

"If I can," she told him eagerly, nodding her head.

"Is there anywhere in town where we might find some communications gear? An electronics shop or network node, anything like that? The kit we need to talk to the other ground teams and the fleet when it comes in was lost when our ship was destroyed. We've got to find another way to get in touch with them about what's happening here."

"Sergeant Mills?" A girl, Vanhi, Mills remembered, interrupted quietly. "Just what is happening here? What about all those people on the road that you saw? What's going to happen to them? You're here to help them, aren't you?"

Mills exchanged an uncomfortable glance with the other members of the team. "Yes, love," he told her, avoiding the question of what was going to happen to the prisoners. "We're going to help them. But to do that, we've got to get the gear we need to talk to our friends."

"The communications exchange?" Amrit, Vanhi's brother, suggested.

Allison shook her head. "The exchange building is still there, but almost everything inside is burned and wrecked. I think our soldiers tried to destroy it."

"That would make sense. They wouldn't want the enemy to get access to it." Danielson glanced at Mills, who nodded agreement.

"There's a gadget shop in town," Allison said slowly, her face a mask of concentration. "A place that has the kinds of things you might need. Comm units and stuff. But it's along Main Street, right across from the town square and whatever those things are the Kreelans are building." She looked up at Mills. "I could get there..."

"But you won't know what we need," Danielson finished. "And I'm in no shape to go with this fu...um, messed up arm."

Allison scowled at him, making it clear that she wouldn't want him with her, anyway.

"I'll go." Valentina smiled at Steph. "I'm the real backup comms specialist, anyway."

Mills nodded. He knew she was the best choice in any case, even had Danielson not been wounded. "All right, then, we'll go in tonight. In the meantime, we'll start keeping a lookout. If that warrior knows where we are, it's only a matter of time before she comes for us herself or sends her dogs after us. I don't want to be caught without any warning."

"We'll help!" one of the children chirped.

Mills grinned. "Is that so?"

All the children nodded emphatically.

"All right, then, we can always use some extra eyes and ears. I'll take the first watch, then Steph and Danielson. Once it's fully dark, Allison and Valentina will head into town, so you two had better get a bit of rest now."

Later, Mills lay prone in some of the barn's wreckage, watching an endless stream of people moving along the road, escorted by yet more enemy warriors.

Valentina came and silently lay down next to him. A young boy, Evan, lay an arm's length from Mills on the opposite side, facing toward the rear of the barn and the fields there, diligently watching for any enemies that might approach from the woods.

The sun was just beginning to droop over the gentle hills to planetary west.

"You're supposed to be getting some sleep," Mills chided.

"Like that's going to happen." She held out her hand for his binoculars. "Anything new?"

He shook his head as he handed them over. "Nothing good." He leaned closer and whispered so Evan couldn't hear. "There's been a constant stream of civilians being herded down the road from the north toward town. And more warriors. Christ, but there's a lot of them."

Valentina frowned as she looked back and forth along the procession moving slowly along the road. There were thousands of people, and their moans and cries sent a shiver down her spine. "My God, where are they going to put them all?"

"I can't see it from here, but if you take a gander over that way," he pointed to a small rolling hill about a kilometer away, "you can see a stretch of road rising up behind that hill just before town. None of the prisoners have passed that way, so the Kreelans are moving them off the road somewhere before that, out of sight from where we are. I'm thinking they're turning off near where you saw all that thermal activity before we were chased down from the hill earlier. I'm wagering the Kreelans have some sort of concentration camp set up there to hold all our people until..."

He couldn't finish the rest. Not just because he didn't want Evan to hear it, but because he had a hard time bearing the burden of being totally helpless when so many people were about to die. He had already seen so much death in this war, but most of those had been in combat, men and women who'd been trained and armed, who could fight back. These poor souls being marched along the road were just regular everyday people who wouldn't stand a chance against the warriors who'd be sent into the arenas with them.

He couldn't do a thing about it. Nothing. And unless Valentina and Allison were successful tonight, he wouldn't even be able to tell the fleet to land Marines here to mount a rescue operation.

He felt Valentina's hand on his arm.

"Don't be so hard on yourself." She understood the anguish he was feeling. While the scale had been vastly different, she had been in more than one situation when she worked as an agent for the Terran Intelligence Service where she hadn't been able to help someone who had been in desperate trouble. Those people had died, some of them under long and agonizing torture. "Take it from me, you can't save everyone, no matter how hard you try."

"I know, but..." He looked away for a moment, wiping at his face, and Valentina saw the glistening of tears.

She'd come to the conclusion over the course of the mission that there was a lot more to Mills that she had ever realized. He would have everyone believe that he was nothing but a big ape, an ignorant jarhead, but that wasn't him at all.

"We won't be able to save them all, Mills," she told him, "but we'll be able to save some, maybe most, if the fleet comes in time. That's what you need to focus on. Not how many we'll lose."

Mills grunted. "And what makes you so worldly-wise, all of a sudden?"

She was silent for a moment, and he was wondering if he'd managed to insult her when she said softly, "Do you know how many people I've killed, Roland?"

"Not if you're going to add me to the list after you tell me." It wasn't quite as much of a joke as he might have liked, and it unnerved him that she was talking about anything related to her operations as a covert agent. It was an extraordinary measure of the trust she'd placed in him.

"I've killed eighty-seven human beings, not counting anyone I killed in the firefights we were in on Saint Petersburg and a few other places I won't mention. But those eighty-seven, they were people I killed face to face. People whose names I knew. I knew everything about them, almost as if we were longtime friends. And do you know how many I've saved?"

"How many?"

"None." It was her turn to look away. "Not a single one. Some of my contacts who were in danger were extracted by other agents. But my own personal salvation score? Zero."

Mills stared at her. "You know, for someone who's supposed to be a brilliant super-spy, you're as dense as a bloody brick."

"What?" Valentina turned to him, a perplexed look on her face.

"We wouldn't be having this conversation if it weren't for you. My mates and I would all be dead back in the government complex on Saint Petersburg had you not shot up half the Russians coming after us. Oh, and let's not forget that minor miracle of how you got all of us off that rock by doing that freaky mind-meld thing with the navigation computer that left you a vegetable for six months." He shook his head in wonder. "My God, woman. Yes, we'll all have to answer for our sins in the end. You've got yours, and Lord knows I've got my own list of dirty deeds. But don't ever tell me again that you never saved anyone, or I'm going to turn you over my knee and spank your bottom."

She grinned. "You'd like that, wouldn't you?"

Mills grinned back. "I could think of worse ways to spend my time."

They were quiet for a while after that, turning their attention back to the stream of people marching down the road.

After a while, Valentina said, "Mills?"

"Yes?"

"Do you know what I'd like?"

Mills snorted. "That's a bit of a loaded question, dearie, but I'll take the bait. What would you like?"

"I'd like a frozen margarita with real strawberries. On a nice beach somewhere under a cloudless sky and a warm sun. I want to be able to just enjoy myself and not be there to kill someone." She glanced at him. "And I don't want to be alone."

Unable to help himself, Mills felt his jaw drop open as he turned to look at her. "Lord Almighty. Are you asking me on a date?"

"Don't get a fat head about it," she told him with a wry grin. "But yeah, I guess I am."

"Bloody hell, woman," he choked, glancing over to see if Evan heard him cursing. "I think I might take you up on that."

"You'd better, or I'm going to do to you what I did to Danielson on the ship and you'll be squeaking like a school girl."

Mills had to bite his tongue to keep quiet. It wouldn't do for the Kreelans to find them because he was laughing his head off. "Well, I guess it's a deal, then. Assuming we get out of this mess."

"Yeah, I guess there's always that." She sighed. "I guess I'll go check on Allison to see if she's getting any rest. I might try and close my eyes, too. Talking to you is exhausting."

"Smart arse." As she began to get up, he reached out and took her arm. "Just promise me you'll be damn careful tonight. Both of you."

"I promise. Allison and I'll take care of one another."

"Okay, then." Mills reluctantly let her go.

Without another word, she got up and returned to the shelter, leaving him to his worrying.

With a sigh, he turned to watch the column of people again, but instead looked up to the sky as he heard the faint but growing roar of an approaching ship.

* * *

Ri'al-Hagir, the First to Ku'ar-Marekh, masked her fear. But inside she trembled, for she knew that Death was very close. Very close indeed. She did not fear dying in itself, for that was the worthy and hoped-for ending for any warrior who served the Empress.

No, she was afraid of what would come after. Or, more precisely, of what might not. To die with honor meant basking in the Afterlife, to take one's place among the spirits who dwelled beyond death in the love of the Empress.

To die without honor, to perish in disgrace, meant that one's soul would be cast into eternal darkness beyond Her love, without hope of redemption. From birth, Her Children sensed the Bloodsong in their veins, an emotional bond with the Empress that was just as real as the blood in their bodies. It was as natural to Her Children as taking a breath.

But that bond could be broken, the lifeline to the river of the Bloodsong severed, both in life and in death. It was rare, yet it did happen. No mere warrior could mete out such a punishment. Only the Empress had that power...and the high priestesses such as Ku'ar-Marekh.

Ri'al-Hagir knelt now before the cold-hearted priestess of the Nyur-A'il, a silent prayer to the Empress on her lips.

"I entrusted you with a simple matter." Ku'ar-Marekh's voice was, as always, empty of all emotion.

Shivering at the words, Ri'al-Hagir braced herself for the eternal agony that would soon befall her. She had been summoned moments earlier by Ku'ar-Marekh to the *Kalai-Il*, the place of atonement that the warriors had been struggling mightily to complete. The sun had long since given its place to the stars, and the great stone edifice was lit by a ring of torches, their orange light flickering in the darkness.

Were it any other than Ku'ar-Marekh, Ri'al-Hagir would have feared only the pain of the lash up on the *Kalai-Il*. Agonizing and potentially lethal as it was, it was a mortal pain. Even if her body died, her spirit would live on.

Yet, Ri'al-Hagir knew that her priestess had never inflicted punishment to any warriors on the *Kalai-Il*. She had either tortured them to death with her powers, or severed their bonds to the Bloodsong.

She could easily accept the former, but greatly feared the latter.

"My life is yours, my priestess," Ri'al-Hagir said, forcing strength into her voice through the fear in her heart. "The *Kalai-Il* is not yet finished as you had commanded. I offer no excuse."

In fact, the delay had been from having to quarry the stones farther away than they had expected. Transporting them to this place using the ancient ways, as custom demanded, had taken more time. The builder caste could have created this monument to Kreelan discipline in but moments, but that was not the Way of their race. The *Kalai-Il* was found on every world of the Empire, and in all of the great warships built in the last fifty millennia. It was built only by the hands of Her Children, using ingenuity and backbreaking labor. For that was the Way, as it had been even before the Empire had been founded a hundred thousand cycles before.

The priestess stood over her, Ku'ar-Marekh's right hand holding the hilt of her sword. "I do not take you to task for the *Kalai-Il*. It is of the humans that I speak."

This so surprised Ri'al-Hagir that she involuntarily glanced up at the priestess, then quickly cast her eyes down again. "I do not understand, my priestess."

"Behold." Ku'ar-Marekh placed a hand on the braids of Ri'al-Hagir's raven hair.

Ri'al-Hagir gasped as she felt herself flying from the *Kalai-Il* to the woods where a great encampment had been built for the warriors streaming here, and the corrals where the humans were being kept.

Not intending any cruelty to the humans, the corrals were nonetheless horrific affairs. Thousands of the human animals had been crammed into the pens, and more were on the way. Many hundreds of those who had been strong enough to survive the march here, a winnowing process to eliminate those unworthy to fight in the arenas, had died, trampled to death by their fellow animals or from lack of food and water.

The stench of their waste and wretchedness reached a full league here to the *Kalai-Il*. In what Ri'al-Hagir knew was the view of the priestess's second sight that she somehow was sharing, the smell was unbearable, and she could sense through the powerful Bloodsong of the priestess how the warriors guarding the animals suffered their duties.

"We do not treat our food animals in such a fashion, let alone those we would face in the arena or in open battle." Ku'ar-Marekh released Ri'al-Hagir, bringing the warrior back to the here and now atop the *Kalai-Il*. "There are millions of the aliens left on this world, and I summoned more warriors here to challenge them and bring glory to the Empress. And this is what they would find when the fleet bearing them arrives on the morrow."

Ku'ar-Marekh paused. Ri'al-Hagir could feel a tingling sensation around her heart, and she shivered in fear.

"The Way of our people is difficult, yet we do not revel in cruelty. We have dishonored Her and ourselves by letting humans we have captured, especially those who survived the difficult trek to this place, die needlessly and in such a fashion, without the chance to fight," Ku'ar-Marekh continued. "What would I tell your sisters when they arrive and see this? What would I tell the Empress? This is not Her will."

Ri'al-Hagir hung her head low, clenching her fists so tightly that her talons drew blood from her palms. "I give my life in dishonor," she whispered, hoping that the priestess would choose to end her life with a blade, and not with the other powers that dwelt within her.

Ku'ar-Marekh's sword sang from its scabbard, moving too quickly to see as it severed the first braid of Ri'al-Hagir's hair. The braids of Her Children were not merely a form of style or ornamentation, but formed a very tangible bond with the Empress. The first braid was the key, for it linked the owner's spirit with the Bloodsong. Were it severed, the bearer might survive physically, but would be doomed upon death to an eternity of darkness beyond Her love.

Ri'al-Hagir cried out as the braid parted, but her voice died as Ku'ar-Marekh's blade flashed again, slicing through the warrior's neck. The severed head fell to the dais of the *Kalai-Il* with a wet thud, and Ri'al-Hagir's body collapsed on top of it in a clatter of metal on stone.

The priestess could sense the sudden silence of her First's Bloodsong as she was carried away into the depths of the cold darkness of eternity. It brought her no satisfaction, but honor had been satisfied.

Ku'ar-Marekh calmly flicked the blood from her blade and slid it back into its scabbard. The warriors around her knelt low to the ground, their left fists over their right breasts in salute. They were terrified.

"Place her body in the forest as a feast for the wild animals," Ku'ar-Marekh ordered. "Then make right what she allowed to go wrong, or you shall suffer the same fate."

As she strode down the wide steps of the *Kalai-Il*, the warriors moved quickly to obey.

* * *

Allison pressed a hand to her mouth to stifle an involuntary gasp as the strange warrior with the dead eyes killed one of her own warriors on the huge stone platform they'd been building.

"What is it?" Valentina whispered from behind her. They'd made better time getting into town than Valentina had expected. The frequent Kreelan hunting parties that had been wandering across the countryside earlier had vanished, and Valentina suspected they were all congregating for the slaughter that must soon be about to start for the prisoners being marched into Breakwater.

"She killed one of them!" Allison hissed. "Cut her head right off!"

"A prisoner?" Valentina sidled up beside Allison where the girl crouched near the blasted-out front window.

"No." Allison shook her head and pointed to where the strange warrior was now walking down from the stone platform. "One of the other warriors. It looked like they were talking for a while, with the other one kneeling. Then Dead Eyes just whipped out her sword and lopped the other one's head off."

"Well," Valentina said grimly, "I guess that's one less that we have to kill ourselves."

"How can they do that, Valentina? How could they just...kill one another like that?"

"Don't think that humans haven't done the same to one another, and worse." Valentina fought to keep a host of unpleasant memories from surfacing. "Let's just be thankful that our friend there is occupied with her own problems instead of coming after us."

"I guess so." Allison watched the warrior disappear from view behind the stone. As she did, the other warriors around her ran to take the body away, then they all disappeared down the street that led toward the woods on the south side of town where the human prisoners were being taken.

In an effort to deflect Allison's thoughts, Valentina said, "You picked a good place here. It'll take me a while to put something together, but I think we've got all the parts for both a radio and a comm link."

"What's a radio?" Allison asked, finally turning from the window.

"Something people used to use a long time ago to talk across distances, before we had comm links. In a way they're the same sort of thing, just that what we have nowadays can carry a lot more information a lot farther."

"Then why don't we just use that?"

"Because sometimes the Kreelans don't let us. We don't know how they do it, but they can make it stop working. They don't do it all the time, but when they do, it's usually at the worst possible moment."

"But they don't bother the radio thing?"

"No, at least not so far as anyone knows. So I want to make sure we have both, just in case." Patting Allison on the shoulder, she said, "I've got just a couple more things to find, then we'll get out of here."

"Okay."

Allison continued to watch, peering out from the corner of the window and keeping as much of her face concealed as possible. The flickering fire from torches illuminated all five of the big rings, arenas, Valentina had called them, and the big stone thing. The sight made her shiver, and she hoped that Valentina would finish soon. She hated just sitting here.

She looked up at the growing roar of an approaching ship, and followed it as it lowered into the woods on the far side of town. Valentina said that while she wasn't sure, she suspected it probably carried more human prisoners. The ships had been coming about every fifteen minutes since Mills had seen the first one a few hours ago.

"Let's go," Valentina whispered from behind her, and Allison nearly jumped out of her skin.

"It's about time."

Together, they crept out the back of the store and through the dark, deserted streets as yet another ship roared overhead.

ELEVEN

"Shit." Danielson looked up, wondering if the children had heard him curse. It had taken him four hours of frustrating labor to try and piece together the device from the parts and tools Valentina had brought back, while she focused on trying to build a radio.

Her task had been just as challenging, as it was difficult to put together a primitive device like a radio with modern technology.

"What's wrong?" Steph had been helping Danielson. She didn't have the technical knowledge to build the equipment, but she could provide a pair of extra hands.

"There's nothing." Danielson glared at the fist-sized collection of electronic components he had managed to fuse together. Two lights glowed on a small panel that was connected to the device. One was green, the other was red. Pointing to the green one, he said, "The thing's broadcasting. I can tell that much. But it's not connecting to anything, not even our headsets." He held up one of the headsets they'd been wearing. They hadn't had to use them much since they jumped down to the planet's surface, as they'd been together most of the time and within easy talking distance.

"Is it just not synchronizing?" Valentina picked up her own headset and working the tiny controls.

"No," he told her, shaking his head. "Those have stopped working, too. The hardware checks out okay, but there's no carrier signal for them to pick up. The network's just gone."

"He's right." Steph was looking at her vidcam. While she hadn't connected it to the team's net, it could see the headset nodes. Now it couldn't. "The Kreelans must have done whatever they do to kill our comm and data links."

"Well, I guess that's that for this piece of crap." Danielson shoved the makeshift comm unit away from him, a look of utter disgust on his face.

"How do they do that?" Steph wondered quietly.

"I think the question we should be asking is why they did it now?" Valentina frowned. "I just spoke to Mills a few minutes ago on my headset."

"Who the hell knows?" Danielson snapped. "I sure hope you had better luck than I did."

"Let's find out." Valentina tapped a few more commands into a small console that she had connected to her own collection of oddball bits and pieces of tech from the gadget store. "Let me have that, would you?" She pointed to a connector attached to the end of a cable that she had run outside the shelter to a wire antenna outside. Steph handed it to her, and Valentina plugged the connector into the makeshift radio.

They were rewarded with the sound of static from the small speaker unit. Valentina touched a control on the console, and the static disappeared.

"I programmed in the alternate radio frequencies we were given" she explained. "All the teams were issued radio beacons. If the other teams have their beacons on, we should be able to pick them up."

"We don't have a beacon, do we?" Steph asked.

"No," Danielson answered bitterly. "It went down with the ship, along with most of our other stuff."

They all stared at the speaker, waiting to hear something.

"What are we listening for?" Steph whispered.

"Bursts of static," Valentina answered, keeping her eyes glued to the console. "It won't sound like anything to us, but I built in a decoder that will break out any transmissions. The beacons are just to let other teams know you're still on the mission. If we pick up a beacon and respond, we'll be patched through to the team and be able to talk to them."

They watched and listened, but heard nothing but silence. One minute passed, then two.

"Are you sure it's working?" Danielson leaned in for a closer look at the device.

Valentina nodded. "We don't have a transmitter that I can use to test it, but at certain frequencies there are natural radio sources like lightning, and gas giants like the one in this system produce a lot of radio signals." She looked up at him. "Those were my test sources. The radio's working, there's just no one out there transmitting."

"Maybe they're too far away?" Steph asked.

Both Danielson and Valentina shook their heads.

"No," Danielson told her. "The beacons were tailored for Alger's World, and all the teams are here on the same continent. If they were broadcasting, we'd hear them."

"And if they're not broadcasting..." Steph looked at Valentina.

"They're gone," Valentina answered with brutal finality.

The three of them sat silently, staring at the equipment on the small table. Behind them, the children slept in a mass of pillows and blankets spread across the shelter's floor. Allison had refused to go to bed after returning from town with Valentina, and had instead gone outside to keep Mills company.

Valentina grinned inwardly. She suspected Allison was quickly developing a crush on the big Marine.

They looked up with a start as the door opened. Mills.

"Why aren't any of you answering your bloody headsets?" he hissed angrily, glancing at the mass of sleeping children.

Danielson held up one of the headsets. "The comm links are out. The hardware's okay. We think it's the Kreelans locking us down."

"They shut down the network only a few minutes after I last spoke to you," Valentina added.

"And none of you thought to clue me in to that little fact?" Mills raised his voice. "Maybe it's because there's a file of warriors from town heading right toward us!"

"Oh, Christ." Danielson closed his eyes and banged his head back against the concrete wall, a small measure of his anger at his own stupidity.

"Get them up," Mills ordered, nodding at the children. "We've got to get them out of here, right now."

"There's something else you need to know," Valentina told him as Danielson gathered up the two comm units and carefully put them into a satchel, while Steph rushed to wake up the rest of the children. "There aren't any beacons from the other teams. They're gone."

"We're it." Danielson gave Mills a sick look as he hurriedly crammed some other essential gear into a pack.

Mills muttered something dark under his breath, not wanting to say out loud what he was thinking in front of the children, who were now all awake and alert.

"Bloody perfect." He fought to calm himself. The children were looking at him with wide, terrified eyes, and he knew that he needed to give them some confidence. Being angry or panicking wouldn't do. "They're probably just busy," he said. When Danielson opened his mouth to say something, Mills cut him off, managing to muster a smile. "I'm sure they're all heading here, as this is clearly where all the real action is. We might even leave a few warriors for them to clean up."

"Uh, yeah," Danielson managed to say, finally catching on. "Yeah. But only if they move their asses and get here soon. I'm not going to hold back just to leave 'em some."

"Valentina, Steph," Mills said, "get the kids out of here. Lead them back to the creek and into the woods and try to get clear. Danielson and I will try to buy you some time."

"Send Danielson with Steph. I'm not leaving you." Valentina stared at him, defiance shining in her eyes. "You know that I can fight better than the rest of you put together."

"Why the bloody hell do you think I want you with the children?" Mills reached out and took her arm. "You may be the only chance they have."

Valentina stared at him for a moment, then slowly nodded. "Damn you, Mills. I…"

"I know," he whispered. "I know." He turned to Danielson. "Give her the comms gear." Turning back to Valentina, he said, "Now you and Steph get your arses and the children out of here. We don't have any more time."

Taking the satchel with the comm units from Danielson, Valentina quickly gathered up her pistol and the extra assault rifle that had belonged to Stallick. "I'm leaving you the sniper rifle. It won't be any good to me in the woods, but you might be able to get some use out of it."

"That I will," he agreed as he held up her pack. She stuck her arms through the straps and cinched them tight. Danielson did the same for Steph.

They were ready. The children stood, behind them, quiet but tense.

"Get going." Mills nodded toward the door.

Allison stood in the stair well, his assault rifle in her hands.

"And what do you think you're doing?" Mills put his hands on his hips, giving the girl a severe look.

"I'm staying to help you." Allison flicked a glance at Valentina.

"Good Lord!" Mills glanced at Valentina, who shrugged helplessly. With a sigh, he bent down so his face was level with Allison's. "Girl, you can't stay with me. You've got to help Valentina and Steph."

"But what will you do if *she* comes?"

Mills's expression hardened. "Don't worry. I've dealt with her type before. Now," he gently took the rifle from her, "we've wasted enough time. Get the devil out of here."

"Here, take this for me, would you?" Valentina handed her the satchel with the comms gear. "We can't let anything happen to it."

Allison, pouting, took it.

Mills slung the assault rifle over his shoulder before taking the big sniper rifle that Valentina held out to him. Then he led the way out the narrow door and up the steps to the burned out barn.

Holding out a hand to stop Allison for a moment, he took a quick look through the sniper rifle's scope toward where he and Allison had seen the warriors approaching.

The Kreelans were about where he'd expected them to be, except now they had fanned out into a skirmish line, swords drawn.

"Come on," he hissed urgently, and Allison quickly ran up the last of the steps and headed toward the back of the barn.

Valentina followed her, pausing until the rest of the children were out before taking the lead as they moved out across the dark field toward the creek.

Then Steph appeared, with Danielson right behind her. Steph knelt next to Mills and squeezed his shoulder. "Good luck, Mills," she said quietly. "And thank you."

"Take good care of yourself, Steph." He grinned, his smile splitting the darkness. "I'll see you in the next turn of the wheel."

She nodded solemnly, then followed after the children, who were moving fast behind Valentina.

"How many of our friends are coming to dinner?" Danielson wriggled into a pile of collapsed timbers from the barn's roof that offered him some cover and a good field of fire.

"About two dozen," Mills told him casually as he snugged the sniper rifle up to his shoulder and put his eye to the scope. The warrior in the center was the same who had been leading the column of warriors when he had first seen them, and he figured she was the leader. She was easy to recognize, as her right ear was gone.

That won't be the only thing you'll be missing in a minute, he thought as he centered the scope's target bead on her forehead.

"Let me know when." Danielson stared through the low-power scope on his assault rifle. "I'll start on the right and work left." He shifted his aim to the warrior who was on the right end of the line.

"I'll take the leader and work left," Mills said. "Good luck, mate."

"You, too, Mills." Danielson's finger tensed on the trigger.

Mills took a deep breath, then let it out. "Let's get to it, shall we?"

He stroked the sniper rifle's trigger, the shot shattering the quiet darkness.

* * *

Steph turned to look back at the farmhouse as the first shot was fired. The building was nothing more than a black shadow against the darkness of the pre-dawn hours, an angular shape that blocked out the stars. She could see flashes of light reflected from the far side of the barn as Mills and Danielson began to fire on the approaching warriors. She could have used the light amplification of her vidcam to see better, but the small projection lens gave off enough light to stand out in the darkness. She knew the Kreelans could see well in the dark, and she didn't want to give herself away.

"Come on!" One of the children took her hand and pulled her along.

Bringing up the rear made Steph feel isolated from the others, but Valentina needed to be at the front in case they ran into trouble, and someone had to make sure none of the children got left behind.

Trying to ignore the frenzied firing now coming from the barn, the rapid staccato of Danielson's assault rifle punctuated with the heavier booms of the sniper rifle, Steph hurried after the young girl who was still holding her hand.

Other shadowy figures shimmered ahead of them as the line of children moved quickly toward the creek, where Valentina gathered them in a circle around her.

"I'll cross first," she told them in a whisper as Steph knelt beside her, "and I'll whistle if it's clear. If you hear anything else, run. Everyone understand?"

There were nods from the ghostly faces, and Steph could see them glance back nervously toward the barn as the alien warriors let loose a bone-chilling war cry.

"If anything happens to me," Valentina whispered into Steph's ear, "get Allison and protect the radio. It's already pre-set to the fleet broadcast frequency. Everything depends on it."

With that, she turned and moved silently into the burbling creek, crouched down low and holding her rifle at the ready.

* * *

"Out!" Danielson ejected another spent magazine and slammed a fresh one into his rifle.

Mills fired again at something moving in the field, but wasn't sure if he hit it. The two of them had taken down at least half the approaching warriors, but he knew that at least some of them must be getting close. Every time he fired, he lost his sight picture and was partially blinded by the rifle's muzzle flash, and he was losing track of his targets without a spotter.

"Check behind us!"

That's when he heard the strange keening sound that the Kreelan flying weapons made. He ducked down just as the thing flew right through his makeshift firing port, making a heavy thunk as it embedded itself in something behind him.

Danielson shoved himself backward with his elbows and peeked up over some of the fallen trusses from the barn's roof to see behind him.

A warrior leaped at him from the darkness.

"Christ!" He fired, the muzzle flashes dancing along the shining blade and gleaming fangs of the alien. The slugs stopped her in midair, and she fell to the ground in a bloody heap.

Four more of the snarling humanoids attacked. Mills barely rolled away in time as a sword slashed right through the timber he'd been next to, and he lost his grip on the sniper rifle.

A warrior was standing right over him, raising her sword again for an overhand cut, the fangs in her mouth gleaming as she roared in triumph.

He kicked one of her legs out from under her, and she fell on top of him, trying to stab him with the sword.

Mills managed to block it, knocking the blade to the side as she fell.

Letting go the sword, she slashed him across the chest, her talons cutting deep into his body armor before he caught hold of both her wrists.

They rolled and writhed until Mills settled for the simple expedient of repeatedly smashing his forehead against her nose and mouth. That stunned her long enough for him to slip his combat knife from its sheath on his belt. He shoved it through the base of her jaw, driving the tip into her brain.

Danielson screamed.

Mills rolled the still-twitching Kreelan away, ignoring the blood that had poured onto him from her punctured throat. Getting to his knees, he saw three of the aliens slashing and stabbing at Danielson. He was holding his rifle, its magazine now empty, by the muzzle with his good hand, using it as a club.

The Kreelans weren't making a concerted effort to kill him, but were taking the time to make him bleed.

Mills grabbed his assault rifle from the black ash and dirt of the barn's floor and fired, killing two of the Kreelans instantly.

The third seemed to somehow dance out of the way of his bullets, moving closer to Danielson. Mills watched in slow-motion horror as the warrior easily parried Danielson's desperate swing with his rifle, then plunged her blade into his chest.

"No!" Mills screamed as he emptied the rest of the magazine into her. The bullets pinned her body to the remains of the barn's wall until his gun fell silent and she crumpled to the floor.

Without thinking, he dumped the empty magazine and shoved a new one in as he crawled through the debris to reach his fellow Marine.

"Stay with me, mate." Mills knelt down next Danielson.

"If my arm hadn't been hurt," Danielson breathed, a froth of blood seeping from his mouth, "I could've whipped all of them."

"No doubt," Mills told him as he moved his hands over Danielson's chest to feel the wound, then reached around to probe gently along his back. The sword had run all the way through the right side of his chest, perilously near his heart. There was nothing Mills could do. "And you'll have a chance to prove you're a macho bastard again after we get you patched up."

"Don't fuck with me, Mills. I'm done, and I'm okay with it." Danielson took Mills's bloodied hand and held it tight. "Just go. Take care of the brats." He coughed, a wet, ugly sound from deep inside his chest. "And good luck with the spy chick, you lucky...bastard."

"Thanks, mate." Mills said quietly, blinking away the wetness from his eyes.

But Danielson couldn't hear him. He was gone.

Mills waited a few minutes, scanning the approaches from town to make sure there were no more Kreelans about. Then he wearily gathered up the remaining rifle magazines from Danielson's combat gear. As an afterthought, he took his grenades, as well.

Picking up the sniper rifle, Mills slung it over his shoulder. Then, holding his assault rifle at the ready, he moved out the rear of the barn and followed after the others toward the creek.

He wasn't quite halfway there when he heard the sound of gunfire and children screaming.

* * *

Valentina waded silently through the water, looking into the forbidding darkness of the woods on the other side of the creek. She stepped slowly onto the soft soil on the opposite bank, taking care that the water in her boots and trousers made no noise.

After she reached the other side, she moved about ten meters into the trees. She paused for a moment behind one of the larger trees and opened up her senses to her surroundings. Nothing suspicious appeared in the computer-generated image of the night vision optics as she looked around, nor did she hear anything unusual over the hammering of Mills and Danielson firing their weapons. Her nose wasn't attuned to the unique smells of the plant and animal life on Alger's World, but she couldn't pick out anything like the faint musky scent ascribed to the Kreelans.

It looked clear. And yet...

The firing at the barn stopped, and she knew that she'd run out of time. If Mills and Danielson survived, they would catch up. The analytic part of her mind told her that she'd probably never see Mills again. Her heart wanted to tear her mind to pieces.

"No time," she whispered to herself. Then she whistled, a low, soft sound amazingly similar to one of the species of birds she'd heard the morning before, welcoming the sun.

Looking back toward the creek, she saw small shadows crossing the water. They stopped and looked back toward the barn as alien screams echoed across the field before a larger shadow, Steph, urged them onward.

Faster now, the children crossed the creek, and Valentina gestured for them to kneel down behind her. She wanted to gather them all together before they moved farther into the woods and make sure she didn't lose any of them.

Seeing that Allison was crossing the creek, followed by Steph, Valentina turned to lead her charges deeper into the woods where they might find a defensible position.

That was when the warrior with the dead eyes appeared right in front of her, out of thin air.

Valentina didn't allow surprise to overcome her. She simply reacted. With barely a conscious thought, she squeezed the trigger on her rifle, whose muzzle was a mere hand's breadth from the warrior's armored chest.

The gun spat rounds at the alien, but the bullets simply fell to the ground in small bubbling pools of molten metal.

Forcing herself to accept the impossible as fact, Valentina swung the rifle in a brutal butt stroke that would have shattered the jaw of a human opponent.

The Kreelan warrior danced out the way, barely, and then held out her hand as if she was going to place her palm on Valentina's chest.

"Oh!" Valentina gasped as she felt her heart pierced by frozen spikes. To anyone else, the pain would have been unimaginable and instantly debilitating, but few human beings had ever endured pain such as Valentina had and survived. It slowed her down, but didn't stop her.

She lunged at the alien, feinting with a lightning-fast open hand strike to her armored chest with her left hand before lashing out with her right elbow at the Kreelan's head.

The alien was taken by surprise, apparently convinced that Valentina would go down from the ethereal attack on her heart. The warrior parried the feint and tried to dodge the strike to her head, but didn't move quite fast enough.

Valentina grinned savagely through the searing pain in her chest as her elbow smashed against the Kreelan's temple, knocking her backward.

But the warrior moved with the force of the blow, pirouetting around to again face Valentina, and the icy grip around Valentina's heart intensified.

Despite all that the implants given her by the Terran Intelligence Service when she had become a covert agent could do, she was still a mortal human. Her heart constricted so far now that it was barely beating at all, Valentina collapsed into the loamy soil, unconscious.

Behind her, the children ran screaming, but they didn't get far. A line of warriors appeared from the woods, clawed hands outstretched toward their victims.

Still in the middle of the creek, Steph watched in horror as Valentina went down and the children were taken. The warriors had some sort of stunning device, and the children crumpled to the ground after being touched with it.

Allison, who had stayed back with Steph to let the younger children cross, was the first to react. Grabbing Steph's hand, she ran back the way they had come, in the direction of the barn, which had fallen disturbingly silent.

Without a word, Steph followed her, the two of them splashing noisily through the water as they ran. In half a dozen steps they had reached the shore.

Then *she* appeared out of nowhere, right in front of them. Steph raised her rifle to fire, but dropped it as her heart felt as if it was being ripped from her chest by an icy hand.

With a cry of agony, she collapsed to the ground and lay still.

"No!" Allison screamed in terrified rage as she charged right into the warrior. She had no weapon, nothing to fight with except the satchel with the precious radio, which was now useless. There would be no one to operate it.

Taking the strap off her shoulder, Allison threw the satchel at the warrior, who simply plucked it from the air and tossed it aside.

Screaming in fury at the loss of her parents, her world, the children she had saved, and now the friends who had come to save them, Allison hammered against the warrior's armor with her fists until they bled.

The Kreelan simply stood there, looking down at Allison her face a dark mask against the night sky.

Finally spent, Allison fell to her knees, sobbing.

She didn't see the warrior take a small wand from her belt. Leaning down, the warrior touched it to Allison's shoulder, and she slumped to the ground beside Steph, unconscious.

* * *

"Lord God, no," Mills breathed as he watched the warriors wade through the water from the woods, bearing Valentina and the children.

Two more picked up Steph and Allison from near the feet of the warrior that he knew must be *her*.

He had dropped to the ground in the field behind the barn as soon as he'd heard the gunfire from across the creek. He quickly exchanged his assault rifle for the larger sniper rifle and its advanced scope while his gut churned with fear and something worse. Self-loathing. He knew the right decision was to stay alive. But it took all his will not to pull the trigger and kill as many of the Kreelans as he could, starting with the warrior who had taken down Steph and Allison, before they came for him.

The thing that stayed his hand was that he had seen the strange warrior toss aside the satchel that contained the precious radio. That was the key to everything, and was more valuable than his honor or his life, because it represented the only chance for Valentina and the others, for any of the surviving humans on this planet.

He watched the aliens through the sniper rifle's scope as the warriors formed a line and slowly marched off through the field to his left, bearing the children and the two women.

When he turned back to look for the warrior with the dead eyes, he found her standing where she had been on the bank of the creek. Except now she was staring right at him.

He pulled his eye away from the scope for a moment to make sure he wasn't imagining things, then looked again.

She was still there, looking right at him, and a shiver of dread ran down his spine.

He had fought another warrior like her who had one of the strange devices affixed to her collar, which seemed to signify some sort of special warrior or class of warriors. That warrior had been huge, nearly a giant compared to Mills, who himself was a big and powerful man. He had fought her twice in hand to hand combat, once on Keran and once on Saint Petersburg. He knew that she had only been toying with him, but he had learned that any warrior wearing a device like that on her collar was one to be feared. This one perhaps more than the big warrior he had fought before. Just as Allison had said, this one seemed to be completely devoid of expression, and looking into her face made him want to turn and run.

She continued to stare at him, but when he blinked his eye, she was gone. He pulled his eye away from the scope, thinking that she was rushing toward him across the field, but there was nothing. No one. She had just vanished.

"Bloody hell." He got to his knees to get a better look, sweeping the scope along the creek and the woods.

There was no sign of her.

His heart in his throat, he turned to watch the line of warriors bearing away their captives. They were heading in the direction of where Valentina had thought the Kreelans had a big encampment in the woods on the far side of town.

After they disappeared down the road, he wearily got up and trudged to the creek to retrieve the satchel. Taking out the cobbled-together radio and the small console, he breathed a sigh of relief as he turned it on and the indicators glowed green. The radio was working, and when the fleet arrived, he would hopefully be able to communicate with them.

Checking his chronometer, he saw that only fourteen hours remained before the fleet was scheduled to jump in.

Switching the radio off and carefully replacing it in the satchel, he strapped the bag to his combat belt and then slung the sniper rifle over his shoulder.

Picking up his assault rifle, he stood for a moment, alone in the empty field, feeling like he was the last free human on the entire planet.

He needed to find a place to hide so he could plan his next move. After a moment's hesitation, he broke into a jog, following a parallel path to the ones the Kreelans and their captives had taken.

* * *

From her vantage point in the shadows of the charred ruins of the human building where the skirmish line of warriors had earlier fought the two humans, Ku'ar-Marekh watched the large human warrior move at a fast trot across the open field.

He had Tesh-Dar's mark upon him, something that the rank and file warriors could not discern, but that to a warrior priestess such as herself was like a mental scent. That he had fought Tesh-Dar in personal combat did not mean that Ku'ar-Marekh could not challenge him. It simply meant that he might prove more worthy of her skills.

She had let him go as an entertainment, to see what the human warrior might do, just as she had indulged herself by following and being followed by the female pup. Such indulgences were all that she had left.

As for the rest of the human pups taken this night, Ku'ar-Marekh had come to the conclusion that her First had been misguided in believing that they should not be put to the arena until they had matured. If the One they sought were here, he - for it had to be a male, Ku'ar-Marekh knew - would stand out in the arena. They sought one not of their race, but whose blood would sing.

There was no trace of the Bloodsong in any of these creatures, and there was no reason to spare them from the blade. Perhaps they would be more worthy to die by a warrior's hand if they were older and stronger, but Ku'ar-Marekh was not inclined to make the conquest of this world into an experiment.

After reaching that conclusion, she had ordered that the children and the humans who had come from the sky be gathered up from their hideout. Unless their blood sang, they would die in the arenas, for that was the will of the Empress.

Waiting until the big human had crossed the road, Ku'ar-Marekh closed her eyes, imagining her spartan quarters in the woods near the *Kalai-Il*.

Then her body vanished, leaving behind only the silent darkness that would soon give way to dawn.

TWELVE

Lionel Jackson watched through hooded eyes as the alien warriors continued to sweep through the concentration camp in a whirlwind of building and cleaning.

They had come late the night before, hundreds of them, seemingly hell-bent on a sudden "do right" campaign to ease the suffering of their human prisoners, and had worked tirelessly by torchlight. The warriors mucked out the human waste and built proper latrines, quadrupled the size of the camp by extending the fences, brought in a supply of fresh water, and now were building what passed for primitive housing.

They'd also brought in a great deal of food, an odd assortment of vegetables and fruits that they must have collected from the farms around the town, along with game animals that they distributed throughout the compound. They even built fires over which the meat could be cooked.

But what came as the greatest shock was that they dropped a few knives, every one of which looked to be unique and with the incredibly sharp blades shared by all of their edged weapons, with each animal they brought, apparently expecting the humans to use them to gut and skin the carcasses.

Of course, a few enterprising souls had gotten the idea that they could use the knives as weapons to fight the Kreelans.

Unfortunately for them, the aliens enjoyed this development immensely. Every time someone had tried to attack one of the warriors, other warriors formed a ring around the combatants, who then fought in a battle to the death.

In two cases, the humans had won, and the Kreelans let them go about their business after hauling away the bodies of the dead warriors.

As for the humans who weren't so lucky, their bodies were hauled out along with the rest of the waste.

The first glow of the rising sun was just visible on the horizon when the gates swung open and a group of warriors entered, carrying two women and eleven children.

Curious, Jackson made his way toward them. He ignored the bustling alien warriors, just as they ignored him.

The warriors shooed away some people who had occupied one of the newly built shelters and carefully, almost gently, lay the two women down on the bed of leaves, then lay the children down beside them before turning and marching away, back through the gate.

Pushing his way through the sudden crowd that had gathered around the new arrivals, Jackson felt his pulse quicken as he looked at the two women. They were wearing Marine combat uniforms.

The fleet's here, he thought, *or it's coming. Has to be.*

He knelt down beside one of them, a blond, and did a double-take as he got a better look at her face in growing light.

"I don't believe it," he whispered.

Someone else pointed at the woman. "Isn't that Stephanie Guillaume?"

A low murmur ran through the circle of people, expanding through the camp as more people came to see what was happening.

"What's she doing here?"

Steph's eyes fluttered open at the sound.

"Miss Guillaume?" Jackson asked. "Can you hear me?"

"Yeah," she groaned, rubbing her temples. "My head's killing me."

Jackson grinned, but there wasn't any humor in it. "It'll pass in half an hour or so." He reached toward the woman next to her, intending to give her a gentle shake to wake her up.

Steph grabbed his hand, stopping him. "Bad idea." Mills hadn't been the only one to read Valentina's psych profile. With Steph's clout and habit of always getting what she wanted, she'd actually seen more than Mills had. "Let her wake up on her own. Otherwise you're likely to wind up dead."

Propping herself up on her elbows, she wrinkled her nose and muttered, "My God, what's that horrible smell?"

"Us." Jackson gesturing at the filthy clothes, rags really, that he and the other prisoners were wearing. While there was now enough to eat and drink, and latrines had been dug, there weren't any showers or other means to wash their clothes or their bodies.

Beside her, Valentina shot to her feet with a startled cry, instantly assuming a combat stance. Everyone around her stumbled backward in surprise.

"Easy," Steph told her quietly as Valentina looked around, wild-eyed. "Easy. We're in a prison camp, it looks like."

"You're okay," Jackson added, impressed and not just a little frightened at the dark-haired woman, her body tight as a steel spring. "You're safe. For the moment."

After taking a deep, shuddering breath, Valentina relaxed. Slightly. "We're in the camp near Breakwater, aren't we?" Her eyes flicking rapidly across the faces around her, then settling on a group of warriors that marched by, carrying yet another load of materials to build more shelters. "My God," she whispered.

"That's doing the Almighty a bit of an injustice." Jackson favored her with a wry smile as he followed her eyes.

"Work of the Devil's more like it," someone in the crowd spat.

Steph took a closer look at Jackson. She judged him to be in his mid-fifties, with close-cropped hair and a body that, despite the deprivations he'd suffered, was lean and tough. It matched the look in his eyes. "Former military?"

He nodded. "Twenty-six years in the Terran Army. I saw enough during the first war with Saint Petersburg and some other actions, and Alger's World looked like the perfect place to start a quiet new life. The homesteading provisions let me settle down on a nice chunk of land." He looked wistful. "It was a nice place until the Kreelans burned it to the ground."

"You weren't in the Territorial Army here, were you?"

"Yes, I was. I was the first sergeant for one of the companies up north, near Gateway." He shook his head. "We killed a lot of warriors, but there were just too many. We got as many people out of the city as we could before it was surrounded and cut off. Most got away, but not all."

He paused a moment, remembering the screams and pleas for help of those who'd been trapped, an eerie, distant keening of the doomed. "The corridor we were holding was the last passage out of the city. But we finally had to get out of there. There were a few more lucky souls who somehow managed to break through the enemy cordon and followed us out, but that was it." He gestured at the people around them in the camp. "I thought everyone we'd left behind had been slaughtered, but they weren't. They're bringing them here."

"What happened to you after that?"

"They began to hunt us down. After we finally broke contact and retreated from Gateway, I had five-hundred people with me who wanted to fight. I divided them up into five smaller groups and sent them out to cause trouble for the enemy in the nearby towns." He shrugged. "I never heard from any of them again.

"Our group did well for a while. We killed warriors in droves, but they just kept coming at us, like they enjoyed the idea of getting killed." He shook his head in disbelief. "Once a group of them made contact with us, they'd stay after us until we wiped them out. They never broke or ran like humans normally would. You know, live again to fight another day? Not them."

"So how did they get you?"

He laughed. It was a bitter sound. "I guess they finally decided they'd had enough. There were only forty-seven of us left, out of the hundred and sixty-five that I started with after I sent the other groups off. They surrounded us and just came charging in.

"But they didn't come to kill us. They came to capture us, just like you. They hit us with those stun batons of theirs and that was that. Then they stripped us of our weapons and had us join that little procession down the main road. Most of those folks are from Gateway and the other towns north of here, although there are a lot of people here from Caitlin, the other big town to the south.

"We marched for three days, day and night," he went on. "The Kreelans left you alone if you kept up. If you couldn't and fell out of line, they just killed you. No whips or yelling. There was just one type of motivation. Some of the folks here had to march longer than that."

About a third of the people in the circle around them nodded, their faces haunted by the horrors they'd seen on the march.

"And that's when the real fun began." Jackson looked at a party of warriors that was hauling in fresh dirt to cover up the sodden, waste-strewn areas of the camp. "They shoved us all in here, into what was nothing more than a huge livestock pen with a crude wooden fence. There were at least eight, maybe ten thousand people here when we arrived, literally with room only to stand. There weren't any latrines, nothing. It was reeking, filthy mass of desperate people. The Kreelans just shoved us in and started closing the gates, and anyone who was in the way, they started cutting them down. That started a stampede, and I don't have any idea how many were trampled to death." He took a deep breath. It was the worst experience, even in combat, he'd ever endured. "And a lot of folks couldn't take it anymore, and decided it would be better to hop the fence and have the warriors put them out of their misery."

Steph turned to look at the fence that surrounded the camp, beyond which stood a cordon of warriors, their attention riveted to the humans in the camp.

"That's when I gave up hope," Jackson went on quietly. "I could feel it dying inside me. I lost my wife and two sons. My friends. Everything that I'd tried to build here. And I knew I was going to die in this stinking cesspool." He looked at Steph. "It took me a day to work my way to the edge of the crowd. I was going to have the warriors work their sword magic on me, too.

"And then, last night, everything changed." He gestured around him. "There were shuttles coming in all night. Some of them brought more humans, but most of them carried warriors. They and some of the others who were already here started cleaning up this pit." He managed a smile. "I guess it must've been for your arrival."

"It doesn't matter," a woman said as she ceaselessly twirled a lock of her dirty hair through her fingers. "We're all dead, anyway."

Everyone else was silent. They looked down at their feet, each a study in total defeat.

Steph turned to her. "That's not true. The fleet's coming."

Only a few people looked up at her words. She glanced at Valentina, who shrugged.

"Didn't you hear me?" Steph said, louder now. "The fleet's coming!"

More looked up at her now, out of curiosity, not out of hope. Steph glanced at Valentina again and saw her frown. "What?"

Valentina didn't speak until another party of alien warriors had passed, then said, "They may not be able to find us, remember?"

"Goddammit!" Steph got unsteadily to her feet. She stumbled, still suffering from the after-effects of the stun, and Jackson caught her arm to steady her.

"People, listen to me!" Anger was burning inside her. The children began to wake up from her shouting. "The most powerful fleet the Confederation has ever assembled is coming here!" She wasn't worried about the Kreelans hearing her. In all the encounters with them so far, there had been no indication that any of them understood any human language, or cared. "It's on its way right now, and..." She glanced at her chronometer. "...it's going to arrive in less than six hours. They're going to wipe the Kreelan fleet from orbit, and then three assault divisions are going to land and do the same to the warriors here on the planet."

"Why didn't they come already?" A man in the crowd shouted angrily as he stepped forward to confront Steph. Valentina moved slightly closer in case he decide to get violent. "Look at us!" he shouted. "Just look at us! Look at what they made us go through, how many of us have died at the hands of those beasts!" Tears were running down the man's face now. "Why should we believe the bloody fleet's coming now?"

"Because," Steph said evenly, stepping right up to the man and placing her hands on his shoulders, "my husband is in that fleet." She looked around at the other faces near her. "Some of you may have heard of him. His name is Ichiro Sato."

Recognition dawned on almost every face. Sato's name was one of the most well-known in the Confederation. While she was estranged from him, she hadn't lost track of what he had been doing. She still loved him. And believed in him. "He's commanding the most powerful ships we've ever built, battleships that are more than a match for anything the Kreelans have. And he's not going to leave until every one of these blue-skinned bitches is dead."

"But why didn't the Confederation come earlier?" the man asked. "Why did they wait so long, until now?"

"Because they couldn't," Valentina answered. "We've been fighting and losing battles on almost two dozen colonies. President McKenna is taking a terrible gamble on this attack by pulling ships away from every one of those systems to put together an assault fleet big enough to beat the Kreelan forces here. She's even stripped Home Fleet over Earth down to the bone." She stared into the frightened, desperate faces around her. "If the Kreelans attacked Earth in any real force, we could lose it. That's the risk she's taking."

"Too bad for them," someone sneered. "They've had it easy."

"Too bad for humanity, you mean," Valentina answered icily. "If we lose Earth, we lose the war. And you should know better than anyone what that would mean. Every colony would be exterminated."

"So what are we going to do?"

The question came not from the crowd of adults, which by now had become a thick ring of hundreds of people, trying to hear and see what was going on, but from the voice of a tired teenage girl. Allison.

"There's nothing we can do," Jackson said quietly. "We just have to..."

"Bullshit," Steph snarled. "We didn't go through hell getting down here just to give up."

"Steph," Valentina interjected, "we don't have a lot of options. The radio's gone. There's no way to communicate with the fleet. Mills and the others..."

She bit her lip, unable to say what she knew must be true. That Mills was gone.

"I don't care," Steph rounded on her, eyes blazing. "I am not just going to be herded into one of those rings and slaughtered like Ichiro's first crew was!" More than anyone else, she understood the nightmare that her husband had endured as a young midshipman when humanity had made its first contact with the Kreelans. He still had nightmares, at least the last time they had shared a bed, months ago now. She bitterly shoved the memory aside, wishing more than anything else that he was here right now to hold her.

But she knew he was coming. And that was enough.

"If we're going to die," she went on, "then let's die doing something worth dying for." She looked at Allison and the other children who were riveted to the ongoing discussion. "At least we can try and get the children out of here."

"*She* won't let us go now." Allison's face, for once, displayed outright despair. While it had been a nightmare in many ways, it had been nothing compared to this awful-smelling place, surrounded by warriors, and knowing that death awaited all of them.

Steph moved over and wrapped her arms around the girl, who returned the gesture, holding on tightly.

"It doesn't matter what that warrior wants," Steph said, her conviction growing with every word. "Somehow, we're going to-"

At that moment a deep gong reverberated through the camp. It was a mournful sound, and it sent a shiver down Steph's spine.

A cry arose from near the entrance to the camp as the gates opened and a phalanx of warriors marched in. Without further ceremony, they grabbed the nearest twenty people before they could run, then herded them out, the gates closing behind them.

Running to the fence near the gates, Valentina, Steph, and Jackson watched the prisoners and their escorts move down the trail that led to the arena complex at the town square. From where the three stood, the top of the large stone construct at the center was just visible through the trees, but they couldn't see the arenas themselves.

Then they heard it, the low murmur of a great number of voices, coming from the direction of the arenas. It had been masked by the moaning and bustle in the camp. But the humans had fallen silent after their fellows had been taken, not wanting to draw attention to themselves as they moved toward the rear of the camp's enclosure.

The Kreelan warriors in the camp continued to work, but all of them periodically glanced in the direction of the arenas.

Fifteen minutes later, as the sun rose full above the horizon, the gong sounded again. Valentina, with her sharp eyes, could see that it was affixed to the top of the stone structure, rung by a single warrior.

Another warrior stood there, silhouetted against the brightening horizon, a cloak fluttering in the light morning breeze. Valentina knew without a doubt who it was. The warrior, the one who had nearly torn Valentina's heart from her chest with nothing but a thought, was looking right at her.

As the sound of the gong faded, the warrior turned away to face the arenas, and a bone-chilling roar from thousands of warriors, unseen beyond the trees, filled the air.

THIRTEEN

Ku'ar-Markekh stood upon the *Kalai-Il*, her eyes fixed upon the unusual human female who held much promise as a challenge to Ku'ar-Marekh's skills. She had decided to face the human animal with only sword and claw, for this would bring the Empress the greatest glory, and would also give Ku'ar-Marekh a chance for an honorable death.

But she would save her own combat until her most junior warriors had blooded themselves against other humans. Those of Her Children who had not yet had a chance to fight one of the animals had been cast first in the lottery of the Challenge. Once they had fought, Ku'ar-Marekh would take to the arena against the female warrior and perhaps some of her companions. Anything less would be no contest at all.

Turning away from the human who stared back at her from inside the holding pen, Ku'ar-Markh faced into the rising sun as the last echoes of the gong faded.

The warriors roared, their excitement over the coming combats pulsing through the Bloodsong.

She gave them a moment to express their anticipation, for Challenges such as this were rare in the Empire outside times of war. The battles fought here would be to the death, and every warrior wanted her chance to fight for the honor of the Empress.

At last raising her arms, Ku'ar-Marekh commanded them to silence. Thousands of warriors knelt as one, crashing their armored left fists over their right breasts.

The litany the priestess spoke was older than the Empire itself. Its words were simple and brief, the core of every warrior's heart.

"As it has been," she began as the human prisoners were brought forth, four of them to the entrance of each of the five arenas where the first challengers already waited, "and so shall it always be, let the Challenge begin."

"In Her Name," the warriors echoed solemnly, "let it be so."

A single human was forced into each arena. They were shown a table that held a variety of edged weapons, and the waiting challenger was honor-bound to choose a similar weapon. They only had a single turn of the small hour-glass that Ku'ar-Marekh's new First, Esah-Kuran, held to decide upon a weapon.

Two chose swords, two refused to decide, and one tried to flee the arena. The one who tried to run was cut down by a *shrekka*.

This prompted the two humans who had not chosen weapons to do so.

Ku'ar-Marekh nodded in approval. They could die like meat animals, or they could fight for their honor. Should a human survive, they would be allowed to rest until the other humans had taken a turn in the arena. Then the survivors again would have to fight.

All would eventually die, unless The One came forth. But Ku'ar-Marekh did not believe that would happen here.

Nor, in her cold heart, did she care.

Another human was brought forward to take the dishonored one's place. This one, seeing its companions in the other arenas, made the choice of honor and chose a sword.

Stepping down from the *Kalai-Il*, Ku'ar-Marekh took the place that tradition demanded atop the dais at the center of the middle of the five arenas.

Looking out upon her warriors and their reluctant human challengers, she bellowed, "Begin!"

* * *

After Valentina and the others had been taken, Mills had taken the risk of running across the fields to beat the group of warriors carrying the women and children.

As he neared the woods, he could hear the pitiful moans and cries of the human prisoners, and his nose was overpowered with the stench of human waste. He forced himself to slow down as he entered the treeline, moving slowly to remain silent.

When he came within sight of the camp, he unslung the sniper rifle and took a closer look. He saw what must have been thousands of people milling around inside an enclosure bounded by a very crude wooden fence. Outside of that stood a cordon of warriors.

As he watched them, he noted that they never turned around to look back into the woods. Their attention was entirely fixed on their prisoners, thinking there was nothing to fear behind them.

"You've got that a bit wrong, dearies." During the run from the barn, Mills had been thinking of different plans he could set into action to help free the prisoners, depending on what he found.

Looking at the camp, he settled on one of those options. A little explosive diversion that he would light off when the time was right.

He had eight grenades, which could be set to detonate a variety of ways, including by remote. He had used them against the Kreelans before during the fighting he'd seen after the original Saint Petersburg operation, and the aliens had never interfered with the detonation signals like they did with other tech like the comm and data links.

Leaving the sniper rifle behind a tree, he crept forward to the trees nearest the Kreelan guards. Moving parallel to what he took to be the rear of the conpound's fence, he set seven grenades at roughly equal intervals, keeping a single grenade in reserve. He didn't expect they would kill many of the warriors, but it would give them a nasty surprise.

He placed the last grenade and was making his way back to where he'd left the sniper rifle when he heard a commotion at the far side of the camp near the entry gates.

Taking out his binoculars, he watched as warriors brought in Valentina and the others, setting them down under one of the newly built shelters. His stomach knotted up at the sight of their limp bodies carried in the aliens' arms, but he told himself that they must still be alive.

Forcing himself to stop lingering and watching for movement from the women and children, he focused on finding a spot in the woods that gave him a good view into the camp, but that wasn't right on top of the Kreelans.

It wasn't easy, but at last he found a small knoll a couple hundred meters from the camp that had a narrow but clear view through the compound up to the gates. He could see the shelter that Valentina and the others were in, and watched tensely through the scope on the sniper rifle the crowd that had gathered around the newcomers. He saw a rustle of movement among the people around the shelter, then saw Steph's face briefly through the mass of bobbing heads.

Then the crowd seemed to flinch back, with some of those closest to the women and children actually falling backward. Mills couldn't help but chuckle as he saw Valentina leap to her feet, her hands raised, ready for a fight.

"That's my girl." He felt like a spring steel band had just been removed from around his chest, such was his relief that she was alive.

He saw the two of them talking to a black man for quite some time, then Steph became agitated and was shouting something at the people clustered around them.

He could only wonder what was going on, but he felt another wave of relief as he saw the children awaken, and smiled when he caught a glimpse of Allison.

Then the gates opened and a group of warriors came in, seizing a bunch of people who were unlucky enough to be in easy reach. The unlucky prisoners were frog-marched out the gates, which closed behind them, disappearing along the trail that led toward the big stone structure and the arenas.

"Hell," Mills whispered. *This is what must have happened at the end on Keran*, he thought. The survivors of the initial slaughter were used as unwilling opponents in the arenas. And when the last had been killed...

Shoving that thought aside, he checked his chronometer. A little less than six hours were left until the fleet jumped in. There wasn't much time. He needed to let Valentina and Steph know he was here, but had no idea how to do it.

Watching through the scope, he saw them return to the shelter from where they had run to the fence. He had a much clearer view now, because almost everyone else in the camp had moved toward the back of the enclosure, closer to him. Valentina was talking to the black man, and Steph leaned down and picked up her helmet. He saw her detach something that looked like a set of eyeglasses and put them on. Then she went to stand a bit behind Valentina, and Allison came up to hold her hand.

She put her vidcam gear back on, Mills realized.

An idea was forming at the back of his brain, but it didn't gel until he pulled his eye away from the big rifle's scope. One of the controls on the tiny panel was for a laser designator that was normally used to provide the exact range to the target. It could also be used to direct guided rounds fired from the rifle or larger weapons from another platform. Unfortunately, it was one of the technologies that the Kreelans frequently nulled out in battle through whatever mysterious means they used.

Mills turned it on, and in the scope an indicator lit up. He put the crosshairs on the head of one of the warriors guarding the camp pulled the trigger back just enough to activate the laser.

The display read 187 meters. The laser was working.

The only trick was that it was completely invisible to the unaided eye.

But Steph's eyes weren't unaided. She was looking at the world through the artificially enhanced view of her vidcam display.

* * *

"Good God." Steph looked toward the commotion coming from the Kreelans gathered around the arenas. She couldn't see anything, for the complex was masked by trees and the buildings on this side of the town square, but she could hear them. Her flesh crawled at the roar of what must be thousands of alien voices.

She felt a small hand take hold of hers, squeezing it tightly. Allison. Her eyes were wide and her face stricken with fear. She had been strong, incredibly strong for someone her age, but she was smart enough to know what awaited them down the dirt path that led from the gates. And she knew that her special relationship with the warrior leader wouldn't spare her.

"Don't worry, honey." Steph had to raise her voice to be heard above the din. Her vidcam was running now, and she planned to just leave it on to record whatever was to come. She would never get the chance to edit it or be able to tell the story of the people here, but with a little luck perhaps the Marines who landed would eventually find it.

She thought of Ichiro and wished more than anything that she could speak to him one last time, just to tell him how much she still loved him. She bit her tongue to take her mind away from the tears she felt welling up in her eyes. "We'll be all right." She squeezed Allison's hand. "I promise."

Allison nodded in jerky movements, and her face twitched in an attempt at a smile, but that was all. She accepted Steph's words for what they were, a comforting lie.

Looking up again as the sound of the alien voices peaked, movement on Valentina's back caught her eye. She was standing just ahead of Steph, and at first Steph thought it was some sort of insect.

Then she realized it couldn't be. It was a small, bright green dot, and it pulsed rhythmically as it moved up and down Valentina's spine.

"What the..." She flipped up the tiny visor that projected an enhanced view of the scene she was recording.

The mysterious dot vanished.

Flipping the vidcam visor back down, the dot reappeared. Now, instead of moving up and down Valentina's spine, the dot was moving slowly from one of her buttocks to the other, pulsing on and off, on and off.

"Oh, my God." Turning around, she looked across the mass of people crushed into the back of the compound, trying to avoid being the next ones to be taken to the arenas.

At first she saw nothing, and then there it was. A bright flash, aimed at her now, coming from somewhere in the woods. "Mills?" Then, realizing that whoever it was couldn't hear her, she said his name again, over-emphasizing the movement of her lips and tongue.

Two flashes.

"You're alive?"

Again, two flashes.

"Blink once."

One flash.

"Valentina!" Steph said, a surge of joy and adrenaline shooting through her system as she stepped backward and reached for the other woman, not wanting to lose sight of the spot in the forest where Mills was hiding. "Valentina!"

"What is it?" Valentina was beside her.

"You're not going to believe this," Steph snatched off her vidcam and carefully placed it on Valentina's head, "but Mills is alive!"

She stepped behind Valentina and gently turned her head toward the spot in the woods. Steph didn't want to draw unwanted attention from the warriors who were still working in a frenzy throughout the camp by simply pointing.

"Steph, you know as well as I do that he's gone." Valentina's voice was wooden with pent-up grief, but she was enough of a realist to know that Mills was dead. She thought Steph had gone off the deep end, even as Steph's hands guided her to look toward the woods. "He couldn't have..."

She stopped, her mouth hanging open as she stood still, staring.

"Do you see it?"

"Yes." A smile lit up Valentina's face as she watched the merrily blinking light coming from the woods. "Oh, God, yes! He must be using the laser designator on my rifle!"

"What is it?" Jackson was looking in the direction that the two women were looking, but couldn't see anything.

"Our team leader." Steph leaned over to speak closer to his ear over the tumult from the arenas. "We were sure he was dead, but he's alive!"

"Thank God." Valentina began to play a game of twenty questions with Mills, who could only answer "yes" or "no."

* * *

Mills gritted his teeth in frustration, wishing that they had a better way of communicating, that he could tell Valentina what he needed to say. He had once heard of an ancient communications code, Morse, he thought it was, that would have worked well for this situation, but neither he nor Valentina knew it. So he had to be content with Valentina mouthing questions in hopes that he could lip-read what she was saying, then he would answer yes or no, two pulses of the laser or one.

Valentina immediately realized that he wasn't there just to let them know he was alive, but that he had a plan to help get them out. After what had seemed like forever, but had only taken about five minutes, she had figured out what he had in mind.

"Beautiful and brilliant." He grinned as Valentina blew him a kiss before turning to Steph and the black man, who had the look about him of someone who'd been in the military, and began to tell them what she'd learned.

Steph made her pause for a moment, then took the vidcam gear from Valentina and put it on Allison. Then she aimed Allison's gaze toward Mills, and he shot her a few blinks with the laser.

The girl put her hands to her face and burst into tears. But when she took her hands away a moment later, he could see that they were tears of joy, and her mouth kept forming his name.

Then Steph took the vidcam gear from Allison and put it back on herself. She gave Mills the thumbs-up sign as Allison gathered the other children around her and began to tell them what was happening, her hands gesticulating wildly. All of them turned to look toward the woods. Toward him.

"Hang in there, sweeties." Mills prayed the fleet would be on time, and that he could contact them. "Just a few more hours."

* * *

"We've got to make sure everyone knows," Valentina told Jackson. "Mills thinks that when the fleet arrives, the Kreelans will be distracted. When that happens, he's going to try to contact the fleet to let them know where we are. That's his first priority. Then he's going to take down as many of the warriors along the back fence as he can."

"Then we make a break for it," Jackson finished for her. He looked around at the people who were still crowded fearfully at the back of the compound. "I don't know how far we'll get with this many warriors guarding us, but it's better than being slaughtered like cattle."

As he spoke, there was a sudden spike in the volume of the nearby Kreelans watching the arenas. Then the huge gong sounded again, and the warriors instantly fell silent.

"Uh-oh." Steph wasn't sure what the silence meant, but doubted it was anything good.

"Get the children back." Valentina took Allison's hand and pulled her toward the rear of the enclosure. As she approached the people at the edge of the crowd, she shouted, "Let the children move to the back!"

"Go to hell." A well-muscled man who stood a head taller than Valentina gave her the finger.

She stepped closer, still holding Allison's hand, and stabbed her free hand, flattened like a blade, into his throat in a lightning-fast thrust. It was a blow that could easily have killed him, but she only intended to make a point. Literally. He collapsed to the ground, gagging. "Let the children through!" "Now!"

Those nearby, many of whom looked at the man with undisguised contempt, stepped aside and offered welcoming hands to help the children.

"No!" Allison begged as Valentina tried to guide her after the younger children. "I want to stay with you!"

"Allison," Valentina told her, kneeling down to look Allison in the eyes, "you can't. What I have to do now..."

"Look!" Steph pointed toward the gate. Everyone looked up.

The warriors who had taken the people earlier had returned. To everyone's shock, one of the men who'd been taken in the first group was with them. He was bloody and battered, but alive.

The gates opened, and they marched in, stopping just inside. One of them motioned for the man to continue inside, and as one the warriors bowed their heads as he moved through their ranks and into the relative freedom of the compound.

The warriors remained where they were.

Valentina waited to make sure the warriors weren't going to rush forward to seize more victims before she ran to where the man collapsed under the nearest shelter. Steph and Jackson were right behind her. As was Allison.

The rest of the crowd hung back, still fearful of being taken by the warriors.

"What happened?" Valentina asked the man, who was slim and wiry, his head clean-shaven. Steph rushed over from where she had grabbed a container of water in another shelter and handed it to the man, who drank from it greedily.

"They made us fight," he explained after chugging down half the water. He had a gash in his scalp and a set of puncture wounds in his left side. Valentina pulled out her medical kit and began applying an antibacterial salve to the wounds as he went on, "It's one on one, to the death. No point in trying to run. If you don't fight, they just kill you and bring up someone else."

"What style of combat are they using?" Jackson asked grimly.

The man laughed. "You choose your own poison, Swords, knives. Other stuff I don't have a name for. Just hands and feet if you like, I suppose. But no guns or anything like that."

"What did you do?"

"I used a knife." He grinned. "That's what I was in for."

"What do you mean?" Valentina asked.

"Prison. I was in for murder. Stabbed a guy. Did the same thing to that warrior bitch in the arena, although she put up more of a fight." He shrugged. "Sort of ironic, huh?"

"I guess you could say that." Valentina accepted the cold logic of it. A killer would stand the best chance of surviving against the Kreelans. In this war there wasn't much of a distinction between killers such as Mills and herself, and a murderer such as this man. Their fight was for more than morality or justice, it was for the survival of the human race. "I can't say that you've atoned for your sins, my friend," she said as she finished with the first aid kit, "but it certainly didn't hurt."

"They're waiting." Steph eyed the warriors, who stared back. The leader stepped forward, a hand on the handle of her sword.

Valentina stood up and looked at them, then at the mass of people muttering nervously behind her. She held up her hand to the warriors, hoping they'd understand, before moving close enough to the crowd that they could hear her.

"I need volunteers," she shouted. "People who can fight hand to hand. The fleet will arrive in a few hours, and we've got to buy some time. If you fight and win," she gestured toward the former inmate who gave them a wave, "you'll get to live." *At least for a while*, she thought darkly, doubting that the Kreelans would simply let go any survivors. "If we don't choose to fight, they'll choose for us!"

A young man, deeply tanned and with shoulders as broad as Mills, stepped forward. Then two more. A woman moved up from behind the front row. Then more.

There was hope now, Valentina knew, seeing the determination in their eyes. Most of those who stepped forward had been fighting the Kreelans since the invasion began.

Valentina took the first nineteen volunteers, then turned and strode toward the warriors, pausing momentarily to talk to Steph. "Get as many of the others as you can organized into groups of twenty for when the warriors come back." Looking at the survivor of the first round, she added, "Hopefully we'll do a bit better than one out of twenty."

"God, Valentina," Steph said, squeezing Valentina's hand. "Be careful."

"Don't go." Allison threw her arms around Valentina. "Please."

Valentina gently pushed Allison away and put a hand on the girl's cheek. "This is the only way we have any control over this. And I have no intention of dying. Not today."

She leaned forward and kissed Allison on the forehead. Then she turned and looked toward the woods where Mills lay hidden.

"I'll be back." She waved at him before turning away and leading the others to where the Kreelans stood waiting.

FOURTEEN

Ku'ar-Marekh watched as the next group of humans was brought forth. She noted that the female human warrior, the one who was of special interest to her, was in this group.

She was pleased, or as close to being so as her empty heart allowed. Ku'ar-Marekh also saw that this group of humans, led by the dark-haired female, whose gaze was fixed on Ku'ar-Marekh, walked with heads held high, clearly proud and showing no fear. They carried themselves like warriors, come to do battle, and were not mere beasts waiting to be slaughtered like most of the animals in the first group.

Around the arenas, the gathered warriors who awaited their turn to fight the humans were quiet in respect, curious as to how this group of opponents would fare.

Warriors gestured for the humans to divide into five groups of four and guided them to the arenas, with the dark-haired female stepping forward onto the sands of the central one. She barely took her eyes from Ku'ar-Marekh.

The first challengers of each of the other groups moved into the other arenas to face the warriors who awaited them on the bloodied sands.

While the priestess could have taken this challenge for herself, a junior warrior had already been chosen by the lottery, and Ku'ar-Marekh would not dishonor her by claiming first right of combat.

Instead, she watched with cold eyes as the warrior, Ayan-Ye'eln, strode toward the human, then gestured toward the table where the weapons were arrayed.

The human glanced at the table, then turned to face the young warrior. Shaking her head in a gesture Ku'ar-Marekh had come to understand as a sign of negation, she raised her hands toward Ayan-Ye'eln, then clenched them into fists.

Tooth and claw.

Interesting, Ku'ar-Marekh thought to herself as Ayan-Ye'eln, understanding the human's intent, bowed her head in acceptance.

With a brief glance at Ku'ar-Marekh, the young warrior began to remove her armor, placing it carefully on the table beside the weapons arrayed there. In a moment she wore only the black garment that formed the under-layer for the armor.

She strode back to her place near the dais, then turned toward the human, flexing her hands, her black talons glittering in the sun.

The greater honor is yours, child, Ku'ar-Marekh thought approvingly. Ayan-Ye'eln was trying to even the odds for the human as best she could by removing her armor, something that was never demanded by tradition.

The human moved forward, coming to stand a few paces away from Ayan-Ye'eln, but her attention remained on Ku'ar-Marekh.

The priestess returned the human's gaze as she again raised her arms, signaling her warriors to kneel and render their salutes.

Then Ku'ar-Marekh once more spoke the words that preceded every Challenge.

"As it has been," she said, her voice carrying across the five arenas and the *Kalai-Il*, "and so shall it always be, let the Challenge begin."

"In Her Name," the warriors echoed once more, excitement plain in their voices, "let it be so."

* * *

Valentina listened as the lead warrior on the dais at the center of the arena spoke, then the other warriors answered in unison.

As they finished speaking, the huge gong sounded again and the warriors rose to their feet.

Unlike with the first group of human victims, when the Kreelans had immediately broken out in a huge uproar at the sound of the gong, this time they remained quiet.

They know we're different, Valentina thought, sensing their curious anticipation. *We're not lambs to the slaughter. Not this time.*

The warrior opposing her turned side-on with one hand extended forward and the other back, both with fingers spread. Her nails, vaguely similar to the claws of a bird of prey like an eagle that Valentina had seen once on Earth, glistened, and Valentina knew they were incredibly sharp.

Have to watch those, Valentina cautioned herself. She knew she could have chosen one of the many weapons arrayed on the table when she entered the arena, but decided not to. She had plenty of experience with knives and had trained with swords in various styles, but for one on one combat, the weapons she knew best were those that were already part of her body.

She suspected that the opposite was true for her opponent. Everything Valentina had read and seen during her brief time here indicated that the Kreelans greatly preferred edged weapons in combat. While hand to hand fighting wasn't unheard of in combat reports, it was rare.

She hoped fighting hand to hand without weapons would help achieve her main goal, which was to draw out the fight as long as she could. She felt confident she could kill the warrior quickly if she wanted to, but the longer the fights went on, the fewer people would have to set foot in the arenas before the fleet arrived.

She stood still, her body relaxed but ready, waiting for the warrior to attack.

* * *

Ku'ar-Marekh watched as Ayan-Ye'eln lunged at the human, trying to grab the animal with her leading hand before impaling her with the talons of her trailing hand. It was a basic attack that typically worked well against the humans, who seemed universally afraid of the talons of the warriors.

The priestess was impressed with the speed of the attack, but was more impressed with the human's response. In a smooth motion, the human animal sidestepped Ayan-Ye'eln's strike.

Then with one hand the human grasped the warrior's leading arm, immobilizing it, before slamming the elbow of her free arm into Ayan-Ye'eln's head.

That probably would have been enough to put the dazed warrior on the ground, but in a seamless continuation of the elbow strike, the human wrapped that arm around Ayan-Ye'eln's head, twirled her halfway around, and flipped her backwards onto the ground in a spray of sand.

It was a fluid, beautiful move, the likes of which Ku'ar-Marekh had never seen.

The human, who clearly hadn't even exerted herself, backed away a few paces as the young warrior fought to regain her senses.

A roar went up from the gathered warriors, not of anger, but of approval. Like Ku'ar-Marekh, none of them had ever seen such a fighting style, and they knew that whoever bested this human, who was clearly a formidable warrior, would bring great glory to the Empress.

That honor shall be mine, my children, Ku'ar-Marekh thought, for she did not believe that any of the warriors here could beat the human in a fair match.

Ayan-Ye'eln got to her feet, and with a roar of anger charged the human again.

* * *

Valentina continued to spar with the warrior, who became increasingly frustrated at her inability to inflict even the slightest injury on her human opponent.

The Kreelan had stopped charging like a bull, but no matter what she did, she always found herself up on the ground, spitting sand from her mouth.

Valentina had no idea how much time had passed, but she knew that the other combats for her group had ended. Seven men and women stood near the entrance to her arena, the survivors of the nineteen who had come with her to fight.

The other warriors, too, had moved in as close as they could, trying to get a glimpse of what was happening in the central arena.

The warrior, her lungs heaving now from exhaustion, came again at Valentina, and again Valentina easily deflected her attack. She hammered the warrior twice in the face with her fists, further bloodying the Kreelan's mouth and nose, before sending the warrior flying face-first into the sand.

"*Kazh!*" The warrior leader bellowed as she raised her arms in the air, and the warriors watching the fight instantly fell silent.

* * *

"Stop!" Ku'ar-Marekh called as the human flung Ayan-Ye'eln to the ground yet again. She did not understand why the human had not simply killed the young warrior.

A strange creature, this one, she thought. But they were all strange to her, their motivations well beyond her understanding or caring.

But it was time for honor to be measured. "Ayan-Ye'eln."

The young warrior pushed herself to her knees, bloodied and exhausted. Her head bowed in reverence to her priestess, and in humiliation, as well. She had fought as best she could, but in this Challenge there was but one acceptable outcome.

"You may choose."

"I choose by her hand, my priestess." Ayan-Ye'eln mustered some pride into her voice as she spoke through her battered lips. Blood ran from them and her shattered nose down her bruised and swollen face as she gestured toward the human.

It was as Ku'ar-Marekh expected, and she nodded her affirmation. "You honor the Empress, my child." She stepped from the dais and strode toward the human, her ceremonial cloak fluttering behind her.

As she drew near the animal warrior, Ku'ar-Marekh drew her sword.

* * *

Valentina tensed as the warrior leader approached, drawing her sword. This one, she knew from her very brief encounter the night before, would be an incredibly hard fight, assuming Valentina was given a chance at all and the alien didn't use her strange powers as she did before.

But fighting now wasn't the alien's intention, Valentina saw. The warrior held out her sword, handle first, toward Valentina, and nodded her head toward the young warrior, who had remained kneeling.

"Kill her!" One of the men shouted from where he and the other six survivors stood, watching the spectacle.

Valentina reached out and took the sword, whose blade shimmered in a way that she had read was peculiar to Kreelan edged weapons. Metallurgists had tried to replicate the metal, which had proven to be far stronger than any man-made alloy, but thus far had been unsuccessful. It was similar in shape to the Japanese katana, with a long, gently curved blade and a long handle intended for two-handed use, although the sword was light enough and so exquisitely balanced that it could easily be wielded in a single hand. The handle itself was a work of art, made of a clear crystal, perhaps even diamond, with golden fibers woven within it. While it looked smooth and should have been slippery, it wasn't. Even with her sweating hands, she could grip it easily. The handle also had an unusual shape, and as she changed her grip slightly, she realized that it was instantly reforming itself to give her the best possible hold, as if it were alive, anticipating how she would hold the weapon.

"My God." She wondered at what magical technology must be at work inside what one could easily mistake for a mere sword.

She looked up at the warrior leader, the one with the dead eyes, who again gestured toward the kneeling warrior, making a chopping motion with her hand.

"Do it!" One of the surviving women called out. "That'll be one less we have to kill when the fleet gets here!"

In her mind, Valentina knew that the woman was right. And while she had killed plenty of human beings, some of whom had been as helpless as the battered warrior now kneeling before her, she had given up a small piece of her soul with every life she had taken that way.

The young warrior who had tried to fight her, if Kreelans aged anything like humans, looked to be little beyond her teens. She would almost certainly die when the fleet arrived and the Marines landed to retake the planet. But she wouldn't die now, at least not by Valentina's hand.

"No." She held out the sword to the warrior leader, who reluctantly took it back.

* * *

Ku'ar-Marekh took back her sword from the human, who stepped beyond the reach of the blade.

The other humans, the survivors of this round of the Challenge, made noises in their language, clearly displeased.

"The animal does not understand the Way," Ku'ar-Marekh told Ayan-Ye'eln as the warriors around the arena again fell silent, straining to hear her words. "She refuses to take your life. She does not understand the honor she would render upon you, if she understands the concept of honor at all."

Ayan-Ye'eln looked up at the human, then reached out a hand to her, palm up. Moving forward on her knees, she came close enough to touch the alien's hand. The alien tensed, but did not move away. Ayan-Ye'eln took the human's hand in hers, then reached out to the priestess for the sword. Ku'ar-Marekh gave it to her, and Ayan-Ye'eln placed the handle in the alien warrior's hand, closing the human's pale fingers around the gleaming living crystal.

Looking up one last time into the human's unreadable gaze, she bent forward, offering her neck. She shivered not with fear, but with anticipation, for when alive all of Her Children, even the males, felt the power of the Empress through the Bloodsong. But in death they became one with it, immersed in Her power and love.

And to die at the hand of a worthy opponent, one who might even challenge the high priestess of the Nyur-A'il, was an honor that few among her race had known since the last great war, fought among the stars many millennia before.

She steadied her breathing, awaiting her release.

* * *

Valentina stood over the warrior, the alien sword now clenched in her hand. She looked up at the other survivors, who had fallen as silent as the alien warriors around them.

How can we fight a race of warriors that wants to die? Valentina wondered. Did winning a battle even matter to them, or did they simply fight until they finally found someone who could beat them.

What if, to them, death was the ultimate victory? What if territory, resources, ideology, or any of the other reasons humans had traditionally fought one another had no meaning to them? How, then, could humanity win, other than by killing every single Kreelan in the universe?

The thought chilled her, more because no one had any idea how large the Empire might be. Even if the Confederation could somehow manage to kill the Kreelans at a ratio of hundreds to one, what if the aliens had thousands, or tens of thousands, of warriors for every human, warriors who simply wouldn't stop until they died?

Valentina looked at the warriors who were intently staring at her, waiting to see what she would do. She realized that in this war, even on as grand a scale as it was being fought, every life would count in the end. On both sides.

With one last glance into the warrior leader's dead eyes, Valentina gripped the sword in both hands and brought it down in a slashing arc, cutting cleanly through the kneeling warrior's neck.

The warriors around them roared their approval as the Kreelan's head fell to the sand and her body toppled beside it. Valentina flicked the blood from the blade before handing the sword back to the warrior leader.

The huge gong sounded again. This round was over.

The warrior leader bowed her head slightly, then gestured with one hand toward the entrance to the arena as she replaced the sword in its gleaming black scabbard with the other.

With a last look at the dead warrior's body, still pumping blood onto the white sands of the arena, Valentina rejoined her fellow humans for the march back to the camp.

Behind her, five other warriors reverently lifted the body of their fallen sister and carried her to a nearby field where the funeral pyres were already burning.

* * *

"Valentina!" Steph shouted as the warriors appeared at the gates and released the eight survivors of the second group. Steph wrapped her arms around Valentina and hugged her fiercely. The men and women of the third group gathered around the survivors, peppering them with questions about how the Kreelans fought.

"I'm okay." Valentina returned Steph's hug briefly. "How long? How long were we gone?"

"Almost thirty minutes. You were gone almost half an hour."

"That was all?" Valentina felt sick. Combat had a time dilation effect, where seconds could seem like hours, and minutes stretched on to eternity. She looked past Steph to the next few groups of fighters lined up, waiting for their turn in the arenas. "We're going to need more people."

Steph ignored her last comment. "What do you mean, 'That was all?' Thirty minutes against them? That's incredible! The first group was gone only ten minutes, and only one survived!"

"The next group will do even better." Jackson came to stand next to Valentina, giving her a brief pat on the shoulder. "It's made up mostly of my people, and all of them have fought hand to hand before." He looked at the warriors, who waited expectantly. "We'll give a good accounting of ourselves, I think."

"You're going?"

Jackson nodded. "I'm not a young buck anymore, but I think I can hold my own in a reasonably fair fight. I'm not just going to sit here on my ass."

"Have one of your people sit out." Valentina headed back toward the waiting warriors, as both Steph and Allison opened their mouths to protest. "I'm going back in."

"Sorry, Valentina." Jackson matched her stride, gesturing for the others in the next group to move up. "You can come along if you like, but none of these folks are going to back out."

The other nineteen people moved past Jackson into the box formed by the warriors, and Jackson joined them.

Valentina walked forward to join them, but the warrior in charge put her hand on Valentina's chest, holding her back while bowing her head.

"I'm going." Valentina's growl did not dissuade the warrior, who held fast while the others turned about and marched out the gates with Jackson's group.

"Don't be a fool, Valentina." Steph took her by the arm and gently pulled her back. "I know you can fight better than any of us, but you can't save us by yourself. That's something we all have to do together. And we're going to need you when Mills gets ready to break us out of here."

Valentina shrugged off Steph's hand. After a moment more of glaring at the warrior who still stood there, barring her way, she turned away and walked back toward their shelter, a silent Allison and Steph following close behind.

The warrior watched her for a moment, then turned and followed her sisters back toward the arenas.

"Here, take this." Steph handed Valentina her vidcam headset. "Mills is talking again."

Valentina put it on and looked out into the woods, where she saw the laser light blinking.

* * *

The half hour that Valentina had been in the arena had been one of the longest of Mills's life. He had cursed her for a fool the entire time using every foul word he could conjure up, knowing all the while that she was doing it to buy time for the others.

Steph and Allison had waited for her along the fence by the gate, now that they weren't afraid of the warriors picking people out at random.

For thirty minutes Mills held still, his eye to the scope as he trained the sniper rifle on the gates. His gut churned, his stomach alternately filled with butterflies and acid.

When Valentina and the others were marched back, he breathed a long, ragged sigh of relief until he saw the altercation between her and the black man. He didn't have to guess what it was about, and he started cursing her again when she tried to join the next group to go to the arenas. Between one of the warriors and Steph, she had her mind changed and turned back to walk deeper into the camp, toward one of the empty shelters.

That's when he started flashing the laser at Steph to get her attention, and Steph gave Valentina her vidcam.

* * *

Valentina tried to smile at the quick pulses of the laser, but couldn't. Instead, she felt an unfamiliar moist warmth in her eyes, and a moment later tears were rolling down her face. She felt Allison's arms wrapping around her, and Valentina hugged the girl tight.

"I'm sorry," she said softly to Mills, taking care to form her words slowly in hopes he would understand what she was saying. "I want to save them. I want to save all of them. But I can't, can I?"

A pause, then one blink of the laser. No.

That was when the gong sounded once more, its deep tone echoing across the camp to signal the next round of bloody combat.

FIFTEEN

"Stand by for transpace sequence in sixty seconds." The artificial female voice of *Orion's* navigation computer echoed through the ship.

Sato was strapped into his command chair, his eyes fixed on the flag bridge displays that showed the computer's estimates of where the other ships in the fleet were in the hyperspace around them.

To the crew on the flag bridge he appeared calm, but his heart was hammering and his stomach churned. He had served aboard three ships that had been lost, two with all hands other than himself. He knew that *Orion* and her sisters would perform well, and that, unless he had completely underestimated the Kreelans, the battleships would outmatch anything the enemy could throw against them. Yet the ghosts of his dead shipmates haunted him still, a peculiar feeling that he hadn't been able to dispel.

His crews thought him a slave-driver, but he had also heard the scuttlebutt, the rumors, that he was a lucky sailor to have survived all that he had. His lips curled up slightly at the thought, wondering if the crew would still think that if they knew how many men and women had died on those ships. In a different age, he might have been considered a Jonah, a curse to his ship and crew.

Not this time, he told himself sternly. *This time it's going to be different.* The ships and crews were the finest in the fleet and the Kreelan forces awaiting them would be terribly outnumbered. This engagement wouldn't be decided by luck or blind fate. It would be decided by superior planning and overwhelming weight of fire.

"Ten seconds." The tension on the flag bridge rose even higher. "Transpace sequence in five...four..."

"Stand by!" Sato's hands tightened on the grips of his chair. The 1st Battleship Flotilla and its escorts were scheduled to jump in first, with the rest of the fleet right behind them.

"...three...two...one..." The computer voice paused. "Transpace sequence complete. Normal space emergence."

The computer generated display on the main flag bridge screen changed to show the actual view of the system, with Alger's World a bright disk taking up nearly half the screen. Green icons representing the other ships of the task force appeared around *Orion* and the three other battleships. They had all made it, and were in tight formation.

"All ships accounted for," the flag tactical officer reported.

"Data links...are working." The communications officer was surprised. "Links are up with the other ships of the flotilla and the escort group."

Sato frowned. "Take advantage of the connectivity, but be ready to cut over to voice and vidcom immediately. Let's not count on something we're almost sure to lose."

"Aye, sir."

"Enemy ships identified, commodore." Sato's flag captain highlighted eight red icons on the tactical display. "Two cruiser class and six destroyer class, just rounding Alger's World on a converging course."

"Inbound contacts!" The tactical officer looked up. "Classify as...friendly! It's the rest of the fleet, commodore. Right on schedule."

Sato watched intently as a cloud of green icons appeared on the display. One of them was a brighter green. It was *Guadalcanal*, Admiral Voroshilov's flagship. The assault carrier group had materialized right where they were supposed to be, in low orbit over Alger's World.

The Kreelan warships altered course, heading toward the carriers and their escorts. Sato saw that his task force was in a good position to intercept the enemy ships before they reached the assault group.

"Inform Admiral Voroshilov that the 1st Battleship Division will engage the enemy formation," Sato said formally to the flag communications officer. Then, to the flag captain, he said, "Have the task force alter course to intercept the enemy. Let's give them a taste of what *Orion* class battleships can do."

* * *

"Acknowledge Commodore Sato's signal," Admiral Voroshilov said to his tactical officer, "and wish him godspeed." He turned to the communications officer. "Is there any word from the ground reconnaissance teams?"

"Nothing yet, sir." She frowned at her console as she worked the controls. "The spectrum's clean. There's nothing from the automatic beacons, no voice contact, no civilian broadcasts. Nothing. We're transmitting the fleet beacon over the normal comm channels and then radio, but..." She shrugged her shoulders helplessly.

Voroshilov's comm panel chimed, and he looked down to see an incoming call from General Sparks, who was with his troops in the assault boats in the carrier's hold. "Yes, general?"

"We're ready to deploy, sir."

"We have nothing yet from the reconnaissance teams, my friend. I will not release the boats until we have targeting information."

"At least let us clear the carriers, admiral. The boats can tag along in formation until we hear something. If enemy warships come calling in strength, I'd rather my troopers...Marines...have a chance to get to the surface than be useless ballast aboard your carriers."

The admiral frowned, considering. The assault force had eight carriers, and had enough boats to drop all three divisions in one pass. While he was reluctant to deploy the boats on the chance that an overwhelming Kreelan fleet appeared, he hadn't come to Alger's World to lose. And when all was said and done, the Navy was here primarily to support the ground operation. Only Sparks and his Marines could actually save the people of the colony, and to do that they had to get on the ground. "Granted, general. I will issue the necessary orders. Prepare your Marines for immediate deployment."

"Thank you, sir!" Sparks was clearly relieved.

As his face disappeared from the small comm screen, Voroshilov looked up again to his communications officer, who shook her head.

Still no contact. His worry grew by the second as he turned his attention to the developing encounter between Sato's battleships and the Kreelan warships.

What had happened to the reconnaissance teams?

* * *

Mills watched the chronometer on his wrist, counting the seconds until the scheduled arrival of the fleet. The last hours had been agonizing as successive batches of people had been taken to the arenas. The longest any of them had lasted after Valentina's fight had been fifteen minutes, and while the first few groups had almost a fifty percent survival rate, the latter ones hadn't fared so well.

Despite Steph's best efforts at rallying their spirits, people were panicking.

"Bloody hell," he hissed, "where the devil's the fleet?" His worry was compounded by gnawing discomfort from the aches in his shoulders, arms, and neck from being stuck in the same position for so long. A trail of native insects, akin to large ants, had made a trail through his hide position, and he could feel a sick tickling sensation as they marched across his back. Fortunately, none of them had decided to take a bite of him. Even if they had, he wouldn't have been able to move.

He held the radio unit that Valentina had cobbled together. When he wasn't staring through the rifle scope to watch the activity in the camp, he was alternately stared at radio and his chronometer.

The fleet's past due. He wondered if the operation had been called off at the last minute. If so, he would still go through with the breakout plan, although the end game would still have every human on this world dead.

The gates opened up again and the warriors returned for more victims. This time they brought four survivors, one of whom was being carried by two of the others.

The people in the crowd surged back toward the rear fence of the camp. There weren't any more orderly groups of twenty people ready to face their doom. The returning survivors had been the last such group that Steph and Valentina had been able to organize. He had watched as Valentina had tried to go with every single group that went, but the warriors always refused her.

The two women, Allison, and the black man went to help the survivors.

The warriors stood waiting, but no one was volunteering to come forward.

"It's time, mate." There was no point in waiting any longer before putting his plan into action. If he didn't do something now, even more people would die, killed by the Kreelans or trampled in a panicked stampede like trapped animals. At least if they were freed from the camp they would have some small chance at freedom.

He pulled the remote detonator for the grenades from a pouch on his combat belt. Flipping up the arming cover, he was just easing pressure onto the button that would trigger the grenades when the radio console blinked.

Looking down quickly, he saw that it was displaying a beacon signal from *Guadalcanal*, the fleet's flagship.

Setting down the detonator, he pressed the transmit button on the console.

"*Guadalcanal*, this is Echo-Six," Mills whispered, hoping the radio had the power to reach the fleet. He knew Valentina wouldn't have put together a hunk of junk, but everything else for this mission had gone wrong, and he was expecting yet another disaster. "Come in, *Guadalcanal*."

His hopes sagged as he heard nothing but silence, and was about to call again when a voice boomed in his ear.

"Echo-Six, this is *Guadalcanal*. Fleet is in position and awaiting targeting information, over."

"Thank you, God." Mills didn't consider himself much of a believer, but he figured it couldn't hurt. He pressed the transmit button. "*Guadalcanal*, target concentration is in the town of Breakwater, located at..." He read a string of coordinates. "Note that we have several thousand civilians being held here. I'm going to try and break them out, but will need help fast to keep the enemy from hunting us down."

"Understood, Echo-Six. Have you had any contact with the other teams?"

"Negative." Mills tensed as saw movement in the camp. Putting his eye again to the rifle scope, he saw that the Kreelans were beginning to move toward the crowd of people to take the next victims. "We've had no contact with them since the drop and assume they've been neutralized. We have no other information on other Kreelan concentrations, but there's a bloody trainload of them here."

Valentina, Steph, and the black man made to intervene between the warriors and the terrified people, but the Kreelans waved the stun wands at them, forcing them to back off.

"Listen, mate, just send a bloody division here to Breakwater as fast as you please. Tell them to expect a very hot reception. I've got to go. Echo-Six, out."

Shutting down the radio and carefully putting it back in its makeshift case, Mills grabbed up the remote detonator and held it in his left hand. Then he snugged the big rifle into his shoulder with his right hand, staring through the scope at the disaster about to unfold in the camp.

Taking a deep breath, he pushed the button on the detonator.

* * *

Ku'ar-Marekh looked into the sky as she felt it, a wave of excitement and bloodlust from the warriors of the ships orbiting above.

Casting her mind's eye upward, she found the human ships that had come to do battle. She sensed the elation of the shipmistresses as they saw that they were not only outnumbered, but that the humans had with them a new class of warship, far more powerful than any of the Imperial ships in this system. They stood no chance of survival, but their deaths would bring great glory to the Empress.

She also sensed…something else. Expanding the reach of her spirit as she slowed time, she flowed through the human ships until she found it. Him.

The Messenger.

Ku'ar-Marekh considered this for a long moment. A Messenger had never been killed, in all the ages recorded in the Books of Time, even in the age of chaos before the Empire.

It was also true that one who had been so marked had never again engaged in battle, for that was part of the Way. Yet this Messenger, as was well known among all the priestesses and many warriors, had fought after he had been marked, and in his last battle had been shown a great mercy by Li'ara-Zhurah, a disciple of Tesh-Dar.

It had brought great honor to the young warrior, but Ku'ar-Marekh was not inclined to be charitable. If the Messenger had again taken up the sword, then he was willing to die by it. It was not the Way of the Empress, but perhaps it was for the humans.

"In Her name," Ku'ar-Marekh whispered, "let it be so."

She turned to the warriors surrounding the arenas, who had also felt the stirring in the Bloodsong. "More humans have come to give battle to our sisters in the fleet. Let us continue the Challenge until the arrival of their warriors."

The peers gave a horrendous roar of joy even as they felt the ecstatic pulses in the Bloodsong of the warriors in orbit as they began to die.

Their roar of blood lust was drowned out by rippling explosions coming from the direction of the holding pen.

* * *

"Targets in range, commodore." The flag tactical officer looked up at Sato, nodding.

On the main screen on *Orion's* flag bridge, icons representing the battleships were joined with the rapidly approaching Kreelan warships with thin lines indicating the targets designated for each ship.

Sato leaned back in his command chair. "Open fire."

As one, the guns of the four battleships spoke. Each ship was precisely aligned along the projected track of four of the six enemy destroyers. A moment after Sato's command was relayed, four beams of intense light stabbed out from the bow of each ship, and an instant later the four destroyers disappeared in titanic fireballs.

Sato felt a sense of deep satisfaction. The pulse cannons had been largely ineffective when mounted in smaller vessels because of their huge energy requirements. The battleships, on the other hand, had power to spare from their four massive fusion plants, and the energy drain on other systems in the ship was negligible. The recycle time was less also than ten seconds before the ship could fire the weapon again.

The remaining two enemy destroyers and the pair of cruisers didn't disappoint Sato. Instead of trying to run, they began a complex evasion pattern as they tried to work their way closer to the carrier strike group.

"Kinetics firing...now."

The twelve thirty centimeter main guns of each of the four battleships fired, sending their massive shells toward the volume of space through which the Kreelan ships had to pass to reach the carriers. The hull of the *Orion* echoed with man-made thunder as the guns salvoed five rounds each.

"Magnify the view, if you please." Sato wanted to see the effects of the weapons on the enemy ships. The optical station at the fore end of the ship zoomed in on the enemy vessels, capturing their rakish lines and haunting runes that adorned their flanks.

The entire flag bridge crew stared at the tactical display, watching the rounds trace their way through virtual space to finally intersect with the four remaining Kreelan warships.

The shells fired by the battleships each contained fifteen submunitions, smaller shells inside the larger casing. Once they reached a certain range from the enemy ships, the larger shells split open, ejecting the submunitions. It was much like a titanic shotgun, and the effect was dramatic.

The Kreelan ships were blasting away at the inbound shells and managed to destroy over half of them, but that still left hundreds inbound.

A cascade of explosions erupted from the enemy ships. One of the two destroyers turned into the storm of shells in what Sato credited as the only reasonable maneuver, as there was some slim possibility it might avoid them altogether. Its point defense weapons were firing desperately until a submunition punched right into its bow. The munitions were set to detonate a fraction of a second after impact, allowing them time to penetrate into a ship's vital areas. In this case, the shell found something vital indeed, as a massive explosion amidships tore the ship in two.

The second destroyer must have run into a closely-packed cluster of munitions. One minute it was there, the next it was gone. There was no spectacular explosion, only the flares of the submunitions as they detonated. The ship was simply torn apart. The debris twirled away, and some of the hull fragments were hit by even more submunitions.

The cruisers fared little better. A hail of explosions marched across their hulls, and while they could absorb more punishment, no cruiser could absorb that much. Both ships lost way and began to stray off course. One of them ran into a chunk of the second destroyer and disappeared in a massive explosion that left only her drive section visible beyond an expanding cloud of gas and debris.

The remaining cruiser simply drifted along, its shattered hull streaming air and debris, its drives torn apart.

Looking at the projected trajectory for the hulk shown on the tactical display, Sato saw that it would eventually enter the atmosphere and burn up. Any members of her crew who might still be alive would come to a fiery end.

Good enough, he thought with grim satisfaction.

The flag bridge crew broke into a cheer that was echoed throughout the battleships. It was the most one-sided engagement, favoring humans, that had yet been fought in the war.

"Incoming from the flag, sir." The communications officer was smiling.

Sato answered the call on his vidcom. "Yes, admiral?"

"I simply wanted to pass on my compliments, commodore." An unusual smile lit up his face. "Please pass on to your crews my thanks for a truly superb performance."

"Thank you, sir." Sato nodded, unable to resist a slight smile himself. "The crews will appreciate that. As do I." He paused a moment. "Sir, what's the situation on the ground?"

That wiped the smile from Voroshilov's face. "It is grim, commodore. We were only able to contact one of the ground teams very briefly. From their report…it is unclear how many survivors there may be, but at least several thousand are in immediate peril. General Sparks is deploying the

10th Armored Division to the contact position indicated by the reconnaissance team, while we hold the other two divisions in reserve. Beyond that...we can only hope."

"Yes, sir," Sato agreed quietly. "Your orders, admiral?"

"Maintain high orbit over the carrier group. I suspect that our blue-skinned friends will bring in reinforcements soon."

"We'll be ready, sir." Sato looked at the bright disk of Alger's World, wondering at the horrors that must have taken place there, and perhaps still were.

Sixteen

"It should be time." Valentina looked at her chronometer, then at where Mills was in the woods. She was wearing Steph's vidcam, but the laser was silent. "Everyone will need to be ready. Whether the fleet comes or not, we're going to break out of here."

"God, I hope they come." Jackson had suffered a few cuts and bruises in his fight before defeating the warrior he'd faced. In a way he'd felt guilty, because she looked like nothing more than a teenager. But his guilt was assuaged by his need to survive. Teenager or not, she'd been determined to kill him.

"They will." Steph looked up, as if she could see the fleet's ships in orbit. *Ichiro will come. I know he will.* "I'll tell the others."

"Is Mills going to get us out?" Allison trailed behind Steph, leaving Valentina to alternate between watching for a signal from Mills and waiting for the warriors to bring back any survivors.

"Yes, honey. You like him, don't you?"

"Yes. He's funny, especially the way he talks. And big. I just wish he were here now."

"It won't be long."

They came close enough to the crowd huddling at the back of the pen for Steph to be heard. "Listen to me!" Her shout got their attention. "The fleet should be here any time now. Some Marines-" She glossed over the fact that there was only one, Mills. "-are going to create a diversion so we can break out of here. When the time comes, go as fast as you can. And if any warriors are in your way, mob them! Even unarmed, there are a lot more of us than them."

"But they'll kill us!" The cry came from deep within the crowd, but was echoed on many faces.

"Yes, they'll kill some of us. But would you rather take a chance dying on your way to freedom, or be killed in there?" She pointed in the direction of the arenas. "Those are you choices! When it's time, head into the woods toward the fields east of town." She and Valentina had decided to send everyone there, as that seemed the most likely place for the Marines to land.

"What about all the warriors guarding us?" Someone asked.

"The diversion will take care of some of them. We just have to take our chances with the rest."

"Steph!" Valentina called. "The warriors are coming back!"

With Allison right behind her, Steph ran back to where Valentina and Jackson stood. The warriors marched back through the gates, but this time there were only three survivors. One of them was so badly injured that the other two had to carry him.

Jackson took the weight of the injured man, with Allison wrapping her thin arm around the man's waist to help, while Steph and Valentina helped the other two, a man and a woman.

"It was a slaughter." The woman was gasping, and there was a deep cut in her side. "Most of the others were finished in a few minutes. God, that hurts."

"I know it hurts," Steph told her, "but you'd better be ready to run. The fleet should be here any minute, and Marines out in the woods are going to start a diversion to help get us out of here."

"Don't worry." The woman managed a smile that quickly turned to a grimace. "You'll have to run fast to catch up to me."

Valentina helped the other survivor, a man whose leg had a long gash but was otherwise uninjured, to one of the shelters. She looked back at the warriors, and could tell that something was different. Their demeanor had changed, as if they were agitated.

I wonder if they know something. Several of them glanced up at the sky, and she looked up herself just in time to see four miniature suns ignite, low on the western horizon.

The crowd of people murmured behind her. They, too, had seen the flashes.

"They're here, by God!" Jackson shouted. "Somebody in low orbit just bought it."

"The warriors!" Allison cried as the aliens began to move farther into the camp, toward the crowd of people.

Valentina, with Jackson and Steph beside her, moved forward to try and intervene. The Kreelans didn't threaten them with lethal weapons, but the leader and several others pulled out the stun batons they had used to take them captive.

"Damn." Jackson pulled Valentina and Steph back. They couldn't afford to be stunned and helpless. Not now.

The warriors were just moving past them to take the next group of victims when the forest along the rear fence of the camp was ripped apart by a series of explosions.

* * *

Mills watched in satisfaction as the grenades detonated, tearing through the line of warriors guarding the rear of the camp. He hadn't actually expected many of the warriors to be killed or wounded, but at least half of them went down under a hail of shrapnel and wood splinters.

He cringed as some of the people lining the fence went down, too, screaming as they were cut and slashed.

There was nothing he could do for them now, and he shifted his attention to the warriors who had come for more victims, and who now were momentarily dazed by his little diversion.

Centering the crosshairs right between the breasts of the leading warrior, he stroked the big rifle's trigger. It fired with a deafening crack, jolting him back with the massive recoil. When he adjusted his aim to where the warrior had been standing, what was left of her body below the midriff was just collapsing to the ground. The rest of her was gone.

He didn't celebrate the shot, but took aim on a line of three warriors, swords drawn, who were running straight at the civilians.

He fired. Two of them went down and the third spun off to the side, all victims of the same shot.

The people along the fence recovered from the shock of the explosions and, following the instructions that Steph and Valentina had given them, tore down the fence and began to run.

"Damn." His sight picture was blocked by the escapees, and he had to take careful aim at the blue-skinned faces working their way toward the mass of civilians.

He fired and fired again, and kept firing until he'd expended the twenty-eight rounds he had for the sniper rifle, dropping at least one enemy warrior with every shot.

After he fired the last round, he looked through the scope, desperately hoping to see Valentina.

He shook his head in wonder when he found her. Covered in the blood of the enemy, she was wielding a sword in each hand, battling the few warriors who remained standing. Even in that brief moment, he saw other people taking up the weapons of now-dead warriors and joining her, hacking and slashing at the warriors.

Tossing the now-useless sniper rifle to the side, Mills grabbed up his assault rifle and charged forward to help them.

* * *

"Now!" Valentina screamed at the top of her lungs to the other prisoners after the booms of the grenades had faded. "Take down the fence and run for it!"

The people along the fence who hadn't been badly hurt by shrapnel from the grenades reacted instantly, tearing the fence apart and running headlong into the woods.

Valentina was just about to go after the leader of the warriors who had come for the next victims, and who was leading her cohorts after the defenseless civilians, when the Kreelan's upper body simply exploded, covering Valentina with blood and gore.

Ignoring the blood bath, she snatched the sword from the warrior's hand as the severed arm fell. Then she pirouetted, driving the blade into the belly of another warrior who was charging past her.

Taking that warrior's sword, as well, she turned, ready to fight. For a moment she had no targets, for the warriors in the camp were systematically being cut down by the sniper fire coming from the woods.

You're almost as good as me, Mills, she thought with a blood-stained smile as one of the few surviving warriors charged her, bellowing a challenge.

Valentina blocked the warrior's overhand cut with an upward block with her left sword before cutting deep into the warrior's thigh with the sword held in her right hand. The warrior went down, and Valentina finished her with a quick stab to the throat.

Jackson was at her side, a sword in his hands, followed by Steph, who held her own captured weapon.

More people armed themselves and joined them, trying to fend off the warriors who swarmed around from the sides of the enclosure to cut off the retreat of the civilians.

Steph watched in horror as the children Allison had saved, every one of them, burst from the stampede of people, heading right toward her and Valentina.

"No!" Steph cried as a group of Kreelans broke through and charged right toward the children. They screamed in terror as the swords flashed down in deadly arcs.

The blades never touched their intended victims. A burst of fire from an assault rifle hammered the warriors backward, revealing the grimy and exhausted form of Roland Mills.

"Good to see you again, girls." He flashed a bright smile as his eyes continued sweeping the area for nearby threats.

"Mills!" A chorus of young voices sounded above the bedlam of the escaping prisoners as the children clustered around the big Marine, as if he were a rock in the middle of a raging river.

"When we get out of this," Valentina said, pausing as Mills blasted a pair of warriors who were getting too close, "I'm going to take you and-"

"Where's Allison?" Steph asked. "She was right next to me!"

All of them looked around, trying to spot the girl in the chaos swirling around them.

"There she is!" Jackson said, pointing.

There was Allison, about twenty meters away, helping a young man who was bleeding badly from his side, the victim of one of the Kreelan flying weapons.

"Allison!" Steph shouted, sprinting toward her.

"Steph, wait!" Mills cried, catching sight of more warriors who had come through the woods and were now vaulting the fence into the camp. "Christ!" Taking careful aim, he fired past Steph, Allison, and the injured man, who were right in between him and the oncoming warriors.

Jackson ran over and relieved Allison of her burden, putting the injured man's arm across his shoulder and his own arm around the man's waist.

Allison had just turned toward Steph, reaching out her hand, when the injured man and Jackson both cried out and pitched forward to the ground. The injured man was now dead, a Kreelan flying weapon embedded in his spinal column. Jackson had one of the weapons protruding from his lower back, but managed to get to his feet using the sword as a crutch, a grimace of agony on his face.

"Run!" Steph screamed, shoving Allison ahead of her, shielding the girl with her body as more of the flying weapons hissed toward them.

Steph's left leg collapsed under her. As she fell to the ground, she could see a deep line of scarlet across her leg where one of the weapons had cut deep into her thigh. She didn't feel any pain yet, so sharp was the blade.

Looking up, she saw Allison stop and turn back toward her. "No, Allison! Run!"

Then she fainted.

Without a thought, Allison ran back to her, falling to her knees and catching Steph by the shoulders as she slumped to the ground.

"Allison!" Mills shouted. "Get out of there! Run!"

With an agonized look on her face, Allison shook her head as she cradled Steph, trying to hold the unconscious woman's head and shoulders out of the churned-up soil. "I can't leave her!"

"Oh, God." Mills saw warriors pouring through the gates from the direction of the arenas. A number of Jackson's people tried to fight them off, but there were too many. He fired his assault rifle into the mass of aliens as Valentina ran forward to help Jackson. She tossed him over her shoulder as if he were a young child and ran back to Mills while he held the Kreelans at bay.

"Take him!" She quickly set the groaning Jackson on his feet next to Mills, who wrapped a powerful arm around Jackson's waist as he fired the assault rifle with his other hand.

Then the rifle's magazine ran out.

"Shit!" Mills looked helplessly at Valentina. "That was all the ammo!"

"Put me down," Jackson wheezed. "Put me down, dammit."

The children, who looked around wide-eyed at the cataclysm unfolding around them, made room as Mills set Jackson down.

"Grenade." Jackson held out his hands.

"Aye, mate." Mills snatched the last grenade from his combat belt and handed it to Jackson. His eyes met the other man's and held them for a long moment.

"Now get these kids out of here." Jackson gave Mills a bloody smile as he popped the safety cap off the grenade.

"He's right." Valentina had to shout in Mills's ear, as her voice was drowned out by the sonic booms of assault boats from the fleet. "You've got to get the children to safety."

"No!" Mills stared at her, his heart hammering with dread. The only other woman he'd ever loved had died in front of his eyes at the hands of one of these alien beasts, and he wasn't about to let it happen again. "I am not leaving you behind!"

"We don't have time." She pulled him down and kissed him hard on the mouth. Pulling away, she said, "I'll see you on that beach someday, Mills."

Then she was gone. Sprinting inhumanly fast, she ran to protect Steph and Allison just as they were about to be overrun. The blades of her crimson-stained swords caught the afternoon sun as a tide of howling warriors swarmed over them.

His heart a cold, dead stone in his chest, Mills gathered up the children and led them away just as Confederation assault boats roared overhead, coming in to land.

* * *

Jackson ignored the agony in his back. He could feel blood pouring from the wound. He'd been hit in the kidney. His vision was fading quickly, but he had time enough.

Warriors had surrounded the women, and more were heading right toward him in pursuit of the fleeing civilians.

Noticing that he was still alive, one of the aliens paused just long enough to raise her sword as the others sped around him.

"Fuck you, bitch." Jackson smiled as he pressed the detonator with his thumb.

* * *

No other human being could do what Valentina was doing, because none had the special implants that poured adrenaline and other chemicals into her system, speeding up her reaction time, increasing her strength.

She wasn't invulnerable, and the warriors could have overwhelmed her had they worked together. Instead, they swept around her, Steph, and Allison to form a ring, an arena bounded by warriors, as more continued to chase after the fleeing civilians.

The warriors took turns, seemingly at random, dashing into the makeshift arena to challenge her. One after another they came, and one after another she killed them, her swords whirling, slashing and stabbing as she danced around Allison and Steph, protecting them.

She had no idea how long she had been fighting when they stopped coming at her. Looking up from where her latest victim was collapsing to the ground, she saw that the surrounding warriors were now kneeling.

"Valentina!" Allison was pointing. "It's *her*."

The warrior leader stood a few paces away, somehow having appeared out of thin air. She was staring at Valentina with her silver-flecked, vaguely feline eyes.

Raising her swords, Valentina prepared to fight.

The warrior held out her hands, and the swords were torn from Valentina's grip, flying as if by magic to the warrior, who deftly caught them. She held them out, and another warrior dashed forward to take them. The warrior leader said something in her language, and eight warriors rose to their feet and came forward.

Valentina tensed, ready for the worst, but none of the aliens drew their weapons. Instead, six came to stand before her, briefly bowing their heads, while the other two knelt next to Steph and carefully lifted her from the ground. The ring of warriors parted as they carried her in the direction of the arenas, and the warrior leader gestured for Valentina to follow.

"Come on." Valentina held out her blood-covered hand for Allison.

"What are they going to do?" Allison got up and clutched Valentina's hand, ignoring the blood.

"I think they're going to let us live. At least for now." The two of them followed after the warriors who carried Steph, and the six other warriors fell in behind them.

Valentina glanced back as she heard the rumble of hover engines from the assault boats in the fields beyond the woods.

The warrior leader was staring off in the same direction as another warrior came up and began to speak to her.

* * *

"My priestess." Esah-Kuran bowed her head and saluted, raising her left fist to her right breast. "The humans land in force around us. We await your command."

Ku'ar-Marekh knew this, of course, for beyond the obvious senses of sight and sound that told her of the human craft landing their warriors, her mind's eye had cast about them, seeing all there was to see, knowing all there was to know.

She saw the many warriors and the great metal machines that were such treasured prey for her warriors descend from the landing craft, even as the tide of humans who had escaped from the pen began to reach them.

"Make sure these humans," she gestured to where the three had been taken to the *Kalai-Il*, "are well-kept until I return."

Then she closed her eyes and opened her mind to the Bloodsong so that her warriors would know her will.

* * *

"Marines!" Mills ran through the field from the woods, panting as he carried two of the younger children, one in each arm.

He had reached the Marines' defensive positions around the landing zone. The empty fields he had crossed the night before were now a beehive of activity as dozens of assault boats disgorged Marines, tanks, and other vehicles and equipment that were part of the 10th Armored Division. Hundreds of Marines were trying to gather up the panicked civilians and get them into boats that were empty of their cargos and ready to return to the carriers.

He was surrounded by Marines offering helping hands, gently taking the children and leading them to a nearby boat.

"First Sergeant Mills." One of the Marines recognized Mills's rank insignia and his name patch and had called it in. "General Sparks wants to see you ASAP."

"Where is he?"

"There, sir." The Marine pointed to a massive M-90 Wolverine tank about a hundred meters away that had a pennant waving wildly from a mast on the turret. "Just look for the guy wearing the biggest damn pistol you ever saw."

"I know him." Mills started off, but paused as a hand gripped his.

It was Vanhi, one of Allison's friends.

"Thank you, Mr. Mills." Then she hugged him. He returned it, biting back the urge to burst into tears.

"Get on the boat, young lady."

She nodded, then turned and went with the boat's loadmaster.

Running to where Sparks's Wolverine squatted on the field, Mills climbed up the track skirt onto the engine deck, then onto the turret.

Sparks was kneeling on the turret roof, surrounded by his staff officers and the commanders of the 32nd Armored Brigade, the first unit to hit dirt.

"Mills." The general's intense blue eyes glittered in the sunlight. "You did a damn fine job. A damn fine job!"

"Thank you, sir." Mills bobbed his head in acknowledgement as he tried to bring his breathing under control.

Sparks held up a display pad that showed a large red swath, like an intense thunderstorm on radar, that circled most of the way around the town of Breakwater, with a large red patch right in the middle of the town. "This is a thermal plot we got of the enemy from orbit. Does this match up with what you've seen on the ground?" With the Kreelans interfering with human technology, seemingly at will, Sparks had very little trust in what any electronic sensors told him.

"Yes, sir." Mills pointed to a spot on the screen where the red was particularly intense. "They built some sort of temple or something in the town square, along with arenas where they were making the civilians fight them. And in the woods around the town there are thousands of warriors." He shook his head. "It's hard to know how many, sir, but I'd say at least five thousand. Maybe more."

"What about the cities to the north and south?" Sparks zoomed out on the map. "Any idea of enemy concentrations there, or how many civilians may be left?"

"We weren't able to find out anything about any other Kreelan forces, sir, but from what we heard from some of the civvies, there are still quite a few people around the cities. But it seems like most of the Kreelans are concentrated here."

Sparks zoomed out more, with the display now showing the entire continent. "We've got recon boats searching all the other major population centers, but so far they haven't reported back."

"Sir..."

Sparks pinned him with his eyes. The general was a thin, wiry man of average height, but the intensity of his gaze commanded respect from every man and woman who encountered him. "Spit it out, first sergeant."

"One of the warriors here, sir. The leader, has...I don't know how to describe it without sounding like I've lost my mind, sir, but she's like a bloody witch."

"Like the one who rearranged your face on Keran and again on Saint Petersburg?"

Mills nodded. "Yes, sir, but not the same one. I don't know much of what she can do other than what one of the civilians..." He had to bite his lip at that point, thinking of Allison's face, looking back at him as the Kreelans swarmed over her. "...what one of the civilians told me. That she can pop out of thin air right next to you. But I believe her."

"Is there anything I can do about this warrior except blow her to bits?"

"No, sir. I just wanted you to know."

Sparks nodded. "Then we'll have to hope that a frag round will do the job when the time comes."

"There's something else."

Sparks stared at him.

"Valentina Sikorsky and Stephanie Guillaume-Sato were..." Mills hesitated, unable to say the word that he knew had to be said. Killed. He couldn't say it, because doing that would have somehow made it real, and it was a reality he simply wasn't prepared to deal with, a reality that he refused to acknowledge.

Sparks saved him from having to cross that abyss. "Damn. I'm sorry, son." He looked toward the town, his expression hard as the armor of the tank on which they knelt. "I guess I'll have to inform the commodore. And Valentina...I'm sorry."

"Yes, sir." Mills felt himself choking up. "General, if it wouldn't be too much trouble-"

An alarm sounded, a piercing siren that wailed from several of the boats and brought all activity in the landing zone to a dead stop.

His comm unit chimed before his operations officer came on. "Sir, we've got an inbound air attack!"

A wave of red dots appeared on the miniature tactical display Sparks was holding.

Then the sensor feed went dark and the red icons disappeared.

Disgusted, Sparks tossed the display into its bin inside the turret and keyed his comm unit. "All units, air action west, I repeat, air action west!"

That broke the spell. Everyone in the landing zone leaped into action, trying to get the last of the Marines unloaded before cramming in the civilians. Boats began to lift off, staying low as they turned away from the approaching Kreelan ships.

The Wolverine tanks of the brigade's armored regiment moved forward, turning to face the threat. The muzzles of their fifteen centimeter guns elevated as the crews prepared for the attack.

The Marine infantry around them fanned out, aiming their own weapons in the same direction. Every one of them knew that their assault rifles probably wouldn't scratch the Kreelan boats, but they would fire if he or she got the chance.

Sparks turned to Mills. "You've done enough here, first sergeant." He gestured to the nearest boat. "Hop aboard and get the hell out of here."

"Yes, sir!"

As Sparks turned his attention to managing the battle, Mills quickly climbed down the Wolverine's flank and headed in the direction of the assault boat.

They're dead. The words kept ringing in his head as he trudged toward the boat. He was tortured with the image of Valentina disappearing into the mass of warriors, trying to defend Allison and Steph as warriors swarmed around them like water flowing past a rock in a river.

The scene played over and over in his mind. He slowed his pace, then finally stopped, staring at the boat's gaping hold as Marines continued to stream out of it.

You didn't see them die. It was an easy rationalization to make, even if it made no sense at all. Steph was down, Allison helpless beside her, and Valentina couldn't have fought so many warriors. It was impossible. There was no reason the warriors swarming into the compound wouldn't have killed them.

No reason...except for the warrior leader. She had let Allison live. She must have known that Mills and his team were hiding at the farm, but she didn't come for them right away. When she did, she took the women and children prisoner when she could have easily killed them all.

It didn't make any sense.

Then his encounters with the huge warrior on Keran and Saint Petersburg came back to him. He had never really understood why she had let him live when she could so easily have killed him any time she pleased, both times they'd fought. The fights had almost been like Saturday night brawls in a pub.

Then it dawned on him. The Kreelans didn't care about winning as humans thought about it. For them, the pleasure was in how the game was played, and the tougher the opponent, the better.

And who could be a more formidable opponent for the warrior with the dead eyes than Valentina?

"You're just making this up, you fool."

Perhaps. But looking at the hold of the boat, he realized that he had nothing to live for, no future but a violent death. He wouldn't have any cushy retirement, reminiscing at the pub with a bunch of other old codgers. No one would in this war. His pension would be the blade of a Kreelan sword through his gut.

He accepted that he was going to die in this war. But if he was going to give his life, he wanted it to be for something that mattered to him. Even if it was only a lunatic idea about an alien's motivations.

"Move it, Marines! We're lifting!" The boat's loadmaster was windmilling one arm as if he were making an underhand softball pitch, urging the Marines to get off. His eyes were glued to the western horizon.

Mills made his decision. Turning and running after the last batch of Marines that had passed by, he caught up to the one he wanted. The platoon's sniper. If his lunatic speculation about the warrior leader was right, there could be only one place she'd take Valentina and the other women. The arenas. And for him to help, he'd need a weapon with a long reach.

"You there, Marine!"

"First sergeant?" The Marine, a sergeant, stepped out of line, his eyes darting to the west as the defensive barrage opened up. Tracers from the Marines' weapons and point defense lasers from the boats arced toward the small but rapidly approaching shapes of the Kreelan ships.

The sniper's squad leader turned and was about to give Mills an earful when he saw that Mills was a first sergeant. Not only that, he was covered in mud, blood, and had a wild-eyed look.

The young Marine snapped his mouth shut.

"Your rifle." Mills pointed at the sniper's weapon, a twin of the one he had used earlier. "Give it to me. And your ammo. Now."

The Marine turned to his squad leader, a helpless look on his face.

"Now, old son. I don't have time to argue or explain." Mills held out his hands.

"Do it." The squad leader had to shout over the racket of the gunfire and roar from the engines of more assault boats as they rose into the air, trying to flee. "I hope you know what the hell you're doing, first sergeant."

"I do, too, lad." Mills took the weapon and slung it over his shoulder, then clipped the ammo bandolier to his combat belt. "Believe me, I do, too."

With that, he turned and ran through the formation just as dozens of Kreelan attack ships screamed in over the trees from the direction of town.

SEVENTEEN

Ku'ar-Marekh opened her eyes after blinding the humans' electronic eyes. It was not something she could accomplish on her own, but she acted as a conduit for the power and will of the Empress. It was a role that only high priestesses such as herself could fulfill, for the surge of raw power through the Bloodsong would kill even the hardiest of her warriors.

Other than the small force guarding the humans for whom Ku'ar-Marekh had special plans, all the warriors here had gathered to welcome the human warriors.

Sensing the approach of her attack ships, Ku'ar-Marekh turned to Esah-Kuran. "Let it begin."

As the attack ships soared overhead, ten thousand warriors charged from the tree line along the edge of the landing zone.

* * *

Lasers and cannon fire from the incoming Kreelan ships tore through the assault boats that were still on the ground, turning half a dozen into flaming pyres of debris in mere seconds. Three more boats were shot down as they tried to lift, and a fourth was brought down just before it reached the relative safety of the low hills to the east.

Sparks stood on his seat in the turret of his tank so he could see out the commander's cupola. He had always preferred to see the battlefield directly, and hated it when he had to button up and close the hatch.

"Anti-air round, up!" The tank's gunner, who was also acting as its commander while Sparks worried about the conduct of the battle, was tracking one of the wasp-like Kreelan ships with his main gun. "Firing!"

The tank rocked back on its tracks as the gun fired with a deafening roar and a huge tongue of flame from the muzzle.

The anti-air round the tank had fired was a huge shotgun shell that was set to go off when it came close enough to a target. It was a relatively primitive weapon compared to the much smarter missiles that the tanks were designed to carry, but Sparks had insisted that each tank carry some. In this war, he had discovered, simpler was often better.

The other Wolverines fired the standard anti-air rounds, small smart missiles that were almost impossible to evade or spoof.

"Son of a bitch." He watched as every one of the missiles followed a ballistic trajectory from the tanks, flying "dumb." None of them maneuvered or came close to hitting any of the Kreelan attackers. "All units, use the anti-air rounds!"

The attacking ships were now close enough that the smaller weapons like the gatling guns mounted on the tops of the tanks and some of the other vehicles began to open up.

One of the ships, then more, started taking hits. The anti-air round Sparks's gunner had fired went off, and they were rewarded with a bright yellow fireball as the target ship exploded.

Sparks was sure the enemy ships would try to evade, but they didn't. They flew straight into the curtain of fire from his Marines.

A chill ran down his spine as he realized what they were doing. "Kamikazes!"

He was partly correct. A third of the ships didn't make it through the defensive fire, and Sparks grimaced as they plowed into the landing zone, killing dozens of Marines and reducing eight Wolverines to burning slag.

The rest of the ships, most of them damaged and streaming smoke as the Marines continued to fire at them, streaked overhead.

Sparks thought they were pursuing the departing assault boats. Then he saw a cloud of black objects leap from the ships, which were about half the size of the assault boats.

Warriors.

His Marines didn't need any orders from their general. The air over the landing zone was filled with thousands of weapons firing at the aliens gliding on thin parasails toward the ground. The enemy wasn't content to just use swords this time around. They had rifles, too, and were lethal shots.

The tanks and infantry combat vehicles swept the sky with their gatling guns. Firing at over a hundred rounds per second, they killed warriors by the dozens while they were falling toward the ground.

A few hundred warriors managed to reach the ground alive, but they wouldn't enjoy the sort of victory they had over the human forces deployed to Keran in the first major battle of the war. Most of the men and women with Sparks had seen combat, and weren't surprised or terrified by the aliens. They met them with blazing assault rifles and, when the Kreelans got too close, unsheathed combat knives.

That's when Sparks heard a roar like the rising wind before a storm.

"General!" His deputy commander was calling over the radio. He was in the command vehicle near the center of the landing zone. It was his job and that of the combat controllers with him to make sure that orders and reports made it to where they were supposed to go. "The southern flank, sir!"

Sparks turned and looked, and for one of the few times in his life, even during the desperate hours of the Battle of Keran, he felt a stab of fear. A massive line of warriors had emerged from the trees and was charging toward the brigade's positions, the warriors howling as they ran, their swords drawn.

That wasn't what frightened him. It was the warrior who led them, who was floating above the ground like a ghost, her arms extended out to her sides as if they were wings. As he boosted the magnification on the vision block in his cupola, it looked like she was staring right at him.

The entire brigade opened up in what should have been a hailstorm of death. Instead, every round, whether fired from assault rifles or the tanks, made a bright flare about a meter short of the line of warriors, then simply fell to the ground, molten or burning. The warriors, incredibly nimble in the black armor they wore, bounded over or danced around the spatters and pools of sizzling metal.

The Marine infantry moved forward while the Wolverines maneuvered back, trying to keep their distance from the oncoming alien horde. Had it not been for the strange shield protecting the warriors, the tanks could have gutted the alien charge. But now the huge vehicles were rapidly coming into range of the hellish Kreelan grenades and would be slaughtered if Sparks couldn't get them clear, and the Marine infantry now had to protect the tanks.

Led by their own angel of death, the warriors ran behind their protective shield right up to the outermost Marine positions, when the shield disappeared. The line of warriors slammed into the Marines like a steel curtain, the air filling with the screams of the dying and those doing the killing, the crash of metal on metal and non-stop weapons fire.

Sparks knew there was no choice. He had to play their game. For now. He looked back toward the middle of the landing zone where the Kreelans had airdropped in. There was still a snarling fight going on, but a company of Marines could finish it. It had only been a diversionary attack.

He contacted his deputy commander. "Move every Marine who isn't involved in the contact inside the LZ to the southern flank and get them into the fight."

"Understood, sir." His deputy's voice was tight. "But if we get hit by more warriors on either end of the line, they could turn our flank. Or worse."

"I'm counting on it, colonel." Sparks saw with approval that the infantry units in the LZ were already moving forward toward the massive brawl. Part of the defensive line was already sagging where the lead warrior was cutting his Marines down like paper dolls, but more Marines piled in, fighting with assault rifles, knives, entrenching tools, and fists. "Just move our infantry forward so I can maneuver my tanks." After a pause, he added, "And get me through to Commodore Sato in the fleet."

* * *

With space above Alger's World secured, most of the crew on *Orion's* flag bridge was watching the secondary display showing a computer-generated depiction of the ground battle. Few could make heads or tails of it, because it resembled nothing so much as a battle between a huge force of red ants and a larger force of blue ants.

Sato allowed them that indulgence because he knew that the tactical and communications officers were fully focused on monitoring the fleet and the space around it, which was blissfully, almost disturbingly calm. For one of the few times since the war had begun, a human fleet had complete and total space supremacy, at least for a time.

He saw the flag communications officer stiffen, then turn to look at Sato. Then he got up and handed Sato his headset.

"It's a direct comm from General Sparks on the surface, sir."

Frowning, Sato put on the headset. "General Sparks, sir?"

"A moment, commodore." Sparks's voice was calm, but Sato could hear a riot of sound in the background, voices shouting orders and reports, punctuated by the unmistakable crack of a large caliber weapon, a tank's main gun. "We're in full contact down here and I don't have much time."

Sato glanced up, seeing the entire flag bridge crew now staring at him. He pointed at the tactical officer and gestured him over. "We're standing by to provide orbital bombardment, general, but it will be terribly dangerous until you can break contact and-"

"Your wife's dead." Sparks paused. "Sorry to sound like a heartless bastard, but there's no easy way to say it."

"General, I don't understand." *Steph, dead?* He couldn't get his mind around the words. Even if it were true, how would Sparks know? Steph was back on Earth.

"She was on one of the recon teams as an embedded journalist, just like she was with my unit at Keran. First Sergeant Roland Mills just informed me that the enemy...got her. I'm sorry, commodore. Damn sorry."

"Yes," Sato answered weakly as the color seemed to drain from the universe around him. "Thank you for letting me know, general." Forcing himself to put some steel back into his voice, he asked, "We're standing by to support you, sir. Just give us the word."

"I appreciate that, son, but right now this is a good old-fashioned slugfest. Godspeed, commodore. Sparks, out."

"Sir?"

Looking up, Sato found his flag captain looking at him, a concerned expression on his face.

"Commodore, is something wrong?"

"No," Sato lied. "I'm fine." He forced himself to his feet, ignoring the vertigo that threatened to take him. "I'll be in my day cabin."

"Yes, sir."

Crossing the flag bridge to the hatch that led to his day cabin was one of the longest treks Sato had ever made in his life. It took every shred of willpower to maintain the appearance of a leader, of a man in control not only of himself but thousands of others. He couldn't allow his crew to see what was happening to him. He couldn't.

As the hatch slid shut behind him, closing him away from the flag bridge, he staggered and barely caught himself on his desk. One of the perquisites of being a commodore was that he had a small private viewport and a couch on which to enjoy the view outside. Slumping onto the couch, he stared through the clearsteel window at the bright disk of Alger's World. At any other time, it would have been a beautiful sight.

"Steph." Her name caught in his throat as his heart hammered in his chest. "It's my fault," he whispered to the world below where the woman he loved had died. And he hadn't even known that she'd been involved in the mission. "If I hadn't pushed you away, you never would have done this. Or if you had, at least you would have told me. I would have known." He clenched his fists so hard the knuckles bled white. "I could have told you how much I loved you one last time."

The beautiful clouds of Alger's World were reflected in the tears of the man who commanded humanity's most powerful warships as he wept, his heart broken.

* * *

After leaving Sparks, Mills had hoped to make his way back to the woods that led toward the camp when the Kreelans attacked. Their air assault trick had given him the shakes, remembering what had happened to his old Legion regiment on Keran, but fortunately he had been clear of that little dance.

He had nearly made it to the edge of the landing zone when the mass wave attack had come from the woods, and he had been caught up in the melee. Luckily, he was on the very edge of the Kreelan line, but he hadn't been able to break contact as he had intended. The senior NCOs and handful of officers in this part of the Marine line had been killed. The Marines were still fighting valiantly, but they had no one to lead them and were quickly giving ground. In only a few more minutes the Kreelans would have been in a position to break through and attack the Marine line from the rear.

Mills had glanced longingly at the woods, then turned his attention to rallying the Marines.

"Stand and fight!" He bellowed over and over again as he waded into the enemy, his head and shoulders standing above most of the warriors. His only weapon was the sniper rifle, and it was useless in a close-in fight.

So he'd unslung it and, holding it by the barrel, began using it like a huge baseball bat. He wasn't killing any warriors with it, but he was able to knock them off balance, giving the other Marines a chance to dive in to blast and hack away at the enemy.

"Bleeding Christ!" Two warriors lunged at him at once. He knocked the first one senseless with the butt of the rifle, but the second used the opportunity to thrust her sword at him. He twisted to the side, managing to keep the tip from running him through, but the blade sliced through the muscle of his right side, just above his hip.

Hissing with pain, he pivoted around, closer to the warrior, too close for her to use her sword effectively. Using the bulk of his body to shove her off-balance, he viciously slammed the rifle butt into the side of her head, sending her flying to the side. He didn't bother finishing her off, trusting the Marines behind him to take care of that little detail.

Another group of Marines had pushed forward, joining Mills and his group in the fray. One of the newcomers had the black bar insignia of a first lieutenant.

"Lieutenant!" Mills's voice was raw, and it was hard to shout loud enough for anyone to hear him beyond a few feet amid the raging shouts and screams around them. "Lieutenant!"

The man turned his head, glancing at Mills, just as a warrior leaped over the top of a trio of Marines and came flying at the lieutenant, her sword pointed at his neck.

Mills could only be impressed as the young officer calmly raised his rifle and blasted her in mid-air.

"Can I help you, first sergeant?" He looked over at Mills as the bullet-riddled corpse of the warrior landed at his feet.

"Would you mind taking over this lot?" Mills nodded at the Marines he'd brought with him. "I have a little something special I'm supposed to be doing with this." He held up the sniper rifle, then jabbed the barrel into the ear of a warrior who was about to get the upper hand against one of his Marines. Thrown off balance, she tumbled to the ground, where the Marine finished her off with a bayonet thrust to the gut.

"Roger that. I relieve you, first sergeant!"

"Thank you, sir!"

After a few close calls, Mills was able to work his way around the end of the melee without drawing undue attention from the Kreelans, who now had their clawed hands full with the Marines.

Fighting against gnawing exhaustion and the pain from the wound in his side, he finally made it back to the woods from which he so recently had escaped.

EIGHTEEN

Valentina, Steph, and Allison had been taken to the dais in the middle of the central and largest arena. There, they awaited their fate, surrounded by alert warriors.

"I think I finally got the bleeding stopped." Valentina wiped her forehead, leaving a smudge of blood. She'd been trying to staunch the blood from the wound in Steph's leg, but all she had to work with was the material from their uniforms. The Kreelans had taken everything else.

She'd torn up the cleanest sections of her uniform blouse to use for bandages to stop the bleeding, then used the lower half of her undershirt and the now-empty combat belt as a final clean bandage, wrapping it around Steph's leg and cinching it tight. "The throwing star must have clipped a vein, but that's the best that I can do."

"Thanks." Steph was conscious again, but very pale and weak, both from the loss of blood and the pain.

"Does it hurt?" Allison knelt behind Steph, letting Steph's head rest on her legs, rather than on the cold stone of the dais.

"Only a little." Steph smiled at her own lie and reached up to take one of Allison's hands, giving the girl a little squeeze that proved to be a herculean effort. Then she turned back to Valentina and nodded her head toward the warriors guarding them. "What do you think they're going to do?"

"Them? Nothing. They're just making sure we stay put."

"They're waiting for *her*." Allison looked in the direction of the landing zone and the sounds of the battle that raged there. The sky beyond the trees lit up with glares and flashes of weapons being fired. She turned to Valentina. "When she's done with the Marines over there, she'll come back here. For you."

"I hate to say it, Allison, but I think you're right." Valentina took a closer look at the warriors around them, gauging her chances.

"Don't even think about it," Steph whispered. "You're good, Valentina, but you're not that good. And Allison and I wouldn't stand a chance."

"You're assuming we have a chance either way."

"All I know is that as long as you're alive, we've got a hope of making it out of this. But if something happens to you..."

"We're dead." Allison finished the thought.

"What about when the warrior with the dead eyes comes back? You know I can't beat her."

"Maybe, maybe not." Steph grimaced as a sudden lance of pain shot through her leg. "But we still might teach the king's horse to sing."

Valentina couldn't help herself. She laughed.

"What does that mean?" Allison had no idea what Steph was talking about.

"She means that she believes in miracles." Valentina smiled and shook her head. "Even now."

"Yes." Steph looked up into the darkening sky as a set of bright points of light that she knew must be Confederation warships passed overhead in low orbit. "Yes, I do."

* * *

Ku'ar-Marekh's warriors surged forward, smashing into the human warriors with a ring of steel on steel, punctuated with the staccato fire of the human weapons.

While some priestesses allowed their warriors to use rifles and other such weapons, Ku'ar-Markeh held them in contempt. The far greater challenge was to close with and slay a superior enemy with sword and claw. Many more warriors died than might have otherwise, but simple victory was not the Way of the warrior. The warriors among Her Children were born to glorify her in battle, and to die with honor.

As she moved forward toward the battle line to blood her own sword against the humans, she sensed the arrival of the fleet bearing the additional warriors she had summoned days before. The new warriors would be pleased to know there were now many human warriors here to fight, assuming the shipmistresses could hold off the human fleet long enough to land the warriors.

It will be an interesting challenge, she thought as she lunged into the melee, her sword drawing its first blood against the humans.

* * *

"Commodore to the bridge!"

Sato sat bolt upright, then got to his feet. The tears were long gone. His heart was dead and his soul was empty, and the computing machine that his brain had become filled the void with a cold yearning for vengeance on the creatures who had taken everything from him.

"Status?" He strode onto the flag bridge, his eyes immediately going to the main tactical display.

"One of the destroyers on picket duty just reported that enemy ships have emerged on the far side of the planet." The flag tactical officer came up beside him. "Ten destroyers, eight cruisers, and four large vessels that appear to be transports."

"Orders from the flag?" Sato focused his attention on the four transports, imagining the massive shells of the *Orion* venting its troop compartments to space and annihilating the thousands of warriors who must be aboard.

"The admiral ordered that we maintain position covering our carriers, sir. He's ordering the cruisers and destroyers from Home Fleet to engage."

Restraining the urge to clench his fists in frustration, Sato only nodded. *Orion* and her sisters were in formation above the precious carriers and the remaining assault boats that had yet to drop to the surface. They had not received any additional targets, only the enemy force that Sparks was engaging near Breakwater. "Very well. Maintain condition two throughout the flotilla and-"

"Emerging contacts!" The tactical officer's call was punctuated with a flurry of yellow icons appearing on the tactical display. "Contacts close aboard!"

The display that showed a video feed looking out over the bow of the ship was filled with a Kreelan cruiser that the *Orion's* captain just barely managed to avoid. The enemy ship's luminous green flanks and rune markings slid past on a reciprocal course, her guns and lasers flashing as she fired. *Orion* shuddered as the shells struck, but her thick armor shrugged them off.

The cruiser had plenty of company. Over thirty enemy vessels had emerged from hyperspace right on top of the battleships and their escorts.

Sato quickly took in the situation on the tactical display as the *Orion's* captain opened fire with the battleship's secondary weapons on the cloud of enemy warships.

But the nearby Kreelan ships weren't what he was most concerned about. A dozen enemy cruisers were pulling away, heading straight for the carriers and the cloud of assault boats, which began to dive toward the surface like a school of terrified minnows.

The destroyers and cruisers escorting the carriers turned to engage, but would be hard-pressed to stop the attacking enemy ships before they were in weapons range of the carriers.

And the carriers were too low in the planet's gravity well to jump away, and were too slow to run.

Sato didn't have any good choices. He could take his battleships after the cruisers pursuing the carriers, which would leave the other enemy warships around him free to overwhelm his escorts and pour fire into the exposed sterns of the battleships as they turned. Or he could fight the Kreelan ships here and hope that the carrier escorts managed to carry the day.

Looking at the balance of power in the looming engagement, the escorts were going to be badly outgunned.

There was one other possibility that he was loathe to do, but there was little choice. He had to split the battleship flotilla. It would divide his combat power, but if he could pin down the enemy ships here with two of the battleships, the other two would be able to maneuver to help the carriers.

Sato turned to his flag captain as the ship staggered under a heavy hit and alarms began to blare. "Order Captain Abdullah to take *Monarch* and *Conqueror* to help protect the carriers. *Thunderer* is to follow us in trail, with our escorts covering her stern."

"Aye, aye, sir." The flag captain's expression made it clear he wasn't at all convinced of the wisdom of Sato's orders, but he obeyed.

Sato called up the *Orion's* captain on his comm panel. She was on the ship's bridge two decks below. "Captain Semyonova, *Orion* is now in the lead of the first division. *Thunderer* is behind us. Make your heading zero-four-three mark seven-zero."

A trajectory line appeared on the tactical display, which was now zoomed in to show the action around the two battleships as their sisters pulled away. The white line curved right through the center of the Kreelan formation, a cloud of red icons.

Sato was going to take the battleships right down the enemy's throat. "*Monarch* and *Conqueror* are maneuvering to protect the carriers, and we need to pin down the enemy here. The flag tactical officer will provide you targeting cues so we don't fire on the same targets, but use your discretion. Fight your ship, captain."

"Aye, aye, sir." The small image of Semyonova's face nodded once, then disappeared.

The ship rang and boomed as enemy shells slammed into her heavy armor, and were answered in turn by her own fire. The secondary guns, as big as those fitted on cruisers, fired non-stop, punctuated by the hum of the point defense lasers as they sought to blast enemy shells before they hit.

As the formation split, *Orion* and *Thunderer* opened fire with their main batteries at the more distant targets of the Kreelan formation, tongues of flame shooting hundreds of meters from the muzzles of the thirty centimeter guns as they sent their massive shells toward their targets.

The space outside the view screen was an enormous pyrotechnic display, with shells and lasers streaking across the darkness, flaring into explosions as they hit their targets.

Sato looked out the forward view screen at the beautiful, yet terrible sight as *Orion* and *Thunderer* advanced with all guns blazing, seeking to tear out the enemy's heart.

* * *

Ku'ar-Marekh's sword whirled and slashed, killing the human warriors who swarmed toward her. She had never been a great swordmistress among the high priestesses. Nonetheless, her skills were far superior to that of the peers. Here, now, her warriors watched in awe as their priestess laid low their enemies in the time-honored tradition.

She had to keep moving or she would have had to reach over a pile of corpses to continue killing. Many of the humans fired their primitive weapons at her, but the projectiles simply melted and fell to the ground. It was a power she could not consciously control. Had she been able, she would have abandoned it, for it might have brought an honorable death sooner.

The humans were indeed worthy opponents, she admitted to herself. Ferocious and fearless, they grappled with her warriors, and with her. Great would be the funeral pyres for the fallen after this day, for even though the humans were soulless creatures whose blood did not sing, she would see that these were honored in death.

To her left, she saw a sudden blaze of lightning as one of her warriors finally reached one of the huge battle machines that were so prized as a kill among her warriors. She felt the warrior's dying ecstasy through the Bloodsong as the machine took her life. Then the humans inside it died in their turn, burned alive by the cyan energy that swept through the machine's metal body.

Emboldened and encouraged, more warriors surged forward, struggling to break through the line of humans who sought to hold them back.

"Forward, my children!" Her bellow carried over the storm of shrieks and curses, the gunfire and explosions that echoed across the smoke-shrouded battlefield.

With a final, massive surge, the warriors broke through the human line. First in a trickle, then in a torrent of swords and claws they broke onto the hallowed ground where the war machines had squatted, useless unless they wished to kill their own kind.

She watched as the things began to back away, their ungainly metal tracks creaking as they sought to escape. They could move faster than her warriors could run, but they would not be able to escape the droves of new warriors who even now were making their final approach to join this battle.

Hurling a *shrekka* and beheading a human who had strayed too close, she stayed where she was, allowing her warriors the honor of the kill as the quickest among them readied their grenades to attack the great machines.

* * *

"Now!" Sparks had his attention focused not on the rapidly approaching wave of howling warriors, but on the Marines they had passed by.

As one, the Marines dropped to the ground, most of them seeking what shelter might be given by their fallen comrades and dead aliens.

Like the other Wolverines, Sparks's tank was backing up, moving erratically, hoping to give the impression they were panicking. The vehicles were moving just fast enough that the warriors dashing toward them were gaining on them.

The timing was going to be close.

Dozens of cyan glows appeared along the approaching line of alien warriors as they readied their hellish grenades.

"Steady..." Sparks's voice was calm, even though his own gut was clenched in a steel vise. He had seen up close what the Kreelan grenades could do to a tank and its crew, but he wanted to let the enemy get in close, to point-blank range. "Steady..."

The nearest warriors cocked their arms back, preparing to throw.

"Now!"

The weapons on every vehicle of the brigade opened up on the Kreelan line in a deafening barrage. The main guns of the tanks spewed flechette rounds that ripped the warriors to pieces dozens at a time, while the gatling guns on the tanks and personnel carriers killed more. Anti-personnel mortars from the tanks popped non-stop, lobbing the small but lethal grenades among the closest attackers, who disappeared in a string of detonations like the climax of a fireworks display.

Even some of the Marine infantry behind the Kreelan line, bravely or foolishly, rose from cover and began firing into the warriors, adding to the carnage.

It was a bloody massacre.

A small measure of what we owe you, Sparks thought. He had not a shred of compassion for the enemy. Were it in his power, he would have killed them all. Everywhere. Because he knew in his heart that would be the only way humanity would win this war. By extinction.

Still, he had to concede the enemy's courage, or stupidity, in refusing to withdraw. Even against the hail of fire that cut them down by the dozens, a few warriors managed to get through. He watched with grim resignation as five of the lightning grenades sailed through the air. Three infantry fighting vehicles and two Wolverines died, consumed by cascades of electrical discharges that left the thick armor plating red hot and cooked the crews.

The firing trailed off, then stopped. It was over. Not because the Kreelans had broken and run, or because they had surrendered, but because there were none left to kill.

"Thank you, God." Sparks surveyed the carnage before him, his eyes taking in the thousands of bodies, most of them enemy warriors, that littered the battlefield. Some were still whole, while others had been blown to pieces. The stench of flesh, blood, and shredded entrails would have been overpowering were it not for the acrid smoke pouring from the burning tanks and the reek of gun propellant that filled his nose.

One of the destroyed Wolverines cooked off, its ammunition exploding from the heat of the flames that consumed its interior. The heavy turret was blown from the hull to twirl twice in the air like a toy before it slammed into the ground, upside down.

Then another sound came, one he hadn't heard before.

It was his Marines, the battered and weary survivors of this brief but desperate battle, who had gotten to their feet beyond the sea of dead Kreelans. Holding their weapons above their heads, they gave voice to the joy of their survival, to victory.

Sparks's heart melted at their spirit, and at how few remained. While he had not lost many of the armored vehicles, the two Marine infantry regiments had been decimated. He guessed from those who were now standing that they'd lost at least half their strength. Nearly six thousand men and women, gone.

It had been a steep price to pay.

"But we won, by God," Sparks whispered softly. He keyed his comm unit to reach his deputy in the command vehicle. "Get the medevacs in here."

"Boats are inbound." His deputy commander's voice carried an edge that immediately worried Sparks. "But they're not medevacs, general. The fleet's under attack, and Admiral Voroshilov is sending the rest of the assault force down to us." He paused. "*Guadalcanal* is also reporting that more enemy warriors are heading our way. Looks like multiple division strength from the number of landing craft heading toward us from some transports that just arrived in orbit."

Sparks's mouth compressed to a thin line under his mustache at the news as he watched infantry fighting vehicles moving toward the line of exhausted Marines to pick them up.

It would be a race between the remainder of his three divisions and the Kreelans. "Damn."

A sudden crack from the direction of town made him look up. It was the unmistakable sound of a heavy rifle being fired. More shots rang out in short order.

The Marine infantry reacted instantly, diving to the ground and turning their weapons toward the sound.

That's when they all noticed her. A solitary warrior, the one who had led the enemy charge and shielded the warriors like some sort of witch, stood behind the Marine line. Unmoving, still surrounded by a wall of dead Marines, she again seemed to be staring at Sparks.

He felt an unaccustomed tightness in his chest, a momentary prickling of needles around his heart.

Then she vanished.

* * *

Ku'ar-Marekh watched as Her Children died in a blaze of glory under the guns of the humans. The challenge posed by the armored vehicles was irresistible, regardless of the odds. Both the hunt and the devastation among the warriors hearkened back to the tales told in the Books of Time from before the Empire, when warriors hunted the wild genoth, the great dragons of the Homeworld. The ancient tales told of battles with the great beasts every bit as horrific as this, and she watched as thousands of warriors ran to their doom, the Bloodsong echoing the ferocity of their joy.

And for those few who survived long enough to attack the great metal machines, even Ku'ar-Marekh could sense their intensity of their ecstasy as they hurled their grenades, just before the humans released them from the bonds of this life.

Great was the glory these warriors had brought the Empress this day, Ku'ar-Markekh knew as the battlefield was lost to smoke and flame. She did not even notice the occasional projectile that immolated itself against the shield of her spirit.

At last, it was over. As the smoke gradually cleared, she saw the human warriors stand and voice a great war cry at their victory.

She looked at the animal she believed to be the leader of the human warriors, sensing the beat of his heart, feeling it in the grip of her mind. It would be so easy, she knew, to take the creature's life.

But what glory would be given the Empress from such a trivial feat?

The loud report of a weapon sounded from the direction of the *Kalai-II*, and she felt the Bloodsong tremble as two of her warriors died. More shots were fired, and more warriors died.

Casting her mind's eye to the great stone edifice, she saw her human prizes in the central arena and watched as the last warriors guarding them perished.

Guiding her spirit through the nearby woods, then the human settlement, she quickly found the attacker. It was the large human warrior who carried the mark of Tesh-Dar, atop one of the buildings.

Sighing in satisfaction, the gesture more of habit than of any true feeling, Ku'ar-Marekh hoped that together the humans would pose a worthy challenge for her when the time came.

But satisfying her personal indulgence would have to wait a short time longer, for she could sense the approach of both the new warriors and the human reinforcements. All were converging here in what would be a glorious and mighty battle.

Closing her eyes, she focused her mind on the leading attack ship, then disappeared.

NINETEEN

Mills was gasping with exhaustion as he ran through the woods, bearing the heavy sniper rifle. He prayed with every step that Valentina, Steph, and Allison were still alive, and that the warrior with the dead eyes had taken them for her own reasons and temporarily kept them safe. He wanted to believe that he would have known inside if they had been killed, but he had been a solider for far too long, and he knew it was only wishful thinking. Yet his heart told him they still lived, and he had to believe it was so. He had to.

"I'm not going to lose you." The words were a ragged whisper through his lips, but were the focus of his entire being.

He ignored the continued roar of the battle now well behind him and instead concentrated on finding a clear view of the arenas and the huge stone construct.

Unable to find a good spot in the woods, he had to run even farther, praying that he didn't blunder into any enemy warriors along the way as he circled to the edge of town nearest the arenas.

He needn't have worried. The town was utterly deserted. He wove his way through the buildings until he was at the central communications exchange, which had a direct line of sight to the town square and the arenas.

Climbing up the service access ladder in the rear, he low crawled on his belly to the mass of antenna supports at the center of the roof.

After unslinging the sniper rifle, he set out the spare magazines so they'd be in easy reach.

Putting the rifle's scope to his eye and aiming in the direction of the arenas, he slowly, carefully, levered himself up along one of the antenna pedestals until he could just see over the parapet around the building's flat roof.

"Thank you, Lord." Relief flooded through him when he saw them all in the center arena, still alive. Steph was on her back, her head on Allison's knees, and Mills grimaced at Steph's blood-soaked leg. Valentina knelt next to them.

They were surrounded by a circle of nine warriors, who were standing at what Mills thought of as parade rest, their attention fixed on Valentina. Even with the thundering racket of the battle raging on the far side of the woods, they never flinched or took their eyes from her.

"They've got your number, love." He grinned as he lined up the crosshairs on the chest of his first target, with another warrior right behind her.

He stroked the trigger, and the big rifle kicked against his shoulder as it fired.

* * *

Valentina happened to be looking right at one of the warriors when the Kreelan's upper body exploded, her arms and head sailing away from the crimson spray that was all that remained of her torso. From the corner of her eye, she saw the warrior who stood beside the first one crumple to the ground, a fist-sized hole in her abdomen.

A deafening crack followed, and Valentina recognized the sound of a sniper rifle. Part of her wanted to turn and see where the firing was coming from, but she had more important things to attend to.

The other warriors reacted instantly. Three of them bolted toward the sound of the firing, while the other four closed in around Valentina. Before they moved more than a pace, she darted forward and pried the sword from the amputated arm of the sniper rifle's first victim.

Another shot rang out, and the warrior who was closest to Valentina died.

Turning back toward Steph and Allison, Valentina leaped forward, raising her sword in time to block an overhand cut by another warrior aimed at Allison. Valentina let her momentum carry her forward, slamming her body into the alien and knocking her off the stone dais and onto the sands of the arena. The Kreelan's sword went flying, landing a few paces away.

As Valentina rolled to her feet, the big rifle fired again, and two of the warriors heading for the sniper's position exploded in a fountain of gore.

"Valentina!" Allison's scream sent an electric shock through Valentina's heart as a warrior grabbed the girl by the hair and stabbed down with her sword, the tip aimed at the juncture of the girl's neck and shoulder.

"No!" Valentina cried as the warrior she had just knocked to the ground sank her claws into Valentina's leg and dragged her down.

Allison's scream ended as the Kreelan's head disappeared in a spray of blood and bone, followed by the now-comforting sound of the sniper rifle's thunder. The blade of the alien's sword grazed Allison's neck as the dead warrior crumpled to the stone dais behind her.

With a roar of fury, Valentina smashed her foot into the face of the warrior who still had her claws in Valentina's calf muscle. Then Valentina twisted up on one knee and with both hands drove her sword into the alien's chest, the glittering blade easily slicing through the black armor, pinning the warrior to the sand.

The fourth warrior who was moving in to attack screamed in agony as the rifle fired again. She only had time to look down and see that one of her legs was gone before she collapsed.

Valentina was just about to write her off as a threat when she saw the warrior pry one of the throwing stars from her shoulder. Valentina was too far away to kill her first, and the sniper - Mills, she knew - was now focused on killing the last Kreelan still dashing toward his position. He was firing round after round at the warrior, who was dodging his aim with stunning agility.

The Kreelan facing Valentina snarled as she levered herself up on her side to throw, and Valentina readied her sword to try and deflect the hellish weapon.

With a scream of rage, Allison was there, swinging a sword at the alien's neck.

Caught totally by surprise, the warrior tried to deflect the blow with the throwing star still clutched in her hand, but she was too late.

Allison's aim was poor, but with a Kreelan blade it made no difference if it encountered flesh or bone. The glittering metal flashed through the warrior's skull, and the top half of her head fell to the ground like a slice of ripened fruit. The body fell back to the bloody sand and twitched.

Allison fell to her knees and vomited just as a shot found the last warrior heading for Mills, blowing the alien apart.

Getting to her feet, ignoring the pain in her calf, Valentina fell to the sand next to Allison and hugged the girl fiercely.

"Are you all right?" They turned to see Steph, who had rolled onto her side and was trying to drag herself toward them.

Valentina and Allison struggled to their feet and went to her. Lifting Steph up to a sitting position, they hugged each other, overjoyed to be alive.

All three of them looked up at a sound like an ape howling. It was so loud that it stood out from the continued thunder of battle beyond the woods.

There, on top of a building with a maze of antennas, stood a familiar figure, a big man wearing a camouflage uniform, brandishing a huge rifle over his head and whooping in obvious joy.

"Mills," Valentina said, shaking her head as she smiled, "you magnificent bastard."

* * *

The *Orion* shuddered as a deafening boom echoed through the flag bridge, jolting Sato so hard that his teeth cracked together. Blood flooded into his mouth from where he'd bitten his tongue. He spat it out before calling to the flag captain. "Status report!"

"The bridge isn't responding, sir!"

Sato hit the button on his comm console. "Captain Semyonova!"

Nothing.

"Get a runner to the bridge to see what's going on. I'm taking the con. Eldridge, you've got navigation. Tactical, assume control of the ship's weapons. Communications, relay our status to *Thunderer* and Admiral Voroshilov."

"Aye, sir!" Eldridge had commanded two cruisers before becoming Sato's flag captain. It had been a long time since he'd been a navigation officer, but he hadn't forgotten how. Sato had despotically drilled him and the other members of the flag bridge crews in emergency procedures, and now Eldridge was glad for it.

The officers acknowledged their orders even as *Orion* reeled from more heavy blows, and her firing slacked off noticeably. While she and *Thunderer* had destroyed at least a third of the Kreelan ships swarming around them, there were still many left that were either undamaged or still able to fight. *Thunderer* had also suffered two ramming attempts, one of which actually hit her, but didn't cause serious damage.

"Commodore, we've got severe damage to the port side." The engineering officer was a young woman whose face was colored scarlet by the reflection of the red status indicators from her display. "We've lost all but one of the secondary turrets on that side, and four of the point defense lasers."

As if to punctuate the statement, the ship shuddered again, and another set of alarms sounded.

"Sir," the communications officer turned to him, her face pale, "the runner reports that the bridge is gone. One of the secondary magazines detonated..."

"Understood." Sato set aside his grief for Semyonova and the others. There would be time to grieve later, if they all survived. "Order *Thunderer* to pull up along our port side and protect our flank, and have her rotate her weakest side to us."

"Aye, aye, sir."

On the tactical display, a trio of enemy cruisers veered toward them on a collision course. All three were seriously damaged, streaming air and debris from earlier hits inflicted by their human foes.

"Tactical, concentrate fire on those ships, if you please." Sato didn't have to point out which ones he meant. "And alert the Marines that we may have company coming."

Everyone glanced at him. The Kreelans had stopped flinging warriors through space at human ships soon after the introduction of the anti-personnel mortars that had proven utterly devastating to boarding attacks. The Kreelans spent their lives easily, but even they didn't have the stomach to waste their warriors that way.

Instead they used warships that had suffered serious damage to ram their human opponents. The warriors then swarmed through the resulting hull breach. It was more effective for the Kreelans, because it was harder for the humans to mount a defense against them before the warriors boarded.

But in most cases, boarding wasn't a concern. The ships were generally moving so fast when they collided that both were totally destroyed.

"Firing, sir."

Sato looked at the main viewscreen, which was now trained to port, following the muzzles of the ship's main guns. *Orion* shuddered again, not so violently, as she began ripple firing a broadside at the approaching enemy ships as *Thunderer* approached from astern.

"Rotate us fifty degrees to port." Sato watched the approaching battleship, whose forward main guns were also firing at the three approaching cruisers. *Thunderer* matched *Orion's* rotation, slipping into place next to her sister to cover her badly wounded flank.

Behind them, the three remaining cruisers and four destroyers of the support flotilla, supported by fire from the battleships' secondary guns, fended off attempts by Kreelan ships to attack the vulnerable sterns of the battleships. It was a desperate battle of attrition, but on balance the humans were winning. Barely.

Sato allowed himself a grim smile, his lips still smeared with blood from his bitten tongue, as he watched the results of the ship's gunnery. The cruiser at the center of the approaching trio bloomed into a gigantic fireball as she was struck simultaneously by no fewer than six main gun rounds from *Orion*, the huge shells tearing deep into the enemy ship before exploding.

A second cruiser exploded, then the third, both the victims of *Thunderer's* guns.

"What's our ammunition level?" Now that *Orion's* mauled flank was protected by *Thunderer's* armored bulk and the most immediate threats had been eliminated, Sato could turn his attention to the ship.

"Twenty-two percent for the main guns, sir. If we maintain our current rate of fire, we're going to be out in another ten minutes." The tactical officer paused. "We're at fifty-seven percent for the secondaries, but that includes the guns on the port side that are out of action. I'm having the ammunition from their magazines shifted to the starboard guns, so we should be in good shape for at least another thirty minutes, even maintaining the current rate of fire."

"And *Thunderer*?"

"She reports thirty-two percent for her forward main guns; the aft guns are out of action. Forty-three percent for her secondaries."

Sato pursed his lips. He knew they could win this fight, but they'd be extremely vulnerable if additional Kreelan ships showed up. "Restrict main gun fire to cruisers or ships attempting to ram. Engage all smaller targets with the secondaries."

"Aye, sir."

On the tactical display, there were still six enemy cruisers and a dozen destroyers left in this group of enemy ships, but nearly all of them were damaged. They had stayed alive thus far by concentrating their efforts on the battleships' escorts in a running fight astern of the big ships where they were comparatively safe from the battleships' main guns and pulse cannons.

Zooming out, he saw that *Monarch* and *Conqueror* had mopped up the cruisers that had tried to attack the carriers, and that the ships from Home Fleet were getting the upper hand in the separate battle against the Kreelan ships on the far side of the planet.

Returning the view to the immediate surroundings and the desperate fight going on around them, he turned to Eldridge. For the first time, it looked like a ship he'd been aboard would not only survive, but emerge victorious from battle. Even at the steep price the ship had paid in the losses of Semyonova and the other members of the crew, it would have been a heady feeling were it not for the knowledge that Steph was dead. He couldn't bring her back, but he could kill as many Kreelans as he could.

"Bring us about as tight as she'll turn with *Thunderer* alongside. Tactical, stand by with the pulse cannon." He paused, his dark eyes taking in the positions of the Kreelan ships. "Let's finish this."

* * *

"We've got to hurry." Mills puffed as he jogged along the road, carrying Steph in his arms. Allison ran beside him, carrying the same sword she'd used to kill one of the guards. Valentina ran a few yards ahead of them, a Kreelan sword in its scabbard tucked into her combat harness and the sniper rifle across her shoulders.

After dealing with the Kreelans, Mills had run from the communications center to meet the trio. After lifting both Allison and Valentina off the ground in an unrestrained bear hug, he had quickly applied a combat dressing to Steph's leg and gave her some painkillers. Then he picked her up and started off for the nearest Marine positions.

Ahead, the pillars of smoke rising from the fields marked the positions of dead ships and armored vehicles, just over the rise outside of town.

"Bloody hill." Mills was struggling, every muscle in his body quivering from exertion as he forced his body up the incline.

Valentina kept an eye all around them, periodically running backward so she could look behind them and make sure they weren't being followed. There wasn't a single warrior in view. *Good*, she thought. "Come on. It's not too much farther."

"Steph, darlin', you need to go on a diet." Mills's dirty, blood-spattered face crinkled briefly into a grin.

"Fuck you, Mills." Steph gave him a weak hug, trying not to wince. Even with the painkillers, her leg hurt like the devil. She also didn't tell him that her wound was bleeding again, the dressing separating from her skin from the rough treatment it was getting.

"Don't let the commodore hear you propositioning me."

Beside him, Allison rolled her eyes theatrically.

Valentina spun around again to check behind them, and stopped in her tracks, her eyes widening at what she saw. A cloud of black specks, just above the flat farmland beyond the town, was heading right for them.

Enemy attack ships.

"Down!" She grabbed Allison and threw her to the ground as Mills, not bothering to ask what Valentina had seen, dropped to his knees beside them, putting Steph down as gently as he could before covering her with his body.

The air was shattered by the screech of dozens of boats, larger ones than had attacked Sparks's Marines earlier, flying over them. The ships were so low that they kicked up a huge cloud of dust and debris from the fields as they passed.

Wave after wave flew overhead. Mills looked up, and could clearly see the garish markings on the alien craft and make out every detail of their wasp-like hulls. While not as large as the assault boats the Marines typically used, he guessed they were still big enough to hold a couple hundred warriors each. Just the ones he counted after the first waves had passed would have amounted to nearly a division's worth of warriors. And there were more, a lot more.

As they passed overhead, the ships climbed higher into the sky.

He glanced over at Valentina, who looked back. She shook her head, grimacing.

After the final wave finally passed over and the roar faded, Mills could hear the unmistakable thrum of gatling guns and the sharp crack of tank main guns firing.

"Come on." Valentina helped him up, then made sure Allison was all right.

Picking up Steph, they walked the rest of the way up the rise to where they could see the battlefield where the Marines had annihilated the warriors earlier.

"Bleeding Christ." Mills felt his hopes of rescue die as the scene came into view.

The landing zone the Marines had used earlier was a scene right out of hell. Hundreds of Kreelan assault ships flew through what looked like a solid flaming wall of defensive fire. Many of the ships began to stream smoke and crashed, while others simply exploded.

But most got through. Seconds later Mills saw the sky fill with clouds of warriors falling from the Kreelan ships.

Beyond them, he could just make out the glint of what must have been Confederation Navy boats, now caught in a brutal slugging match with the Kreelan ships.

"I guess we're not getting out of here yet."

Mills and Valentina exchanged a glance at Allison's words.

"Looks that way, hon." Mills knelt down, and Valentina and Allison helped him put Steph, unconscious again, carefully on the ground.

The big man was overcome by a wave of exhaustion, and nearly fell over before Valentina caught him.

"I'm fine," he rasped, trying to push her away.

"No, you're not, you idiot." She undid his equipment harness and pulled his uniform tunic aside to look at the wound in his side from the battle earlier. "You've lost a lot of blood."

"Give me a pint or two of beer to make up for it." He tried to laugh, but it ended up little more than a cough. He felt Allison's arms around his neck, hugging him tightly. "I'll be okay," he told her.

Valentina, frowning at his bravado, quickly did what she could for the wound, slapping a coating of the liquid bandage over it and hitting him with a painkiller and some stims while silently cursing Mills for not having done it himself earlier. "Idiot."

Then she checked on Steph, noticing that her leg was bleeding again. She'd lost too much blood, and if they couldn't get her to a corpsman or sickbay soon, she was going to die.

"What are we going to do, Mills?" Allison, her arms still around his neck, was watching the fireworks over the battlefield, her voice nearly lost in the booms and cracks that followed the explosions and gunfire.

"We're going to hope that General Sparks kicks their little blue arses. And soon."

TWENTY

After the fleet had informed him he could expect more Kreelans, Sparks had quickly gathered his staff officers and regimental commanders to his tank to regroup after the battle and get ready for the one that was yet to come.

"This is good ground, right here." Sparks pointed to a spot on a laminated map he'd pulled out of a tube and unrolled on the back of his Wolverine's turret. The location he was pointing to was a huge expanse of farmland that was only broken by a few scattered stands of trees. The farms around Breakwater were bordered fairly close-by with woods, but five kilometers from town, where Sparks was indicating on the map, the gently rolling farm land opened wide like a river delta.

"The main thing is going to be who gets here first, our reinforcements or theirs." The operations officer looked up. "It's going to be bloody close."

"And we have no idea where the Kreelans are going to come from. It's not like they have anyone left here to reinforce. They could approach however they please, so we don't have a known axis of attack." The intel officer's observation failed to add any cheer to the conversation.

Sparks nodded. "That's true, but the Kreelans seem to do things very direct." He took a pen from his pocket and set it down on the map, near the margin, in the upper left corner. The tip pointed in the direction of the area where Sparks wanted to deploy, the imaginary line passing right over Breakwater. "The fleet intel pukes said the enemy boats were coming from roughly this direction, did they not?"

The intel officer nodded. "Yes, sir. Their approach vector is a steady one-four-zero degrees toward us. But they could break off at any point and encircle our position."

"They could, but I don't think they will. I think they're going to come straight down our throats and play their favorite little air drop game." Sparks took another pen and set it down on the map in the rough center of the open expanse of farmland, turning the point to face the direction of the Kreelans' approach. "This is our center point and axis, ladies and gentlemen. I want our forces here, facing the enemy's approach vector. It's a risk, but we don't have enough firepower to cover the entire LZ, and we're going to need to get the rest of our folks on the ground."

"It's going to be a madhouse." The logistics officer shook her head. "Has anyone ever landed three divisions simultaneously?"

"At Kirov they landed six," the operations officer replied. "But they had weeks to plan the op and there weren't any Kreelan reinforcements inbound to screw things up." He glanced skyward. "We've just got a big gaggle of boats coming down in a race to see who gets here first."

Sparks looked at the logistics officer. "I want a straight up answer. Are you going to be able to get those boats down without making a big charlie foxtrot?"

The young woman returned his gaze evenly. Charlie foxtrot was the phonetic term in military-speak for a cluster-fuck, and she had served under Sparks long enough to know that he never tolerated bullshit. "Yes, sir. We can handle this. We'll get them down."

Satisfied, Sparks nodded. "Good. I want the center of the LZ to be right here." He pointed to a small stand of trees on the map, and the logistics officer noted down the coordinates. "Any questions?" The young woman shook her head. "Then get in your track and get over there to set up the welcoming committee."

"Yes, sir!" She climbed down the flank of the Wolverine, then ran to her own track, which was a field support vehicle based on the same tank chassis, but with a much larger superstructure and no turret. It was only armed with a gatling gun on the commander's cupola. Shouting a warning to the nearby infantry, she climbed into the cupola and in a few seconds was off, the tank's tracks throwing out big rooster tails of mud and dirt as it sped away.

"I want the rest of the brigade on this line here." Sparks turned his attention back to the map, drawing a line along a slight rise that was perpendicular to the Kreelan's approach vector. "Space out the two armored regiments evenly, and I want a company-size reserve...here." He made an X near another stand of trees about two kilometers behind the main line. "I'll be with the brigade on the center. XO, I want you with the reserve."

His executive officer nodded as he jotted a note on his data pad.

Sparks turned to the man who was the commander of what was left of the Marine infantry. The brigade had started the day with two mechanized infantry regiments, but had lost over half their total strength in the first fight. The highest ranking officer who had survived was a captain, who stared at the map with bloodshot eyes.

"Captain, I want you to divide your Marines evenly along the line. Don't worry about making it clean, just divide up your folks as best you can and get them moving, pronto. We don't have much time."

"If I may, sir?"

Sparks glanced at the intel officer, a young man who had graduated from college only six months before, but had already made two previous combat deployments. Sparks had given the youngster a hard time during training, but only because he had respected him and had great expectations for the him as an officer, assuming he lived long enough to make his next promotion. "Shoot, son."

"If the Kreelans do try another one of their air drop runs, I'd suggest deploying some of the empty infantry combat vehicles forward of the main line..."

He took a pen and drew a line on either end of the line where Sparks wanted the armored regiments, forming a squared U shape with the open end pointing toward the Kreelans' expected approach vector. "They can provide some flanking anti-air fire with their gatling guns, then pull back through these depressions here and here."

Sparks looked up at his operations officer. "Thoughts?"

"I like it. Anything coming through that corridor would hit a solid wall of lead, and we've got plenty of empty ICVs." He saw the Marine infantry officer wince. There were a lot of empty vehicles because so few of the infantry had survived the earlier attack. "Sorry, Hermann."

The captain made a dismissive gesture with his hand, but said nothing.

"Agreed." Sparks turned to the intel officer and nodded in approval.

"Anything else from anyone?"

There wasn't. Sparks ran his eyes around the tight circle, meeting the gaze of each of his officers in turn.

"Good. But let me remind you of something, ladies and gentlemen. We are not retreating. Either we beat the Kreelans here or we die. Make sure your people know that."

"With our shields or on them, sir?" The operations officer, who had a love of ancient literature, paraphrased Plutarch.

Sparks did something he rarely did in the field. He smiled. "Damn right. Now saddle up."

* * *

Selan-Kulir stood silently next to the high priestess of the Nyur-A'il as their attack ship streaked through the sky toward where the humans awaited them. As tradition demanded, Selan-Kulir had offered to become the First to Ku'ar-Marekh when the priestess materialized on their ship. The priestess had declined her offer with no more than a shake of her head.

To some, it would have been a great dishonor to have been denied the duties of First.

To Selan-Kulir, it brought not shame, but relief. She had sensed the fate of Ri'al-Hagir, the echo of fear in the Bloodsong as her soul was cast into the pit of darkness. Esah-Kuran, who had followed in the ill-fated Ri'al-Hagir's footsteps, had not long survived, but at least had met an honorable end in the great charge against the human warriors who had landed on this world, and against whom she herself would soon fight.

She glanced at Ku'ar-Marekh, who stood as still and cold as the stones of the *Kalai-Il* beside her. Her Bloodsong, as with all the priestesses, was strong, powerful. But instead of providing the warm fire that would ignite into flame during battle, it was a frigid wind that blew upon the souls of the peers.

Shivering involuntarily, Selan-Kulir returned her attention to the ship's forward view port, looking beyond the craft's pilot. Their ship led the entire formation, which stretched out for half a league on either side, and as much again behind them. She knew that the transport ships that had brought them had already been destroyed by the humans in orbit, and that while the battle still raged in space above, the Imperial warships were doomed to die under the guns of the human fleet.

This, too, brought no shame, for the warriors of the fleet had fought valiantly and well against a worthy foe, and had brought much glory this day to the Empress. Their deaths were merely the next step in the Way of Her Children. Death was a part of life, and for a warrior, to die for Her in battle was to have lived well, earning a place in the Afterlife, basking in Her love.

"That is what I, too, desire."

Selan-Kulir snapped her head around to look at Ku'ar-Marekh, who was staring at her. Realizing the breach of protocol, Selan-Kulir lowered her eyes. "I beg your forgiveness, priestess."

Ku'ar-Marekh went on as if she hadn't heard, shifting her eyes to look well beyond the young warrior, to something only she could see. "To die with honor in Her glory, to awaken on the other side of death and join those who have gone before. To feel again, and be warm..."

Selan-Kulir bowed her head and saluted, mystified by Ku'ar-Marekh's words. She had never known a priestess to act so.

Turning to look out the view port, Ku'ar-Marekh watched as the ship flashed up over a sharp rise. Off to their right, she caught a glimpse of four tiny figures collapsing to the ground as the landing force passed overhead. She sent forth her second sight to confirm her suspicion, and a moment later a cold smile graced her lips, revealing her ivory fangs.

It was her humans, the ones she wished to face in personal combat. They had survived.

"Good," she murmured to herself. She would attend to them soon.

Ahead, she could see the positions the force of human warriors had taken along a slight rise in the terrain. Beyond them was a cloud of human assault ships, racing in to land.

With a last glance at Selan-Kulir, she turned to the warriors gathered in the hold of the ship. "Prepare yourselves!"

Beyond the view screen, the fiery streaks of cannon fire rose to greet them.

* * *

With the rough battle plan made, Sparks's officers dispersed to their own vehicles to rush off to their units.

The tanks didn't wait, knowing that the infantry could quickly catch up in their fighting vehicles. After their orders were passed down, the big vehicles spun around in place and tore their way across the farms and fields toward their new positions, the air filled with the sounds of the racing turbine engines and the creaking of hundreds of tracks.

A few minutes later, half the infantry vehicles followed, carrying the Marines who had survived the first battle.

The infantry vehicles manned only by the drivers and vehicle commanders divided into two groups and headed toward their positions to form the mouth of the U, into which Sparks hoped the Kreelans would fly. Their orders were simple. Train their gatling guns toward the center of the formation, elevating them high enough that the shells would fall beyond the vehicles on the far side if they didn't happen to hit a Kreelan ship, and open fire on order.

"About time." Sparks squinted into the sky as he heard the rumble behind him, heralding the arrival of the rest of his Marines. The assault boats were streaking down toward the landing zone the logistics officer had set up five kilometers behind the line of tanks facing the Kreelans, right where he'd wanted.

"Looks like we beat them." The voice of his XO, who was now with the reserve tank company behind the main line, said in his headphones as the first boats, still smoking from the heat of their reentry, set down and quickly began disgorging their troops and vehicles.

"Incoming!" The operations officer broke in from his command vehicle. "One of the forward observation posts has sighted incoming enemy ships."

Sparks had sent out three infantry fighting vehicles well ahead of the main battle line to give warning of the Kreelans. The ships in orbit had been providing the intel officer with a rough plot of the Kreelan attack ships, but being voice only, it lacked the clarity of the datalink-fed displays. Besides, Sparks liked to have human eyeballs on the target, not just orbital sensors.

"Count?" Sparks demanded.

"Stand by..."

There was a sudden series of explosions in the direction of the approaching Kreelan ships.

After a long pause, the operations officer said, "Sir, the OPs just went off the air."

"Damn."

At the landing zone, the first wave of assault boats lifted while more came in to land. The sky beyond the LZ was thick with the ungainly ships, but somehow the logistics officer was keeping them organized. Vehicles quickly formed up into their company formations and headed off at full speed to their assigned combat positions along the edge of the landing zone.

But there were so many more boats to get down. So many.

"Sir! Look!" Sparks's gunner had been keeping watch in the direction of town. The general looked at the display in his cupola, which was slaved to the tank's main gun sight.

Hundreds of enemy ships were now streaking toward them, their rakish prows and gaudily painted flanks reflecting the glow of the afternoon sun.

"Well," Sparks muttered to himself, "at least they're coming from the direction we wanted." He just hadn't anticipated so many of them. *Just more to kill*, he told himself.

Thumbing his radio control to the corps command frequency, which would broadcast to every vehicle in the formation, he said one word. "Fire."

The land echoed with thunder as the brigade's guns opened fire.

* * *

"Fire." Ku'ar-Marekh's order to her pilot was not relayed through the formation by voice or data, for there was no need. Every warrior sensed her will.

As one, even as they entered the curtain of steel thrown up by the defending human vehicles on the ground, the attack ships began firing. Not at the enemy warriors on the ground, or even the boats bringing in more humans, but at the ships leaving the battlefield. It was a small honor compared to besting a foe with sword and claw, but it gave those who piloted the attack ships an extra chance to bring Her glory while the humans landed more of their own warriors.

Around her, ships and warriors died. The cannon fire the humans were putting into the sky was brief but incredibly intense. Many of the attack ships were destroyed as they passed through the stupendous barrage, but those that survived were free to wreak havoc among the humans behind their main battle line.

Those ships that were mortally wounded found glory in destroying their foes on the ground, guiding their ships in as they might a sword, striking at the enemy's heart. Three tens of ships fell in the brief span of time the formation passed through the humans' fire, but nearly all of them destroyed at least one of the greatly prized human vehicles.

Ku'ar-Marekh caught Selan-Kulir's look of exhilaration.

On impulse, she reached out to the young warrior, gripping Selan-Kulir firmly on the shoulder. Selan-Kulir's eyes widened in surprise. "May thy Way be long and glorious, my daughter."

Then Ku'ar-Marekh turned to the pilot. "Now!"

The sides of the craft disintegrated except for the framework. The warriors, a fierce battle cry on their lips, leapt into the air. Moments later, flying wings sprouted from packs on their shoulders, and they began to glide rapidly to the ground.

Ku'ar-Marekh leapt with Selan-Kulir, but when the younger warrior's wing deployed, the priestess simply vanished from the sky to reappear on top of a human war machine on the ground below, and the priestess again began to kill.

* * *

"Move, move, MOVE!"

On Sparks's shouted order over the radio, the tanks and infantry fighting vehicles turned and began racing away from the cloud of warriors descending on top of them.

Sparks was tense, but unafraid that this battle would devolve into a debacle as had been suffered by the *Légion étrangère* on Keran.

This type of attack had become typical for the Kreelans when making assaults from orbit against massed human defenses, and Sparks had been counting on them repeating it here. While the tactic had proven devastating in every instance thus far, it had one major weakness. The parawings could only carry the warriors so far before they reached the ground. Once the Kreelans jumped from their ships, always at low altitude, their ability to maneuver was extremely limited. The descending warriors couldn't cheat gravity.

Most of the fighting in the war thus far had been in urban areas on more populated worlds, because the Kreelans attacked where they could find the most people. Unfortunately, the most powerful human land weapons, the tanks, were highly vulnerable in the confined streets of a city.

But here, outside a small town on a backwater planet, Sparks had found a near-perfect fighting ground for his tanks, and he intended to make the most of it.

His head sticking out of the cupola as his tank tore across the fields, he watched with satisfaction as the other vehicles around him maneuvered at breakneck speed away from the center of the Kreelan drop zone.

Every gatling gun and assault rifle in what was now over a division, with more boats coming every minute, swept across the sky to kill enemy assault ships and warriors before they could touch the ground. Dozens of Kreelan ships fell in flames, and Sparks gritted his teeth in anguish as many of them became lethal weapons, guided by their dying pilots to destroy his tanks and infantry fighting vehicles.

A swirling battle involving the assault boats developed as the Kreelan ships that had dropped their load of warriors swept in to attack.

Massive explosions shook the battlefield as ships on both sides died.

Above, warriors spun crazily in the air, trying to avoid the streams of cannon and rifle fire coming from the ground. Those warriors who were close enough hurled their lightning grenades at the fleeing armored vehicles. Some hit their targets, turning tanks and fighting vehicles into flaming pyres.

But most missed their mark, and the warriors found themselves landing in a field that was empty, save for the ships that had crashed and a couple dozen destroyed vehicles.

Sparks took it all in, his mind tallying up the butcher's bill as his driver guided the big Wolverine to their destination. The gunner kept up a steady stream of fire from the top-mounted gatling gun, firing it remotely. He punctuated the gatling's fire with shots from the main gun, flechette rounds aimed into the densely packed cloud of descending warriors.

The sky rained blood as the enemy was ripped to shreds.

"They're committed now, by God," Sparks told his operations officer as the last of the Kreelan ships dropped its warriors, then turned to attack an assault boat.

The boat's defensive lasers fired, and the Kreelan ship dove straight into the ground, sending up a tremendous pillar of flame. Warriors who had been coming down nearby burned like mosquitos on an electric grid.

Sparks keyed his microphone again. "Have the logistics officer shift our remaining boats to land three kilometers to the east. That'll keep them from taking too much fire, and we'll use those troops as a reserve. The rest of the formation here is to keep moving outward from the LZ until we're clear of the Kreelans' drop radius. Then we're going to turn back on them in a full envelopment and blow these blue-skinned bitches to hell."

"General, we've just gotten word that the fleet can provide direct fire support from *Conqueror* and *Monarch!*"

That news sent an electric shiver of relief through Sparks. "Are our people clear of the center of the LZ?"

"Aside from a few stragglers, yes sir. All units have made it beyond where the warriors landed."

Sparks spared a quick prayer for the few Marines who might be left in the ant's nest of warriors the former landing zone had become. They'd likely be dead long before the first shells from the fleet arrived.

"Have the fleet open fire on the center of the drop zone with a kill radius of three kilometers." Sparks raised his field glasses to his eyes, thankful that the driver had stopped. The Wolverine now stood facing the landing zone. It was swarming with thousands of warriors, running toward the iron ring encircling them.

Surrounded by two Marine heavy divisions, the enemy was being systematically annihilated.

Sparks was pleased. But he was also a man who believed in using all available firepower. He wanted the enemy dead.

"Have the fleet open fire."

* * *

Ku'ar-Marekh beheaded the human who had been sitting half-out of a hatch in the vehicle she'd chosen to land on. Kicking the corpse down into the bowels of the machine, she sheathed her sword and leaped down after it. Using only her claws, she made short, bloody work of the humans inside, even as the vehicle continued to race across the land.

Climbing back out, her armor covered in blood and the scent of it filling her sensitive nose, she jumped from the vehicle just before it went over a small hill and overturned, its tracks thrashing at the empty air.

Rolling gracefully to her feet, she surveyed the carnage around her. While some of the human vehicles were burning and tremendous pyres marked the final resting places of many ships, both human and her own, precious few humans remained in the kill zone.

The ones being killed now were her warriors. Nearly twenty-thousand had been dropped over the human positions, but the animals had run away as her warriors drifted down from the sky. And as the warriors descended on the flying wings, the humans raked them with fire.

On the ground, her warriors were trapped within a ring of weapons. The circle of human vehicles and troops surrounded them like an armored hand that would squeeze the life from Ku'ar-Marekh's legions.

Over the ceaseless roaring of the human guns, Ku'ar-Marekh heard the screams of pain from the dying, and rage from those who even now charged toward the humans, spending their lives fruitlessly. The Bloodsong echoed their feelings, a bright stream of cold light in Ku'ar-Marekh's heart.

"My priestess." Selan-Kulir appeared at her side, gasping. A hunk of flesh was missing from her right shoulder, and she shivered with pain and loss of blood.

Ku'ar-Marekh saw that there was blood on the young warrior's blade, as well, and nodded in satisfaction. She had found at least one human to kill.

"There is no honor in this!" Selan-Kulir dodged behind Ku'ar-Marekh as a fiery stream of cannon shells swept over their position, blasting divots of dirt from the ground. Three of the shells fell to the ground in front of the priestess, sizzling and burning.

"I agree." Ku'ar-Marekh did not feel fury or anger. It was merely duty that motivated her. It was honorable to give advantage to the enemy in battle, to prove one's worthiness against a superior opponent; this was a fundamental part of the Way by which Her warriors lived.

But there had to be balance. Just as the warriors of the fleet had learned when making boarding attacks against ships armed with the hellish anti-boarding weapons, Ku'ar-Marekh had to redress the overwhelming advantage the humans had, just as she did during their initial attack against the human forces earlier in the day.

Honorable advantage was one thing. Even waves of warriors dying for the honor of slaying the monstrous vehicles was a worthy way to die, as long as the warriors had at least a slim chance.

Slaughter, without a chance to even come within sword range of the enemy, was something entirely different.

Raising her hands out to her sides, palms up, Ku'ar-Marekh closed her eyes. Unlike the Empress, her own powers were finite. Even Tesh-Dar, great as she was, nearly died when her powers failed in her last battle with the humans. She would have died, had the Empress not intervened by sending Pan'ne-Sharakh to save the great warrior.

Ku'ar-Marekh silently prayed that the Empress would not show her the same mercy when Death's hand closed around her own heart.

Selan-Kulir watched in awe and fear as the smoke and dust around them stopped swirling upon the wind and began to move outward. Above, the sky darkened as the tiny motes in the air gathered together, blocking out the sun.

The circle of the wall of smoke and dust expanded. Slowly, at first, and then with gathering speed, darkening with every passing moment as it grew less transparent, more opaque. The warriors it passed felt nothing more than a brush of air, but the shells fired by the human weapons simply fell to the ground when they touched the expanding wall.

Sensing in their blood what their priestess was doing, the warriors ran as fast as they could toward the humans, whose weapons were now all but useless.

Dozens of streaks appeared in the sky, falling toward the battlefield like fiery meteors.

Selan-Kulir hissed as she realized that they were massive shells from the human ships in orbit. She held her hands up to her ears in anticipation of the sonic booms before closing her eyes, awaiting death.

But neither sound nor destruction came. Looking up again, she saw the shells, each as big as a several warriors, stop as they hit the darkening shield Ku'ar-Marekh had spawned over the battlefield. The weapons did not explode or even melt, they simply fell from the sky, great lumps of inert metal that the warriors easily evaded as the shells dropped to the ground.

Looking back at her priestess, Selan-Kulir saw that blood now trickled from Ku'ar-Marekh's nose and eyes, and her body trembled.

While she knew that the priestess might have considered it an affront, Selan-Kulir knelt beside Ku'ar-Marekh and reverently placed a hand on one of her sandaled feet.

The physical contact brought a surge of power through the Bloodsong from the priestess that overwhelmed Selan-Kulir. The young warrior cried out, lost in an ecstasy that she had never before felt, and never would again.

* * *

"What the devil?" Sparks whispered as he saw the dust and smoke that shrouded the battlefield begin to move toward him. As it did, moving faster and faster, it became opaque, a black wall expanding outward from the center of the Kreelan positions. It was like the shield the alien warrior witch had used in the previous fight, and the rounds from the Marines' weapons fell to the ground as the wall swept onward.

Behind the wall, he knew with chilling certainty, would be the warriors. He switched to the corps broadcast frequency. "Marines, prepare for close contact! The warriors are going to be right behind that..." He was at a loss for words. What exactly was that thing?

"General, fleet reports incoming fire!" The voice of his operations officer, coming to him over the staff channel, diverted his attention.

Sparks looked up as the contrails from the shells fired by the battleship guns signaled their imminent arrival. He raised his field glasses again, hoping he could see the shells when they detonated. They would be submunition rounds, the big shells nothing but containers for thousands of smaller bomblets that would turn any living thing in the target zone into mincemeat.

The shells came in...and stopped in mid-air. Then they just fell toward the ground. He couldn't see them hit because of the ever darkening wall that was racing toward him.

"Dammit!" To his crew, he said, "Be ready. There's going to be a lot of pissed-off warriors right on top of us when that thing blows past. We'll have to be quick."

After one last look to either side, seeing that the crews in the other tanks and fighting vehicles had buttoned up, he reluctantly gave in to his own apprehension and dropped into the cupola, slamming the hatch shut above him.

The wall was racing at them now, so thick it was nearly black. He only hoped that his theory was correct and the thing would pass by them, rather than simply smashing them to pieces.

"Steady, now..."

Closer it came.

Sparks could feel the big tank trembling as the ground shook, and tightened his grip on the handholds inside the turret, wondering what could possibly create such a phenomenon.

"Steady..."

His last thought was that the dark, swirling mass looked as if it were alive.

TWENTY-ONE

"That's the last of them, commodore. We did it."

Sato watched the last red icon representing a Kreelan warship blink and disappear from the tactical display as *Orion's* final salvo echoed in the flag bridge. No Kreelan warships were left in the entire system, only tumbling heaps of metal and frozen bodies that even now clanged off of the battleship's armor as she changed course, *Thunderer* still alongside, to rendezvous with their twin sisters.

"Yes, we did." Sato's voice held an air of satisfaction mixed with sorrow. The Confederation had won the battle and the new battleships had certainly proved their mettle. But the cost had been high. Eight cruisers and thirteen destroyers had been lost, most with all hands.

"Sir," the communications officer called, "incoming from Admiral Voroshilov."

"On the main display, if you please."

The Saint Petersburg admiral's bearded face appeared on the forward viewer. "My congratulations on a battle well fought and won, Commodore Sato."

"Thank you, sir." Sato bowed his head, wincing as he looked back up.

"You are injured, commodore?"

"Minor burns, admiral." Sato gestured with his left arm, where the sleeve was still smoking and his left hand was heavily bandaged. An electrical fire had broken out on one of the command consoles, seriously injuring his engineering officer. Sato had dragged her away and batted out the flames covering the woman's upper body with his hands while other members of the flag bridge crew extinguished the fire. His hand was covered with second degree burns, but he barely felt it now after the surgeon had injected him with painkillers. "It's nothing, sir. We've lost far more."

"Which brings me to the next question, commodore. What is the status of your ships?"

"*Monarch* and *Conqueror* suffered only minor damage and no casualties, and remain fully combat capable. I've ordered them to rendezvous with the munitions ships to rearm. That should take roughly four hours."

Voroshilov nodded. "Very good. Go on, please."

"*Thunderer* suffered moderate damage. Half of her main batteries are out of action and she's lost her secondary sensor array. She's also very low on ammunition. I've ordered her to detach and head for the resupply ships as soon as *Monarch* and *Conqueror* are finished. As for casualties, she suffered twelve dead and fifteen wounded, sir."

"And your flagship, commodore?"

Sato's expression hardened. "*Orion* is no longer fit for combat, admiral." Those words hurt him, but he was buoyed by the knowledge that at least *Orion* had survived. "Two of our main batteries are out of action, along with half our secondaries and point defense lasers. The armor along the starboard side has been compromised, and the hull has been breached in five places. Damage control parties have contained the damage and are shoring up the hull around the breached sections.

"Casualties…" Sato paused, thinking of the smoking wreckage that was all that was left of the ship's bridge, and the silent vacuum-filled tomb of engine room number three. "Casualties were high, sir. We lost eighty-seven members of the crew, including Captain Semyonova and the other personnel on the ship's bridge. My condolences, sir."

Voroshilov closed his eyes for a moment. Semyonova had served under him while they were in the Saint Petersburg Navy. "Thank you, commodore."

"Admiral, if I may ask, what's happening on the ground? I know that *Monarch* and *Conqueror* conducted a direct fire bombardment, but we haven't heard what happened."

"Absolutely nothing happened, commodore." Voroshilov's mouth twisted as if he were about to spit. "The shells did not detonate. Tracking indicated they were precisely on-target. But optical sensors showed them simply…stopping, and falling toward the surface."

"Impossible," Sato breathed, knowing even as he said it that it that anything seemed to be possible for the Kreelans. He knew that better than anyone.

"Yes, just like neutralizing radioactive isotopes as they did during our battle at Saint Petersburg. Impossible. Yet it happened."

"And there's been no word from General Sparks?"

"None since just after the bombardment commenced."

No one else on the flag bridge would have caught it, but Sato had worked long enough with Voroshilov that he could tell the admiral was worried.

"The combat zone has become obscured and we have lost all contact with the general and his Marines."

* * *

With a cry of agony, Ku'ar-Marekh collapsed.

Selan-Kulir, her body tingling from the power of the priestess's Bloodsong, still had the presence of mind to grab hold of the priestess's armor and help to ease her fall.

"My priestess?"

Ku'ar-Marekh stared at the eerily darkened sky as the shield she had woven began to rapidly disperse. Blood now ran freely from her nose and eyes. She coughed, and droplets of blood sprayed from her lips. The pain in her body was nearly as bad as the fire that had engulfed her during the Change when she had become a priestess.

"I will get you to a healer." Selan-Kulir closed her eyes to focus her need through the Bloodsong, but felt Ku'ar-Marekh's hand take her wrist.

"No, child. There is no need."

"But..."

Ku'ar-Marekh shook her head. "There is no need." Gently pushing the young warrior's hands aside, she managed to get to her feet.

Selan-Kulir stood close beside her, uncertain. She forced herself to keep her hands at her sides as her priestess swayed on her feet.

"The battle is again an honorable one." Ku'ar-Marekh could see her warriors charging the humans that surrounded them. The humans still held a decisive advantage if they could recover in time, but her warriors would no longer be slaughtered like meat animals with no chance for glory.

The two stood there, alone among the screaming wounded and the silent dead, the smoke from the destroyed ships and vehicles again wafting across the field of battle.

Above, the sky began to clear. Ku'ar-Marekh cast her second sight upward to the human ships, and quickly saw that their weapons were no longer prepared to bombard her warriors, for they were too close now to their human opponents.

In the distance, all around them, the howl of the warriors grew as they came within striking distance of the human animals. The sound was slowly punctuated by weapons fire as the humans regained their senses. Their rate of fire picked up quickly, but no one would know until the battle was over if it would be quick enough.

"You will return to the fleet," Ku'ar-Marekh ordered quietly.

"But, my priestess, what of the battle?" Selan-Kulir could conceal neither her confusion, nor deep disappointment. She had been wounded, yes, but could still wield a sword. "I wish to fight!"

Ku'ar-Marekh turned to her. "And fight you shall, child, but not this day. Our lives are spent easily in war, but do not waste yours. This," she gestured around them, "will be over before you could reach the battle line, and if the humans win, you will simply die an empty death. I do not wish this, and it brings neither honor to yourself, nor glory to the Empress."

Selan-Kulir, chastened, bowed her head as Ku'ar-Marekh went on. "You did the Empress great honor by standing by my side this day. The last day…"

She faltered, and Selan-Kulir reached out to steady her.

"…the last day a high priestess of the Nyur-A'il shall walk among Her Children. After me, there shall be no more, for all eternity. You are my last witness, and I wish you to live until you can die with honor. Do you understand?"

"Yes, my priestess." Selan-Kulir looked up, the skin under her eyes black with mourning for what the Empire was about to lose. Ages before the foundation of the Empire, all of the martial orders had maintained unbroken lines of high priests and priestesses. After the passing of Keel-Tath, there were only priestesses, for the males had been left barely sentient by the Curse.

But the most ancient orders, such as the Nyur-A'il, had fewer and fewer disciples since those ancient days. Two of the orders now had only a single priestess, Tesh-Dar of the Desh-Ka, and Ku'ar-Marekh of the Nyur-A'il.

And this day would see the passage of the Nyur-A'il from history, something that had never happened in all the ages since the first Books of Time.

Holding out her hands, Ku'ar-Marekh took the young warrior's forearms in a tight grip, the formal greeting, and parting, of warriors. "May thy Way be long and glorious, Selan-Kulir."

And then she was gone.

                         * * *

Sparks shook his head, trying to clear his vision. The last thing he remembered was his helmet slamming against the heavy metal frame of the cupola display.

The Wolverine was dark and deathly quiet. All the displays were out. The engine must have died and the power had somehow failed.

"Crew! Status?" He didn't bother with the intercom, but shouted so his crew could hear him through their helmets.

"Christ, sir, what was that?" The driver was still disoriented.

"I don't know and I don't care," Sparks snapped. "Can we move or is the tank dead?"

"Hang on, general..." Sparks relaxed slightly at the change in the driver's tone of voice. He was snapping out of it.

The interior lights snapped back on, and Sparks heard the whine of the starters for the tank's twin turbine engines.

"Gunner?"

"Sir, primary fire control is off-line, but we've still got optical." He paused, then looked up at Sparks from where he sat, below and ahead of the general. Sparks could have reached out and tapped the man's helmet with his foot. "Jesus, sir, they're right on top of us!"

"Hell!" Sparks popped the hatch. Shoving it open, he stuck his head out and looked to their front. His skin crawled at not only the sight, but the blood-curdling screams of thousands of alien warriors who were now less than a hundred meters away. "Do we have radio?"

"Negative, sir." The driver muttered a curse. He couldn't move the Wolverine until the turbines had reached operating temperature. It didn't take long, only a minute, but it was a minute they didn't have. He could see the cyan glow of lightning grenades held by some of the approaching warriors. He was a veteran of the ongoing campaign against the Kreelans on Saint Petersburg, and knew painfully well what those hellish weapons could do to his vehicle and its crew.

"Guess we'll have to wake everybody up the old fashioned way." Sparks manually aimed the gatling gun at the approaching horde. "Open fire!"

The gun spat a solid stream of shells that tore into the front ranks of the warriors, mowing them down by the dozens. Other tanks and fighting vehicles, their crews recovering from the strange phenomenon that had hit them, began firing, as well.

The Wolverine's main gun spoke, sending a flechette round straight into the Kreelan line. Normally a devastating weapon, the enemy was so close now that it simply punched a deep but narrow hole into the mass of warriors that was quickly filled by more.

"Driver!" Sparks paused momentarily in his firing so he could hear his driver's response. "Back us up! Fast!"

"The turbines aren't up yet, sir!"

Sparks cursed as he fired again, sending over a hundred cannon rounds every second into the enemy in a desperate attempt to keep the Kreelans away.

Next to him, the antipersonnel mortar began to fire, sending the small bombs arcing into the alien horde.

The first volley of lightning grenades rose from the approaching warriors, and the tanks on both sides of Sparks were hit. Webs of cyan energy engulfed the weapons as soon as the weapons touched the metal, the flickering tendrils leaving white-hot scars across the armor. The commander of the Wolverine on the left managed to get out. His uniform was on fire, and he only lasted a few seconds before a Kreelan flying weapon cut him down. The other members of his crew and that of the tank on the right were burned alive.

A pair of lightning grenades sailed up from warriors in front of Sparks's tank just before his gunner blew the Kreelans apart with another round from the main gun.

"Driver!" Sparks gritted his teeth in resignation as he kept on firing, waiting for the lightning to take him.

"Hang on, sir!"

Sparks barely had time to reach out a hand to brace himself after the driver's warning when the Wolverine lurched in reverse, throwing up a huge geyser of dirt into the faces of the attacking warriors.

"Please, God." Sparks prayed as he watched the two grenades arcing down toward them. He mashed down the trigger again, blasting more warriors into oblivion.

One of the grenades missed completely, sending out a flurry of lightning bolts as it hit the ground.

The other hit the edge of the glacis plate, the very front armor of the tank.

"Oh, shit." The driver's words echoed the thoughts of all three men as the grenade began to arc against the tank's armor.

But as the metal around it began to melt, the grenade fell away to sizzle harmlessly on the ground

"Driver, we're running out of room!" Sparks glanced behind them. The tree line was approaching fast. The woods here were too thick for the tank to drive through without the risk of throwing a track and being immobilized. Right now, mobility was life. "Spin us to the right and get moving forward. We'll run parallel to their line and pour fire into 'em!"

"Yes, sir!"

As the driver answered, the Wolverine did exactly as Sparks had wanted, coming to a skidding stop before spinning in place in a perfect turn that lined them up parallel with the approaching aliens.

The gunner turned the turret to the left and began raking the enemy with the tank's guns. Behind and ahead of him, the other surviving tanks and infantry fighting vehicles were doing the same, following the lead of the Wolverine that flew a red pennant with three gold stars.

Sparks shook his head in grudging admiration at the endurance showed by the alien warriors. Even wearing armor and carrying weapons, they had sprinted almost half a dozen kilometers and were still coming on strong.

"General, we're going to run out of room."

Looking to his right, toward the tree line, Sparks saw that the driver was right. They wouldn't be able to keep far enough away from the Kreelans without going into the woods.

"Just keep firing." Sparks figured that if he had to die, this was as good a place and as good a way as any for an old cavalry soldier like him.

That's when he heard a sudden, massive barrage of cannon fire.

Looking up, he saw a line of tanks and infantry fighting vehicles burst over a rise just to the east, in the direction they were heading, every gun hammering at the mass of alien warriors.

"The reserve," Sparks whispered, relief flooding through him. These were the Marines his logistics officer had brought down farther away from the LZ, and they had been beyond the range of the strange... phenomenon. "Driver, wheel around as they pass and join their line."

"Yes, sir!"

For the first time, Sparks knew for certain that this battle was theirs. More of his Marines would die before the day was through, but he knew they were going to win.

TWENTY-TWO

Mills, Valentina, and Allison watched the strange dark wall consume the battlefield like a sandstorm.

Above, they saw the unmistakable streaks of incoming shells from an orbital bombardment, and clapped their hands over their ears at the deafening sonic booms.

Mills knew the shells were from the new battleships, which had special munitions that Commodore Sato had helped design. Mills had witnessed the gunnery tests over a deserted expanse of Siberia on Earth. The effects on the target area, which had been covered with dummies designed to simulate the alien warriors, had been devastating.

"Come on! Blow them to bloody kingdom come!"

The shells simply stopped in mid-air. He could see the glint of the metal casings, red-hot from reentry, hanging above the target.

Then they simply fell toward the ground, out of sight behind the rapidly expanding darkness.

"My God! That's bloody impossible!"

The dark cloud, whatever it was, swept over the Marine positions surrounding the landing zone.

Then, as suddenly as it had appeared, it began to dissipate.

Taking his hands from his ears, he could hear the voices of the warriors, tens of thousands of them. A mass of black-clad bodies ran through the clearing smoke as they charged the human encirclement.

"Start shooting, you buggers!" Mills bellowed at the top of his lungs.

As if the distant Marines heard him, a gatling gun growled, followed by the heavy crack of a tank's main gun firing.

In a moment, the battlefield was consumed by weapons fire as the human defenders came alive.

"It's going to be close," Valentina said from beside him. Her eyesight was better, and she could see how close the Kreelans really were. The Marines were mowing them down in droves, but the aliens were right on top of them. "If the Marines don't…"

Right in front of them, *she* was there. The warrior leader.

"Look at her," Mills whispered.

The warrior's face was covered in blood. It ran like tears from her eyes, which themselves were a bright red from burst blood vessels. It dripped from her chin onto the pendants that hung from her collar, then onto her breastplate. Streaks of crimson ran down the bright cyan rune on her armor.

She swayed for just a moment, then steadied herself. She looked at each of them in turn, her gaze lingering on Allison, before she fixed her eyes on Valentina. Then she slowly drew her sword.

Mills began to step forward, but Valentina held out a hand to stop him. "No, Mills. I've got this. Keep Allison and Steph safe."

He wanted to argue, but knew that she was right. He was at the end of his rope physically and could barely stay on his feet. And the only thing he had left as a weapon, besides his massive fists, was his combat knife, although Allison still held onto the sword she'd taken from a dead warrior. "Be bloody careful."

With that, Valentina moved forward, and the warrior took a few paces back to give them both some room.

Drawing her own sword, Valentina fought to clear her mind, hoping only that the warrior wouldn't use any of her supernatural powers. If she didn't, Valentina thought the fight might just be even, especially since the warrior was clearly injured.

With her blade held at the ready, she waited for the warrior to make the first move.

* * *

Ku'ar-Marekh was disappointed. One of the humans was grievously injured, and the others clearly wished to fight her one at a time. She had hoped they would attack her simultaneously to provide more of a challenge. Fighting each of them alone, even as badly wounded as her own body was, could have only one outcome, and would give little opportunity for her to bring the Empress the glory She deserved.

It also allowed for the chance that Ku'ar-Marekh herself might survive.

If that is to be my Way, she thought, *then so be it.*

With the roar of gunfire echoing from the distant battlefield, Ku'ar-Marekh raised her sword, her hands tightening around the living crystal of the handle, the tip of the blade glinting in the fading sunlight.

Staring into the eyes of the human, she attacked.

* * *

Valentina thought she was ready, but the strength and ferocity of the lightning-swift cut of the alien's blade caught her by surprise. The alien was far stronger than her battered appearance let on.

She managed to parry the attack, the blades singing as they collided, but the force of the blow knocked Valentina off-balance.

Using her momentum instead of fighting against it, she fell backward and rolled, springing to her feet just in time to block a thrust aimed at her heart. The alien missed her intended target, but Valentina hissed with pain as the alien's blade sliced deep into the flesh along the ribs under her left arm.

Baring her teeth and focusing her anger and frustration, she launched herself at the warrior, her sword whirling in a series of strikes that drove the alien back. Adrenaline and stimulants flooded into Valentina's system from her implants, and the sword in her hand was a blur as it slashed and cut at the Kreelan, trying to get past the alien's devilishly fast defense to land a telling blow.

The alien made a sudden overhand cut, and as Valentina blocked it, she whirled to one side, intending to land a disabling kick to the alien's knee when a sudden, white hot pain exploded from her left shoulder.

She turned to see the claws of one of the alien's hands buried in the fragile joint.

With a cry of pain, Valentina shoved the alien back and tried to slash at the Kreelan's exposed wrist.

The alien warrior pulled out her claws and used her armored fist to deflect Valentina's blade.

Then the Kreelan rammed her sword into Valentina's unprotected stomach, shoving it in up to the golden hilt.

* * *

"Valentina!" Allison cried.

"No!" Mills screamed as Valentina froze, her face echoing shock and surprise as she stared down at the sword that had run clean through her body. The blade, glistening with her blood, protruded from her back.

Filled with murderous rage, Mills charged the warrior, armed with nothing but his bare hands.

The Kreelan deftly sidestepped his charge, even as she still held Valentina pinned on her sword.

A victim of his own momentum, Mills tumbled to the ground, but was back on his feet in an instant. Like a bull who'd missed the matador on its first pass, he came at the alien again.

This time, when she looked at him, he felt his heart constrict, pierced by thousands of icy needles.

Gasping in agony and clutching his hands to his chest, Mills sank to his knees.

He saw Allison, a feral snarl on her lips, rise up from beside Steph. Holding the Kreelan sword in both hands, she ran at the alien.

While the girl's attack had spirit, it was no match for the Kreelan. The warrior batted the sword's blade downward with her free hand, then with a powerful backhand blow sent Allison sprawling backward. She tripped over Steph and fell to the ground, still clutching the sword.

Get up, Mills told himself, sensing the pain ease slightly as the alien turned her attention back to Valentina. The warrior stared into Valentina's eyes as she deflected Valentina's weak attempts to strike the warrior with her good arm, the sword having slipped from her grip.

"Get up, you bastard…" Mills forced himself to his feet, his heart desperately trying to work within a constricting cage of ice.

With a wet hiss, the warrior yanked the sword from Valentina, who slowly fell to her knees, a thin line of blood seeping from the corner of her mouth.

Then the Kreelan raised her sword, intending to take Valentina's head from her body.

Grimacing in agony, Mills charged.

* * *

Steph awoke with a start, her heart racing. She'd been having a nightmare, a terrible dream of swords and death. But as her subconscious gave way to conscious thought, the details blissfully faded into oblivion.

She was curled up in bed, surrounded by all the familiar things of home. The scent of freshly brewed coffee drifted in from the kitchen down the hall, where the automatic coffee maker was percolating away.

Early morning. It had always been her favorite time of day, the brief moment out of time when the world hadn't yet intruded, when she had no duties or obligations. A moment when she had time to herself to do absolutely nothing.

Beside her lay Ichiro. She watched the rise and fall of his well-muscled chest, the slow rhythm of his breathing as he slept. She was so happy he was home, that they were together again. She had hated being separated from him, had wanted him back so badly. But he was here now. Everything was again as it should be.

Watching him sleep, she marveled at what a handsome man he was. Despite having what amounted to a sedentary job, he still kept himself in excellent shape, and she smiled as she ran her eyes over his arms and shoulders, his chiseled abs. He was quite a bit younger than she was. It was a fact she never made any to-do about in public, but that she secretly allowed to serve her vanity. And as motivation to stay in great shape herself.

Young though he might be, he had been made far older and wiser by the dreadful experiences he'd had since first contact with the Kreelans. He'd suffered through more than any man should have to endure, having lost so many of his shipmates and his beloved ships to the enemy.

Her mind filled with visions of the blue-skinned horrors rampaging across the human sphere, a plague in shining black armor, killing everyone in their path. She heard the cries of rage and pain as men and women fought the enemy for their lives, defending their homes, themselves, and their children.

They fought, yes. And died under the enemy's sword.

The thought made her shudder, gooseflesh breaking out all over her skin. She snuggled closer to Ichiro, rearranging his arm so she could lay up against him, her head on his shoulder.

But as she clung to him, her visions of the loathsome aliens intensified, and Ichiro's body seemed cold. So cold.

She began to shiver uncontrollably, and one of her legs throbbed with pain.

Propping herself up so she could see Ichiro's face, she saw that it was deathly pale.

No, not pale, she decided. His face was…fading. He was disappearing before her eyes.

"Ichiro?" she whispered, her heart hammering with dread.

His eyes snapped wide open, and he spoke, but it wasn't his voice. It sounded like Roland Mills.

"*Valentina!*"

* * *

Steph screamed and blinked her eyes open. She lay there in the dirt, disoriented, wondering where she was.

Beside her, she saw a young girl staring at something. Then she heard a man, not Ichiro, bellow "No!"

Turning her head, she saw a huge man in a camouflage uniform running toward an alien warrior, who was standing next to another woman.

"Valentina," Steph whispered, recognizing her. But she realized Valentina wasn't just standing next to the alien. The Kreelan's sword was sticking out her friend's back. "Oh...God..."

The big man - Mills, she realized, fighting through the fog in her brain - ran at the warrior, who dodged aside. He turned around to attack again, but before he took more than two steps he clutched at his chest as if he were having a heart attack, then crumpled to the ground.

Beside her, Allison charged the alien, brandishing a sword. But the Kreelan deflected the girl's sword before knocking her backward. Allison tripped and fell over Steph, sprawling in the dirt beside her.

Grimacing in the pain from her leg and fighting the dizziness that threatened to again leave her unconscious, Steph reached down to her combat harness and pulled out her knife. Her mind had caught up with the reality around her. She didn't expect to survive, but wasn't about to allow the Kreelan to kill her without putting up a struggle.

"Allison!"

The girl was next to her in an instant. "Steph? Oh, God..."

Steph grabbed the girl's hand and held on. "Listen to me. You need to run. Get away."

"No! I'm not leaving you!"

They both looked up as Mills roared.

Valentina was on her knees, the warrior standing over her, sword raised, as Mills ran at the Kreelan. Her blade whistled through the air, and the big Marine grunted as the sword slashed deep through his right shoulder, effortlessly slicing through muscle and bone.

But that didn't stop him. A hundred and twenty kilograms of solid muscle slammed into the warrior.

While the warrior was shoved back, right up next to Steph, she somehow managed to stay on her feet.

Mills grappled with her, his good hand yanking the braids of her hair. He levered her head back and bit into her neck above her collar, his teeth sinking deep into her flesh even as she battered at his head with the handle of her sword.

Shoving Allison out of the way, Steph cried out in pain as she forced herself over on her side, plunging her knife into one of the alien's sandaled feet and pinning it to the ground.

With one final, titanic heave, Mills threw the warrior off-balance, and the two of them crashed to the ground.

* * *

Allison watched in terror as Mills, blood streaming down his chest from the terrible sword wound, clung desperately to the warrior. Behind them, she could see Valentina, still on her knees, watching the spectacle as her life drained away.

Allison gripped the alien sword in her hand, determined not to run, but afraid at the end to die.

That's when Steph shoved her backward, away from the struggling titans, and rammed her knife into one of the Kreelan's feet.

The alien gurgled a cry of pain, half her throat torn out by Mills, before he finally shoved her over, making her fall.

Right on top of Allison.

Without thinking, Allison propped up her sword, the handle on the ground. The blade pierced the alien's back armor as the warrior fell right on top of it, and the glittering tip burst from her chest armor only a few centimeters from Mills's neck.

Allison gasped as the Kreelan and Mills slammed down on top of her, driving the air from her lungs. But Allison didn't have to suffer their full weight. Most of it was supported by the handle of the sword.

After a moment, the weight lifted as Mills rolled off to one side, dragging the Kreelan with him.

"Bloody hell, girl," he gasped as he struggled to his knees. "Bloody hell." Mills grabbed his right shoulder with his left hand, literally holding the flesh together. The sword had cut clean through his collar bone and part of his shoulder blade, and he could tell from the wet rasp of his breathing that his right lung had been punctured, as well.

He looked up as a shadow fell over him, and Valentina, blood soaking the front of her uniform, slowly sank down beside him. Her face was deathly pale. "Ready for that margarita on the beach?"

Then she closed her eyes and slumped against his chest.

"Jesus," Mills whispered, fighting away the darkness that threatened to take him.

"You've got to get help, Allison." Steph pointed toward the battlefield, where the sounds of the guns had reached a crescendo of growls, staccato pops, and booms, mixed with the fading roar of the warriors. "Hurry, honey."

"Just ask…" Mills could barely get the words out as his right lung filled with blood. His heart was as broken as his body as he cradled Valentina, who lay lifeless against him. "Just ask…any Marine…for General Sparks."

"General Sparks," Allison repeated, and Steph nodded.

But as Allison rose to her feet she felt a clawed hand grip her arm.

With a cry of fright, she looked down to see the warrior, staring up at her.

* * *

Ku'ar-Marekh felt the life flowing from her body. She knew the blade held by the human pup had severed one of the major arteries inside her, and she would bleed to death in but moments.

Beyond the pain, the thought gave her a sense of peace.

Instead of the chill she expected as death came for her, she felt a growing warmth. It wasn't simply a trick of her dying body, but was from the Bloodsong. She could sense it more fully as her blood soaked the loose earth beneath her. She began to feel the emotions of her sisters again.

And the Ancient Ones. She could sense them now, as well. All who had lived and died since the days of the First Empress were bound in spirit to She Who Reigned. Ku'ar-Marekh could feel them now, as clearly as those who now fought and died against the humans here on this world.

The humans. She had not expected them to best her, but she did not regret their victory.

The small one, the child who had held the killing blade, was next to her. As the child made to stand up, Ku'ar-Marekh reached out and took her arm.

The young human made a small noise of fear and surprise, but did not attempt to flee.

Ku'ar-Marekh released the child's arm and instead held out her hand, palm up. Much to her surprise, the human slowly took it.

"In Her name, may thy Way be long and glorious, little one."

Giving the human's hand a gentle squeeze, Ku'ar-Marekh let go before closing her eyes and letting the warmth of death enfold her.

* * *

Allison had no idea what the alien had said, but in the moment that she spoke her final words, her eyes changed. Allison saw life in them, just before they closed for the final time.

As the alien's hand slipped away, Allison stood up and ran as fast as she could toward the sound of the guns.

* * *

Many light years away, the Empress stood upon the dais at the top of the pyramid of steps in the great throne room on the Empress Moon. She cast Her eyes upward, beyond the transparent crystal that formed the top of the gigantic pyramid that housed the palace, looking out at the stars.

And at one, in particular. With a second sight that could see beyond time and space, She watched Ku'ar-Marekh's last battle, and felt the priestess's pain as the sword pierced her.

The Empress opened Her heart wide as Ku'ar-Marekh's life bled away, releasing her spirit from the bonds of life, and the last priestess of the Nyur-A'il took her place among the Ancient Ones.

Across the vast stretches of the Empire, a vast wave was cast through the Bloodsong, an echo of the sorrow of the Empress.

TWENTY-THREE

Allison had never run so far, so fast. Exhausted as she was, she knew that every second counted, and that the lives of her three friends depended on her. Even as she sucked air into her lungs, she bit her lip to drive away the fear that they would all be dead by the time she could get help.

She had never seen so much blood on a person who was still alive as she'd seen on both Mills and Valentina. And while Steph's wound wasn't as bad, she'd been bleeding a long time now. All three of them, Mills especially, looked like something right out of a vid about zombies that she had seen once with her older brother.

God, please don't let them die. She forced herself to go just a little faster, wishing with every step that she had Race, her brave, dead horse to carry her. Wishing the Kreelans had never come to her world. Wishing them all to Hell.

As she ran, heading right down the road past her farm, she came upon more and more bodies. Most of them were Kreelans, but there were many humans, too. Marines, like Mills.

And there were ships, both human and Kreelan. Many of the wrecks still burned, while others were nothing more than smoking piles of melted metal and plastic, surrounded by bits of debris. The stench of it, combined with the smell of blood and other bodily things she didn't want to even think about, made her want to gag.

Around her, there were no cries for help or screams of agony from the wounded or the dying. None here, human or Kreelan, were left alive. The humans had all been killed, and the Kreelans, she had read, committed suicide. None had ever been taken alive.

With a yelp, she dove to the ground as a stream of cannon shells whipped past her, stray rounds from the fight up ahead.

She looked up after a moment, and found herself next to a Kreelan warrior whose dead, sightless eyes were open, as if staring at her.

"Get up, Allison!" She looked away from the nightmarish blue face, mustering the courage to go on. She couldn't stop. Too much depended on her.

With a grimace, forcing herself to not be sick from the horror around her, she pushed herself up from the sticky pool of blood that the road had become and again started running.

Mills, Valentina, and Steph. I have to save them. I won't let them die. She kept repeating that mantra, over and over, with every step through the nightmare landscape around her.

She slowed momentarily as the gunfire, which had become deafening the closer she'd come to the battle, began to taper off, then stopped.

The silence that descended gave her a chill until she heard something she hadn't heard in what seemed like years: people cheering. She could see Marines on their big tanks and on the ground, holding up their arms and giving voice to their victory.

"We've won!"

The thought gave her a new burst of energy, and she ran toward the tank that was nearest her.

* * *

Sergeant Emilio Sanchez sat in a small patch of grass in the shadow of his tank. He was on the side facing away from the gruesome mass of dead aliens, leaning against one of the big road wheels. He could make out the smell of the charred paint and scorched metal from what was left of the tank's skirt, a sheet of relatively thin armor that was meant to protect the vehicle's vulnerable lower hull.

A Kreelan had thrown a lightning grenade that had stuck to it, and Sanchez had been sure they were done for.

They would have been, had not a lunatic commanding an infantry fighting vehicle driven alongside them, shearing off most of the skirt, the grenade along with it, just as the thing detonated. Both vehicles were scorched, but had survived.

Sanchez had every intention of making sure the crazy bastard got a medal and a case of beer as soon as he could figure out who it had been.

Taking another drag on his cigarette, he stared blankly at the original landing zone, toward the town, idly watching the columns of smoke rise from all the destroyed ships and vehicles there. Behind him, his crew and most of the others around them were hooting and hollering, celebrating their victory.

Sanchez just wanted to find a bar somewhere and get drunk, but he knew there probably weren't any bars left open on the entire planet, and Confederation warships were "dry," not allowing alcohol on-board.

"Navy prudes," he muttered, disgusted.

Taking a last drag on the cigarette, he flicked it away. Following it with his eyes, he noticed something moving in the distance, coming closer. *No, not something, you idiot,* he chided himself. *Someone.*

"Pikula!" Standing up, he called out to his gunner, who was sitting on the turret. "Pikula!" he shouted, louder.

The woman turned around. "What is it, TC?" Her smile faltered as she caught the movement. "Holy shit! It's a civilian!"

"It's not just a civvie, it's a kid!" Sanchez was already running toward the grimy, blood-spattered girl, who was gasping for breath as she staggered more than ran toward him. "Get the medikit and some water!"

As he reached the girl, she collapsed in his arms, her chest heaving.

"Take it easy, kid. I've got you." He sat her down on the ground and knelt in front of her. "You're okay now. Nobody's gonna hurt you here."

She shook her head. "Need…to talk…to General Sparks."

He leaned back, shocked that she knew of Sparks. "Well, sure. We'll get you up to see the general when we've got you taken care of. You've been roughed up a…"

"No, now!" She leaned forward and grabbed his combat webbing with both hands and shook him, a look of desperation in her eyes. "I have to talk to him…right now!"

Sanchez rubbed his chin, thinking for a moment as Pikula dropped to her knees beside him, offering the girl a canteen.

Taking her hands off Sanchez, the girl grabbed it and took a single, greedy swig, before handing it back.

"Now," she begged him. "Please, there's no time! My friends are dying, or already dead. They need help."

"Right." Sanchez clicked the control for his unit's general channel. "Captain Kamov, this is Sanchez. I've got a civilian here who needs to talk to General Sparks." Looking into the girl's pleading gaze, he added, "It's an emergency, sir."

"Roger that." Kamov's response was instant. Sanchez had had his disagreements with the man, but one thing the captain wasn't was indecisive. "Stand by."

Barely a few heartbeats had passed when a voice came over Sanchez's headset. "This is Sparks. Go."

Sanchez took off his helmet and gently set it on the girl's head. "Just talk, honey. The general will hear you."

* * *

Hands on hips, Sparks stood at the ragged edge of the killing field where tens of thousands of dead Kreelans lay, his cavalry hat shading his eyes from the sun. While on the whole it had been a massacre, the aliens had managed to kill another three thousand of his Marines. He shuddered to think what they could have done if they had chosen to fight with more modern weapons. In some battles, they did, and others they didn't.

Like everything else about the Kreelans, Sparks didn't understand it, and that bothered him more than anything else. *How can we ever defeat an enemy we don't understand at all?* The thought further depressed him as he looked at the carnage.

"Nothing except a battle lost can be half so melancholy as a battle won." The operations officer, his face bandaged where a piece of shrapnel had sliced his cheek, murmured the words spoken by the Duke of Wellington centuries before.

"At least at Waterloo the end was in sight." Sparks gestured at the mass of bodies that lay sprawled in death. "This here was just a sideshow."

"Maybe so, sir, but we still won. That counts for something."

"I wonder," Sparks murmured. Turning to the other man, he said, "I assume you didn't just come over here to cheer me up, especially since you didn't bring a damn beer with you."

The operations officer smiled. "No, sir. I just wanted to pass on that Commodore Sato's coming down to pay his respects."

"And look for his wife, I imagine." Sparks had worked with Sato during the planning for this mission, but held him in high regard for another reason. Sato had saved Sparks's life, and that of his men and women, during their escape from the Keran disaster. And Sato's wife, Steph, had been right with Sparks and his regiment there, and had in her own way been very much a hero. Sparks planned to render every assistance to Sato to try and find his wife's body. He owed both of them that much. "Damn, that was an awful thing."

"Yes, sir. I won't argue with that." He looked out at the battlefield, following his general's gaze. "God, what a mess that'll be to clean up."

Sparks was about to reply when a voice sounded in his comm headset that was draped around his neck.

"Sir, I think you need to take this," his communications officer told him.

"What have you got?"

"Sir, it's an emergency call for you. I'm cutting you over to Sergeant Sanchez, a track commander in the 47th Armored Regiment."

There was a pause, then a beep, indicating the channel was open. "This is Sparks. Go."

He was surprised to hear the voice of a young girl.

* * *

"General, sir, my name is Allison Murtaugh..." She paused, not sure how to say the right words to this stranger. The voice on the other end, the man, seemed as hard as steel.

"Go on, honey," the voice said, much softer. Even though his accent was different, one she had never heard before, his voice reminded her of her father's.

"Sir, my friends need help. Sergeant Mills and Valentina are terribly hurt, and Steph is, too. They're dying. Mills told me to run here and get you, so I did. Please help them!"

There was a brief pause before the general spoke again, the steel back in his voice. "You can count on it, Allison. Now please put Sergeant Sanchez back on."

Relieved to be rid of the weight of the helmet, Allison handed it back to Sanchez, who quickly slipped it on.

"General, sir?"

"Sanchez, crank up your track right now. Take Allison and have her show you where Mills and the others are. And if there are any corpsmen nearby, take them, too. If not, have your medikit handy. I'll be with you as soon as I can. Got all that, son?"

"Yes, sir!"

"Then ride hard and fast, trooper! Sparks out."

Sanchez pulled Allison to her feet and headed toward the tank. Pikula was just disappearing down the hatch to her position in the turret.

"Tibbets!" he called to the driver over the tank's comm link, "crank her up!"

As he helped Allison climb up the front of the tank, vibrating now from the power of the vehicle's big turbine engines, he told her, "Little lady, you're about to have the wildest ride of your life."

* * *

Sato sat in the passenger compartment of the shuttle from the *Orion*, desperately trying to shut off his brain, to banish the dark thoughts that clouded his mind.

With *Orion* severely damaged, he would be shifting his flag to *Conqueror*. Before he did, however, he had one last duty to perform as *Orion's* acting captain, burial services for his dead crew members. It was a task he dreaded, but like his other duties, he would perform it to the very best of his abilities. Semyonova and the others deserved no less.

In the meantime, a duty much closer to his heart called. He had to look for Steph's body. He had to bring her home. It would be a grisly task, looking over the thousands of bodies around the town of Breakwater, but he would do it. No matter how long it took or what he might find, he would do it.

He couldn't tell himself that she never would have come here had he not pushed her away, because that wouldn't be true. Steph was an adventurer, as he was in his own way, and she probably would have come, anyway.

"Commodore?"

He turned to see the copilot, standing in the doorway to the cramped flight deck.

The copilot handed him a headset. "Sir, General Sparks is calling for you."

"Thank you." He took the headset and slipped it on. "Sato here, general."

"Ichiro, get your ass down here. Steph and some other members of her team may have survived. I've got some troops on the way to them now. Head toward the western edge of Breakwater, and I'll send you exact coordinates as soon as I have them. You'll have to evac them. We don't have any boats left down here that can fly. You got that?"

Sato sat, staring wide-eyed at the forward bulkhead, not believing his ears.

"Sato?"

"Yes...yes, sir! We're on our way."

"Let's hustle, son. Sparks, out."

"Pilot!" Sato ordered. "Take us down, now! Emergency descent!"

* * *

Allison didn't know if she should be terrified or elated. She was standing in the commander's position in the big tank as it raced along, going so fast it sometimes went completely airborne when they came over a rise in the ground. The commander, Sanchez, stood behind her on the engine deck, clinging to handholds on the turret for dear life.

"A little to the left!" Sanchez had fitted her with an extra helmet so she could talk over the tank's intercom and guide the driver. She pointed to a spot about a hundred meters away now, where a few figures were visible on the ground.

"It's them!" Sanchez told the driver. "Pull up close and stop."

The tank slowed at the last possible moment, then slewed to the side and came to a stop. The driver was careful to make sure that the dust and dirt the vehicle kicked up didn't hit the blood-soaked bodies.

"This is Sanchez. We found 'em." He didn't wait for his company commander to respond before he linked the coordinates to the division's net. Sparks would be able to find them easily now.

Sanchez helped Allison out of the turret, then hopped down to the ground. Pikula and Tibbets, both with medikits, were right behind him.

"Holy Jesus," Sanchez whispered, crossing himself. The blond-haired woman, who he knew by sight was Commodore Sato's wife, lay on her back, eyes closed. The only major injury he could see was her leg, but that was enough. It was a mass of dried and matted blood.

The other two were far worse. A huge Marine - Mills, he must be, from what the girl had said - lay on his back. There was a horrible wound in his right shoulder, as if he'd had a run-in with a bandsaw and lost. His face was covered in blood.

In his left arm he cradled a woman who had been stabbed clean through with a sword, with another set of stab wounds in one shoulder.

There was blood everywhere.

"Sanchez…" The tone of Pikula's voice echoed his own thoughts. They were all dead.

Allison stood there beside Sanchez, shivering as tears brimmed in her eyes. "I was too late."

Sanchez knelt down next to Steph first and reached out with a pair of fingers to her throat to feel for a pulse. "She's alive. Barely." He gestured to Tibbets. "Get a fresh bandage on the wound and shoot her up with some antibiotics and stims."

Then he turned to Mills and the other woman. "What's her name?"

"Valentina." Allison slowly knelt beside her two entwined friends. She had been too slow. Too slow. Steph was still alive, but they were dead. "No."

Again reaching his fingers out, he touched Valentina's throat.

He shook his head and was just pulling his fingers away when he stopped. "What the hell?" He tried again, waiting longer. "Son of a bitch! It's slow as hell, but she's got a pulse! Pikula, get a patch on the wound in her back, then we're gonna roll her off this guy."

Then he checked Mills for a pulse. "I don't believe it. He's still alive, too."

Ripping open the medikits, Sanchez and his crew did what they could to patch up Mills and the two women.

As they worked, Allison heard another sonic boom and looked up. A small ship glinted in the sky, and as she watched, it headed right for them.

Rescue had come.

Smiling, hope rekindled that her friends might yet live, she turned back to watch as the tankers gently rolled Valentina off Mills and put a dressing over the wound in her stomach.

That's when she noticed that the Kreelan who had nearly killed them all, the one with the dead eyes, was nowhere to be seen. Steph's knife was still stuck in the ground where she had impaled the warrior's foot, just as it had been, but there was no sign of the alien's body.

She was gone.

* * *

The first thing Steph noticed was the vibration. It was rhythmic and steady, but seemed...hurried.

After a moment, she realized that she was being carried.

The second thing she noticed was her left hand. Someone was holding it, and she could tell just by touch whose hand it was.

Her eyes fluttered open, and she looked up to see a familiar face looking down at her. It was the face of the man she loved. Beyond him she could make out the interior of a small ship, and the shapes of people she didn't know, carrying her along.

"Ichiro," she breathed as she was gently lowered onto a foldout bunk in the ship. "I knew...you'd come."

"The whole Empire couldn't have kept me away." His hand tightened on hers. "And I'll never leave you again."

Just before she drifted off into a painless, dreamless sleep, she felt the warmth of his lips on hers.

EPILOGUE

On the open plain of Ural-Murir, an island continent in the southern hemisphere of the Homeworld, stood the temple of the Nyur-A'il.

As with all the temples of the seven orders from the ancient times, it had long since fallen into ruin. The stone of which the buildings were made was eroded and crumbling, the runes and glyphs of the Old Tongue long since erased by wind and rain.

The dilapidated state of the temple was an illusion, however. For the true nature of this place, as with the other ancient temples, lay beyond mere stone. It was in the spirit of the Ancient Ones, the high priests and priestesses now dead, whose spirits dwelled here.

The Empress stood on the worn dais of the temple's *Kalai-Il*, Her white robes and hair reflecting the gentle magenta hue of the sky as the sun began to set. Around the edges of the massive central stone base, torches flickered in anticipation of night's fall.

Before Her lay Ku'ar-Marekh's body on a carefully constructed pyre of wood. Each piece had been brought by one of the warrior priestesses and clawless mistresses who now stood upon the weathered stone rings of the *Kalai-Il*. They had come from all over the Empire, brought here by the will of the Empress.

As had Ku'ar-Marekh's body. She was the first high priestess to fall in battle since the last great war with a soulless enemy among the stars. And, as She had done since the time of Keel-Tath, the body of a high priestess would always be given the last rites, and would never be left behind for an enemy.

The difference between this ceremony and those in ages past was that Ku'ar-Marekh was the last of her kind. This had never before happened in the long history of the Empire. There would be no more disciples to follow in her footsteps, to keep alive the Way of the Nyur-A'il.

For this, the Empress mourned, and the skin below her eyes was black with the tears of Her soul.

Around the pyre stood five high priestesses of the surviving orders. The sixth, she who would have stood at the right hand of the Empress representing the Desh-Ka, was absent. Tesh-Dar, the greatest living warrior of the Empire, remained cloistered in her temple, and there would remain until the Empress again summoned her. When it was time.

To the left of the Empress stood Pan'ne-Sharakh, the oldest and wisest of the clawless ones. All of the high priestesses had weapons crafted by the ancient armorer, who could shape the living steel of their blades like no other, and make each a unique work of art worthy of display in the throne room on the Empress Moon.

Her hands clasped in the sleeves of her black robes, Pan'ne-Sharakh stood, head bowed in silent thought. The Empress knew that she mourned for Ku'ar-Marekh, but that the ancient mistress's heart mourned far more the silence in the Bloodsong of Tesh-Dar. The two had long been close, perhaps closer than the Empress had been to the great warrior before ascending to the throne, even though Tesh-Dar and the Empress were sisters by blood, born from the same womb.

Around the high priestesses, filling the dais, were the senior clawless mistresses of the castes from among Her Children. From porters of water to the builders, they represented the spirits of those who had been most loyal to the First Empress in Her darkest hour. All now stood in honor of the fallen high priestess of the Nyur-A'il.

Beyond the massive platform of the *Kalai-Il*, on the concentric raised rings of ancient stone stood the hundreds of warrior priestesses and acolytes of the five orders. There were none from the Desh-Ka, as Tesh-Dar had no disciples.

An even greater tragedy, the Empress thought darkly, before turning Her gaze upon the warriors watching from above, remembering from ages past how there once had been many thousands.

Never would such a time come again, She knew.

And yet, solemn as the occasion might be, the Empress's heart was warmed by Ku'ar-Marekh's spirit. Her soul, complete now, had at last taken its rightful place among the warriors of the spirit.

"My Children," the Empress began, "we grieve the loss this day of the high priestess of the Nyur-A'il, not because she fell in battle, for she did so with great honor, but because she was the last of her kind. Never again shall there be another. For with her death, the ancient crystal that dwelled here, one of the seven that formed the heart of the ancient orders, has become dark and cold. Never again shall a warrior experience the fire of the Change in the temple of the Nyur-A'il."

She paused, looking around the inner circle of high priestesses. "Never before has this happened, in all the pages of the Books of Time. The Nyur-A'il was fated to be the first to pass into the darkness, but it shall not be the last." She glanced at the empty place to her right where Tesh-Dar would have been standing.

"In this, the Last War, all of us shall succumb to the same fate unless we can find the One and the tomb of the First Empress. Even then, most who stand here before Me now shall fall in battle, as is your honor and your right.

"I wish My Children to survive the dark night that is falling over us, borne by the Curse of Keel-Tath. Yet even the ancient prophecies from the oldest of the Books of Time do not speak of our salvation, only what we need to achieve it."

The warriors and clawless ones nodded. All of them knew the peril in which the Empire found itself, and realized that they were all bound to the same fate.

Sensing their darkened spirits through the Bloodsong, the Empress caressed Her belly where Her next child was growing in Her womb. It was a female, for which She was thankful, but would be born with silver talons. Sterile. While the Empress would give birth to new life, She knew that it would only bring Her Children one step closer to extinction.

"The humans," the Empress went on, looking up at the stars. "They are the key. We know much about them from the first of their ships that came to us, and from others since, lost in battle. We have pressed them hard, driving our blade deep.

"Yet, this is not prey we wish to kill quickly. They now build greater, more powerful ships and are training legions of warriors that will bring you much honor in the coming cycles. But we must bleed them slowly; I do not want to overwhelm them and break their courage. And no more shall we take them to the arenas. It is clear they do not understand the honor we accord them."

The high priestesses nodded their understanding. The pace of the offensives against the humans would be slowed. It did not upset them, but gladdened them. For the humans were worthy opponents, and letting their soulless race live longer would give greater opportunity for the warriors of Her Children to bring honor to the Empress. And all of them had seen by now that the arenas were nothing but slaughter pens for most of the humans, slaughter in which there was no honor, nor glory for the Empress.

"The world where Ku'ar-Marekh and her legions fell, we shall leave to the humans in her honor, until the time comes when we have found the One, or until we perish from the cosmos."

"In Thy name," the assembled warriors and clawless ones intoned, "shall it be so."

The Empress watched as the sun set over the distant white-topped mountains, beyond which lay the great sea of Tulyan-Ara'ath. The sky rippled with fiery hues of red and orange, yellow and violet that glittered in her silver-flecked eyes, eyes that opened onto an ageless soul.

"It is time."

Acolytes handed torches to the five high priestesses and Pan'ne-Sharakh, who stepped forward and set alight Ku'ar-Marekh's funeral pyre. As the flames grew, the wood crackling and throwing sparks into the air, they stepped back and watched as their sister's body was consumed.

As the smoke rose into the sky, the Empress focused Her love on the once-tortured spirit of Ku'ar-Marekh, whose soul now rested in the peaceful stillness of the Afterlife.

* * *

The beach was perfect. The sand was white and fine, the water clear blue and warm. A light breeze blew in from the ocean, carrying with it the sound of the gently rolling surf and the voices of the children playing in the waves.

Valentina took a sip of her margarita, savoring the taste of the tequila and strawberries as she sat in a beach chair under a huge umbrella. She watched Allison, hopping up and down in the waves and screaming with delight as she and some other kids she had found to play with splashed each other.

Not having any other relatives on Alger's World, and not wanting to stay there, Allison had come back to Earth. Ichiro and Steph, who had recovered quickly from her leg wound, had taken care of her while Valentina and Mills were in the hospital.

But when Valentina had been well enough for visitors, Allison had asked if she could live with her and Mills. Permanently.

"You two are going to get married, right?" The girl had gone straight for the jugular with an assumption about something that Valentina had only just been giving some thought to. "And well, I thought maybe you could adopt me. I promise I won't be any trouble!"

Valentina had been taken completely off-guard, and the girl's expression tore at her heart.

She was a great kid, and Valentina would never be able to have her own. The injuries she'd sustained in the battle at Saint Petersburg had seen to that. She'd never considered adopting, because she had never really given much thought to being a mother. But after all that had happened...

Adopt Allison? Why not?

Looking into Allison's expectant eyes, Valentina knew she couldn't say no. Instead, smiled and said, "Okay. We will."

Allison had been elated, but that was nothing compared to her delirium after meeting Valentina's parents, Dmitri and Ludmilla Sikorsky. That's when she discovered they owned a horse farm, and Allison could ride as much and as long as she wanted. And she was in complete heaven when they presented her with her very own horse.

Marrying Mills, on the other hand, had been something that Valentina had been a lot less certain about, and so had he.

While they had been living together after they got out of the hospital, they hadn't discussed anything more serious than what Valentina had originally promised him. Some time together on a beautiful, sunny beach, sipping margaritas.

They had Allison along, of course, albeit sleeping in an adjacent room at the hotel. She didn't seem to mind, and was happy to let Valentina and Mills have a little privacy.

"Looks like she's doing well enough." Mills, sitting next to her, was watching the kids, too, and when Valentina glanced at him, she could see a look of fondness on his face. While he was still a bit of a tough guy on the outside, she knew that he couldn't have loved Allison more if she'd been his daughter by birth. "Tough kid."

Valentina smiled, thinking of how happy the three of them were now.

It hadn't been that way at first. Both of them had gone through hell the last few months since returning from Alger's World, but Mills had gotten the worst of it. While her own injuries had been bad enough, her implants had shut down her body's systems after the warrior had stabbed her, preventing her from bleeding out. She had lost a kidney and suffered some other internal injuries, not to mention the damage to her shoulder joint, but had recovered relatively quickly. She still experienced some pain, but knew that over time it would fade away to nothing.

The worst of it, she thought wryly, was that she'd never wear a bikini again. Her body had too many scars.

Mills, on the other hand, almost hadn't made it. Surgeons on the *Guadalcanal* had worked on him for six hours. His heart had stopped three times, and the surgeons would have given up on him the last time, except for Sato's impassioned pleas for them to try to resuscitate him one last time. Just as they were about to give up, his heart started beating.

His survival had been little short of a miracle.

After that he'd had to battle a series of infections, and then the ultimate torture of physical therapy for his right shoulder, which had to be completely reconstructed. Many had been the nights when she'd held him, his body shivering from the pain. He refused to take any painkillers after leaving the hospital. At first she had thought it was because he was trying to be a macho fool, but gradually realized it was because he was afraid of becoming addicted. As a big, powerful man, a trained killer, he had very few fears, but that was one of them.

Finally his condition reached a tipping point. The pain eased off, his strength and range of motion dramatically improved, and after the last of the dressings and restraints had been removed, he was again able to sleep.

Among other things, she thought with a sly smile.

"What's that look for?" He squinted at her, as if trying to read her thoughts. "God, but you're a randy wench."

Valentina couldn't restrain a laugh. "Well, in that case, I guess we needn't have a repeat of last night."

"Well," he said quickly, "you wouldn't want to deprive me of some great physical therapy, would you?" He made a show of moving his right arm, flexing the muscles that, between his physical therapy and increasingly tough workouts, were quickly growing back to their earlier massive size. Unlike her, he had no reservations about displaying his battle scars for all to see. He liked the attention.

His flexing drew more than a few appreciative glances from some of the bikini-clad women nearby.

"You're hopeless." Rolling her eyes, Valentina took another sip of her margarita, turning her attention back to Allison.

"But you love me, anyway."

"Yes, you idiot. God help me, but I do."

* * *

Ichiro came into the apartment and closed the door behind him, puffing a breath out through his lips. It had been a long day at Africa Station, as most days were, overseeing the repairs of *Orion* and the construction of the next batch of new battleships. Eight of them were being built at Africa Station, with another six in the yards at Avignon and four at Ekaterina. The new class was only slightly changed from the *Orions*, but the next battleships that were now being designed would be even larger and more powerful.

It was exhausting work, but it was no longer the focus of his life. He called Steph at least once a day to tell her he loved her, and made sure he did at least one little thing each day when he came home to prove it. And sometimes a big thing or two.

But his work week was over. While he was technically always on call, unless Earth were attacked, he was looking forward to an uninterrupted weekend that he fully expected to enjoy.

His wife, too, had made more room in her life for their marriage. She was back working on the president's staff, but this time as a coordinator for the agency the president was establishing to handle the massive refugee problem. The goal wasn't to simply find a place for refugees to go, but to use those who were willing to establish new colonies on the edge of human-explored space.

While that was an option for adults and families, it didn't help the war orphans like Allison and the other children from Alger's World. That was a much harder problem to solve, and is what Steph concentrated her energies on while at work.

Her first success had been placing the children Allison had saved in foster homes. The children had been on one of the boats that had escaped to reach the fleet, and the kids had first class accomodations in Admiral Voroshilov's living quarters aboard the *Guadalcanal* for the trip back to Earth.

After the story of what Allison had done hit the press, Steph's department had been deluged with thousands of inquiries from people offering to adopt. After personally interviewing the families that seemed most promising, Steph had placed Amrit, Vanhi, and the other children with families on Earth, and had stayed in touch with them to make sure they were getting the love and care they deserved.

"Steph?" He called out again.

No answer.

Frowning, he quickly hung up his uniform jacket in the foyer closet, then walked down the hall toward the living room.

He wasn't worried, although Steph had been acting a bit odd the last couple days. He hadn't been able to put his finger on it, but she'd seemed unusually anxious.

Walking into the living room, he saw her there, seated on the couch. She was leaning over, her elbows on her knees, with her chin propped up by her hands. She was beaming at him, but she had wet streaks down her cheeks.

Ichiro stopped, confused by her behavior. "Steph, are you all right?"

She nodded as she stood up and came over to him, reaching for his hands. "Yes, we're just fine."

Cocking his head, Ichiro asked, "We? You mean…"

"Yes." She nodded, a look of uncertainty on her face. "I'm pregnant. I know we hadn't exactly planned it, but-"

She didn't get a chance to finish as Ichiro threw his arms around her.

"I'm going to be a father!" Lifting her gently from the floor, he whirled her around, his heart filled with joy.

* * *

"It worked, by God." Secretary of State Hamilton Barca's deep voice carried the mixture of pleasure and relief he felt at the news he had brought to the president's cabinet meeting. "Every government that was even whispering about secession before the Alger's World operation has stepped back from the proverbial abyss. They remain concerned, obviously, but nobody can argue now. The Kreelans can be beaten. And the real key to it was the footage that Steph gathered. The stuff with those kids surviving until the Marines got there, and the recounting of the young lady - Allison, correct? - who helped kill the warrior leader..." He shook his head in admiration. "Along with the combat footage, it was some incredibly powerful stuff that really helped turn things around on the diplomatic front." He grinned at the president. "Your speech didn't hurt, either."

At the head of the table, McKenna blew out her breath and leaned back in her chair, a huge weight lifting from her shoulders. The news about the operation had received a lukewarm reception from the Confederation planetary ambassadors until the video footage had been released. It had been heavily edited, of course. Steph's assistant had compiled a documentary from the mass of footage Steph had captured, and McKenna and her defense counsel had been the first to see it. Some of what they had seen had been disturbing, to say the least. In particular, the phenomenon that had nearly led to General Sparks's forces being defeated.

Those things, McKenna had decided, the public did not yet need to see.

With Steph's help from her hospital bed where she was recovering from her leg wound, the raw footage had been transformed into a documentary that had left McKenna with her heart in her throat, overcome with pride in the men and women she had sent there, and in the people of Alger's World who had fought to survive.

Most of the planet's population had survived, although the butcher's bill had still been enormous. Fifty thousand civilians and Territorial Army soldiers had died. Another eight thousand sailors and Marines had been killed in the fighting, with hundreds more wounded.

But it could have been far, far worse.

"The reconstruction effort on Alger's is moving along well," Barca continued. "A number of other worlds have even stepped forward, volunteering to send workers and supplies to assist in the effort." He cocked an eyebrow at the president. "That, Madam President, is a first."

"They feel confident enough to send some of their own resources off-world in troubled times," said Vice President Navarre. "That is indeed a good sign."

"How are things going on the production front?" McKenna turned to Defense Minister Sabine and Admiral Tiernan.

"Aside from some supply problems we're having with certain components, things are actually going amazingly well," Joshua Sabine told her.

"Supply problems?" McKenna leaned forward. "Who do I need to lean on?"

Tiernan and Sabine exchanged grins. "No one this time, Madam President," Tiernan told her. "The problem is simply that our growing building capacity has outstripped our ability to produce certain parts, mainly for the hyperdrive engines. We had anticipated that problem and were already establishing additional production facilities, but our shipwrights and yard workers have been, shall we say, excessively efficient."

"So what's the projection for the fleet's strength?" McKenna asked.

Sabine smiled. "We'll double the number of ships and nearly triple our warship tonnage in the next eighteen months."

"And that's a conservative estimate," Tiernan added. "More importantly, by that time we'll have naval shipyards established in sixteen systems, four times what we have now. So in case the Kreelans give us another sucker punch, we won't have to worry so much about its impact on our shipbuilding."

McKenna nodded, impressed. "And what about the Marines and Territorial Army?"

"We've found a candidate world that we'd like to set up as a primary Marine training facility," Tiernan told her. "We'll expand the Corps as the Navy builds its transport capacity, as that's really the limiting factor beyond raw manpower. We certainly don't have any shortage of volunteers."

"And the Territorial Army is rapidly expanding, as well." Sabine paused, considering how far they'd come from the chaos three years before. "We've got cadres fully established on every Confederation world now, and some of the bureaucratic interference we were starting to get from the governments considering secession has pretty much vanished since the Alger's World operation."

McKenna nodded in satisfaction. They had bought the Confederation some time to bind itself together and better prepare its defenses. It was time she desperately needed, because she had no doubt that this war, more than any other ever fought by humanity, was going to be a long, bloody affair.

We'll win in the end, she thought. There was no other option. Because in this war, the only alternative to victory for humanity would be its extinction.

DISCOVER OTHER BOOKS BY MICHAEL R. HICKS

The *In Her Name* Series
First Contact
Legend Of The Sword
Dead Soul
Empire
Confederation
Final Battle
From Chaos Born

"Boxed Set" *In Her Name* Collections
In Her Name (Omnibus)
In Her Name: The Last War

Thrillers
Season Of The Harvest

Visit AuthorMichaelHicks.com for the latest updates!

ABOUT THE AUTHOR

Born in 1963, Michael Hicks grew up in the age of the Apollo program and spent his youth glued to the television watching the original Star Trek series and other science fiction movies, which continues to be a source of entertainment and inspiration. Having spent the majority of his life as a voracious reader, he has been heavily influenced by writers ranging from Robert Heinlein to Jerry Pournelle and Larry Niven, and David Weber to S.M. Stirling. Living in Maryland with his beautiful wife, two wonderful stepsons and two mischievous Siberian cats, he's now living his dream of writing full-time.

CPSIA information can be obtained at www.ICGtesting.com
Printed in the USA
BVOW07s1514101113

335935BV00001B/29/P

9 780984 673032